EAL

1314000613156 8

D0537683

FOR

BY ADRIAN GOLDSWORTHY

The Vindolanda Series
Vindolanda
The Encircling Sea
Brigantia

Non-Fiction
Hadrian's Wall
Philip and Alexander

For Robert

EAST AYRSHIRE LEISURE	
1314000613156 8	
Askews & Holts	
AF HISTORICAL	
BELLFIELD	

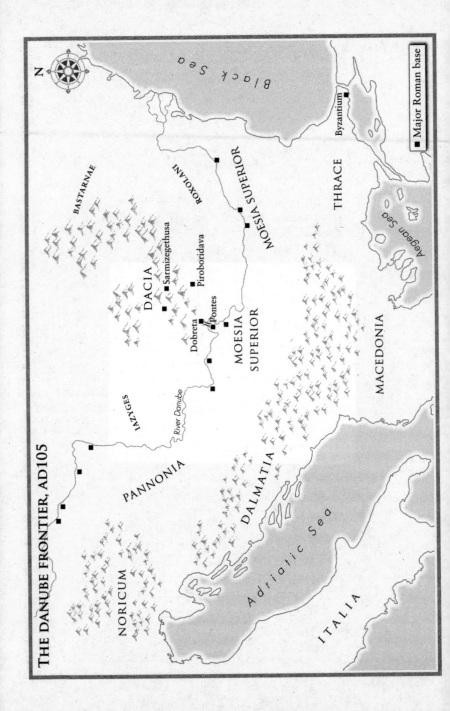

THE DANUBE FRONTIER, AD105

N

■ Major Roman base

Black Sea

Aegean Sea

Byzantium

THRACE

ROXOLANI

MOESIA SUPERIOR

MOESIA SUPERIOR

BASTARNAE

DACIA

Sarmizegethusa
Piroboridava
Dobreta
Pontes

MACEDONIA

IAZYGES

River Danube

PANNONIA

DALMATIA

Adriatic Sea

NORICUM

ITALIA

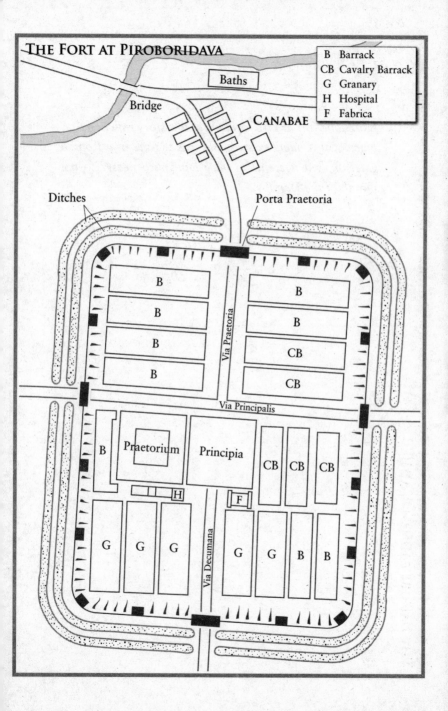

Note: The fort at Piroboridava in this story is fictional. A place of this name existed, and was the site of a Roman garrison, but it seems to have lain much nearer to the mouth of the Danube.

Near the cave of the prophet
Outside Sarmizegethusa
At the winter solstice

THE DRUMS POUNDED, *on and on, the beats echoing back off the peaks and valleys. It was the sound of thunder, rolling across the mountains and bringing the cleansing storms, but tonight the sky was clear of any cloud.*

Brasus looked up at the vast field of bright stars and tried to focus. They seemed to move as he watched, or perhaps he moved or his eyes were sluggish from the draft given to him by the priest. The drumming felt as if it was inside his head, the throbbing a part of him, and perhaps he was already being lifted out of this world. The choice would be soon, so he and the other two Messengers waited, sitting cross-legged in the snow. Brasus' breath steamed, making a tiny cloud. The man beside him was waving his hand in the mist, frowning as he stared at it. The Messengers each wore only a pair of bright white trousers, and yet Brasus did not feel the cold. He was close now, although his mind was too clouded to make full sense of it.

A warrior took a brand from the great fire and used it to light the tallow wrapped around the shaft of an arrow just behind the head. He walked across to the edge of the cliff, where a tall bowman waited. The bowman took it, nocked and drew in one swift motion, and then loosed.

Brasus watched the arrow arch high into the air, the flames flickering. They did not go out until the missile dropped out of sight into the valley below. The drummers stopped as one man, sticks held up high, and waited as the echoes faded away until there was only silence. Brasus blinked and still the stars moved, dancing their endless dance through the Heavens. Then he realised that he heard everything as if the sound was new – the breath of each man, the soft whimpering of the strangers kneeling in their chains, and the great crackle of the fire.

'Is the message prepared?'

The words were appallingly loud, though the man spoke in a whisper. He had asked the question three times before and received no answer, so that the drums had begun again and a fresh arrow been sent to ward off the storm clouds.

'It is ready.' The priest had answered. He was a tall man, clad wholly in black – boots, trousers, tunic, cloak and tall hat. Even his face was painted black, so that he was no more than a vague shape as he stood beyond the fire.

'Is the truth pure?' A warrior almost as tall asked the question. He wore an iron helmet and armour of bronze scales, both glinting red from the flames, but he carried no weapons. He was the Eyes of the King, his duty on this night to speak to the priest.

'Truth is always pure or it is not truth.' The priest never spoke above a whisper and yet Brasus heard each word sharply. He bowed his head and waited for the choice.

'Which is the messenger?'

The priest said no words and must have pointed or made some other gesture. Brasus and the other Messengers waited, heads down and eyes closed. After a while they heard the sound of boots crunching in the snow and sensed the Carriers were passing them and making ready to play their part.

Suddenly the man on Brasus' left stood up. There were men behind them, their tread as loud as their breathing and they had come for the man on the left. Brasus sighed, and raised his head, for the choice had been made and he was not to be the First. The Romans were being led past him, and he saw them closely for the first time. Two were soldiers, their unbelted tunics hanging well beneath their knees, and the third was familiar. He saw the jowly face, thick neck and the white scar on the forehead. His mind was sluggish, each thought taking shape as slowly as wood carved by a blunt knife. The man was a merchant, a secret friend of the king, but his odd foreign name would not come.

He did not see the First Messenger being led away, for the king had arrived and Brasus bowed low as was proper. Then he heard someone walking towards him and a hand touched his bare shoulder, then moved to lift his chin. It was Decebalus, and the great king smiled at him, his teeth white against his thick black beard, the widening streaks of grey hidden by the night.

'You do not bow to me,' he said. 'Not on this night.' Instead the king bowed to him and hushed Brasus when he tried to say that this was wrong. 'The Messengers are above the lords of men,' Decebalus told him and made Brasus all the more disappointed that he had not been chosen to be

3

First. Then he tried to banish such jealousy. A Messenger must be pure or the journey could not be made.

Brasus waited. He could not see what went on for the ritual was conducted behind him. He had never seen it done, although the last time he had stood with the king's main escort some way down the path. Yet he knew what was to be done and imagined the twelve Carriers standing beneath the great boulder in four rows of three. The Messenger was led half way up the path and there his hands were tied behind his back. After that he walked alone, for this was a journey only he could take and that was a hard walk barefoot because the ground was littered with sharp rocks. He must not speak or utter any sound.

Beneath the great rock the Carriers drove the spiked ends of their long spears into the hard ground, and then held them at a slight angle, the great broad heads pointing up. The Messenger would reach the boulder some twenty feet above them. Then he would jump.

Brasus heard the screams and shuddered. The First had failed, and failure meant that he was not pure enough for the journey, which meant that a Second would go instead and then, if necessary, a Third. The drums beat once again, building up slowly this time, so that the last wails of the First carried above them until his throat was cut. On and on the drummers pounded the hollow trunks, and again the bowman shot into the sky to ward off clouds and storms.

Twice more the Eyes of the King asked the question, and the second time the priest answered. Brasus was not the Second, and instead the other man went, and again Brasus waited. This time it seemed to take longer.

'It is done!' The priest had his arms in the air and for the first time shouted. 'The Great Lord of the Heavens has taken the Messenger into his arms!'

Brasus felt his eyes moistening, and his clouded mind struggled to know whether this was frustration at not having ascended or a shameful relief that he had not gone – or worse yet, been tested and failed. Was this uncertainty why he had not been chosen?

'Rise, boy.' Decebalus had come to him again. 'I shall have need of you.'

Brasus shivered, feeling the cold, and his eyes were so glassy that he could barely see. He heard a dull grunt, then another, but did not see the axeman standing behind the two Roman soldiers swing down or the merchant staring wide-eyed at the corpses beside him.

Decebalus walked over to the black-clad priest and the man raised his arms and called in his hoarse voice. 'The Lord of the Air has spoken. The pure shall live free!'

'Then it is war,' the king shouted. Brasus thought that he looked happier in that moment than he had seen his ruler for many months. The waiting was almost over, the pure would ascend, some to glorious blessedness and those left to freedom.

I

*The fort at Piroboridava, Province of Moesia Inferior
Three days after the Ides of Februarius, in the consulship
of Julius Candidus and Caius Antius (AD 105)*

S NOW STARTED FALLING again as they reached the top
of the tower, the big flakes tumbling slowly through the
still air to settle on the timbers. Two sentries were on
watch, their drab cloaks dotted with flecks of white, and the
men stiffened to attention when their centurion appeared.
Sabinus, round faced, looking far younger than his twenty-
seven years, was a relative newcomer to the legion and
indeed the army, commissioned after several years on the
council in his home town in Baetica, but was well liked.
He grinned at the two legionaries, and gestured for them to
stand at ease.

'All well, boys?' Sabinus asked them, knowing the answer
already.

'All well, sir.' The 'boys' were both veterans, only a couple
of years away from the end of their twenty-five years with
I Minervia, and glad not to stand on ceremony. They pulled
their cloaks tight and assumed the well-practised stare of
sentries doing their job, apparently oblivious to the centurion
and the officers with him, while making sure that they heard

anything that might be useful or worthy of gossip. Rumours that they were to be relieved and allowed back to civilization had been doing the rounds of the garrison for weeks, and the arrival of the four riders at noon today was taken as a good sign. It was happening. No matter that it seemed odd to change garrisons before the winter was out, and no matter that it seemed even odder to replace a predominantly legionary garrison with a band of irregulars from the wilds of Britannia. If it meant that the *vexillatio* of I Minervia could return to their base – or anywhere other than here – then what did it matter if the army was making even less sense than usual. They were going, and soon by the look of things, and that promise helped to keep a man warm as he paced up and down on top of this tower.

One of the Britons' boots skidded where snow had been trodden into sludge. The man next to him steadied him and then nodded as if to reassure his comrade. They were clean shaven, smart and might easily have been decurions in a regular *ala* of cavalry, true auxiliaries rather than half-barbarian irregulars. Each had a fine iron helmet with the shallow neck guard safer for a horseman than the wide ones on an infantry helmet. Both were slim, rangy men, with a stiff yellow plume atop each helmet adding to their height. The third was built along the same lines, but taller, the skin on his face so taut that even with his drooping moustache it looked skull-like. He seemed to sneer at the man who had almost fallen, although that may simply have been his usual expression. Swathed in a thick tartan cloak, with an old-fashioned army issue helmet, but no mark of rank, he struck Sabinus as more bandit than soldier.

The fourth man was slow to follow, but as he was the most important of the party – indeed the only man of account among them – Sabinus waited for him to appear. At long last the high transverse crest of the centurion's helmet came up through the open trap door. Flavius Ferox was another Briton, but he came from a legion, even if currently put in charge of a band of cut-throats. From the start of the tour of the garrison the younger officer had done his best to be amiable. Ferox was senior to him, and by all accounts had a long, even distinguished, record, and it never did any harm to be pleasant to someone who was – or one day might become – a useful acquaintance. Pity the fellow was so surly.

'The *scorpio* below,' Ferox said abruptly before he was even off the ladder, 'how often is it checked?' On the level below there was a light bolt-shooting engine, covered as usual against the weather.

Before Sabinus could answer, one of the sentries slammed his boots down on the planking as he came to attention. 'Cleaned every third day, sir!' the man shouted his report. 'Springs checked daily, sir!'

Ferox grunted, and Sabinus hoped that his gratitude to the soldier was not too obvious. He would have remembered the answer eventually, but had gone blank.

'Can you reach the bridge with it?' The fort lay beside the main track where it crossed over the river.

'No,' Sabinus replied, confident of this at least. 'With luck and the right wind, you might get close now and again, but not with any accuracy. It's just over two hundred and fifty paces from the gate to the first plank of the bridge. Two hundred and fifty-three to be precise,' he added, having supervised the survey himself.

Ferox nodded. 'So even putting one up here wouldn't make much difference.'

'Not really.'

Another grunt, and the centurion climbed off the ladder and stretched. He was a big man, only slightly less tall than the bandit, but broader across the shoulders and giving a sense of brooding power. His eyes were grey and cold, although as he turned his head to look around, Sabinus thought he could see some pleasure. After the best part of two hours spent exploring the buildings and narrow streets of the fort, it was a relief to be up here. Even in the snow the view was magnificent, with the steep valley sides climbing to the north east towards the pass through the mountains and winding away in the opposite direction on the road to the great river.

Sabinus decided that this was a good opportunity to revive everyone's spirit, so he strode towards the front parapet and waved his arms to gesture at the grandeur around them.

'Well, there they are,' he said, his round face more boyish than usual. His helmet, the crest running crosswise like Ferox's, although in his case black rather than white, seemed too big for him and added to the impression. It was an annoyance wearing the thing on such a routine duty as giving a tour of the fort, but when the senior officer kept his helmet on Sabinus had no choice but to conform.

'Yes, there they are,' he continued. 'Every last one, every tree of regulation height and shape and at its station!' He chuckled theatrically. 'Actually, I do believe that there are a dozen more of the buggers since yesterday. ... That one for a start.' He pointed. 'And the oak tree beside it. I'm sure it's twice as tall as when I last looked.'

'That's a beech, sir,' one of the sentries corrected. 'Begging your pardon, sir.'

'Dear me, is it, Maternus?'

The legionary nodded. 'And it is the same height as yesterday.' A veteran was granted more licence than an ordinary soldier, especially with a good-natured officer like Sabinus.

'Really? ... Well, you know best, I'm sure,' the centurion resumed. 'A beech, eh? Shows you can't trust the devils to know their own mind from one day to the next.'

Disappointingly Ferox did not smile, and instead brushed aside the snow so that he could lean on the parapet at one of the low points and stare out. His instincts were telling him that the report was right, and that the attack could come at any moment. Yet it was all silent and peaceful out there, without the slightest sign of any danger lurking close by. Perhaps he was wrong or perhaps not. He had only lived as long as this by trusting his feelings and, through a good deal of luck, which made it all the more worrying that this place did not feel lucky.

'You need to be careful,' the centurion told him, the words so in keeping with his thoughts that it took an effort not to react.

'Careful, Sabinus?' Ferox had to appear unconcerned and off his guard, so gave a wry smile, before turning back to the view.

He had not said much all morning, so even this reply was very welcome to his guide. 'Yes, sir,' Sabinus said, 'careful not to try counting the trees. Not good for a man's peace of mind.'

There was no more response, and after a while the one

who looked like a bandit sniffed. 'We have trees in Britannia. What's so special about these?'

'Vindex, isn't it?' Sabinus had remembered the name because of the senator who tried to depose Nero and died in the attempt. The bandit muttered something impudent, but he decided not to notice in his relief that someone had spoken. 'Yes, well, Vindex, these woods are special. Aren't they, Maternus?'

'Yes, sir,' the sentry responded, obviously having heard all this before. 'If you say so, sir.'

'I do say so, Maternus, I do indeed, and so will these fine Britons when they have been here as long as us.' He beamed a broad smile. The bandit leered back, but then the rogue's face was locked in a permanent leer, not helped by his prominent teeth.

'We will, will we?' The Latin was clear, with the clipped accent common in the northern provinces.

'No doubt about it,' Sabinus assured him. 'Meaning no disrespect to the woods and forests of your native lands, my dear fellows – or to the sprites and nymphs who dwell in them – but they are as far away now as my own homeland, and might as well be in India as far as we are concerned.

'We are here, my friends, at Piroboridava, and we are alone. People don't live up here – at least no one with any sense. And they don't pass this way if they can help, least of all in winter. So all this garrison sees are those trees. Day after day, you look out and there they are. It's the closest we get to company.'

'Company?' One of the clean-shaven Britons had spoken.

The man was frowning, and appeared almost on edge. Sabinus struggled to recall the man's outlandish name. Mobacus or Molacus? Something uncouth, he was sure.

'Yes, my dear fellow.' That seemed wiser than risking getting it wrong. Sabinus beamed at him and the others, resigned to the lack of interest shown by Ferox and making the most of the rest as the only audience on offer. 'Although you may not believe it, you will grow fond of those trees. Once you have been here a month you will surely grow to love them. When you have been here two months you will start to talk to them.'

Ferox, knowing what was coming, had to force himself to keep staring out, apparently without a care in the world.

'Talk to them?' That was Molacus, always too quick to speak and too ready to show scorn.

'Most certainly,' Sabinus said, enjoying his little game. Ferox could imagine the centurion's serious expression. 'You will indeed talk to them – all of us do.' He paused, drawing out the moment. 'But it is only after you have been here three months that the trees begin to answer.'

There was an amused snort from Vindex, prompting a delighted chuckle from Sabinus, and at long last the other two joined in. The sentries were not officers, and were not involved, and like Ferox they must have heard this so many times before. It was an old joke, even by army standards, told of countless forts and outposts dotted around the empire, and sometimes it was sand dunes, mountain tops or even sheep instead of trees. He let himself smile, out of nostalgia as much as anything else, then saw the movement beyond the bridge and grinned in satisfaction. They were coming and soon he would know.

'Riders, sir!' Maternus shouted. 'Two, no, three of them, leading another pair of horses.'

Ferox stood up straight and faced back towards the others.

'Yours, sir?' Sabinus asked.

'Vindex?' Ferox already knew the answer, but needed to play his part.

Vindex squinted, shading his eyes. 'Aye,' he said. 'It's Ivonercus and the other lads. Coming slow, so maybe the mare is still lame. ... Could just be the ice though.'

'Wise to be careful.' Ferox smiled. 'Now, my dear Sabinus, perhaps we could take a look at the ditches.'

'The ditches, sir?' The centurion had hoped that the new arrivals had already seen all that they wanted so that he could escort Ferox to his quarters and then return to his own.

'The ditches,' Ferox repeated. 'I had better see all the defences of my new post. And perhaps we will stroll down to the bridge as well.'

Sabinus led the way, hoping that his disappointment did not show. They went down the two ladders, then out onto the main rampart and down the stairs. The fort's defences were of earth and timber rather than turf, no doubt because the grass nearby was thin and the earth brittle, while the woods that so fascinated the centurion were handy. There were smells of any army base, of horses and sweat, damp leather and wood, overlaid with smoke. Everything was familiar to Ferox or anyone else who had soldiered for even a short time, not simply the scents and the sounds, but the layout. As they came down onto the flat they could see straight up the main street to the *principia* and other key buildings, just as you would anywhere else. Army bases tended to be almost, but not quite identical, and from Ferox's experience the similarities could make it harder to remember the differences. Part of his mind was trying to settle the plan in his memory. That would only matter if he was wrong or if he was right, and survived the rest of the day.

The right-hand gate was open, so they went that way. Ferox glanced back when they were outside, at the big painted sign between the two arches announcing that the *praesidium* had been built by a vexillation of Legio I Minervia and another from *II Adiutrix*. He wondered whether this was a good omen. The men of the Second had built the tiny outpost in northern Britannia from which he had acted as *regionarius* for the best part of a decade. All in all it had been a happy, simpler time, left to his own devices to keep peace in his region. Still, the legionaries had made a shoddy job there, and he had to hope that they had been more diligent here.

'You are no stranger to this part of the world, I am told?' Sabinus once again tried to make conversation. They had to walk carefully, because the track was uneven where deep ruts had frozen solid. Someone had not bothered to maintain it properly before the winter freeze and that was sloppy.

'It was a long time ago, when I was new to the army.' Ferox felt a little guilty for his coldness towards the man. Sabinus seemed a decent officer and his eagerness to leave this place was obvious, which made it unfortunate that Ferox was carrying orders that would keep him here for a good while.

'Is it true that you were at Tapae with Fuscus?'

Ferox nodded.

Sabinus searched for the right words. 'That must have been rough?'

A commander killed along with most of his army, Ferox thought, yes, I guess you could say that. He had been in charge of the scouts and had tried to warn Fuscus, but no one had listened until it was too late. He had got away, with his own men and as many others as he could gather, just as he had got away a year earlier when the legate of Moesia had got himself chopped to pieces, and then a couple of years on when another legion marched to disaster. A philosopher, and for all that it was unlikely now a very good friend, on listening to the tale of his career suggested that it was proof of remarkable luck, or perhaps that the gods enjoyed watching him squirm. Ferox smiled at the memory, which pleased Sabinus, who took on most of the conversation as they walked past the double ditches, answering questions about the recent war against the Dacians.

'Well, I missed it, just my luck,' the centurion explained. 'Got accepted by the army and posted to Minervia in the last weeks, but did not get here until it was all over.'

'Any trouble since?' Ferox asked, half listening. The ditches were in pretty good order, with only a little rubbish and spoil at the bottom. A day's graft would clear that out. He was trying not to stare at the horsemen, who were now a quarter of a mile away, still coming on slowly. The riderless horses were not a good sign.

'No, not really. As I say, this is a quiet spot. The local Dacians are the Saldense, but they mainly live lower down. Hardly anyone winters up here. Come the spring and summer we will see the herdsmen arrive, travellers on the road, and even a few hunting parties of Sarmatians. The game is good around here.'

Sabinus nodded at the lone auxiliary who stood as picket beyond the ditches. That was regulation outside every base, set down a century ago by the divine Augustus, although far older than that. The rules said that there should be a dozen or more on duty outside the main gates of a fort this size, but it was rarely enforced, especially when things were quiet.

'One man can see as well as twenty,' Sabinus said, as if reading his thoughts.

'True enough.' Ferox could not help wishing that they had stuck to the rules. Still, perhaps it was better that way. He had to give them their chance. 'So the camp was built during the fighting?' he asked, continuing to stroll down towards the main road and the bridge, and forcing Sabinus to follow. There were rows of stakes and pits in front of the ditches, all suggesting that there had once been a real prospect of attack.

'Yes,' Sabinus said. 'In the second campaign of our Lord Trajan, he sent a column this way, and another bigger one to the east, heading for the pass of the Red Tower. They had to storm a couple of strongholds as well as drive in bands of enemy. This place was built to store the supplies they might need and then care for all the casualties. Those Dacian castles are a bitch to take, as I'm sure you know. Hence our big hospital and all those granaries.'

Ferox nodded. The buildings had been one of the most striking peculiarities of the base, especially because they were half empty. He stopped for a moment. They were half way to the bridge, and he noticed that the riders had reined in and were waiting on the far side. Well, that seemed to settle it.

'Vindex, perhaps you would see what is keeping Ivonercus and get his news. I can't see anyone following them, but you never know.'

'Lazy bugger,' the bandit snorted, leaving Sabinus unsure whether he meant the rider or his commander, but since Ferox did not make a fuss he was not about to interfere.

'Your bath house is finished?' Ferox asked as the lanky Vindex trudged away through the four-inch deep snow. The long building was over to the right, close to the river but some way from the bridge and the centurion turned to face it.

Sabinus gave a wry smile. 'Almost. Everything is taking much longer to dry in this cold. They say in another week they'll be able to light the fires for the first time. Not that it will do us much good, but your lads ought to enjoy it.'

'Don't move, centurion!' Sabinus gasped as he felt the point of a sword pressing into his side where his cloak had fallen back. He was wearing mail, but the tip was already inside a ring and a strong thrust would punch through. 'Say nothing and you will live.' It was the Briton Mobacus or whatever the barbarian was called. The other man had his sword pressed against Ferox.

'Take out your sword and drop it. Slowly mind,' the other decurion said.

'You too, sir. Nice and easy,' Molacus added. 'No fuss, no sudden moves.'

'Better do as they say,' Ferox said.

Sabinus wondered if this was some strange joke. It seemed too bizarre to be anything else. The one called Vindex was still plodding down to the bridge and did not appear to have noticed.

Sabinus' *gladius* grated on the metal mouth of his scabbard as he drew it, holding the pommel with just his finger and thumb. Ferox's sword, one of the longer, old fashioned types, dropped to the ground first, so he felt no shame in letting his own blade go.

'And the *pugio*. Gently now.'

'I don't carry one,' Sabinus said. 'Now just what—' He stopped as the sword was pressed harder. Glancing nervously to the side, he saw Ferox slide an army issue dagger from his right hip and drop it.

'Do what we say and it will all be fine,' Molacus said.

'This is absurd,' Sabinus snapped until the point was pushed in just a little more. His side started to ache from the pressure.

'Sir?' The soldier on picket duty called, no doubt wondering what was happening.

'Taranis!' Molacus had noticed that Vindex had stopped and had glanced back at them.

'No need to harm the centurion,' Ferox said, his words steady. 'You've got to go over the rampart now anyway and one more witness won't matter. Your oath was for vengeance, not murder.'

'As long as he does what he's told,' Molacus said and then added something more in a language Sabinus did not understand. He gulped, but the point of the sword drew back a fraction. Sabinus wanted to ask again what all this was about, but his throat felt so dry that he doubted the words would come.

'We must do it now!' the one behind Ferox said. Vindex

was walking back towards them. Behind him, the riders kicked their horses to move, but they were still a hundred yards away from the warrior.

Ferox sighed. 'At least let me face you,' he said. 'We let your king die as a warrior.' He stepped away from the decurion, who let him go. Ferox turned very deliberately, and his voice was resigned. 'And I'll make it easy.' He unfastened the knot holding together the cheek pieces of his helmet. 'Sabinus, you will obey my orders. When all is done let these men go.'

'My lord?'

'And tell your men to do the same.' Ferox lifted his helmet off his head, taking the woolly hat he wore inside with it. He held the iron helmet in both hands, twisting it round. 'Only just bought this,' he said ruefully and grinned at the decurion facing him. 'Waste of money, eh?'

Sabinus felt the sword pulled away from him and let out a long breath. No one protested when he edged away, and he saw that Molacus was watching Ferox, his sword held in a low guard.

'Can I help, my lord?' The sentry called, closer to them now. Vindex had started running, and was clumsily drawing his sword as he tried not to slip. Behind him the riders were closing, one ahead of the others.

'I'd rather not kneel,' Ferox told them. 'And I'd be obliged if you do a neat job. Just like I've trained you.'

The one facing him licked his lips as he pulled his arm back, sword out straight, ready to lunge at Ferox's face.

'My lord? Shall I give the alarm?' The auxiliary on picket duty had stopped, his voice more than ever uncertain. Sabinus saw the leading horseman was just a few paces behind Vindex, his horse in a clumsy canter. The fugitive swerved away from the track and it was a moment before the rider dragged his horse round to follow.

Molacus looked at Sabinus. 'Tell your man to stay at his post.'

Vindex had turned, pulling his cloak off and waving it with his left arm in the hope of frightening the horse. He had a long cavalry sword in his right hand and they could hear him taunting his attacker. The animal flinched, pulling away, and the rider fought the beast, forcing him on at a walk. It gave time for the other two to close.

'Give the alarm!' Sabinus shouted, amazed that the words came out and were so loud.

'Bastard!' Molacus spat the word and slashed wildly at him. Sabinus felt the wind of the blade, stepped back and his boots slipped under him and he fell on his bottom.

Ferox went half a pace forward, his helmet held firmly in both hands, and slammed the edge of the neck guard into the decurion's throat, driving into the little gap between his cheek pieces and scarf. The man gasped, head snapping back, eyes wide, and Ferox spun to the left, helmet in one hand and struck at Molacus, a glancing blow on the side of the face as he dodged. The Briton went back, raising his sword high, but Ferox was quicker and swung the helmet again, breaking Molacus' nose so that blood jetted down his face. The man staggered and Ferox struck again, using all his strength and worrying less about aim. There was a dull ringing sound as his iron helm hit the front of the decurion's helmet, twisting it to cut the forehead. Molacus went back again, and the next blow produced a crack as a hinge snapped and a cheek piece of Ferox's helmet flew off. The decurion sank to his knees.

Sabinus realised that his gladius lay beside him and he snatched it up as he stood. The other Briton was clutching at his neck, swaying as he gasped for breath. Ferox had pushed Molacus down and was sitting on him, left hand clamped around the man's sword arm and the other using his battered helmet to pound his face again and again. The auxiliary was coming, but as his fear turned to anger Sabinus went over to the gasping Briton and thrust his sword into the man's belly. He felt the resistance of the iron rings, pressed harder, his rage growing, and felt the metal snap and the point slide in. The decurion seemed to stare straight at him, eyes desperate and imploring, so Sabinus pushed harder, using both hands to force the sword deeper, until he punched through the rear of the man's armour and the tip erupted from the Briton's back.

'Sir?' The auxiliary had reached them. He was a youngster, his confusion obvious. Sabinus let go of his gladius and let the man fall. Down the slope one of the riders was stretched on the ground, unmoving, but Vindex was also down, rolling and dodging the two horsemen as they struggled to reach him with their swords.

'Give me your spear, boy.' Ferox was up, his face, arms and chest all spattered with blood. He snatched the shaft from the auxiliary and ran towards Vindex and the others. 'Mongrels!' he screamed at them.

Sabinus' hands were smeared red. He glanced at Molacus and wished that he had not, because there was just bloody pulp where the man's face should have been. Neither he nor the other decurion were moving. Sabinus struggled to accept that for the first time he had killed a man. It had all been so sudden with no time to think.

'What's happening, sir?' the soldier asked.

Ferox raised the spear as he ran to help his friend. It was a sturdy *hasta*, too heavy to throw all that far, so he pounded down the slope to close the distance. Vindex had lost his sword and cloak as he scrambled to avoid their attacks, but at least he was still moving and at least neither of the men had spears. From horseback it was hard to reach a man on the ground with only a sword – hard, but not impossible.

'Come on, you mongrels!' he screamed again, trying to distract them. 'Your king was a pimp and a coward!'

They heard him. As one man reined in, his mount reared and for a moment Ferox thought that the rider might be thrown, until he recovered. It was Ivonercus and, like all Brigantes, he was a fine horseman. You had to give them that, and that they were easy men to like and admire.

'Bastards!' Ferox bellowed, not checking, but pulling the spear back a little more to give the throw as much force as he could. Ivonercus hesitated for an instant, and Ferox could sense his urge to charge and finish it once and for all.

'Come on!' It was Sabinus, leading the lone auxiliary, and perhaps that made up his mind, for Ivonercus turned and fled, calling to his companion to follow. Ferox pelted towards them, desperate to close the distance before he made his one throw. They were still forty paces away, and slowed as the horses turned. He gained just a little, left arm out straight to help, aiming at Ivonercus who was closest as well as the one who really mattered.

Then just as he threw, his hobnailed boots slipped on ice and his feet flew from under him. The hasta went high, almost straight up, as Ferox hit the ground hard.

Vindex cackled, trying to sit up, until the laughter grew

too strong and he lay back down. Sabinus was waving Ferox's sword high as he reached them.

'Are you hurt, sir?' he asked, his face a mix of concern and obvious excitement.

Ferox sighed. 'Only my pride – and I've never had much of that.'

'Shall I get them to muster a patrol to go after them?'

Ferox pushed himself up, brushing off some of the snow as he stood. The two Brigantians were in plain sight, although he doubted that there was any chance of catching them by the time pursuit was organised. The cheeky devils had even stopped to catch the two riderless horses. 'No harm in trying,' he said.

Sabinus sent the auxiliary running back to the fort with the message, as Vindex came over to join them. 'Reckon we'll see 'em again?' Ferox's expression made an answer unnecessary. 'Aye, that oath.'

'Oath?' Sabinus asked.

'To kill us both or give their lives in the attempt,' Vindex explained. He bared his big teeth. 'The centurion has a knack of making friends wherever he goes.'

'This has happened before?' Sabinus was struggling to keep pace.

'Only a couple of times. Most just mutter among themselves, and probably not more than fifty have taken the oath.'

'Fifty?'

'Give or take,' Vindex conceded. 'And three less now.' Taking pity on the shocked officer, he decided to explain. 'They're Brigantes and we killed their high king. Made his men a bit angry, you might say.'

'He was a rebel and we were acting under orders,' Ferox spoke for the first time.

'Oh aye,' Vindex allowed. 'Still their king though.'

'Not anymore.'

'Well, there is that.'

Ferox gestured towards his sword and Sabinus was surprised at feeling a moment of reluctance before handing it over.

'Let's go then,' Ferox said and set off up the slope to the fort. There were dozens of men on the ramparts, watching them, so the alarm had been given, but he doubted that a patrol would be ready before the hour was out. He walked quickly, leaving the others behind.

''Course,' Vindex began to explain, 'many of the other lads may want to kill the centurion on account of his sunny disposition. As I say, he has a way with people.'

II

Rome
The same day

THE PRAETOR WAS in a hurry, as usual, but Rome was Rome, and the crowds saw too many magistrates to be that impressed by the pomp surrounding one. His lictors did their best, threatening when their mere approach was not enough to make people clear a path, and steadily they made progress, acquiring the inevitable tail of boys and idlers hoping to watch a few arguments or perhaps even a fight. The Flavian amphitheatre towered over them, quiet today – or at least as quiet as anywhere could be when it was surrounded with hawkers and stall holders. Rome was never quiet during the daylight hours and not much better at night, although after yesterday's Lupercalia by rights everyone ought to have been subdued, if they were awake at all.

They pushed their way through, and as they began to climb the slope of the Caelian hill the crowd changed, thinning a little, and more and more of them obviously the slaves and freedmen of the wealthy going about their duties. Litters stopped to make way for them, as was fitting for the symbols of a magistrate, their occupants hailing the praetor with greetings and invitations.

'Will you dine with me, Aelius?', 'May I call on you, praetor?', 'Best wishes to you, my lord, and to your good lady.'

Some of the passengers were women, and some of what they said was barely audible, since no fine lady should shout in the streets. Twice words were unnecessary, and the obvious longing of one mature woman and the giggles of a younger one made clear that there was more than respect for rank and family. Each of the women was a senator's wife, and all the lictors knew their master's reputation there. The praetor could be very charming when he wanted, was a good height, athletic and with dark, soulful eyes. His neat beard was not fashionable for a man of rank, and had not been for centuries, but that was a sign of his immense self-confidence, pronounced even for a senator. He had celebrated his twenty-ninth birthday last month, was approaching his prime, and for a bored or neglected wife he can only have seemed a dashing figure. They dreamed of love, and he learned about their husbands, filing the information away in case it one day was useful. None of the lictors knew whether these stories were true, but they had seen his prodigious memory and the interest he took in individuals. On the first morning the praetor addressed each one by his name, whereas some magistrates never got very far past 'Hey, you!' in their twelve months of office.

The *castra peregrina* lay in the Second Region of the city, joining onto the old walls. Few magistrates came this way, let alone visited the 'camp of the foreigners', which was smaller and less impressive than the barracks of the praetorians, or the new ones that Trajan was having built for his cavalry bodyguard, the *singulares Augusti*. This camp was more of a *mansio* on a grand scale than anything else. It was the base of the *frumentarii*, centurions and other ranks from the legions on attachment from their units with the staffs of provincial governors. They helped supervise the provision of grain for men and animals, as well as other foods and material to the army, especially when these could not be found in adequate quality and quantity from local sources. These days much of their time was spent carrying messages and reports from governors back to the emperor and then from the emperor to the governors. There were usually a couple of hundred at the camp, drawn from the thirty legions dotted around the world, hence the talk of 'foreigners'. These were a mix of men lately arrived, those waiting to travel back to a province and sufficient others to ensure that there was never any shortage of messengers at a time of emergency.

Today there were two men forming the picket on guard outside the gate, just as in any fort, even though the likelihood of rioters in such an affluent part of the city was unlikely, and the approach of foreign enemies absurd. Yet the men stood there, replaced every two hours, their equipment burnished until it almost glowed, with tunics bleached a brilliant white, and the drab cloaks of the frontiers, albeit new and perfect, because no one was about to let any of the pansy, play-acting soldiers in Rome find the slightest fault.

'Halt!' One of the guards was quite short and the shoulder bands of his gleaming segmented armour made him look almost square. 'Who goes there?' The man's rectangular *scutum* was red, and emblazoned with the lightning bolts and wings of Jupiter painted in gold. A lot of the legions used similar insignia, but the praetor knew that this was the badge of *Legio X Fretensis*, based in Judaea.

'The noble Aelius Hadrianus, praetor, with an appointment to see the *princeps peregrinorum*,' the lictor responded, careful to say exactly what he had been told. His master made it clear that precision was important.

The two legionaries stamped to attention, sparks flying on the paving stones as their hobnailed boots slammed down.

'You are expected, my lord,' the second soldier said, eyes curious even if his voice was not. This man also had a red shield, with a white Capricorn and *LEG II AUG* beneath the boss. That meant that the man was detached from the garrison of Britannia. 'If you would like to go through the gate, there is a man waiting to take the noble praetor to the princeps.'

Once the lictors and the litter had passed, the two soldiers exchanged wondering glances, before resuming the impassive stare of a sentry. A couple of grubby infants who had trailed the magistrate for the last half hour waited for a while, until they realised that sticking their tongues out at the legionaries provoked no response and decided to shuffle away.

By this time, the commander of the garrison was a little less worried. His guest had accepted a cup of wine and given sufficient sign of enjoyment to justify the purchase of so expensive a vintage. He had also eyed the slave who had brought it as the boy had left, which suggested that some of the rumours about the man were true.

'Thank you for seeing me at such short notice, my dear Turbo,' the praetor said abruptly. 'By the way, I trust that your brother is well? He was very kind to a young and naïve tribune when I served with II Adiutrix.'

Turbo had not known of the connection, for his brother had not mentioned it – well, who bothered to discuss the antics of the aristocrats doing their five-minute stint as broad stripe tribune with a legion. Interesting that the praetor had not mentioned this in his letter.

'He is well, my lord, hoping to be made *primus pilus* before too many more years.'

'Does not surprise me. He will make it too. The best soldier I ever saw.'

Turbo wondered whether the prefect always spoke in such clipped sentences or whether the man was posing as a bluff soldier. He could detect no hint of an offer to assist his brother's ambitions – or indeed his own – in return for some favour.

'My letter must have worried you!' Hadrian said abruptly, and grinned, his informality as shocking as his words. He raised a hand at Turbo's instinctive denial. 'Please, do not trouble yourself.' The grin was back again. 'It certainly would have worried me if I was in your place. Some senator – a praetor of all things – nosing about an army base and wanting to talk to the *numerus*. What's the bugger up to, you must have thought? Can't be up to any good, and more than likely doing something that might compromise your sacred oath to the emperor. Even these days that looks suspicious, under as beneficent and wise a princeps as the Lord Trajan.'

That was indeed what Turbo had thought, and under ordinary circumstances he might have made excuses, pleaded other duties or just refused and asked the praetor to submit a formal request via the consuls if he needed information for a trial. The problem was that the circumstances were not normal. Hadrian was not simply a praetor, but the great-nephew of the emperor. If Turbo was not sure how far Trajan's favour extended, that did not matter. At the very least it placed this young man close to the highest levels of the Senate, which meant that he could scarcely do less than meet him, after such a courteous request. At the same time, he had filed the letter and formally recorded the appointment.

Hadrian reached over and patted him on the arm. 'My dear fellow, I really am sorry to trouble you, but my intentions are in no way improper. That is why I have come so publicly – to show that neither of us have anything to hide.' The praetor's eyes were fixed on him, as if reading his innermost thoughts. 'I believe that you can help me, and that in turn will permit me to serve the *res publica* more effectively in my small way. Please forgive me for taking some of your valuable time.'

'An honour, my lord.' Turbo glanced down at the tablets on his desk, less because he needed to remind himself of what they said than to break away from the intensity of Hadrian's gaze. 'Your letter explained that you are returning to the eagles.'

'That's right. Instead of the usual year as magistrate, I am to hand over my responsibilities next month and go out as legatus to Legio I Minervia. No one ever likes a changeover of command and getting used to a new commander's little ways – I lived through that twice while I was tribune. You must have experienced it even more often?'

'Yes, my lord. A fair few times.' Turbo was a centurion, with eighteen years of service in a succession of legions before his appointment as princeps peregrinorum. 'Soldiers are creatures of habit. Discipline may be petty, but at least you know where you are.' Turbo wondered whether Hadrian's clipped manner of speaking was infectious. Apart from his connections, this was clearly a man to watch. 'A new man has a tendency to change things, usually little things, but they are the ones that can get under the skin.'

'So I would like to learn as much about my legion as I can before I arrive, in the hope of making the transition as painless as possible. That way, the only changes I shall have to introduce will be those essential to honing the Minervia's efficiency.'

Poor bastards, they don't know what's going to hit them, Turbo thought in momentary sympathy. 'Of course, my lord, but why come to me? There must be more information kept in the *Palatium*. We only deal with food and other supplies. While we carry messages to and from provincial *legati*, no copies are kept here.'

'It is because of that that I am here. The latest strength return they have is almost a year old. A new one is due anytime now, but they do not have it yet.' The grin was back. 'But if I'm any judge the men must have eaten since then, and your frumentarii are bound to have been involved in supplying any substantial detachment. In the last return there were vexillations from the legion scattered all over the place and I should like to know where they all are now.'

'Well, as you know, sir, the depot is at Bonna in Germania Superior, and around one thousand men are there or nearby. Then there are two cohorts at Viminiacum, and the equivalent of three strong ones at Dobreta working on the bridge.' The grin broadened at this point, although Turbo could not guess why. 'Both in Moesia – Superior that is.

Can't quite get used to one province being split into two, begging your pardon. Then a couple of smaller vexillations.' He handed a tablet across to the praetor.

'Thank you.' Hadrian scanned the list. 'Three hundred with two centurions at the praesidium of Piroboridava?' He frowned, but before Turbo could explain, went on. 'That's Dacia isn't it? Well, on the fringes at least, and across the Ister. I'm guessing they are not the only ones in garrison?'

A few hours ago Turbo had forgotten the name if he had ever heard it, but the warning had at least served that purpose and given time for information to be gathered. 'They're the biggest contingent, but there is also a parcel of auxiliaries. No whole units, although a mixed contingent is on its way. Yes, here we are, *Brittones sub cura Titi Flavii Ferocis*, no more specific than that, but all I know for sure is that there will be a lot more horses in the garrison soon, so that they will need barley and straw as well as wheat. It may mean that some of the troops already there will be withdrawn.'

'Two hundred and twenty at Sarmizegethusa,' Hadrian read, 'and one hundred and sixty at Buridava.'

'Also beyond the Ister, my lord. The ones at Sarmizegethusa are part of the observation force, keeping an eye on the king. If you remember the thinking was that detachments from several units could do the job, without leaving men of just one legion so exposed.'

'And do we expect trouble from Decebalus?'

'Not my field,' Turbo said. 'The frumentarii carry reports of that nature, but do not read them – not if they want to keep their jobs. However, judging from the shipments we oversee, we aren't expecting anything big this year.'

Hercules' balls, he thought, realising that he may have been indiscreet. 'Still early days though,' he added, hoping to muddy the matter.

Hadrian gave a pleasant smile, not in the least triumphant. Turbo realised that he was drumming his fingers on the table and stopped.

'Are all the detachments beyond the Danube composed of *veterani*?'

'My lord?' Turbo's fingers twitched again, but he just managed to restrain himself from tapping the wood. He considered for a moment. 'No idea, if I am honest. We do not get that sort of information. Could be, I suppose – well, some anyway. They're excused fatigues of course, but still liable for garrison duty.'

'Not to worry, it was just a thought. How many men from Minervia do you have here at the moment?' Hadrian asked.

'Just three. A couple set off for the Rhine a few days ago and a few may arrive by the end of the month. Journeys take longer at this time of year.' Turbo wondered whether he saw brief annoyance at his banal explanation.

'Quite so.'

'One is waiting outside, in case you wanted to have a word. Name is Celer. He's served thirteen *stipendia*, and this is his second as a *frumentarius*. Shall I call for him?'

Hadrian nodded, so Turbo rang the little bell standing on his desk. Almost immediately a slim soldier marched into the room, wearing tunic, weapons' belt and boots and slammed to attention.

'At ease, Celer,' Turbo told the soldier. 'This noble gentleman is soon to take command of the legion and wishes to talk to you.'

'Sir!' Celer slackened his shoulders ever so slightly, while continuing to stare over the heads of the seated men, avoiding making eye contact.

'My apologies,' Hadrian said affably. 'I regret interrupting your duties or even worse taking you away from well-earned rest. I know you frumentarii have to travel hard and fast – and then be willing at a moment's notice to set out again.'

'Sir.' An experienced soldier sheltered behind that short word as he did his shield.

'And you do not need to speak in praise of I Minervia. I know their reputation from my time as tribune and from when I served in Lord Trajan's campaigns in Dacia. ... I also appreciate that your duties take you away from your comrades and the legion, but am sure that you have friends with whom you keep in touch? Or relatives?'

Celer gave what might have been a shrug. 'A brother, sir.'

'Older?'

If he was surprised then Celer concealed it. Turbo was wary enough of his visitor to do the same, but could still not work out what was behind this interest.

'Yes, sir,' Celer said. 'Eleven years older. He's one of the originals.'

'The first recruits when Domitian formed the legion?'

Turbo suspected that his mouth twitched at mention of the last of the Flavians, an emperor now formally damned by the Senate, his statues cast down and name erased from monuments.

'That's right, sir. Done twenty-two years, all with Minervia, and awarded *dona* twice.'

'Any rank?' Turbo asked.

Celer shook his head. 'Doesn't have the learning for it

– or the brains truth be told. But he raised me and made sure I could read and write well before I joined up.'

'Sounds a fine soldier – and a good brother,' Hadrian said. For the first time Celer smiled. 'Where is he now?'

'Out of the way hole called Piroboridava, sir. They sent a few hundred veterans to keep an eye on the Dacians after they packed it in.'

'The legion has more than its fair share of veterans?'

'Fifteen hundred or so, sir.'

Turbo was surprised and guessed that Celer was as well, although the soldier did not show it, but finally understood. If he lasted the course, a legionary soldiered for twenty-five years, the last five with the status of veteran, and then took honourable discharge with the emperor's thanks, best wishes and a decent bounty – or failing that a plot of land in some benighted colony. Most legions had been around for generations, the majority since the days of the Divine Augustus more than a century ago. That tended to give them a good spread of ages in the ranks, if always weighted a little towards the young because of the toll taken by war, the ravages of disease, desertion and those accidents that always happened. A new legion was different, since apart from a few soldiers transferred in from elsewhere, you began with everyone enlisting over the course of a few months.

'Yes, I thought the number would be something like that. I was a tribune with II Adiutrix and the older officers talked of the shock caused when they had to discharge all the men enlisted when it was formed by Nero.'

Turbo almost sighed, and instead made a sign to ward off the evil eye, holding his hand under his desk so that no one else could see. It seemed unlucky to mention a second damned emperor in as many minutes.

Hadrian could not have seen, and yet he glanced at the centurion and gave a brief smile before he continued. 'Meant we lost a lot of experience in a very short time, although things were pretty much back to normal by the time I was posted to them. So someone realised that Minervia had more than its fair share of *veterani*, far more than could be attached to *cohors I*, so decided to send the poor devils off as garrisons? Wonder how your brother and the rest feel about that?'

'They're soldiers, under discipline, and will do their duty.' Turbo's tone was almost defiant, for he was not about to see one of his men tricked into indiscretion by some aristocrat.

'Pia fidelis, sir,' Celer added, shoulders stiffening back to attention.

'Of course.' Hadrian's smile was open, apparently without malice, but unable to conceal the conceit of a man who knew himself to be smarter than others. 'Pius' and 'faithful', he thought to himself. The titles had been awarded to the legion by Domitian, because they quickly abandoned a provincial legate who had rebelled against him. They were also named Domitiana, but had quietly forgotten that after his fall and it would be impolite to mention it now.

'Of course,' he said again. 'I did not mean to imply anything less. Legio I Minervia will always do its duty and more, I know that. That's why I am so proud to become its legatus. It is just...' He gave an earthy laugh. 'Well all the best legionaries I have ever known have bitched like mad. Moan, moan, all the time, and then they fight like heroes and endure more than Hercules.'

Celer smiled, until Turbo glared at him. The praetor was speaking the truth, but that did not mean they had to admit it.

Hadrian stood up. 'To be frank, I have always felt that with senators in charge, our lads have plenty to bitch about!'

Celer's face was rigid, although his eyes were sparkling, and Turbo struggled to keep his own features as blank. With well-mannered apologies for disturbing them both, and thanks for their assistance, the praetor left. Both sentiments insincere and unconvincing when combined with the immense self-assurance of an aristocrat, but then what else were manners for save to conceal otherwise unpalatable truths. Turbo was glad to see the man gone. He did not believe that he had compromised himself in any way or done anything improper. Still, he dictated an account of the meeting to a clerk and had it copied and filed just in case.

III

Piroboridava
The same day, the third hour of the night

A BLIND MAN could have followed the tracks left by the horses, not that it mattered. The fugitives were well mounted, had two spare horses, and far too much of a lead. A month or so earlier, when the snow was deeper, they might not have made it up the valley to the pass at all, but Ferox reckoned that they would get there during the night if they pressed hard or at the latest tomorrow morning.

The pursuers did their best for two hours and did not see the quarry once, only the hoof prints in the snow. There was also a spear, point driven into the hard ground so that it stood upright, and surely a sign rather than an accident, but it was not one that Ferox had ever seen before.

He was disappointed by the cavalrymen provided by the garrison, or strictly speaking by their mounts, although that was really the riders' responsibility. It was always hard to keep horses in condition during the winter, when they had to spend so many hours in their boxes and the chances to exercise were so few. Yet even allowing for that, these were in poor shape. Several looked old, almost as old as their elderly riders, and it was obvious that no one had ridden far or often even in the last few weeks when the paths were slowly becoming easier. There was a flabbiness about men and animals, infecting spirit as well as body. Not that it mattered, because he had known that the pursuit was hopeless from the start, but it was a bad sign. Even on the tour of the fort he had sensed so much that was wrong with the garrison. This was an odd place, the men stationed here bored, angry and frustrated, and none of that would help him in his task.

Ferox turned back before night started to fall, and at least the men rode with far more enthusiasm and even a little more speed on the way back to Piroboridava. The horses knew their way, knew they were going back to warmth and food and it was an effort to keep them together in a group when all were itching to race.

The Brigantes had escaped. No doubt they had heard that Decebalus was ignoring the treaty and once again welcoming army deserters into his own army, giving them rich rewards and promotion. If they played it well, then in a few months each of the fugitives could have rank, a farmstead and a pretty grey-eyed wife. That might be enough for contentment, and was better than the punishment awaiting them if ever the army caught up. Yet there was still the oath, pressing around each man's soul. Ferox was relieved not to have to kill any more Brigantes today. Let them run, and hope never to see them again.

'They'll be back,' Vindex said, breaking a silence that was unusual for him. The fort was in sight, a dark shape against the glow of the snow. 'You know Ivonercus.'

Ferox grunted in reply, sure that his friend was right, but

not wanting to talk about it. He had enough on his mind without thinking about the future. So much seemed wrong, which just meant that he was not looking at everything in the right way. There was design behind all of this, and he had to hope that he could see the truth before what he did not understand killed all of them.

Latinius Macer sighed, and only in part because he found Ferox irritating. As the current commander of the garrison, he had naturally invited the centurion to dine with him, and given the shocking events earlier in the day, a conference was all the more important.

Macer had a tidy mind, decades of experience in the army with its regulations and routine, and this was neither tidy nor very military. Instead it had the makings of a scandal, perhaps even a disaster, all caused by a succession of foolish decisions. Those choices were not his, and by the time the worst happened he should be far from this place, but the crassness of it all offended him. He was too old to expect fairness from the world any more than sense from the army, so the risk that his name would become associated with it all simply because he had handed over the command was just how the world worked. Still, he would make sure that he had done all that he could.

'So, please help me to understand,' he said, trying again. 'Your own men want to kill you?'

'Some of them.'

Macer had planned to leave Piroboridava as soon as his successor arrived, and was wondering whether or not he could still do this in the circumstances. If his health had been better he might have jumped at the excuse to stay on. Forty-three years in the army was a long, long time, and he wondered about life as a civilian.

'Just some,' Macer said after waiting a long time for a fuller answer. Every unit had its unpopular officers, the tyrants, the floggers, the extortioners and the ones who preyed on the soldiers' women, or worse yet, their children. They were rare, and it took weak or lazy superiors to let matters get out of hand. Then there were mutinies or murders, and people died, sometimes even the man or men who had caused it all in the first place. It was hard to tell, but Ferox did not strike him as that sort of officer. 'Just some,' he repeated.

At least the meal was nothing special. Macer was no slave to his stomach, but had come to enjoy the comforts of rank and decent wealth. However, without his even making the suggestion, his steward had provided campaign meals for his last few days with the eagles. It reminded him of when he was young, fighting those crazy, brave rebels in Judaea under Vespasian and Titus, or with the heavy scent of pine resin as they chased the Chatti through their forests.

Ferox did not seem to mind being given a bowl of thick stew, flavoured with salty bacon, along with cheap posca to drink. The fine-grained bread was a concession, but having hard tack biscuit with his meal would have been going too far. Still, they sat on camp stools on either side of a folding table in one of the side rooms – the walls were colourful, but only painted in fairly simple geometric patterns. Another luxury was the warmth. As one of the few partially stone buildings in the fort, the commander's *praetorium* had its own bath suite and the rooms butting on to it were always warmed by the constantly tended furnace. That was a luxury, and one that he would never have ordered for himself. Macer had come here prostrated by fever in the last weeks before the Dacian king made peace. This had been the closest base with a big hospital, and he had spent weeks there in peril of his life and months recovering. In the meantime the legionaries had decided to build a far more comfortable house for the fort's commander than was normal on a site like this. He took it both as a complement and a sign that they understood how the army worked. When he recovered, he was by far the most senior officer in the area, already present at a fort with such a mixed garrison, while I Minervia were scattered and there was not really a main camp for him to supervise. So the army put him in charge here, and thanks to the enthusiasm of the soldiers he had lived in as much comfort as such a bleak spot could offer. Over the months and years his health had recovered a little, and it was nice to be his own master on a day-to-day basis, rather than deferring to aristocrats, who were either lazy, stupid, or just interfered in things they did not understand. Yet the appointment also told him that there would be no offer of another post after this one. His time with the eagles was done, at least if he could bring himself in all conscience to leave, now that a replacement had arrived.

Macer tried again to get at the truth. 'Sabinus tells me that you killed their king.'

'Yes.' Actually Vindex had done the killing, but they had both hunted the man down and Ferox had been in charge.

'Youthful high spirits, I presume?' Macer's temper was rising and he fought it down. Instead he sighed again, took another spoonful of the stew, savoured it, and then put the spoon down. 'You do not know me,' he began, 'but I spent two years as a *cornicularius*, then five as *principalis* before being raised to centurion. I did not have influential friends, but I kept on climbing, slowly, but steadily. I led my own cohort, and at long last got the step to primus pilus and now *praefectus castrorum*. I am an *eques*,' he held up his hand to show the ring, 'and own an estate near Lepcis Magna. I grew up there, the gap-toothed lad of a tanner, and I'm going back to lord it over them and serve on the council. Now do you know what all that means?'

'That you are a damned good soldier,' Ferox said, his admiration genuine.

Macer grunted at the compliment. 'What it really means is that I have seen it all and done it all. And one thing I have done more times than I can remember is bullshit to senior officers, and I'm not about to sit here and let you do it to me. So talk. Who was this king and what happened?'

'His name was Claudius Aviragus, from the royal line of the Brigantes, they're the—'

'I was three years with *XX Valeria Victrix* under Agricola,' Macer cut in.

'He was from their royal house, and he or his sister in line to rule, assuming Rome decided to let the tribe have a king or queen. He'd been educated in Gaul and Rome, served as equestrian officer...'

'Useless bastards every one of them,' Macer muttered.

'Aye. ... Well this one got ambitious, started talking to men plotting to overthrow the Lord Trajan, and rebelled. We beat him – in the end, that is – and Neratius Marcellus, the *legatus Augusti*, sent me to hunt Aviragus down and bring back his head.' Ferox shrugged. 'I obeyed my orders.'

Macer nodded. The emperor had already been on the Danube by the time news of the rising reached Rome. An official report was read in the Senate and then published, which merely stated that there had been disturbances in Britannia, principally the north, and that after some fighting the miscreants had been killed or arrested. No one had even suggested that Trajan be hailed as *imperator* for the success of his local commander, implying that it was all a minor affair, and then soon the big war with Dacia had begun and everyone forgot about some problems with brigands in a distant province.

'The Brigantes are known for their loyalty,' Macer said. 'So am I right in thinking that the ones wanting to kill you served this Aviragus?'

'There was a royal ala and cohort trained and equipped like regular auxiliaries. Aviragus commanded the cavalry, but all of them followed him when he raised an army.' Ferox did his best to explain, deciding that Macer was sensible enough to treat with respect. So he talked about how the rebels had announced that Trajan was dead and Neratius Marcellus trying to make himself emperor, which meant that they were not revolting against Rome, only against a usurper. He even mentioned the rout of the first column sent against them, and the desperate battle to break the rebel army, only won when enough loyal Brigantes came to the Romans' aid.

'How many of the king's men survived?' Macer asked.

'More than half were taken prisoner more or less unscathed. The wounded were sent home, others fled and were not caught. Apart from the leaders, no one was too interested to go hunting for them.'

'How many were executed?' Macer's tone was matter of fact. Both men knew the fate of rebels. 'I take it that they did not just tell the prisoners that they were conscripted into the army and place you in charge.'

Ferox gave a wry smile. 'Not quite. At least, not straightaway. But this was not a war, you see, not a rebellion, however it looked. Too many important people were connected, more or less distantly, and with the emperor about to win glory on behalf of the res publica, public trials and executions would not have fitted with the spirit of the age. All this was just a disturbance by bandit leaders, a few good men turned bad, and nothing to threaten the peace and stability of the empire.'

Macer grunted, but was sensible enough to let Ferox tell it in his own way, now that he had started.

'A couple of dozen died, the executions private and quick – no crucifixions or trips to the arena. About a hundred were condemned to the mines, although in the event most ended up working on the salt beds. I would guess as many more were vouched for by loyal leaders, most of all Aviragus' sister Enica, who had been staunch throughout, and they took a fresh oath to Rome and to serve her. That left almost three hundred, all of whom were given a once in a lifetime opportunity to enlist in the army.'

'And they are your men?' Macer rubbed his chin, an old habit he had never quite shaken off.

Ferox had a surprisingly musical laugh. 'Would that it were so simple? Most were sent off to one of the cohorts or alae of Britons, as long as the unit was stationed well outside the province. Some settled in, and some were trouble. I have a score of recaptured deserters from that lot, and fifty mutineers. Then I have ninety of the ones from the first batch that were not sent out to a unit – maybe nobody wanted them, as some are old or speak no Latin and seem too dull to learn. I am not especially popular with any of them and none are too keen on army life in the first place. After that it gets really funny, because it was decided after a couple of years to let the ones condemned to hard labour have a chance to rehabilitate themselves through military service.'

Macer whistled softly. '*Omnes ad stercus.*'

'They added a couple of hundred men from the loyal clans, and just to season the mix all the waifs and strays recruited in Britannia, including a fair few caught thieving and invited to join up. On paper there is a mixed force of two hundred horse and four hundred foot, but in practice they haven't yet been all brought together in one place. Half were concentrated in Pannonia back in the autumn. Neratius Marcellus' brother is legatus Augusti there, so was easily convinced of the wisdom of the whole thing. The appointed commander drowned while they were being ferried along the river.'

'An accident?'

'I suppose that is at least theoretically possible. ... And so they thought of me, and here I am.' Ferox shrugged. 'Guess I have tried to bullshit too many senior officers over the years.'

Macer laughed. 'They probably told you that it was because of your exceptional abilities as a leader.'

'Something like that. They said a Briton would best understand other Britons, but that's just because they can't tell the differences between the tribes. And they promoted me to *pilus prior* of cohors VII.' There was no enthusiasm in Ferox's voice.

'That will make you senior here,' Macer said. His mind was made up, even if he was not quite sure why. The orders brought by Ferox stated that he was relieved of command at the fort. He was free to leave as soon as he chose, and could take an escort of up to fifty men – including a dozen specified by name and intended for other duties – with him. The rest were to stay, and come under Ferox's command. His annoyance at the man was replaced by a fair bit of sympathy, but it seemed clear that hanging around would risk Ferox getting murdered before he was gone. The orders would stand and he could – and officially should – leave and let command pass to Sabinus, who was the next in seniority. Yet people would talk as they always did, and they were bound to say that he had run from responsibility. He knew that it would bother him, even far away on his farm, revelling in the African warmth, so he would go first, as ordered, before anything else could happen. It would mean a hard journey because of the weather, but a day ought to take them down the valley far enough to ease the cold.

Macer's intent gaze fixed on Ferox. 'Why are you still alive? And don't bother to say that you have no taste for philosophy. You know what I mean. A lot of your men want you dead – and this Vindex – and there is always the dark of night and the quiet moment in camp or on the march. If these men were truly as determined as Britons can be – or any men consumed by hate – then we wouldn't be having this conversation and you'd be floating down the Ister or cold in a ditch somewhere.'

'Two tried right at the start, but I was faster.' Ferox

rubbed his chin where new stubble was already forming. He sighed. 'That made the others think, and I am careful and maybe it is just luck, but I know what you mean. There would always be a chance if they did not mind too much the risk of arrest and death. Reckon the ones who are left would prefer to live.'

Macer nodded. 'So here, where they can run off to a cushy billet with Decebalus, they're more willing to remember their oath and their hatred.'

'That's how I see it.'

Macer made up his mind. 'I'll go the day after tomorrow at dawn,' he announced. It could not be sooner, for he needed to assign the men and make sure that they drew rations, tents and baggage animals. Only a storm would stop him. 'We can carry out the formal handover tomorrow. Will the rest of your men have arrived by then?'

Ferox shook his head. 'I expect that they will cross your path as you make your way to Dobreta. That's the half of the unit already in province, of course. The rest won't be here for a month or so.'

Privately the praefectus was relieved, since no more assassination attempts were likely until the others arrived. There did not seem any reason to expect these Brigantes to be hostile to him and his party. He had not cared much for Britannia during the time he had spent there, although the campaigns had at least gained him a step in rank. The Britons were odd folk, even for barbarians. Ferox's Latin was perfect, better indeed than his own, for all his family had struggled to give him as good an education as they could afford and for all his efforts to fit in. Yet there was an air about him, something not quite right, not quite civilized.

Macer had learned that he came from the Silures, a tribe of the south west with a reputation as vicious bastards, and perhaps blood still told after all these years. They were supposed to be hard to kill, and it had taken the army more than twenty years to batter them into submission. For a moment, he wondered whether there was a grain of sense and purpose in the plan of sending Ferox and this ragbag of rebels, bandits, deserters and rival tribesmen to this place. Probably not, he decided, and it was just the army being even more like the army than usual.

'You have told me how, my dear Ferox, and for that I thank you, but I confess that I am still baffled as to why you and your men are coming here.'

'A friend truly learned in philosophy said to me more than once that there is much in life to convince you that the gods have a sense of humour. Or that they just don't like some people.' He shrugged again. 'The Brigantes are good fighters. They're of more use to Rome fighting its enemies than dead. Killing them would just be a waste of resources, so the idea is to make use of them and only kill them if that does not work. ... But that's only part of the story and the rest is political, so beyond a mere centurion. Aviragus' sister is eager to be queen of her people and confirm that her family will rule for as long as their line lasts, so they say that she begged the legatus to release the prisoners and make them soldiers, and pressed for a unit to be formed combining the different factions of the tribe.'

'What are her chances? A decision like that would have to be made by the emperor, but he would surely listen to the legatus.'

'No idea,' Ferox lied. He was not about to start discussing Claudia Enica with a stranger. 'I'm not paid enough to have an opinion.'

IV

*Near Vindobona, Province of Upper Pannonia
Thirteenth day before the Kalends of March*

I T WAS LATE for travelling, especially for such a fine coach, a fashionable, well-sprung and expensive *raeda* pulled by four mules, and the tall man grunted in satisfaction from his hiding place a few hundred paces away. He had feared a few armed escorts and he needed to be quick for this was too far within the empire for his liking.

'Told you,' Sosius said, crouching beside the tall warrior in the ditch running next to the road. 'No guards. Just an old man driving, a boy to help with the horses and a couple of other slaves.'

'Not the brightest, is she?' Quiet country roads were rarely safe, let alone at night. 'Any cutpurse could take her.'

'She's discreet and married, as is her lover. He's waiting a couple of miles down the road in the farmhouse. Expect she's all dressed up for him. You know what these fashionable ladies are like.'

'Only from a distance. They'd never have looked at a common soldier like me.' The tall man grunted again. 'Doesn't matter if she's dumb, Catualda isn't after brains. You sure she's pretty?'

'A goddess. Twenty-five, skin still like alabaster, and everything where it should be. Knows how to use it too, well broken in by husband and lovers. And fancy, if that's what he wants, then he couldn't find a fancier, unless he wants to send you to go to Rome itself.'

'Hair? The king believes all Roman ladies have black hair.'

'Redhead, but if he's that keen on dark hair there's always dye. What does it matter if all he wants is to hump a fancy Roman lady?'

That was why the tall man was here, hired by the king of a clan two hundred miles beyond the *limes*, far enough out of Rome's reach if he could only find one and get her past the army's outposts and far enough away before anyone found out or could catch them. He had been hired because he had once been a soldier of Rome, and a good one too, until a decurion wanted his woman and he had killed the man and run. Twelve years on, he could barely remember the woman's face, let alone her name, but he had survived, first in Dacia and now among the Marcomanni, Quadi and the peoples to the east. He sold his sword, killing as he was bidden, with half a dozen good men at his side. Catualda liked the silver dishes and the pale blue glass of the empire, and listened with fascination to traders' tales of the greater wonders of Rome. He was rich by the standards of the tribes, for his clan controlled large salt beds and lived in hill country hard for others to attack, but through which one of the best of the old trade roads passed. For whatever reason, Catualda wanted a Roman lady to add to his wives, and had promised them plenty of gold if they brought her. The king reckoned that a one-time soldier of Rome was best suited to the task – and since the tall man was known as a bandit and raider, no one was likely to ask too many questions if he was caught. Even if he revealed the secret, the Romans had never come as far as the King's lands and were not likely to start now.

A man came running out of the woods on the far side of the road.

'Help! Help!' he shouted, waving his arms. 'Please help me!' The carriage was fifty paces away and no one seemed to be paying any attention to the man.

'They're not going to stop,' the warrior hissed. 'Why in Hercules' name should they?'

'They will,' Sosius whispered. 'She's a kind lady.'

'If you think so much of her why are you selling her to me?'

'Business,' Sosius said. 'Only business.' They had been lucky to come across Sosius, the freedman of a rich Roman who acted as his agent inside and well beyond the province. He traded in luxuries, favours and information, and for the right price it was said that he could find anything someone wanted. The truth of that rumour was about to be tested.

The driver shouted something and a woman they could not see replied from inside the raeda. Hauling hard on the reins, the team slowed from trot to walk and then halted. Sosius and the warrior slid back down in the ditch so that they could not be seen, even by the driver and the boy sitting on top of the carriage.

'Thank you, lords, thank you,' the man who had called to them said. 'May Minerva and Vesta bless you and your families.' They heard a scrabbling sound as he went down into the ditch and came up on the road.

'Ask him what this is about?' a woman's voice said. It was a nice voice, refined and yet caring, and if the warrior had still had a conscience he might have felt a doubt. Instead he waited for the right moment, trusting his men to follow the plan.

'What do you want, fellow?' the driver shouted.

'Protection, sir and noble lady. I was set upon by bandits, beaten up and robbed of money, most of my clothes and my donkey. My friend is hurt far worse, and I wish to go and find help so that I can return to him. Are we near an inn or village? We got lost, you see, and no longer know where we are. There would be someone who might help if you would carry me that far, I am sure of it. I beg you to help.'

'Lady, he wants a ride,' the coachman shouted. 'But I don't believe him. Bandits often tell such tall tales. We should have waited for the cavalry to reach us, as I said.'

'Never speak to me like that!' The kind voice was shrieking, and the warrior half smiled. Good luck to Catualda bringing this one into his hall. 'Don't you dare!'

'Hoy! Let go of that harness!' The coachman ignored her and was yelling. His long whip cracked and there was a yelp. 'I said let go, you mongrel!'

'Now!' the warrior shouted and began to push up the side of the ditch. Something hit him hard on the leg, knocking it from under him and he slid down the muddy bank. Sosius was over him, and his cudgel struck again, striking the warrior on the wrist so that he dropped his sword. He tried to get up and this time the blow was on his head and knocked him flat again.

'Lie still, you dumb bastard!'

There were shouts, a woman's scream, a brief clash of steel and the dull thunks as blade sank into flesh.

'Enjoy the moment, slave,' the warrior said, not caring

that the man had been freed, for his men were good and would soon deal with the travellers. He had told them that the lady was not to be marked, let alone touched in any other way. The slave girl was another matter, although he wanted a good look at her before he decided whether they could have some fun with her. If she was a virgin and pretty, then she might command a high price if they kept her that way. What mattered now was to grab the mistress and the girl if they could and get away as soon as they could. If they were lucky, they could sneak through the line of towers along the frontier before the sun rose the day after tomorrow, and be safe from pursuit if they rode hard for another day.

With one last cry of agony, the fight was over.

'Get up!' Sosius said, his club held ready, although what he expected to do with that against five good warriors was anyone's guess. The tall man's grin of satisfaction changed to shock when he stood, nursing his broken wrist, and stared across the road to see that all his men were dead. A slim boy not yet twenty was wiping the blade of his gladius in the cloak of one of the corpses. Beside him a girl, who was a little older and wearing a short tunic, was feeling the balance of the sword taken from another of the dead men!

'All done?' It was the lady's voice and she appeared from around the mules, clad in a long dress that shimmered in the moonlight. There were dark stains on the material and more on her face and they could only be blood, for she held a curved *sica* in her hand and the blade was dripping. A short figure pattered up behind her, and the warrior thought it was a child until it spoke with a deep voice.

'How positively disgusting,' the dwarf said. 'I told you we should have gone to the feast instead, but would you listen?

A nice girl who likes to play with swords will soon find she doesn't get any more invitations like that.' No one seemed to pay any attention to him.

'All done, my queen,' the boy said. 'Five of them, all dead.'

'Good,' she said. 'Well, Sosius, are you satisfied?'

'Yes, lady, it is a good start.'

That was Sosius, the warrior thought ruefully, sell anything or anybody if the price was right. He still could not fathom why he would be worth the trouble of catching.

'There is another one with the horses, about a quarter of a mile back in the trees. Follow the brook and you'll find him. Bran had better deal with him.'

'Aye,' the boy said, striding away, and without being asked the girl in the tunic followed.

'What now?' the lady asked – or the woman since the warrior could not help wondering whether this killer was a fighter from the arenas in disguise. She was beautiful though, even with the blood, so Sosius had not lied about that, but it seemed odd that a proper lady would speak with such respect to a slave.

'He will give me the name of the man I need.'

'Bugger I will. Why don't you go hump yourself? I'll entertain the slut.'

Sosius swung the cudgel against the man's kneecap, and the warrior dropped.

'He will tell me,' Sosius said, ignoring the groaning man beside him. 'Then as agreed I will take the boy and the lass and we will find that man and learn what we can. If all goes well, we will take him alive and bring him back.' Almost absent-mindedly, he slammed the club down onto the man's other knee. 'Will take a month, perhaps two or more and we should be back. I may send them to you if I am needed elsewhere. Then you should send word to my master.'

'It is agreed.'

'My master is a good ally, lady.'

'I said it was agreed. Now I had better get to the fortress before we are missed.'

'Are you sure, lady? These roads are not safe and I am taking your two warriors away.'

'I shall manage with Achilles to defend poor little me. And I do not care to see what comes next.'

'Very wise, lady.' Sosius swung the club again. After a little while the coachman's whip cracked and the warrior heard the wheels grating on the stones of the road as it drove away. Above him Sosius drew a long dagger in his other hand. 'Now,' he said. 'Do you want to make this hard or difficult?'

The warrior spat his contempt, so Sosius hit him in the mouth with the club.

'Fair enough,' he said. 'We have plenty of time.'

The Tower of the Ox
The next day

*B*RASUS WAS THE *first to see the riders, and they were not the ones he was expecting. They were Romans though, drinkers of wine and unclean of soul, and they were soldiers. He whistled softly and one of his warriors looked up. They were below, two on either side of the gaping hole where the gate and the wall for ten paces on either side had been demolished, hiding behind the mounds of rubble. From down there they could see much less than he could from the window in the tower. The riders were a quarter of a mile away, only just over the brow of the ridge and invisible to the warriors. There were two of them in sight, leading two horses, and so far no sign of any more. They were too far away to hear his whistle, but he did not want to risk gesturing from the window and had to trust that his men would do the right thing now that they were alerted to trouble.*

The Romans stopped and Brasus wondered whether to climb down to join his men, before deciding that it was better to watch the enemy. They were staring at the tower and the ruined walls around it. For the moment the driving rain had stopped, and Brasus sensed that the storm had passed and that the night would be dry. He doubted that the Romans understood the land well enough to realise this, and with little more than an hour left before nightfall, they were surely wondering whether the tower offered safety and shelter. Were there more of them? As far as he knew no patrols had come this high up towards the pass since the early autumn, which did not mean that one had not come now.

After an age, with Brasus regretting not having climbed down to join his men, the riders walked their horses forward again. They did not seem agitated, but one had a spear and the other had drawn his sword, and they moved with care.

There was no one behind them, or if there were, they were staying too far back to be of any help. Never before had the man come with soldiers or sent them to carry his letters. Perhaps he would not come today, delayed by the storm or wary if he had seen the cavalrymen. Brasus thought back to the solstice and the sending of the Messenger, when the Roman merchant had knelt as a captive with the two legionaries. For years the man had helped Decebalus, bringing him information, much of it secret and carrying letters back and forth so that the king could speak to Romans of high rank. Their treachery was contemptible, but useful, and perhaps no more than could be expected of such vermin, eaters of red meat and drinkers of wine. The merchant was paid for all this, paid with gold for the risks he ran and the shrewdness with which he performed his tasks.

Brasus wondered whether Decebalus had ordered the fat man taken to the ceremony to frighten him. Yet that was a risk. There were three captives because there were three Messengers prepared to carry word of the world of men to the Lord Zalmoxis. Yet there was risk, for as many captives were fated to die as Messengers, and the Second might have failed the test so that Brasus would become the Third, which meant that he would end his life on this earth to travel to the Heavens and also that the merchant would have been killed.

Less than fifty paces from the old gateway one of the Romans stopped, holding both the riderless horses, as his comrade trotted forward.

Brasus wanted to believe that fate and the will of the Lord Zalmoxis had decided that night, but the doubts kept bubbling up as the months had passed. The merchant was too valuable to the king to be killed, unless he wanted to prove his devotion by the worth of the offering. Brasus had liked to think that he was chosen by the god because of his own merit. Although only twenty, he was a chieftain, a proven warrior and leader of men, head of a family loyal to the king and pure of life and heart. He had been flattered to be chosen as Messenger, and though passion was vanity, he had to admit that there had been a thrill at the thought of transcending this body to join the god. Such a death was more blessed even than a death in battle.

The Roman was coming closer. Brasus saw his men waiting, weapons in hand. One was an archer and as he watched the man reached into his bag for an arrow. If there was a fight, then Brasus would shout down to him to shoot the one left behind and stop him getting away.

Brasus knew the tower well, which made it a shame to see it abandoned and in disrepair. His father had held this place for the king for many years. He remembered parting with the old man and sensing how strongly he yearned to defend it against the invaders in the last war with Rome. For the first year he was frustrated, until in the second the Romans came and his father fought them and held them for seventeen days before they breached the wall. As his men died fighting, his father had taken his own life in devotion to the god. That too was a good death.

Fate and the will of Zalmoxis, those were the drivers of men's lives, and the pure accepted this truth and embraced their destiny. Yet now he struggled. He had been chosen as Messenger and yet not chosen to go to the god. The other two men were brave warriors, but neither was pileatus, neither a noble or leader of a clan. As reward the king favoured him, even promising to give Brasus one of his daughters in marriage. Instead of passage to the Heavens, he would receive land and power and a royal bride. Accepting this as his just fate might have been easier if it had not seemed so convenient. A loyal nobleman was honoured and rewarded, his devotion to the king confirmed, and the only Roman of value was spared to serve Decebalus. Was that simply the will of the god? If so, then the Lord Zalmoxis was very obliging. The thought was disturbing, gnawing away at his old certainties like a worm burrowing into fruit, but would not go away. He had seen too much in battles and all the little fights of the last war to be certain about anything. So many of the pure failed to act as they should, while other lesser men outshone them like comets – and even Rome and its creatures sometimes showed true purity.

The rider was almost at the rubble piled outside the breach in the wall where the gate and its towers had once stood. He had a yellow crest on his bronze helmet and that was the mark of a junior officer. Still there was no sign of anyone else. If they were not alone, then these men were taking a great risk.

'We are friends!' The man shouted in Latin. He had a strong accent, which Brasus did not recognise, and then he switched to a dialect of the Keltoi, so perhaps he was from one of the tribes of Gaul. 'Friends!' he tried in guttural Greek. The man held his sword high and then dropped it into the snow. 'Friends!'

Brasus could see no sign of a trap, and revealing his own presence did not betray his men. He leaned forward out of the window and shouted down. 'Friend!'

The cavalryman started at the reply, having probably decided that the tower was empty. Brasus gestured to him. 'Dismount and come in! Slowly!' Whether or not he understood the words the Gaul or whoever he was saw the beckoning arm. He swung down from his horse, dropped his shield to lie by the sword and walked up the rubble, arms spread wide to show that they were empty and that he was no threat.

'Call the other!' Brasus pointed at the distant rider and beckoned again. The man nodded, and shouted something back at his comrade, who came on. Then he gasped as warriors appeared on either side of him.

'Just watch him!' Brasus shouted to his men. 'And wait for me.'

By the time he had come down the second cavalryman had come in. One of the warriors held their horses while the rest watched the prisoners.

'Says his name is Ivonercus and this is his servant,' the oldest of the warriors told him. He spoke the Celtic language and they had managed to communicate a little. 'They're both Britons and have run from the Roman army.'

'Why have you come?' Brasus asked in Latin.

'To serve Decebalus,' Ivonercus told him. 'And to fight for him.'

The king always welcomed deserters. If their story was true then they would be taken into his service, but that was for another day. For the moment he explained that they were prisoners and would be guarded until they crossed back through the pass and reached safety. Only then – if they answered all questions satisfactorily – would they be given back their weapons.

'I understand,' Ivonercus assured him. The man seemed desperate to please.

'Take them there,' Brasus ordered, pointing at one of the out-buildings that still had most of its roof, 'and guard them. Bring their horses inside so that they cannot be seen.'

'Yes, my lord.' The older warrior did not say anymore, but the question was obvious from his expression.

'We will wait another day for the messenger. Perhaps two if nothing else seems wrong.' Brasus smiled. 'One man watches the prisoners and another on guard – in the tower during daylight. There won't be a lot of sleep.'

'Two awake, two resting,' the old warrior said. 'It could be worse.'

'There are five of us, and I shall take my turn like everyone else.'

'My lord.'

V

Rome
Tenth day before the Kalends of Martias

'PLEASE, MY LORD, read this!' The old woman thrust a writing tablet out in her right hand, while her left elbow jabbed into a man trying to push her out of the way to present his own petition. For all her grey hairs, she was plump and powerful, and the victim dropped his rolled papyrus as he doubled over. One of the toga-clad praetorians scooped to pick the scroll up and then took the woman's tablet as well. Other guardsmen in cloaks and tunics, but carrying big oval shields and *pila*, formed a cordon to mark the line beyond which the crowd was not permitted. A good princeps ought to be accessible, so like the divine Augustus, Trajan walked whenever possible, even on occasions like this when he was to dine at a friend's house, itself another mark that he was servant of the res publica and not a tyrant. The journey was unannounced, a social call rather than for some ceremony or to attend a session of the Senate, so the crowd was not as big as on other days. These petitioners were only the ones who had waited hour after hour and sometimes day after day outside the main doors of the *Domus Tiberiana*, the house of the princeps, on the off-chance that he would appear.

The procession did not stop, everyone taking their cue from Trajan, who whenever he went into the city took pride in maintaining the steady, regulation drill pace of the army. Hadrian could almost hear the instructor calling out the time and tapping his stick or the butt of a spear onto the parade ground as he did so. It had amused him in Dacia to note how often all the *comites*, the senators like himself who accompanied Trajan to war to advise and serve him, unconsciously fell into step alongside their leader. The emperor had his toga carefully draped over his left arm, his back was as straight as a spear shaft, and you could see the effort as he forced himself to glance around him now and then rather than striding on, concentrating only on the task in hand.

Hadrian wondered whether the divine Augustus had been more affable, at least until his great age and poor health meant that he had to be carried in a litter on all save the shortest journeys. Trajan often invoked Augustus, and even when he did not acknowledge the fact tended to make the first princeps his model for his decisions and behaviour. Yet his love was for the camp rather than the city, *militiae* rather than *domi* – and deep down he wanted everyone to see this. In his youth, long before anyone could have guessed that he would be raised to the purple, Trajan had served more than the usual spell with the army, much more, but Hadrian guessed that his former guardian felt that this was not enough and still needed to prove to himself that at heart he was a soldier. Hence the steady pace, and acting always as the bluff, no nonsense military man, who demanded even greater discipline from himself than his subordinates, and pretended to less education than he possessed. Perhaps after all these years the act was all there was, and that made Hadrian wonder about the nature of a person or thing, and whether it could be changed by circumstance or desire. The deepest joy of philosophy for him was that there would never be a final answer, only further speculation. Still, one thing that was certain was that there would be another great war, and the only question now was when. Hadrian believed that he already knew where, and hoped that his own appointment had this in mind.

A slave walking behind the emperor took the petitions from the guardsman, scanning through them quickly. He whispered something to Trajan, who nodded, and a boy doubled back with a coin for one man and a little purse for the old woman. This slave was about thirteen or fourteen, with a dark complexion and smooth unblemished skin. He was also quick, moving well, if without the polish provided by training in the gymnasium. A lot of the imperial slaves were good looking like this one, and a fair few encouraged to preen and think highly of themselves.

'Don't get any ideas,' a voice said from just behind his shoulder.

'Good evening, noble Laberius,' Hadrian replied, as the former consul came alongside. They kissed on the cheek in greeting and smiled with everything apart from their eyes. Until now Laberius Maximus had been near the rear of the little procession, talking with men of his own age.

'We do not want any more awkwardness, do we?' Laberius gripped Hadrian's right arm just above the elbow, a gesture that always annoyed him. 'Good, good,' he went on. 'Youthful indiscretion is one thing, but you are a praetor now.'

Hadrian smiled. Just before the first campaign in Dacia he had taken one of the imperial boys as a lover. It was not rape, or even coercion beyond the fact that one was a slave and one was an aristocrat. He had wooed the boy, given him presents as an older man should, and been kind. Yet Trajan's rage had astounded him and for a while he feared that he might be sent home in disgrace, favour forever denied. Men closer to the emperor had placated him, mature men with good military records like Laberius, the sort of men Trajan liked and trusted, and in the end Hadrian had been forgiven, at least publicly. There was no need for reminders, for he was not a man to make the same mistake twice, but it had put him under obligation to Laberius and the rest.

The whole business was a nonsense and Trajan's anger a mystery. The emperor must have known that gossip throughout the empire, let alone among the aristocracy, was amused by his fondness for having lots of pretty boys in his household, just as they were by his habit of drinking heavily when he was the host at a dinner. Hadrian had nursed plenty of merciless hangovers as a result, for like most guests he felt obliged to match their leader. Yet he did not know for certain that Trajan had ever used any of the boys in that way, whether casually as slaves or with kindness. It was so hard to tell. Maybe this was all part of play-acting the tough soldier, and, realising his own appetites, the emperor rigidly exercised self-control, denying himself the slightest concession to human frailty and vice. Then again, maybe he was very, very discreet. Either way, the Roman aristocracy would approve. Excesses denied were admirable, indulgences concealed were pardonable, as long as the secret never escaped for such was the hypocrisy of the senatorial class. Trajan had never done anything unwise or acted badly while drunk, so that was also no weakness or flaw, and the same attitude stretched to the boys at court. If ever anything dishonourable happened, then no one saw it.

Hadrian did not know the truth, and after all these years could not claim to understand Trajan. That, indeed, was the root of the whole problem. Hadrian's father was the emperor's cousin, and when both his parents died, Trajan had become Hadrian's guardian, back in the days when he was no more than a prominent senator. He had been efficient, stern and distant, and had softened only a little in more recent years.

Laberius kept alongside him, and they exchanged the usual empty pleasantries, asking after relations and friends. Hadrian sensed that the former consul wanted something, but manners dictated that they chat about nothing first.

'You are off to the army soon.' It was a statement, not a question.

'I am.' Hadrian was conscious that he slurred some words and cursed himself for doing it now, especially when Laberius gave a faint smile. Men said that it was the accent of Hispania, but since Hadrian had spent barely a year in the province and only when he was already fourteen, he doubted it.

'You do not care for the courts?'

'Acting as judge may teach a man something,' Hadrian conceded, 'although it seems largely a question of discerning which side is lying the least.'

This time Laberius' smile had less mockery. 'A good

training for life, I should have thought. Still, soldiering may be a little more straightforward. The Minervia have earned a fine reputation in what is still a short history. It is a good command, albeit a scattered one at present, as you have no doubt learned from your investigations?' He paused, and stared straight into Hadrian's eyes. 'That is unusual diligence – or something else perhaps? Still, I am sure you know your own business.'

Hadrian had expected the matter to be raised at some point during the evening, and wondered only how soon and who would bring it up. The emperor had surely learned of his visit to the camp of the foreigners before the day was out. It was probably better that someone was speaking openly to him about it.

'I wish to serve the princeps and Rome well.'

'Indeed, and such an honourable intent must be praised. But why talk to the frumentarii?'

This time Hadrian smiled. 'Because I wonder whether we do not take sufficient advantage of their knowledge. Where else in Rome will you find men from every legion, recent arrivals most of them and sent back in due course? Apart from the lists of numbers, locations and supplies, those men have knowledge and news beyond the written reports of legates and procurators. They could all become eyes and ears, reaching out across the globe.'

Laberius was sceptical. 'Common soldiers, though. I'll grant they can all read and write in a good hand, but they are not selected for intelligence or insight.'

'But they could be.'

The former consul nodded several times, his head moving slowly as if it confirmed an obvious truth, but Hadrian could tell that he was thinking. A lot of good ideas appeared so simple once someone had explained them, and there was no doubt that Laberius Maximus was now exploring the possibilities.

'That is original,' he conceded at last. 'Although perhaps we should be cautious in turning so many simple soldiers into spies. The gods only know how much they might discover, and how inconvenient it might prove.'

'For the good of the res publica.'

'An expression frequently employed by the last of the Flavians – as even you may be just old enough to recall – so of meagre comfort. After all, we all have our little secrets, do we not?' The stare was intense. 'And would prefer that they remain just that, harmless indiscretions known only to ourselves. Trust is important. To trust the men picked by the emperor or appointed by the Senate to do their jobs to the best of their ability, without having to be told step by step how to go about them. A degree of ignorance does little harm if it fosters trust.'

The crowd had thinned and as they went downhill several senators joined them, hailing the emperor and then the rest of the party. Hadrian was always amused to see the slaves doing the same thing with the slightest of nods and gestures. Theirs was a small world as well in many ways, as attendants of great men.

'You are in need of a new tribune,' Laberius commented once they had resumed.

'Yes.' Hadrian had suspected as much, for the stripling in the post had done six months and on brief acquaintance had struck him as the sort never to do more than the barest minimum. No doubt Laberius was better informed.

'Anyone in mind?'

That was surprisingly direct and strange for the matter was not really up to him.

'I would guess that the legatus will find someone suitable.' That was the usual way, with the governor of the province putting forward a name to the emperor for approval, more often than not recommending someone who had in turn been recommended to him.

'Wouldn't do any harm if you wrote to him with a suggestion.'

More petitioners clustered where the road turned, and this caused a little delay. In front of them, an older senator was telling a story about Augustus and a poet who had waited outside the palace for weeks, hoping that he could get the Caesar's attention for long enough to recite a composition in his praise. 'Well Augustus spotted the ragged fellow, and made sure to ignore him, always turning away. He wanted money, of course, they all do. When did you ever hear of a rich poet who did not inherit his wealth?'

Hadrian half listened, for the old senator had a carrying voice and either did not realise how loudly he was speaking or did not care. It took an effort not to chip in with half a dozen examples of poets whose verse had earned them considerable wealth.

'Perhaps I could think of someone,' Hadrian said softly. If Laberius wanted to play little games then why not make it hard for him.

'Day after day it went on,' the senator continued, half shouting. 'Sun and rain, there the poor fellow was and each time the divine Augustus strode past. Took to coming earlier and earlier and finally to camping out to be closest to the edge of the road.'

'Perhaps you could,' Laberius said. 'And perhaps even better you would consider Licinianus – I mean young Crassus Frugi, or Piso as he likes to be known.'

Hadrian had a good memory for names, even long names like Caius Calpurnius Piso Crassus Frugi Licinianus. It was a point of pride never to forget, especially if he had met someone, but even so it was a moment before he could picture the face. It was not a pretty face, speckled with moles, some of them large, the expression dull and sullen. 'An admirable young man, I believe,' he said, lying fluently. 'I did not know that he was eager for service. He must already be twenty-two.'

They had to pause because Trajan had slowed and was showing pleasure at the story, listening as he gave instructions to the young slave to dole out more bounties to the crowd. Seeing his interest, the old senator spoke even louder. 'So after a few more days, Caesar Augustus decides to have a game with the rogue. Next morning, instead of ignoring him, he strides right up to the little fellow and declaims a verse of his own.'

Hadrian smiled. It was a good story.

'Maybe the man ought to have been an actor rather than a peddler of verses, for he reacts well, praising the poem to the skies. Then out with his purse, pulls the string open and pours out the contents into Caesar's hand. Only a couple of asses there. Well, that's why he was begging. "I wish that I had more with which to recognise your art," he says, "but here, you must take my last coins as well as my praise and blessing!"

'Augustus liked a joke and knew when he was beaten. Clapped the fellow on the shoulder and sent a boy to give him a full purse!'

Trajan laughed. A few began laughing at the same instant and the remainder took their cue from the master of the world. Laberius contented himself with a wry smile, but he was an especially old and trusted friend.

'I do hope that there are no poets here today,' the emperor declared, producing more laughter.

'I know a good one about Priapus!' someone shouted from the crowd.

'Quick, give him some money to keep it to himself,' Trajan called to the boy, the loudest instruction he had given, and there were cheers.

After a few more minutes, they were almost at the house of their host, the doors of the *atrium* standing open and the welcoming party visible.

'It would be a wise gesture,' Laberius said, and the merest flick of his eyes towards the emperor's straight back was sufficient to show that he was not speaking solely for himself.

'And the father's injudicious actions?' Hadrian asked. The elder Crassus had plotted to overthrow Nerva, the old man made an emperor by the Senate after the murder of the unlamented Domitian seven years ago, who had in turn adopted Trajan and raised him to the purple. He was now in exile, albeit a comfortable one at Tarentum rather than on some bare rock out at sea.

'Almost forgotten and not the fault of his son. Let the youngster have a chance to prove himself and redeem the family.'

'I see.' Hadrian thought for a moment. The father was

a fool, his plot a badly run farce easily discovered and defeated. The son certainly looked a halfwit, but with the legion dispersed in so many detachments, it should be easy enough to keep him at a distance. Stupidity was tiresome to observe in detail. 'I daresay I could find work for him somewhere.'

'Not too far away,' Laberius said as if reading his thoughts. 'As you might say, keep eyes and ears on him.' There was clearly more, but by this time they had arrived and there was no more chance to talk for some hours.

The dinner was pleasant enough. Their host, a noted epicure, knew the emperor well and had judged his tastes nicely. The food was fine, but not so fine that it was too exotic or ostentatiously expensive. The wine was decent, some of it scented as Trajan liked, and all of it plentiful. All of the guests were men, for the host's wife had died years before and he had never taken another. Conversation flowed easily, with much merriment and jokes at the host's and guests' expense. A few of those present knew Trajan well enough to mock his habit of eating too fast or his abrupt, martial way of speaking and other idiosyncrasies that the emperor himself liked to laugh at. All was perfectly balanced, as was the talk, most of it innocuous, yet to the discerning observer helping to confirm the pecking order of those nearest the princeps. Little was serious, even less important, and Hadrian as the youngest man there said less than the others as was proper, refrained from correcting a number of ill-considered statements, and listened whenever there was something that truly mattered.

Another war with Dacia seemed likely, perhaps even inevitable, for there were more and more reports that King

Decebalus was violating the treaty. Sosius' most recent letters had told Hadrian even more than the emperor seemed to know, speaking of envoys of the king ranging widely to seek allies. That letter had come weeks ago, and another was surely due. Still, experience taught that it was best to trust Sosius and let the man go about his dark business without close supervision.

'We will prepare this summer,' Trajan said after a question from their host about the rumours. 'Get most of the men and stores in place by the end of the year. Then next spring I will march into the mountains again and smash Decebalus if he won't see sense. Ought to know by now that he is no longer dealing with Domitian.'

The diners voiced agreement more or less loudly. Most of them had served with the emperor in the previous war.

Hadrian, relieved to hear that there would be a campaign before his spell as commander of the legion was up, was even more pleased when Trajan followed up by addressing him.

'My cousin will precede us all,' he declared, voice slightly louder than necessary and words just a little slurred. Trajan rarely spoke of Hadrian as a relation, so that too was welcome. 'I shall expect you to take a good look at the situation and report to me. Put that nosiness of yours to good use for a change, eh?' Trajan tapped his own nose as the company laughed, and Hadrian tried to seem abashed but good humoured.

Trajan suddenly jabbed a finger towards him. 'Find out what that Dacian bugger is up to! That's what I want you to do!' He turned to his host. 'He's a clever bastard, you know.'

Hadrian was not sure whether the emperor was referring

to him or Decebalus. After that the talk drifted away to other matters, most of them trivial. There was less and less need to pay close attention as the evening wore on. A Trajan full of wine loved to tell long stories about past campaigns.

Nature called, and Hadrian was shown by a slave girl the way to the lavatory. Noticing that Laberius had risen and was following, but pretending not to have seen the other man, Hadrian slapped the girl on the rump. She gave a little squeal, but had the subdued expression of so many slaves and even this show bored him.

There were three wooden seats, the sound of water trickling constantly from below and a strong scent from incense burning around the hanging lamp to cover almost all the smell. Laberius came in, lifting his tunic to sit alongside and soon started to talk. Hadrian wondered how often matters of state were discussed by two men defecating, but paid close attention.

The next morning Laberius went to call upon the emperor and was given a private audience, rather than being received with others obeying the same courtesy.

'You spoke to him?' Trajan's voice was gruff, but then it often was. There was no sign of the after-effects of last night's wine, even though any man must have felt them.

'I did.'

'And explained.'

'As much as he need know.'

'Good.' Trajan had a habit of rubbing his chin. His hair was dark and thick, and Laberius knew that he often was shaved more than once a day. 'Let's hope the little shit can do his job.'

'You really do not like him, do you, my lord?'

Trajan shrugged. 'Don't have to like him, he's family.'

'But he is capable,' Laberius said, 'and very bright indeed.'

'Exactly. How can you trust a man as clever as that?'

'Spoken like a Roman, my lord, if you will forgive me for saying so!'

The emperor's laugh was rich and deep. He liked that. 'Well, thank you, but I had better get back to work being polite.' He clapped Laberius on the shoulder. 'You can go back to sleep again, if you like!'

'Good advice, my lord, but I have to be at the Senate in an hour.'

'Best place to sleep, if you ask me!'

Laberius was almost at the door, the chamberlain opening it for him, when the emperor called to him.

'Well done,' he boomed, before lowering his voice. 'Old friend, I am so glad that I can trust you.'

The former consul left, wondering how he should take that.

VI

Piroboridava
The first day of the festival of the Quinquatria

LATINIUS MACER LEFT three days after his dinner with Ferox, for the storm the prefect had feared blew up suddenly from the west and kept him waiting longer than he had hoped. To his considerable satisfaction, no one killed Flavius Ferox. At the same time the snow turned to sleet and then to rain, all driven in by ferocious winds, and cleared altogether by the next dawn, leaving the ground with less snow than there had been for months. Ferox suspected that the men would be riding or marching through mud by the time they were lower down the valley. A lot of off-duty men gathered to see Macer and his escort set out, whether from fondness for the old man, envy for those leaving with him or a mixture of both.

Two days later the Brigantes arrived. Ferox had left one hundred horsemen and one hundred and sixty infantrymen to wait their turn for the ferry over the Danube at Dobreta. Twenty-seven, about half of them cavalry, failed to arrive.

'They just vanished, sir.' Ulpius Cunicius told Ferox, struggling to meet his gaze. It was a sorry tale, if no great surprise. Once over the river they were almost out of the empire, with few garrisons, and a warm welcome waiting from the Dacians or the chance to rove free among the other tribes if they chose. One entire picket of four horsemen had ridden off during the first night.

'Did you chase them?'

'We tried,' Cunicius said weakly. Ferox could guess that no one had been that keen. After all, what were they to do if they had caught the men? 'But I called it off quickly. There was no hope of catching them and I wanted to press on and join you.'

'Without losing too many more,' Ferox added to himself. Ulpius Cunicius was a decent man, the son of a chieftain who had stayed loyal to the right side during the rebellion, although had not been directly involved in the fighting. The reward was citizenship for the family, hence taking Ulpius, the family name of the emperor, and then a little later appointment as centurion to the irregular unit. He was the only centurion with the party, and now there was only one other decurion apart from Vindex. Others would appear if ever the rest of the force arrived. Cunicius was twenty-five, long limbed and narrow faced like most of his kin, but was still feeling his way into his new role. Ferox could not blame him, since he did not really know what was going on and how to turn the disparate mob into a useful unit before someone killed him or half of the rest went over the wall. In truth Cunicius had done well to lose so few on the way to Piroboridava. Now that they were here, it became a little harder to desert than it had been on the march, while opening up a whole new set of problems.

The first fight broke out on the evening of the day after the Brigantes had arrived, and Ferox was surprised that it had taken so long. He did not see it, nor did anyone else of high rank, and what had happened only came out after there were more arguments over the next few days, culminating in one that left a veteran of I Minervia with a bad knife wound to the stomach and a Brigantian hit so hard on the head that he remained unconscious and would not wake. Both men were carried to the hospital, along with half a dozen more with lesser injuries.

'They're not happy,' Sabinus conceded.

Ferox had summoned his senior officers to a meeting in his office in the principia, the headquarters of the fort. Thinking about it, he supposed it was now his principia, just as they were his officers. Neither thought felt natural and he wondered whether they ever would. He had been in the army for the best part of twenty years, more than half his whole life, but the only garrison he had ever commanded was the tiny outpost at Syracuse not far from Vindolanda in northern Britannia. There his duties had been modest, the administrative work light or trivial enough to be left to a junior. Here there were some six hundred soldiers to oversee, feed, and keep healthy, as well as sick men in the hospital, army slaves like the *galearii*, private slaves and no doubt women and children belonging to the rest, although there seemed far fewer of these than he would have expected. The Brigantes had not been permitted to bring families or slaves, apart from one servant for each of the officers.

'Not happy?' Ferox asked. He understood the mood of the men already in garrison, but needed to get a better sense of their officers. It would have been nice to think that only the Brigantes were discontented, but even a few hours at Piroboridava was enough to get a sense of the wider frustration of its garrison.

'Yes, sir.' Sabinus glanced nervously at Sertorius Festus, the only other centurion from I Minervia, eager for his support.

'They're fed up,' Festus said. He struck Ferox as capable enough in his way, without imagination or spark. It was hard to know why either man was posted to this vexillation and whether it was chance, their turn on the roster, or more deliberate than that. Outposts often received the men no one wanted anywhere else. Both centurions were understandably and very reasonably loyal to their men, putting them on the defensive and making it hard to admit that their legionaries were anything less than bursting to do their duty.

'Rumour was that we were all being relieved.' That was Julius Dionysius, the remaining centurion left in the garrison. He was a small man, his movements precise and very controlled. His dark complexion and delicate features marked him as an easterner, and as an auxiliary centurion he was junior to the other two, although ranking above poor Cunicius. He had a young, open face, even though he must be nearly Ferox's age, and hard, intelligent eyes. When no one else said anything, he continued. 'Everyone expected to be relieved as soon as you and your men reached us. Then they found out that only a handful are to leave and the rest are to stay. Indefinitely for all they know.'

'That is not our fault,' Cunicius said defensively. Ferox was glad he had the confidence to speak up.

'Of course not.' Dionysius's smile was disarming. 'But you are here and they have no one else to blame.'

'And your men need to show more respect,' Sabinus declared. 'These are not simply legionaries, but veterans.'

'We are Brigantes,' Cunicius replied, defiant in his pride. 'We step aside for no man.'

Festus sneered. 'You are barbarians.' He was not a tall man, but very broad in the shoulders with long, powerful arms. Ferox had not been at the fort long before he heard legionaries calling the centurion 'the ape'; he was not sure whether or not Festus knew of his nickname. Probably not, as the man lacked subtlety. Still, this was getting them nowhere.

Ferox drummed his fingers on the wooden table. The silence was immediate. None of them, not even Cunicius, knew him at all well and all – with the possible exception of Dionysius – were nervous of their new commander.

'Soldiers fight,' Ferox said, speaking softly. 'I suppose that is why they pay us!' Even Festus laughed and whether they were genuinely amused or felt obliged did not matter so much. 'When there are no enemies they will fight each other. If there were only your legionaries here, then I daresay in time men who had served in one cohort would band together against those who had spent their time in another, or the Spaniards against the Italians or even the Blues against the Greens. You know how devoted the fans of each faction can be. So they will fight if they are bored and have time on their hands. That is the key.' He scanned the faces. Cunicius doing his best to seem eager, but still unused to the army and its ways and smarting at the contempt shown by Festus. The 'ape' had his chin thrust forward belligerently waiting to be told what to do. Sabinus seemed to understand, while Dionysius had clearly heard it all before.

'So we will not give them any time. The weather is breaking and spring on its way. From now on we work, day in and day out. Sabinus.' Ferox nodded at the man.

'Sir.'

'I want that bath house finished and running before the end of the month. You are in charge.'

'Sir.'

'I also want the ditches cleared, roofs repaired where they need it, and then we go through all the stores and equipment here and make sure they are in perfect condition. That's your job, Festus.'

The ape nodded.

'Both of you will take work parties from all the units here. You know how it's done. Put them into teams and make it a competition over who can do a job best and fastest. Prizes will be extra wine in their ration, and extra passes to bathe or to visit the *canabae*. I know it is small, but there are a couple of bars.' He did not need to add, that in the bars there were bound to be at least a few girls available for hire.

Festus coughed. 'Our men are veterani, sir. They are not obliged to work or perform fatigues.'

'The craftsmen won't mind, and all of them will be happy to help with the bath house. The rest will do the lighter jobs, but we will mix up the teams. Give each party some auxiliaries, galearii when they can be spared from their own duties, and a score of Brigantes to help. Then it's about making their Britons do a better job than the ones with the other teams. We will make sure there are men with decent Latin in every group. See to that, Cunicius.'

Festus and Sabinus still looked dubious.

'And the Brigantes are also going to drill like they have

never drilled before. I want some of your best legionaries to act as instructors and tell them not to go easy. Let 'em pass on all those years of experience. And the workshops can make sure all the kit is up to scratch. I'm also putting you in charge of that, Festus. See if you can turn those barbarians into proper soldiers. You deal with the infantry.'

Festus was grinning now. 'A pleasure.'

'I want them exhausted, not dead, mind you.'

'Do my best, sir.'

'And never strike them. Not ever!' Ferox could see the centurion's look of disappointment. 'Do that and we will have a mutiny. Scream at them, insult them, but they are warriors and if you touch them they'll try to kill you for honour's sake. So warn your men. And tell them that as soon as they start training with practice swords they can pound on them as much as they like – if it's in a fight, even a training fight, then a blow is no insult.'

The ape bared his teeth happily.

'Julius Dionysius?' Ferox wondered whether the man really was a citizen. A lot of educated easterners were a good deal more civilized than many a Roman, and if they enlisted often gave themselves Roman names to make people think that they did have the franchise. No doubt it was in his records, but he was not sufficiently curious to check.

'Sir.'

'You see to the cavalry. And I want all the horses and other animals in the garrison fit again. Get as many out exercising as you can, every day you can. We only stop for the worst storms. Nothing else.

'And finally, we are all going to stretch our legs as much as we can. Patrols. Every day from now on. On foot and on horseback. Up and down the valley. We'll start short and make them longer, each of us leading one in turn. For the moment each will return to the fort by nightfall. In the future, we'll see. ... We can see who is about and what is happening in the world. There's never any harm in that. At the very least, Sabinus here can get a chance to converse with his trees.'

Sabinus chuckled and the rest laughed. He must have told Cunicius at some point since he had arrived.

'Drive them hard, and don't let up.'

'Sir?' Sabinus spoke with obvious reluctance. 'What about the Britons, sir? Are they going to run?' He turned to Cunicius, spreading his hands in apology. 'Sorry, but it sounds as if many of them are even less happy.'

Cunicius seemed about to speak, but then said nothing and just shrugged.

'Some are bound to try,' Ferox told them. 'Fatigue will help, and now that they are in the fort it is harder to slip away.'

'What about the pickets – and these patrols?' Dionysius seemed the sharpest of the group, and Ferox was already glad to have him. 'Perhaps we should make sure that there are always reliable soldiers to watch them?'

Ferox shook his head. 'We need to show trust if we are to earn it.' Festus sniffed, Sabinus and Cunicius both showed concern, while Dionysius' smooth features were impassive. Ferox liked him all the more. 'However, we can work up to things. For the moment, we jig the duty roster so that only the men and groups we trust get faced with temptation.'

Dionysius gave the slightest of nods. 'Have many men run from the garrison since it was established? We all know the promises offered by Decebalus and so do the men.'

'None of Minervia.' Festus' chin thrust out even more, and his little eyes were belligerent.

Sabinus coughed. 'A couple of men vanished last autumn.'

'We don't know they ran,' Festus maintained. 'Bandits had been seen, and the Red Alans were on the prowl.'

Ferox kept his face rigid. 'These are dangerous lands.' He remembered the Roxolani, the Red Alans, from his years on the Danube. They were Sarmatians, horse folk, always on the move until the snows made it impossible, not just brave warriors, but clever ones – and thieves and marauders. He had liked them, apart from when they had been trying to kill him. In some odd way – odd because their lifestyle was very different – they had reminded him of his own tribe, the Silures of western Britannia.

There was another awkward silence. 'Before the vexillation from I Minervia arrived, there were some desertions,' Dionysius explained, for he had been at the fort the longest. 'The vexillation was chosen for its reliability, as were many of the other troops sent here. We have a lot of experienced men, a good few of them only a few stipendia short of retirement.'

Festus preened at the praise of his men. 'Good men, all of them. Sensible too. No sense in buggering off and losing that fat bounty they'll get on discharge.'

'And I take it their families were left back in Germania at the main castra?' Ferox guessed at least half the men, and probably more, had 'wives' and children. Army regulation said that soldiers were not to marry, but men were men, and few wanted to wait out twenty-five years before finding the right woman and starting a family. The army turned a blind eye, knowing that it was better that way.

'Well, it's rough up here, the winters savage,' Festus said.

'And they were told that we would not be here long enough to make it worth putting the families through the hardships of the journey,' Sabinus added, his tone dubious. 'And...' he trailed off, before rallying. 'A few were allowed to come anyway, and a dozen or so more made it up here with the last big supply convoy.'

'Soldiers' women tend to be a tough bunch,' Ferox said. He did not add what Sabinus, Dionysius and many of the veterans – if not perhaps Festus – understood. Fear of losing the discharge bonus due in a couple of years was one incentive to keep the legionaries away from the temptation of running. Even bigger for many was the knowledge that running meant that they would most likely never again see their families, and that these would be evicted by the army and sent away with nothing. Someone high up had worked this out, realised that I Minervia had more than its share of men nearing the end of their enlistment, and formed this vexillation – and another sent further to the east – to serve in this out of the way, bleak outpost in the belief that they were least likely to be lured away into Dacian service. The same was true of most of the auxiliaries, notably sixty men from *cohors I Hispanorum veterana*, whose main base was far away in Thrace, and all of whom had served at least twenty-three stipendia.

It was a bright, if cynical, idea, and had worked well, at the cost of creating a garrison of elderly soldiers, all of them, to quote Sabinus, 'not happy'. There was almost none of the laughter and life that women and especially the children brought to most big army bases. Piroboridava was quiet, not helped by the fact that it had been built for a garrison twice the size of the one there now, even including the Brigantes.

The place of his men in this grand design still puzzled Ferox. If someone had decided that the old sweats sent to Piroboridava were the men least likely to desert, then why add the Brigantes, full of men almost bound to run, if they did not mutiny first. Were they seen as such a nuisance that senior officers wanted them to desert and rid the army of a problem? Or was this a test of him and the men, to see how they coped, challenging them to come to heel and redeem themselves. Then again, maybe someone judged that the veterans would keep the Brigantes in line. Ferox was not sure, and did not ignore the possibility that this was all a mistake, that a senior officer had written the wrong destination on the order and no one had dared correct him. He almost smiled at the thought – almost. With the army you could never quite be sure, but his instincts all still told him that somebody was playing games, and using them all as pieces on a board.

'Well,' he said and let himself smile. 'That is the broad plan. Now let us see about the details.'

'I can tell you one thing, sir,' Sabinus announced after they had spent an hour drawing up lists and plans. 'We are not going to be very popular.'

'Just blame the new commander,' Ferox told them. 'I hear he's half barbarian and a right tyrant!'

★★★

The garrison sweated. Ferox drove the officers hard to make them drive the men just as hard. All of the regulars, legionaries and auxiliaries alike, bitched and moaned, and the veterans, with all their long years of experience, were very good at it. They complained as they worked, and afterwards, and plenty of comments were just loud enough for Ferox and the other officers to hear, if never sufficiently clear to justify a formal charge.

To his surprise the Brigantes resented the labouring jobs less than he expected. The deserters and mutineers had done it before, if unwillingly, and the former prisoners had lost a fair bit of pride toiling in the mines. None were happy, but they did what they were told as long as someone was watching or there was fear of punishment. The rest of the men from the royal units, let alone those sent by willing chieftains, resented work fit for peasants not warriors. Vindex and the forty horsemen he had brought from his own clan, the Carvetii, were a rough and ready bunch, less sensitive about such matters.

'We're wondering how best to kill you,' Vindex told him. 'Don't want to make it too quick, after all.'

'I am sure it's just talk, sir,' Cunicius added. He seemed more worried with every passing day.

'Tell them to wait their turn,' Ferox said. He made them work, all of them, because he could not afford to have parts of the units seen as more favoured than the others. Most began cleaning the barracks allotted to them. The veterans had done a cursory job, once the roofs were decently repaired, afterwards justifying this as only for a mob of Britons. That meant the Brigantes had to scrub and paint, bring in new straw and rushes to cover the floors, and clean the little chimneys so that the smoke did not choke everyone inside. The nights stayed cold, giving them a more personal incentive, and that helped to speed the work. At the same time they all showed the tribe's deep love of horses by working with even greater will on the boxes in the stables.

Then things started to vanish. The veterans liked their comforts, and had done their best to fit out their quarters with luxuries and ornaments. Some were stolen, then stolen back. Ferox gave orders that anyone caught was to suffer full punishment for robbing a comrade, but did not hold his breath waiting for arrests. There were a few more fights, and these had less venom than the earlier ones. They did not end the thefts, although they may have made some of those involved a little more careful. The centurion Sabinus had brought a bronze statue of Venus. It was about a foot high, had cost more than its modest aesthetic charm merited, and showed the goddess surprised while bathing, modestly crouching to cover her nudity with her hands to the small extent that this was possible. One morning the statuette was suspended by a little loop of rope from one of the stubby chimneys on the roof of a barrack block occupied by the Brigantes. Returned to its rightful owner, on the next morning it was atop the roof of another building, this time occupied by the legions. After that, the goddess travelled all over the camp, every day finding a new home. At least one of the thieves was a craftsman, for Venus also acquired a carefully made little helmet just like the ones worn by the legions, and later on a belt with a gladius in its scabbard hanging from her left hip. Whoever had made it must have decided that a deity ought to hold high rank, so had put it

on the side where centurions and more senior officers wore
their swords.

'Where is Venus?' became the first question most men
asked in the morning, and bets were soon being placed
on where the statuette would turn up next. Other thefts
dropped off, and there was more laughter to be heard.

'I can't think how anyone knew I had it,' Sabinus said.

'Thrash your slaves,' Festus advised, but could not
convince his colleague.

'I always heard that the Silures were the greatest thieves
in the world,' Vindex commented. The others were getting
used to Ferox's willingness to let decurions and other juniors
speak out with some freedom, although neither man liked it.

'Never heard of them,' Festus grunted. 'Are they some of
your Britons?'

'No,' Cunicius replied.

'We won't take just anyone,' Vindex added.

Ferox did not bother to say anything. For most Romans,
even those who had served there, anyone from Britannia was
a Briton. There was simply no point trying to explain that
many peoples lived there and all were different. Vindex was
leering at him, and not simply because that was his natural
expression. It was hard to tell whether he was fishing for the
answer or really knew that Ferox had been the first to steal
the statuette.

The days passed and the laughter helped leaven the
constant complaining. A couple of times men let things fall
during their work whenever an officer, and especially Ferox,
passed by. He was spattered a few times by dirt or sand,
and narrowly missed by a pile of heavy shingles which had
slid off the high roof of one of the granaries. They missed,

if narrowly, and perhaps had fallen by accident. The men working up on the roof were only using ladders, not full scaffolding for Festus had declared the job an easy one, and the two Brigantes up there were not men he expected to risk killing him in public.

Ferox was more wary on the patrols out of the fort, although he loved those days for the sense of space that they gave him and the freedom from lists and reports. He went out more often than anyone else, usually with the cavalry, so that he could range further afield and get a sense of the wider area. Contrary to Sabinus' verdict, there were people all the year around living not so very far away and more would come as the weather improved. Ferox had come up this valley almost twenty years ago on a long patrol, albeit in the summer, and now and again there was a view that he remembered. Memories were coming back, and he tried to fit them into place and learn all that he could about the locals. None of the officers at the fort showed much curiosity, let alone knowledge of these people. They were Saldense, as Sabinus had told him, and were not Dacians at all, but Getae, although few Romans would bother to note the distinction. The closest were the tough ones, the ones who lived in the area throughout the winter and they were neither hostile nor friendly. For the moment, his smattering of half-remembered words and the locals' even thinner knowledge of Greek meant that the few encounters were short and conversation simple. Still, it was a start.

They had to build up gradually whenever a patrol included horses from the garrison, working on them to make them stronger and fitter each time. In March they did not go far up the valley, and instead tended to go down, where the slopes were gentler and the snow less. There were more farms down there, although the people were not much more forthcoming. Instead they remained wary, as such folk always were when any bands of armed men arrived, let alone strange soldiers come from far away.

A few horses went lame, and Ferox doubted that all would recover, while another bolted for no reason anyone could see and plunged into the river, smashing through the thick ice and being swept away by the current. The rider had leapt and landed well, but the animal was a pitiful sight when they found it, lying on the bank a mile downriver, forelegs broken and ribs smashed. They put the poor beast out of its misery and then cut off a foot as proof that army property had been destroyed – a practice followed by the cavalry in Moesia which Ferox had forgotten.

One man died on the next patrol. Sabinus said that the cavalryman had been showing off, and put his mount at the low wall encircling a ruined farm. The horse balked at the last minute, and the rider kept going, sailing over to slam into the ground. It was luck, simply bad luck, but he fell badly and broke his neck. In the days that followed there were more accidents, with a couple of falls and the mistakes with ladders, pulleys and other tools that were always a risk when you set soldiers to building and especially when you made them work quickly. One of the Brigantes even managed to drive an eight-inch nail through the hand of a comrade who was holding a beam in place.

A day after that Ferox took out another patrol and at one point led a dozen horsemen away from the main column to practise searching through the fir woods. Soon they lost each other, as was bound to happen. He was taking a chance and knew it, but his instincts were good and the man's aim was bad. Some sense warned him and he twitched at the reins, making his horse lurch into a canter going to the left moments before the javelin whisked past and hit the trunk of a tree. The animal stumbled, almost fell, throwing his weight hard against the front horns of the saddle, and by the time he had recovered and turned the mare around all he could see was the darker shape of a horseman vanishing into the shadows.

There was the soft thud of hoofs on years of dried pine needles from behind and he turned again as one of the Brigantes appeared, a man named Vepoc, one of those who had been sent to the mines. He had a javelin in his hand and his face was impassive. Ferox's cloak was around him, and he gripped the hilt of his sword.

Then Vindex appeared, from off to the side.

'Hullo, who lost that?' The thrown javelin had not driven deeply into the wood and was hanging down limply.

'Not mine,' Vepoc said, lifting his up as proof.

Ferox walked his horse over until he could grab the shaft and pull the weapon free. 'No harm done,' he said. 'But time we went home.'

'Home?' Vindex muttered. 'Oh, you mean the fort.'

Ferox let Vepoc ride behind them and before long they were back with the rest. None of the Brigantes or anyone else with the patrol was missing a javelin and no one had deserted. Rain started to fall and for two hours they rode back, gusts of wind blowing the drops hard against them. No one said very much and by the time they rode up the track to the main gates they all felt numb with cold.

Sabinus was waiting for him, and let the hood of his cloak fall back as he hurried over to see Ferox. The news was not good.

The ape was dead.

'**T**HAT IS FEROX,' the Briton said and spat.

Brasus could see the centurion at the head of a couple of dozen riders. He was no longer surprised by Ivonercus' hatred of his former commander. The Briton did not appear to feel much resentment to Rome, and his hatred was deeply personal. According to him the centurion and his friend had killed Ivonercus' king and destroyed his family, taking lands from his father so that the broken man died in poverty.

'And the pig Vindex beside him.'

They were too far away to make much out. Both were tall men by the look of it, even compared to the long-limbed Britons who made up half of the patrol. They must have been higher up the valley, which meant that it had been right to stay in the trees and walk rather than ride. The Briton had resented that, saying that it was easy to ride amid a forest like this, but had obeyed. He was being tested and he knew it. If Ivonercus ever wanted to be more than just a soldier for Decebalus then he needed to demonstrate that he was useful in other ways. So Brasus had brought him to help scout the Roman fort at Piroboridava – and brought two of his most trusted warriors along just to be sure. Fifty more men were waiting back at the tower and soon there might be more. The walls were to be rebuilt and the king's presence in these lands restored. There was a plan. Brasus knew a little of it, and understood that the king wanted to learn more before he gave orders. The time was not yet right, but the first preparations were under way.

'How many men does he command?'

Ivonercus showed a flash of anger. 'As I have told you before, between five and six hundred. Maybe a quarter cavalry. Half of the rest are legionaries.'

'You do not remember more?'

'How can I? As I have said again and again, I never reached the fort. We tried to kill Ferox outside, but failed and I escaped with my servant.'

'Ah yes, your servant.' Brasus wondered whether that was true, as the men seemed very familiar with each other. The Britons said that this was from hard labour together in the mines and the custom of his folk. They had left the man behind at the tower and he would be killed if they did not all return. Ivonercus knew this and if he did not understand the words he must also have appreciated the sense of Brasus' orders to the warriors with them. 'Kill him if he does anything suspicious. Anything at all. A wrong look, a wrong gesture, and this Briton dies. He can be useful to us, but this is all too important to risk discovery. One day we will fight, perhaps here. That is not today. Today we are the eyes and ears of the king.' He had regretted the phrase immediately. Yet this was his duty. Fate or calculation would guide Decebalus, and his part was simply to obey and live or die as one of the faithful should.

'So tell me again about this Ferox.' The Roman patrol was heading down towards the bridge and the fort. Brasus could *see a cluster of houses and buildings outside the walls, and one big one almost beside the river. He had seen something similar at Sarmizegethusa where the Romans had a garrison outside the walls of the king's fortress. That one was even bigger and fires were stoked all the time so that the Romans could pamper themselves with baths. Odd how a people who neglected their souls wished to scrub their bodies.*

'He is one of the Silures,' Ivonercus said the name as if it should mean something. 'The wolf people, the cruel people. One of their royal house, though they do not have kings. When his tribe was beaten by the Romans they took him and raised him in their ways. He has been Roman longer than he was a Silure, but the wolf still lurks in his soul.' Ivonercus' Latin was good, in spite of his thick accent, and they had found this the easiest way to speak. The Briton knew no more than a word or two of Greek.

'Wolves hunt in packs,' Brasus said. He was studying the fort as best he could from this distance. The ramparts were earth and timber, the towers quite high – with the highest over the main gates – but after the Roman fashion they were set back into the walls. Outside was a double line of ditches, and though he could not see them there were bound to be the usual traps and stakes. All in all it was like most Roman forts he had seen – not laid out with cunning, not impossible to take, but not easy either. He could see no spot obviously weaker than the rest. The fort was quite big, especially for six hundred men and that would stretch the defenders thin.

'Mostly,' Ivonercus conceded. 'Ferox is like the lone wolf, and they are dangerous. He is a ferocious and merciless fighter. He will not give in, even if the cause is lost, so that you must wonder whether he despairs of life. They say he

had everything and yet threw it away because he does not value life or happiness. The queen...'

Brasus grabbed the Briton's arm to silence him, although the man had already stopped in mid flow. One of the warriors had hissed a warning and they waited and listened. There were steps approaching.

Ivonercus had not spoken like this before, and part of Brasus wanted to know more. If the man had been speaking his true thoughts then it did not matter. Ferox was beginning to sound interesting. Perhaps he was one of the creatures who was different. Not a pure man, since that could not be, but a stranger who sensed or by chance followed something of the right path. That would not matter to the king, who would only care that this was a commander who would fight hard and by the sound of it skilfully. So be it. Such knowledge might change the way things were done rather than the plan itself. Brasus was beginning to think that it could work.

There was the sound of a man singing softly, his rather nasal voice wandering either side of a tune that was as old as the hills. One of the warriors smiled, for it sounded like one of the Getae.

Brasus drew his curved dagger and showed it to the warrior. The smile died, but the man nodded in understanding. They knew the instructions. If the wanderer did not find them then he was free to pass. Even seeing their tracks would not matter. Yet if he saw warriors, men he would guess were men serving the king, then he must die. The folk in this valley had sometimes been loyal and sometimes not. He might tell the Romans deliberately or by accident and for the moment the secret needed to be kept.

The warrior crept until he was leaning against the thick trunk of a beech tree. His own knife was in his hand.

Brasus looked again at the fort and wondered about this Ferox and wondered about the queen the Briton had mentioned. He sensed that Ivonercus regretted speaking of her and doubted that he would willingly tell more. The queen must be the sister of the king the man had served and Ferox had killed. The Briton had rarely mentioned her, and only ever with awe, perhaps fear, as if it was unlucky to speak of the royal house.

The singing faded, getting further and further away. Brasus kept them there for a long while, but they heard no more of the wanderer. Night was falling.

'It's time to go,' he said.

VII

THE STORY WAS simple enough. Manius Sertorius Festus had walked over to the parade ground to watch as some of his veterans marched groups of the Brigantes up and down. The warriors were formed into groups of thirty, mixing the men who had served in the royal cohort or other units with the rest for whom all this was new. After a slow start, progress was good, not least because everyone had realised that this was easier than labouring. Within a few days, they began to drill with weapons, which helped them all to feel more like warriors again. Festus had chosen instructors well, helped by the fact that many of the veterans had done this before and did not need to be watched every moment. They treated the Brigantes with a respect denied to raw *tirones* in a legion, picked up a few words of their language and taught the Latin commands simply, so that the whole squad and not simply the Latin speakers knew what they were supposed to do. Somehow, they made the warriors laugh, the humour simple and often crude, but enough to make the barked orders and even louder reprimands acceptable.

On this day, for the very first time, they had begun picking men from the squads to take over and drill the rest. They started with the senior soldiers, the experienced ones, and they did not do too badly. Then with the two hours of drill almost at an end, they asked if anyone else wanted to try. There were plenty of volunteers, for Brigantes were rarely short of confidence.

The centurion arrived just as they were starting, with four squads in a line along the long edge of the parade ground and the fifth and sixth formed opposite each other on the shorter edges. Festus came to stand beside one end of the main line, gesturing to the instructors to show that he was merely there to observe and did not want to take over.

'Silentium!' One of the Brigantes chosen to lead had a deep, powerful voice.

'Siwentium!' The other one was tall, the most corpulent man in the whole unit and one of the least bright. His voice was high pitched, and as he shouted turned into a squeak as he mangled the command. One of the instructors had picked him to remind the rest that this was not easy, and because a few laughs at the end of two hours of stamping and marching would do no harm.

There were sniggers from behind Festus.

'Iunge!'* The squad shuffled into close order, doing the manoeuvre well enough.

'Lungee!' The second squad was no less proficient in spite of the order. Behind Festus a man laughed, louder than all the others. The centurion glanced and saw that it was a tall, good-looking young recruit.

---

* Close ranks.

'*Parati!*'*

'*Rapatii!*'

There were giggles now, and the youth was cackling, his face red. Festus glared at them and then at the closest instructor, who was not looking in his direction. With an effort, he stopped himself from interfering, but resolved to have a word with the instructors after the parade was over. This sort of behaviour would not do at all.

'*Move!*'† The first squad stepped forward as one, prompting a satisfied grunt from the centurion. Done well, Festus found drill a very moving, almost spiritual experience.

'*Mole!*' The second squad responded almost as well, although he could see some of the soldiers were grinning. Behind him there was more laughter, the boy closest to him barely able to control himself. Festus gripped his slim vine cane with both hands to stop himself from intervening. The squads were marching towards each other, until they were fifteen paces apart.

'*Sta!*'‡ The first squad halted, stamping their feet as one, shields and javelins not jostling too much considering how little drill these men had received.

'*Tsss!*' The command was a piercing squeal. Grinning, and fully aware of what they were doing, the second squad ignored him and kept marching forward.

'The daft bugger's forgotten the order,' someone said from the ranks behind him.

'Quiet there!' an instructor ordered, although he could not keep the amusement out of his own voice.

---

* Stand ready.
† March.
‡ Halt.

'*Transforma!*'* The first squad wavered a little, transfixed by the sight of the other group bearing down on them, before managing a ragged about face.

'*Taaa!*' The second squad were no more than eight paces away, still marching. '*Steeee!*' The man's voice somehow managed to become even higher. All the men behind Festus were laughing.

'Move!' The first squad started marching away, although some of the men in the rear rank were turning their heads to see behind them.

Instead of trying to remember the order, the big man ran in front of his own squad, waving his arms to make them stop. They quickened the pace instead. Sensing or seeing this, the first squad also began to take longer strides, the ranks becoming ragged.

'Oh, that fat mongrel!' The boy closest to Festus managed to say before he could say no more for laughter, made worse as the second squad began to run, and everyone else ran to get out of their way.

Then the youth dropped his spear. It fell forward, the point close enough to twitch the hem of Festus' cloak before it hit the ground. The centurion's response was a reflex, as he spun around and swung his cane in his left hand, letting go with his right. If he was thinking at all, he probably meant to hit the soldier's shield. Instead, the lad was already leaning forward, whether from laughter or to pick up his spear. Held wrong way up, the gnarled top of the centurion's cane slammed into the youth's mouth, so that he staggered back, blood coming from a split lip.

---

* About turn.

'Stand to attention, man!' Festus yelled. 'And pick that up!' He turned away, and his temper rose again because the parade was a shambles, the two squads mingled together, some running, some barging each other with their shields.

'You!' Festus almost screamed at the instructors. 'Sort that disgrace out!'

There was a thud as the youth dropped his shield onto the grass and the scrape of a sword being drawn. Festus turned, frowning, small eyes staring and saw the youth coming at him, gladius held low, blood on his chin and growling. The centurion raised his cane, while his mouth opened to shout, but it was all so fast, so absurd. He was not wearing armour that day, because for much of the time he had supervised building work and had not wanted to be encumbered. Driven by rage, the triangular point of the gladius slid easily through his two tunics and undershirt into his stomach, angled up to thrust under his ribs. He grunted with the shock, as the boy made more animal noise and grabbed the centurion by the shoulder to pull him onto the blade. The cane fell from Festus' hand and he gasped.

No one else had moved. There had been no warning and no time. The boy was screaming, trying to wrench his sword free and only then did other men drop their shields and spears and pull him away. Festus slumped, gave a long sigh and died.

'Oh shit!' the soldier standing next to the boy said.

The facts were simple, and Ferox understood what had happened very quickly; the boy, whose name was Andoco, had been struck by the centurion and had killed him in reply. Even so, he spoke in turn to all the instructors and all the Brigantes who had stood close enough to see and hear what had happened, and then to the *medicus* from the hospital who had examined the corpse and confirmed the obvious cause of death. Then he saw Sabinus, Dionysius and Cunicius, telling them all that he had learned in case they had anything to add. Cunicius testified that Andoco was a good soldier, too young to have been in the rebellion although sent by a family who had joined Aviragus' rebels. So far his record was unblemished, and as a well-educated and intelligent lad, there was some expectation that in due course he would be promoted.

Sabinus added that he believed Festus was rather sensitive about his weight, fearing that middle age was turning muscle to fat, so that perhaps the boy's comment about a fat mongrel provoked him more than usual. 'Pity he spoke in decent Latin or all he might have got was an order to be quiet.'

'Perhaps, but how often does Festus – did Festus – use his cane?'

'Quite often,' Sabinus admitted. That was common enough, especially in some legions and cohorts, and the only restriction imposed by regulation was that a centurion was not allowed to inflict serious injury without making a formal charge against a soldier.

'I am sure that you recall my telling Festus how important it was never to strike one of the Brigantes.'

'Yes, sir,' Sabinus conceded. 'And I heard him repeat the instruction most forcibly to our men and up until this moment all obeyed.' The centurion's round face was worried, but determined. He took a deep breath. 'Nevertheless...'

Ferox sighed. 'Nevertheless.'

There was no easy way out, for a soldier could not simply fly into a rage and kill a centurion without being punished, and there was only one penalty for such a crime. An offence to personal honour was no excuse, and the only real question was how it was to be done.

Ferox went to see Andoco, his cell guarded by one of Vindex's Carvetii and an auxiliary. The boy had chains around his wrists and ankles, and that was necessary, at least for the moment. With effort he stood when Ferox entered, as a proud warrior should in spite of his terror. Andoco had very pale, innocent eyes, adding to his childlike appearance, and Ferox knew from the records that he was eighteen.

'I was angry, and struck in haste, but he should not have treated me that way,' was all that he would say when Ferox asked him to explain what had happened.

'I am not afraid,' the boy added, lying well enough in the circumstances.

Half an hour later Ferox strolled down to the river, Vepoc beside him, neither man speaking. Vindex and a couple of his men, along with three other Brigantes, followed twenty paces behind. The rain had stopped, the clouds scattered and a crescent moon gave enough light to see with ease. None of the men carried shields, though all had a sword in their belt. By now the picket was far behind them and they passed through the dozen or so buildings of the canabae without seeing a soul. They were alone, and Ferox knew that he was taking a risk. Vepoc was Andoco's older brother, the other men their cousins. At least this way the numbers were equal and whatever happened would be fair.

They reached the bank about twenty paces from the

bridge and stopped. Ferox bent down to pick up a stone, hefted it and then lobbed high, hearing a splash when it landed. There was little ice left now. For a while he waited, for he must give Vepoc and the others their chance in case they wanted to take it. His own tribe were raised to cherish silence, so he did not feel uncomfortable, although the rare occasions when Brigantes were silent – and awake – were strange.

'Blood calls for blood,' Vepoc said eventually.

'Aye.'

Vepoc was about Ferox's age, and had served in the royal ala, rising to the rank of *duplicarius*, a 'double-pay man' second only to the decurion in each *turma*. There were stories that before that he had been a famous warrior and raider, which in truth meant much the same thing. He had killed warriors from other clans and tribes – and Romans – and lived to tell of it, just as he had lived through the hardships of the mines and kept his pride and his strength.

'Just as a wrong calls for vengeance,' he said.

Ferox did not know whether Vepoc spoke of the killing of Festus, or was referring to Aviragus. He had certainly fought for the king, and been considered dangerous enough to be sentenced.

'If Andoco was a legionary,' Ferox began, 'then he would be flogged and beheaded, his head placed on a stake and the rest of his corpse denied proper burial. That is the way of the army, as you know.'

'We are not Romans.'

'Yet you are here.' Ferox leaned over and found another pebble. 'And you are oath sworn to serve the Lord Trajan.'

'If you kill him then I must kill you.' Vepoc did not mean

the emperor. 'The centurion was a fool.' He had his hand resting on the pommel of his sword. He did not move, and was not tense or giving any other sign that he was about to spring.

Ferox tossed the stone up and caught it. 'There are many fools in the world, and plenty of them are chieftains and lords.'

'Andoco is my brother. Oath or not, I must avenge him, and so must our cousins.'

'I know. The Silures understand the calls of blood.' There was no harm in speaking as one of his own folk, and not as the citizen and centurion.

Vepoc sniffed in contempt. 'Silures know nothing of honour.'

'Yet any folk who have wronged us know how much we are driven to vengeance.' Ferox reached back and threw the stone as far out as he could. There was no sound, so either he had reached a patch of ice or the far bank. 'The choice is yours.' He spread his arms wide and turned to face the warrior. If Vepoc wanted to kill him he had a good chance of drawing his sword and striking before Ferox could answer.

Vepoc did not move and was silent for a long while.

'We will do it,' he said at last. 'Kin will slay kin on the orders of a chief so that justice will be done. Then there is nothing to avenge, since the man who gave the first insult has already gone to the Otherworld.'

Ferox lowered his arms to his side. 'You have a day. I can give you no more.'

'The Silures are a cruel folk,' Vepoc told him. 'To make a man wait so long for the end.'

'The Silures are cruel folk, as all men tell,' Ferox said. 'Shall we go?' Without waiting for an answer, he began walking back up the slope. Vepoc was one of the king's men as were his cousins. If they wished to avenge the king's death then they still had a chance, and could kill them if they were able and vanish into the night. On foot it would be harder to escape pursuit, but it was possible. He wanted to show them trust, and at the same time readied himself to dodge and fight if the attack came.

It did not, and Vepoc followed him for a few paces before speaking again. 'One thing I must ask.'

Ferox halted and listened. 'So be it,' he agreed after hearing the explanation.

The next morning Andoco's head was impaled on a spike over the *porta praetoria*. The boy had been freed from his chains and handed over to Vepoc and the others as soon as they all returned to the fort. Ferox had let them have a room in an empty barrack block that was being cleared for the rest of the unit when it arrived. The older brother and his cousins prepared a meal, and over the next hours men came to offer gifts or pay their respects to the courage of the young man. They were not just others who had served the king, and as men went to the room, paid their respects, ate a morsel and left, others saw and joined. Even some of the legionaries went, although this was not their custom. Sometime later in the night, Andoco kneeled down outside, bowed his head, and let his brother slit his throat. That at least was the story, for no one apart from the cousins were there and none of them said a word. Rumour also said that the boy was brave. Afterwards they cut off his head and carried it to the main gateway, where the sentries had been warned and Ferox was waiting. Vepoc said nothing, and with his own hands rammed the head onto the spike, for this was where enemies and criminals were to be displayed. No words were spoken. He caressed the dead man's hair just once, and then left.

'I do not like any of this, sir,' Sabinus said. 'It is so irregular.'

'So are my men,' Cunicius replied, and Ferox was glad to hear the hardness in his voice.

At sunset Ferox returned to the gate tower and waited for the Brigantes. Before they arrived he prised the head from its spike and wrapped it in a cloth. Then he stood, holding it in his hands.

Vepoc had painted his face white, so that it shone in the torchlight. On the road below waited his cousins, all mounted and carrying spears and shields. Andoco's corpse lay across the back of another horse led by one of them, while each of the others drew a mule, one bearing provisions, the gifts given to the dead man and his weapons, and the other with bundles of wood and tools.

Once again no words were said, and the sentries had the sense to keep their distance and stay silent. There was something uncanny about the whole business, as if the entire garrison was holding its breath, unsure what was about to happen.

Ferox offered Vepoc the head, and the Brigantian took it. The centurion bowed and the warrior left, taking care as he went down the ladders.

'I do not like this,' Sabinus whispered as the Brigantes

rode out through the gateway into the night. 'How will we report it?'

Ferox did not answer, but leaned on the parapet as he watched them go.

'The record will show that five men went on patrol,' Julius Dionysius told him. 'If pressed, it may be noted that one of the men was dead. The roster already shows the death of our lamented colleague, and the arrest and execution of his murderer as a warning.'

'There'll be questions,' Sabinus went on. 'There are bound to be.'

'The responsibility is mine,' Ferox said, still staring out, even though the horsemen had long since vanished into the darkness.

'What if they don't come back?'

'Then we have a few more deserters,' Dionysius said airily. 'Or say they have been eaten by lions.'

'They will come back,' Ferox said, hoping that he was right. 'The oath will hold them.'

'The pledge to kill you?' Sabinus was thinking back to the sudden, appalling burst of violence on the day Ferox arrived.

'Perhaps,' Ferox said, 'or another.'

'Brigantes keep their word,' Vindex said. Sabinus started, for he had forgotten that the tall head of scouts was standing in the shadows. 'Not like Silures,' he added in the language of the tribes.

Ferox sighed. 'Silures keep their word. It's just that they hardly ever give it and promises don't count.'

Sabinus shook his head, for Ferox had spoken in Latin. 'I do not understand.'

'I don't think we are supposed to,' Dionysius said.

On the following morning a pyre was prepared for Festus on the far side of the track opposite the parade ground. He had not been popular, for he lacked charm and his moods had been a little too unpredictable for the soldiers to accept him as a character. Yet there was grudging respect, a feeling that his death was a ghastly mistake, and also the desire of the veterani of I Minervia to see one of their own sent off in proper style. The centurion had liked things done to the letter of the regulation, so that is what they did.

In the afternoon they burned his corpse, and the preparations proved good because the heat was immense before the shelf collapsed and the centurion's remains dropped into the flames. All, save the legionaries on guard duty or other essential tasks, were present, parading in their finest tunics, armour gleaming, leathers spotless, and those who had them wearing their dona and other decorations. Ferox was also in full uniform, the harness worn over his mail shirt heavy with medals, a torc at his neck and smaller ones around his wrists. Preparing all the gear was a task close to the heart of his freedman, Philo, who had done an exceptional job even by his standards. Up until now Ferox's distinguished record was largely a matter of rumour and no more, and seeing all these awards for valour impressed even the most grizzled veterans, at least a little. Yet they were more satisfied to see that he was showing appropriate respect for the dead man and thus their legion.

There was no wind, so the black smoke climbed straight into the blue heaven and the sun's warmth made it uncomfortably hot even some distance from the blaze. The last of the snow had melted down in the valley, although the heights remained white and that was unlikely to change for another month or more.

Ferox watched Festus burn and wondered how the mood of the garrison would change. They were still shocked and unsure, but that would not last forever. No one had stolen Venus since the day of the killing. At least the weather seemed to have turned as spring came slowly to the highlands and that ought to help. He would have to keep driving them, and that made him wonder about how to replace Festus. Ferox had not cared all that much for the dead man, finding him boorish and lacking in imagination. Still, he had met plenty of officers who were worse, and in many respects Festus had done his job well. From now on, he and the others would have more to do.

The sound of hoofs on the planking of the bridge made him turn. A rider was coming, an auxiliary trooper riding a foam-flecked horse. He recognised neither the trooper nor the mount, so this was a stranger and surely a messenger. He tried to push down the thought that any news or orders arriving during a funeral were unlikely to be good.

'Dismiss the parade!' he ordered Sabinus. 'Let the fire burn out and we can collect the ashes in the morning.' Festus was not to be buried in the small cemetery on this side of the road. Instead the ashes were to be carried to his widow and family in Narbonensis. Ferox had still not got over his surprise at hearing that the dead man was married, and felt guilty at not having bothered to find out more about his subordinates. Not only married, but the man had seven children. Festus had never spoken of them, but then Ferox was not one to speak of his own life outside the army except with his closest friends, and even then, only rarely. The news had made him regret the centurion's death even more and it was a relief to discover that Festus' estate was considerable and had gone entirely to his widow and offspring.

'Did you ever meet her?' Ferox asked later that night, as he once again leaned on the parapet above the main gate and stared up at the slim moon and the vast field of stars around it. He had taken to coming here whenever he wanted to think and could find no excuse to leave the fort. Sabinus was on duty that night, and inspecting the sentries.

'No. There is a picture in his quarters. She looks...' Sabinus struggled for the right words. 'A little ferocious? I am sure that the fault is with the artist. Some women have an enigmatic beauty and Festus spoke very highly of her as wife and as a mother.'

Ferox had not realised that the two men were as close, for they seemed so different, although spending a long winter at Piroboridava was likely to make a man eager for any company. Down below the pyre was no more than a red glow in the night.

'I have written a letter to her and will forward it with my report with the request that it be sent on. The ashes will have to wait until we can find someone able to take them.'

'Merchants will start coming through soon,' Sabinus said. 'A few of them at least. The track through the pass isn't the easiest, so most take one of the other routes. The bridge may make a difference though – when it is finished that is.'

Ferox nodded. 'In the meantime we shall soon have some other visitors. Your new legatus is coming in a few weeks and sends word to expect him and a large party. Says he wants to inspect as many of the vexillations of I Minervia as he can, now that he is taking over.'

'*Omnes ad stercus*,' hissed a legionary standing guard a few paces away.

'Quite,' Ferox agreed. 'And more immediately the despatch rider said he saw some Roxolani lower down the valley, so we had better double the guards whenever any horses or mules are put out to graze – and tell them to keep a close watch.'

'I thought that we were at peace,' Sabinus said. 'There were a few about at the end of last summer and they weren't any trouble.'

'Shouldn't be trouble,' Ferox told him, and wondered why a little voice in his head was telling him not to be a fool. 'But they are Roxolani. They like horses. If they can steal one they will – and see it as our fault for not taking more care of our property.'

Two days passed and there was no sign of the four Brigantes. Ferox could tell that Sabinus was convinced that the men were gone for good, but did not want to say as much. After another day even Vindex showed concern and suggested riding out to take a wee look. Ferox waited. He might have been able to pick up their trail, but he doubted that anyone else had the skill and he did not wish to be seen to lose faith in Vepoc and his relatives. The rituals ought to have been completed some time ago, as both he and Vindex well knew.

That evening the regular patrol up the valley returned with two men riding double.

'I cannot make them out,' Sabinus said, shielding his eyes with one hand. Ferox wondered at the man's eyesight.

He could not make out the faces, but the way the men sat made it obvious to him that they were Brigantes. Once they were closer he saw Vepoc and one of the cousins. When they reached the fort and reported, the Brigantian spoke of sudden ambush and hurried flight. One man died instantly, a second bled to death as they fled, and all their mounts were lost or killed. The last cousin had his thigh pierced by an arrow, and they had fled on foot, Vepoc carrying him half the time. Throwing off pursuit they had begun the long walk home, with little food and less hope if their attackers found them again. They had been walking for two and a half days when they ran into the patrol instead.

'Roxolani?' Sabinus asked, holding the arrow in his hands. The medicus had managed to extract it in the hospital and claimed to be optimistic about saving the leg.

'No, Dacian.' Ferox took it from him and fingered the fletches. Their shape was as distinctive as the bare wood of the shaft. 'I think we may be in for some trouble.'

In hiding

*T*HE ARCHERS WERE *still young, the oldest barely twenty, and all three had spent the whole of the last war in a garrison in the far north west of the kingdom. There they had watched over a gold mine, and that was an important service to the king whose gold it was, but months passed, one year faded into the next and the Romans never came near. One of the men had shot an arrow at a bandit trying to steal a donkey. He missed. The rest of the time they watched and they trained for a war that never came. That was something the king believed could be learned from the Romans, who were so formidable in war because they spent the peace practising. Warriors called up to serve him from the clans were expected to train, learning to use their weapons, to stand together in line and prepare for the clash of battle, much of the time taught by Roman deserters. This was not the discipline of the pure, where all of life was devoted to excellence, but Brasus had to admit that it had great value. The biggest problem was that you could not train eager young men forever while denying them the chance to use what they had learned. So when the time came and enemies wandered into range, the archers had shot.*

Brasus had known about the Romans soon after they rode to within a few miles of the tower, for he kept sentries along the treeline, all told to remain out of sight and some perched in the high branches. His men were keeping a good watch and in most respects they were obedient and thorough. The watcher had seen the riders and noticed that they had brought a dead man and were treating the body with reverence. To make sure and to try to understand better these men he must one day fight, Brasus had gone the next day, although since Ivonercus struck him as too clumsy, he had watched from the undergrowth on the edge of the forest. The Briton had confirmed what seemed obvious; this was a funeral of a friend or relation. They were not close enough to recognise them, other than to say that there were more Brigantes, more of Ivonercus' kin. With great care they built a platform of wood they had brought and branches they cut. The warrior who had watched them said that they had gathered a great deal, and it seemed that they had enough for they did not return to the edge of the forest during the day.

There was no pyre, as Brasus had expected, and Ivonercus told him that his kin did not burn the dead, but raised them to the Heavens. That was interesting, and Brasus watched for longer than he had intended, given that these men presented no real threat at the moment. He watched as they fashioned the platform, saw them lift the corpse onto the top.

'The soul must be freed,' the Briton told him. 'Then it can find its path to the Otherworld.'

'Do they leave him there?'

Ivonercus was reluctant to talk about it, but when pressed at last gave an answer. 'There are places in our homeland, places touched by the gods, where the boundaries between worlds are thin. No man visits such a place unless bringing the remains of kinsman or friend, so the treasures given to the dead rest undisturbed. Here it is different. They will let the sun rise and fall twice, and before the next dawn they will dig a hole and put him in it.'

'So he will be buried?'

The Briton looked at him as if he was a fool. 'By then he will have gone on his journey. All that is left is the empty shell and that has no value. They may just scrape a hole and chuck it in.'

Brasus sensed that there was more, much more to this, but did not press. The ways of the unenlightened were a curiosity and no more, so he fought down the urge to stay any longer or return and contented himself by sending men to pay particular attention in case these Britons wandered anywhere they should not or showed an inclination to defect. He sensed that Ivonercus guessed who they were, but when questioned the Briton had simply shrugged.

'They might come over,' he said. 'Or they might not.'

So warriors had watched them, and two of the archers had used the excuse of a hunting trip to join their friend who was on watch. The Britons had let their horses stray near to the forest, trusting the animals not to run. Their faith was justified, but when they wandered over to collect them, the warriors had not been able to resist using the bows given them by the king against human targets. Each was a beautiful creation, the two arms curving deeply. When unstrung the arms bent forward and then when strung they bulged back, so that when a nocked arrow was released it was driven with great force and speed. To hold one was to wish to loose a dart, and for eager young warriors the chance to shoot at a real enemy was too great a temptation to resist.

At least they had practised well. All three of the first

arrows they shot found a mark, two in the flanks of one horse and the other in the throat of one of the riders. Then it got messy as men panicked in surprise and animals bolted.

Brasus had told his men that there were situations when they must kill if it would prevent their presence being revealed. If this happened, then he had also told them again and again that no one must escape, for one mouth could tell as much as a dozen, just as two eyes could see as much as hundreds.

The three warriors had tried. More arrows brought down a mule and another horse, throwing its rider badly.

'After that it was as if they were blessed,' the oldest warrior explained. 'They came back to save their man and we shot, but it was as if the arrows flew wide by some magic or if they struck did no harm.'

Or your aim wavered when the targets were not helpless, but coming at you, Brasus thought to himself.

'One, an older man, scooped up the one on foot and set him behind him. The other threw a javelin at us – he was that close. He missed and so did we, until as he was almost out of range an arrow struck his horse on the leg.' The warrior licked his lips nervously. 'There was one horse still grazing, so I ran to it and jumped up to give chase. It proved a good one, and though they rode like Sarmatians I began to catch up. Closer and closer.' He was warming to his theme again, recalling the thrill of the chase. 'I reckoned that I had a chance so reined in and jumped down. I only had three arrows with me – the others had spilled from my bag – but I nocked the first and let fly. Missed with that, but the second hit the horse with two men on its back. Beast must *have been turned for I skewered the neck and it dropped, throwing them.'*

Brasus had not said anything, and simply waited.

'Well, I was a long way out and on my own. And it was getting dark. Had one arrow and a dagger and there were still three of them left. So I...' He hesitated.

'You were wise to come back,' Brasus told him, almost saying prudent until he judged that this might come across as a rebuke and drive the warrior to fresh recklessness in the future. Nor was there much point in telling the man that it would have been wiser still to have left the Britons alone.

The next day Brasus sent men to follow the trail of the Britons. They found both of the horses and not much further on the corpse of one of the soldiers, who had taken an arrow in the thigh. It was strange that none of his archers had claimed to score this hit and reminded him of his own chaotic memories of past fights. So much happened that it was hard to see everything, let alone recall it afterwards. Brasus' warriors obeyed their orders and did not go any further, for there was too much to do. He had to reckon on the last two men getting back to Piroboridava on foot, which meant that the Roman commanders – this Flavius Ferox that Ivonercus had told him about – would send out patrols to search. With regret Brasus decided to abandon the tower for the moment and set up camp amid the pines up near the pass itself. As far as possible he got them to remove every trace of their presence. Better for the moment that the Romans not know that the king was thinking about this valley and the path down to the river. They would learn soon enough, but the whole plan relied on surprise, catching the enemy on the wrong foot. So today they would copy the archer and do the prudent or wise thing and run away. The men did not like it, but none protested openly. That changed when he told them to wait for him and set out alone. The oldest warrior, a trusted man and one whose past valour granted him licence, wanted to come along, but he was the best man to keep order while Brasus was away. Instead he took the archers, allowing each no more than a knife and a little food, as well as a few loops of rope. Their bows stayed behind and they walked rather than rode, staying always in the treeline.

Brasus positioned each man with great care. All were in trees, for this was an important skill to practise.

'As you have seen, the first shot can be the deadliest, which makes it vital to wait for the right opportunity.'

Four men could only see so much, so he placed one in the woods on the opposite side of the valley to the tower, and the others spaced out a mile or so further on. Brasus found a tree not far from the place where the youngsters had attacked the Brigantes. He did not hurry to climb, for he doubted that any Romans would appear until well after noon. Yet his senses told him that they would come today and that they would come here and he would learn.

The tree was not at the edge of the woodland, but about twenty paces in. Brasus climbed when the time felt right, and found a sturdy branch with others on which he could fasten the loops of rope to use as rests for his feet. He could just glimpse the ground beyond the treeline and the dead horse, its belly already bloated as it decayed.

Romans appeared an hour or so later. He heard the sound of horses and equipment, for the wind was blowing towards him, and at the same time caught the stale smell of leather and sweat.

Brasus waited. He heard voices without catching more than the odd word and at last glimpsed a rider by the dead horse. Another man appeared, walking in a crouch and staring at the grass. He was big, bare headed at the moment showing a mop of black hair, and when his cloak parted there was the gleam of mail and the pommel of a sword. Another horseman rode in front of him, talking to the man, and by the time he moved the first man was out of sight. There were shouted orders and the sound of jingling harness, growing fainter, which meant that some were riding away.

The floor of the forest was a mass of needles, most faded brown and dry and they muffled the sound of the horse's feet until they were very close. They came closer. Brasus glimpsed the black-haired man riding a grey horse towards him. The Roman came closer and closer, passing out of view. The only way for Brasus to see down would have been to shift his feet from the ropes and move, but that was bound to make noise. If he stayed absolutely still then he would be very hard to see, even if the man thought to look up – hard, but not impossible. He doubted the Roman would come up after him, but there must still be soldiers close by and they could wait for him to come down or perhaps reach him with javelins or arrows.

'Trying to get killed, are we?' Another Roman was approaching from the opposite side. He spoke good Latin with an accent much like Ivonercus, so was probably another Briton. 'Wandering off on your own.'

'Maybe I'm luring you away. Reckon the price on your head must be even higher now.' That was the first man, now

almost below him. His voice was deep, with a different, almost musical intonation. 'You know what Silures are like.'

Outlandish though it was, the name had stuck in Brasus' mind. This must be Flavius Ferox, the man hated and feared by Ivonercus.

'Bastards the lot of them,' the other man said. 'Can't trust 'em for a moment.'

They said no more for a long while. Brasus heard the soft footfalls of their horses as they moved around close beneath him. He tried not to imagine faces searching upwards, of enemies grinning because they had seen the man hanging from the branches. One of the horses whinnied, then shook its head and blew noisily.

'So what do you reckon happened?' the second man asked. Brasus wondered if this was Vindex and his instincts told him that it was. No chance had brought him here today. Fate was at work and the will of the Lord of the Heavens. He had known that this was the place and that he needed to be here, and the same instincts told him that he would not die today.

'Someone shot arrows at them.'

There was a pause. 'That it?' Vindex said. 'Might just have worked that one out on my own.'

'Given time,' Ferox conceded. He waited and then sighed. 'The arrow came from the sort of bows the king issues to his warriors. Bit like our army ones and almost as good. The men were on foot – three, maybe four of them. Don't think they planned it, or if they did they didn't plan it well. Probably just saw a chance and took it. Wanted to prove their courage, I guess. They killed all the horses apart from one, so if they wanted those, then they made a mess of it.'

'So what does it mean? You still reckon war is coming?'

'Never doubted it for a moment. Why send us here otherwise?'

'The lass is trying to please the Romans by giving them men.'

'The lass?' Ferox sighed again. 'She's your queen. Haven't you Carvetii always been the queen's folk. Still, given what you used to call her, guess it's an improvement.'

'Calling her the queen only makes me sad. You really buggered up there.' Vindex sniffed in contempt. 'More than usual, I mean. She's my queen all right, and a wise one, but… So you reckon the Romans want soldiers from her to help fight a new war. Haven't they got enough soldiers without this mob?'

'Maybe they want to keep the good soldiers alive?'

'Cheerful sod as usual. So we're humped again.'

'As usual,' Ferox said.

'Aye, as usual,' Vindex agreed. 'But everyone's been telling us since we got here that the war is over.'

'That's the old war,' Ferox told him. 'We get the new one that hasn't started yet. Your people never fought the Romans.'

'Not while anyone was watching.' Vindex chuckled. 'No, not really. Too smart for that. We made friends. Had enough enemies already without finding a new one. And they've treated us right enough since. Left us alone most of the time, which is the main thing.'

'The Dacians are special,' Ferox said. 'Remember that farm we passed last month? The one where the people were sobbing and wailing?'

'Aye, but I still don't get it. You said a baby had been born

– a boy too. Who is mad enough to mourn when mother and child both survive?'

'They celebrate a death. Birth means a life of toil, sorrow and imperfection is ahead. Death means that the soul goes to their god and lives in blessedness forever.'

'Daft buggers.'

'Means they don't fear death. Not the true faithful at least, and especially not the nobles. You haven't met any of them yet, nor true Dacians rather than Getae. They're brave and they're smart – and their king is the smartest of the lot. You can't beat folk like that or a leader like that in a couple of years, so there is a war coming, it's just a matter of when. This year, next year, the one after that? We'll start it if they don't, but you know the Romans, they like to say the other lot started every war.'

'Do they? Haven't they noticed that they own most of the world.'

'They'd say that they are just very good at defending themselves, wouldn't they? Still, makes me wonder whether Trajan wouldn't mind if a couple of his garrisons get attacked and massacred?'

'And we took an oath to this high chief?' Vindex said something else in what sounded like the Celtic language, but Brasus could not understand. However, the tone made the general meaning obvious. 'So we're the bait, are we?' he went on, switching back to Latin. 'Shove a few hundred useless Brigantes who want to kill each other and us in a fort in the middle of nowhere and wait for the wolves to gather?'

'I could be wrong.'

'You often are,' Vindex said without any conviction.

'Hey, what are you doing?' There was the sound of a man dismounting and then a scraping. 'Trying to blunt it are you?'

'Just checking,' Ferox said. 'And then we need to go and take a look at that Dacian fort up near the pass.'

'No one was there last time.'

'Then let's make sure it's still empty. Are you coming?'

'Miserable git. No wonder the lass kicked you out.'

'Aye, well, as you say, she's wise.'

Brasus listened as they left, letting himself breathe naturally at last. Fate had brought him here and times like this took away all the doubts. This Ferox was indeed one of those unusual, dangerous Romans, and that thought kept him in the tree long after he was sure that they had gone. There was only an hour or so left of daylight when he climbed down, but even in the shadows beneath the trees he could make out the shape this Ferox had carved in the bark of the tree. Brasus' blood ran cold.

VIII

Piroboridava
Nonis of April

'WHAT! BASTARD WAS up a tree all the time!'
Vindex was as angry as he was surprised. He
and Ferox were up on top of the gate tower,
and they spoke in the language of the tribes because the only
sentries nearby were legionaries.

'It's an old trick in these parts. They hide scouts or archers
up in the trees. They use ropes so they can stay for a long
time – even tie themselves in place. Then they wait. Some of
them are good at waiting.'

'And you didn't say anything.'

'No point. And it took me a while to be sure. Only
glimpsed him once even then. He did not try to kill either of
us, so maybe he did not have a bow, or maybe the angle was
wrong or he just wanted to stay hidden up there. In that case
showing that I'd spotted him might just make him think a
shot was worthwhile.'

'Why didn't we scrag him?'

'Mongrel was up a tree. Remember Mona?'

Vindex sucked in a deep breath, his big teeth making his
face more horse-like than ever. 'It gets worse. Why bring up

that dark place? Of course I remember, no matter how hard I try to forget. You kill the last great druid, so that's bound to bring us all wonderful luck!'

'You helped,' Ferox said, 'and we are all still here.'

'Here – in this fort you reckon is on the brink of being overwhelmed by hordes of enemies! That's good luck!'

'Perhaps,' Ferox spread his hands. 'I may be wrong.'

'Aye, but when it comes to predicting misery you have a knack of being right, don't you?'

'It's usually a safe bet. At least it has been in my life so far.'

'All right, I'll bite,' Vindex said. 'What has the sacred and terrible island of Mona got to do with a Dacian bugger hiding in a tree?'

'Back on Mona I had to climb that big oak, remember? On my own because you reckoned you couldn't climb. ... So I don't reckon you've been practising much in the last five years. Which meant I'm on my own, trying to find and kill or catch him without falling out and breaking my neck. Let's say I didn't like the odds and did not feel my story should end that way.'

Vindex again sucked in air through the gaps in his teeth. 'Aye, suppose so. More likely to end when a close friend bludgeons you to death in frustration.'

'No doubt about it,' Ferox agreed.

They were interrupted by the arrival of Sabinus and Dionysius, followed by one of the veterans. At morning orders, Ferox had outlined his suspicions, and changed the routine, so that patrols would regularly go up as far as the abandoned Dacian tower and fort, just to check that it was abandoned in accordance with the treaty. Although he had seen nothing when they had taken a look, Ferox's instincts told him that someone had been in the place, and not simply wanderers or hunters looking for shelter. He had carved another symbol in the wooden frame around a doorway just in case.

'Well,' Ferox began once the other three had joined them. 'Let's try to imagine that we are the enemy.' Vindex pulled a face and the others grinned. 'That should make it easier. But let's say we have ten thousand prime warriors at our command and our king has ordered us to capture Piroboridava or face his wrath.'

'Why?' Sabinus asked.

'Probably wants Venus!' Dionysius quipped.

'Does not matter why,' Ferox told them. 'Not for the moment. What matters is how – and what we can do to make their life hard. You're Fulvius Naso?' he asked the soldier.

'Sir.' The veteran's beard was more white than grey, his voice hoarse but steady, giving nothing away.

'Spent a lot of your service with Minervia's engines? Good. I want your thoughts on how best we can use artillery from the towers and even the walls, if practical. But let's start with the basics – walls, towers and ditches. How can we improve them?'

Sabinus coughed. 'Excuse me, sir, but should we not advance to meet the enemy in the open?' His voice quavered, but that was the way the army was taught to operate. Dominate the enemy. Always attack regardless of odds, because you are Roman and you have discipline and they are just rabble.

'Let's say they surprise and attack before we are ready or

there are too many to beat in the open. Somehow or other we are inside and there are a lot of them outside trying to get in. Our problem is stopping them.'

'What about the bridge?' Dionysius asked.

'Could be the reason they come, but let's think about that later. How do we stop them pouring over these walls like a wave.' So they talked of ditches and obstacles, of the height of the rampart and towers and how far a man could throw a missile. Ferox ordered Dionysius to set the workshop to making as many things to throw as they could.

'*Pila muralia*,' Naso said. 'Nasty things at close range, but they're worth the effort of making. They can start with any ordinary pila we have that are broken. Bend the shaft back at an angle and sharpen it.'

'You've made them before?' Ferox asked. Naso nodded. 'And we want stones for throwing, as many as we can find. Chip up any building material left over. They have to fit in a man's hand. Once we have them we practise – all of us – throwing as far as the outer ditch.' Ferox grinned. 'Then we go down and pick them up for next time – and keep the ditches clear while they're at it.'

'That'll make you even more popular, sir?' Sabinus said, and then looked embarrassed.

'Nothing new there,' Vindex commented. He had said almost nothing during the discussion up to this point.

'They already call me "the Bastard", don't they?' Sabinus blushed. It had taken some cajoling to get him to admit to knowing the nickname. Ferox had already known, but wanted to see how honest his subordinates would be when asked a direct question.

'Among other things, sir,' Naso added.

'Hmmm. Well, let's turn to the engines. There is a scorpio in each of the gate towers. Do we have any more?'

'Half a dozen in the workshops that could be decent given a little work. As many more if we could get new washers and frames.'

'That's something. See to it.' Dionysius nodded as Ferox glanced at him. 'And they'll need plenty of ammunition. What about the trophies?' Sabinus showed his surprise. When Ferox had first arrived he had done no more than point at the buildings, but had seen no useful purpose in going inside. They were a pair of former granaries, left empty of food during the last campaign of the war and empty until the Dacians handed over dozens of war engines as part of the peace treaty. Why they had been brought to Piroboridava no one seemed to know and Sabinus could not guess, but here they were, slowly rotting away and no doubt forgotten by everyone. He had kept quiet about them rather than have Ferox create even more tasks cleaning and maintaining what was probably no more than junk. They said more than half were local made rather than machines captured from the Romans or donated by the Emperor Domitian when he had bought peace with Decebalus so that he could go off and fight the Suebi.

'Don't know, sir.'

'We've kept them locked up as ordered,' Sabinus said, unwilling to let the old soldier take responsibility for something over which he had had no control. 'But no one has told us what to do with them.'

'Then no harm in taking a look to see what we have.'

'Waggons coming, sir!' one of the sentries shouted out his report.

Ferox had seen the dust a while ago, and turned back to see the five brightly painted waggons, each with a high cover, as many more ox carts, a single coach and long lines of pack mules.

'That's Tettius Crescens, sir,' Dionysius said. 'Almost to the day he came last year. The lads will be pleased.' Even from this distance women's voices could be heard from the passengers in the waggons, even if little could be seen under the vehicles' covers. Vindex was leering, and Naso barely less interested.

Ferox was unimpressed. 'I'll see this merchant later. He asked for an appointment to see the commander, but not until it is convenient for me.'

'He does have friends, sir,' Sabinus reminded him. 'Who wrote on his behalf.'

'I'll see him, but first I want to look at these Dacian catapults and see if there is anything worthwhile stored in those halls. If nothing else, there may be timber we can use or iron and bronze to melt down. Dionysius, you stay and keep an eye on things. Tell this Tettius that he is invited to dine with me.'

'Poor devil,' Vindex muttered.

'Well, I need to do something about that as well, with our distinguished guests coming before too long. But that's for later. Now let's see what the Dacians pretended was their best artillery when they handed it over.'

There was far more equipment than Ferox had expected, but it was hard to make much sense of it. Both granaries were crammed with artillery and machines of one sort or another, all swathed in dust and cobwebs, arms and beams overlapping or piled in heaps. Beneath the filth some of them were painted red, blue or green, something he had never seen done on artillery before. He saw a good few *scorpiones*, some other bolt shooters that seemed to be of a different pattern, but similar size, and many more larger pieces, some of them truly huge. Naso whistled as he reached up to touch the huge bronze washers and the ends of twisted sinew on one piece two or three times taller than he was.

'Throw a three mina stone at the very least,' he said. 'Not sure about the cord though – looks half rotted away. Like a lot of the others. Not sure how many ever worked in the first place, come to that.'

'Any idea what these are?' Ferox gestured at a couple of strange devices that were more like cranes than catapults, each with a thick boom pointing upwards.

Naso shook his head. 'Buggered if I know, sir.'

'They're big whatever they are,' Sabinus said, and then broke down coughing as he swallowed dust. Ferox patted the centurion on the back.

'I want a full inventory. There must be more *veterani* who have at least a little experience of artillery or who can learn fast. Find as many as you can, Naso. Tell them the Bastard wants this lot sorted out – and then point out that it's lighter work than clearing ditches and digging pits. But I want to know if there is anything that we can put to use. So tell me what works, if any of it still does, what could do with a little attention, anything else that might be made to shoot and then whether there are parts or scrap we can use for anything else.'

'I have a book about engines,' Sabinus said, finally recovered from his bout of coughing. His tone was apologetic. 'My father presented me with a small travelling library of military manuals before I set out for the army. To be honest, I haven't paid much attention. All seemed a bit dry and abstract when I tried.'

'I would appreciate a loan, if I may,' Ferox said.

'Of course.' Sabinus hesitated. 'Do you really think we will be attacked, sir?'

Ferox doubted that the man would understand about instincts. He had already explained what he knew and what he thought it meant that morning and if that did not convince the man, then saying that he 'knew' it would happen was not likely to make a difference. Yet he did, and the feeling grew stronger every moment. 'Yes,' he said in the end. 'I hope that I am wrong, but I am sure I am not.'

Sabinus was saved from answering by another bout of coughing. Vindex patted him this time. 'The centurion tends to be right about things like that,' he said as Sabinus recovered. 'But also has a way of winning when all the odds are stacked high against him. And usually those of us with him get through as well.'

'Begging your pardons, my lords,' Naso said, his rough voice a croak in this dusty atmosphere, 'but if the commander is right then we are royally humped. No way in the world that less than six hundred of us can hold a place as big as this against two or three thousand let alone ten. Not if they're determined.'

'Dacians usually are,' Ferox said. 'And they're not just barbarians when it comes to sieges.' He waved a hand around the great hall with its piles of artillery. 'They've learned too much.'

'Then should we hold at all, when…' Sabinus swallowed. 'If they come.'

'And go where, sir?' Naso was like a father talking to a nervous child. 'There's nowhere to go. Only thing between us and the Ister is a lot of nothing.'

'That's why we've got to try,' Ferox said. 'We've got time, so let's use it.'

As they walked out onto the loading platform at the front of the granary and turned for the steps at the side leading down to ground level, Vindex walked alongside Sabinus and gave one of his sinister grins. 'If it's any help, since I've known the centurion I have expected to die more than a score of times. But as he says, I'm still here after all that. He's a hard man to kill, and there's a lot to be said for having him around.'

Sabinus managed a thin smile.

The dinner was a poor affair. As commander, Ferox occupied the big praetorium, but he had not brought a great household to run the place. There was just Philo, his wife Indike, and a rather slow Brigantian boy, an orphan, who had nowhere else to go. In the past, even this modest staff had seemed excessive, not least because of Philo's relentless pursuit of cleanliness and determination to make something better of his master. The boy – and Ferox still thought of him as a boy, even though he was now twenty-five and his freedman rather than slave – was a Jew from Alexandria. He was slim, dark skinned, dark eyed, and always immaculate, somehow bleaching his tunics until they were whiter than even the most eager *candidatus* standing for election at Rome. Indike was smaller, even slimmer and darker, and had come originally from India even though she had been sold into slavery and shipped to the empire when she was an infant. A former dancer, most recently in Londinium, she had ended up being looked after by Philo, and the pair had fallen in love, so that Ferox had let them marry and then given both their freedom. If anything this increased their devotion and determination to run his life if possible, and at the very least turn him into a respectable, well dressed and groomed officer. It was an uphill struggle, but both had as much patience as willpower. Even so, there was only so much they could do with the limited help offered by the boy and fatigue parties of soldiers. Philo's expression was a constant reminder that Ferox had ignored his advice to acquire more help before they came to Piroboridava.

Lucius Tettius Crescens registered no more than mild surprise at the modest array of dishes on the table between the couches, and even less at the absence of anyone else to occupy the *triclinia*. From his paunch, heavy neck and jowls, this was a man who enjoyed his food, but his tone was practical, and neither ingratiatingly humble or with the excessive pride of a man who had made his fortune. Dionysius had told Ferox that the merchant was a Sardinian, that he had undertaken contracts to supply the army during the last war, had bought large numbers of the prisoners taken to sell on, and had done a lot of business in the Dacian capital Sarmizegethusa, even with Decebalus himself. Tettius knew a lot of people, and plenty of them had written recommending him and asking good Romans to assist him. To his surprise, a few letters addressed directly to Ferox had preceded the man's arrival.

'I plan to stay for a few days, if that is acceptable,' the merchant said after brief pleasantries. He spoke loudly and his voice echoed around the big, almost empty dining room. 'My apologies.'

'None needed.'

Indike appeared, bearing piping hot stew on a tray. Tettius watched her, as most men would, for she had a rare, delicate beauty and even her slightest movement had grace. The man watched, but did nothing gross, whether from respect for his host or innate decency, and Ferox was glad because he did not wish to have to rebuke a guest. 'Would you care to stay inside the garrison? I am sure that we could find some rooms, although they may be a little basic in their comforts.'

Tettius' eyes flicked around the room. 'I do not need much, but would be grateful for what you can offer. Most of my people will remain outside in the carts or stay in the *vicus*.' The collection of a few decent buildings and plenty of shacks outside the fort was scarcely worthy of the term, which was usually reserved for the more formal and organised communities around a base. 'Some of the carts are well suited to our business.'

'You will not be short of customers, especially for your girls. I trust that the prices are clear and fair.'

'Of course. All as they should be, approved by the legatus Augusti, and all recorded so that taxes will be paid. After a few days I intend to press on with some of my people, but wondered whether ten of the girls should remain? I would wish my property to be under your protection.'

'Give a statement at the principia, with witnesses to vouch for its truthfulness.' Ferox was relieved that this was a straightforward request, easy to grant. 'Will they stay at the tavern?' In smaller outposts, it was common enough to hire a prostitute and give her a room in a barrack block to ply her trade. Men in a bigger base liked the relief offered by walking out through the gates to take their pleasure, where they felt free of the army for just a short while.

'Yes. The owner will watch them – after all he works for me.' Tettius gave a thin smile. He had thick hair, which hung down almost to his eyebrows. Once or twice he brushed it with his hand and touched a pale scar that was concealed the rest of the time. He did so now, and Ferox could not decide whether this was sheer habit or a mark of nervousness. 'You have had trouble I hear.' The change of subject was abrupt. 'Men killed, I mean.' Again his fingers pushed hair out of the way and scratched the scar.

'There has been an incident,' Ferox conceded, wondering how the man had learned of this.

'Julius Dionysius told me,' Tettius explained. 'Do not blame him, I beg you. I am going that way so naturally I asked if all was safe. I have a few men in case of trouble, but no real protection against bandits or worse.'

'You travel over the pass and to Sarmizegethusa?'

'Yes. My girls will find plenty of work with the garrison there and I have luxuries for the officers and the royal courts – as well as other business. It is a great deal to ask, but I wondered whether an escort might be possible?'

That was it then. It was a significant favour, although not an unreasonable one for a man with so many friends willing to speak on his behalf. 'Certainly. Although they must rest at Sarmizegethusa for no more than a day before they return.

Unless you are ready by that time, you shall have to find other protection for your return journey.'

'That is more than generous, and I thank you.' The merchant raised his hand and pressed it against his own mouth, presumably a gesture from his homeland, for Ferox had never seen it before.

'In turn, I hope to purchase a few things from you,' Ferox said, 'for as you may have noticed, my hospitality is meagre.'

Tettius made a dismissive gesture. 'I assumed merely the disdain for luxury of a simple soldier.'

Ferox began to explain what he wanted. 'All in all, something more appropriate for my rank and responsibilities is now necessary, not least because a senior officer is soon to pass this way.'

'The legatus of I Minervia? Do not show surprise, it is my business to know things, so that I am best placed to provide services and goods as they are needed.' He scratched the scar again, as if in thought. 'Yes, yes, and it is no ordinary senator, but Publius Aelius Hadrianus, cousin to our princeps. You did not realise?' Tettius must have sensed the surprise although Ferox did not think he had betrayed it. 'Well, once again it is good for my trade to know such things. He is a man with high standards, although not too demanding beyond the requirements of military discipline. Is there good hunting at this season? I hear that he is fond of the chase. Well, well, I am glad to repay your services to me so easily. Let us consider what you need. How well do you wish to entertain the noble legatus?'

'Sufficient for courtesy,' Ferox said. 'And please understand that I mean to pay. Your escort was a duty, not a favour.'

'I would not insult you by suggesting otherwise, noble Flavius Ferox. But I can give my personal attention to this matter, so tell me what precisely you want.'

IX

THEIR LITTLE CAMP was a shambles when they returned, the blankets scattered, bits of food everywhere and the horses wandered off to crop the grass. In the centre the girl sat by the dying fire, staring out blankly. She had a thick woollen blanket pulled around her and was clutching it tight just as she clutched her own knees. She shivered even though the sun was now very warm.

One man lay with his hand in the fire, the skin long since blackened and the smell of cooked meat heavy in the air, mingling with the reek of blood. Another corpse had its trousers down around its ankles and a great gash across the chest. The third was barely recognisable for once having been a man for it had been hacked into pieces where it lay.

The captive tried to raise his hands to touch the amulet around his neck before remembering that they were tied to the horn on the saddle. He whistled in amazement. 'That Chrauttius? And his brothers? They were a tough bunch of lads.'

Three spears had been driven into the ground and on top of each one was a severed head.

'You said that you trusted these men,' Bran said bitterly.

Sosius shrugged. 'I was wrong. I thought that they would want what I had promised them enough not to do anything stupid. And I thought that she could handle them.'

Bran leapt down from his horse.

'We got the man we wanted, and she's alive,' Sosius said. 'That is enough. It was a gamble, but no real harm done, is there? Without them we'd never have got what we wanted.'

Bran paid no heed to the freedman and walked slowly towards Minura as she sat. She gave not the slightest sign that she saw him or the others, so he sat down beside her.

Minura stopped shivering and became still, and that was almost more unnerving, as she stared out at something no one else could see. Bran could see that she had bitten her lip and the blood had dried on her chin.

'I am here, sister,' he spoke each word softly, as if to a child, although the woman was a fearsome warrior and older than he was by several years.

'Reckon he might kill you,' the captive said, watching them. 'The lad's good with a sword.'

'She's better,' Sosius said, knowing that it was best to keep back for the moment.

Bran reached over and touched Minura's hand softly.

'I am here, sister, you are not alone anymore.'

Her hand moved and her fingers closed tightly around his.

'And you are avenged on them,' he said.

'The joy of revenge is brief.' Minura did not look at him, but her words were steady. 'I am glad that I killed them, but I should not have been taken off guard. They were bad men, and such men never believe that a woman can fight and at first I could not.' The words started to pour out and Bran sensed that she was on the verge of tears. 'One was joking, trying to get me to drink with them while we waited and he seemed a harmless fool. Then another grabbed my arms from behind, and although I jumped and kicked the one in front, the other then caught my legs and they wrestled me down.' Bran could see her torn tunic lying on the ground. 'They took me, one after the other and I screamed and screamed for my courage left me, and when they were done, they cast me aside and sat around the fire as if nothing was happened.'

'Warriors can be cruel,' Bran said. 'But they have paid. There is only one more to punish.'

'Not yet, brother,' she said, knowing what he meant. Sosius had brought the men to their camp, spoken to them and then left her here with them as they went to catch the man he had come for. The freedman cared for no one, but used others as counters in some game which only he – and perhaps his distant master – understood. They had seen his ruthlessness many times since they were sent off with him.

'I will kill him,' Bran whispered.

'Not today, little brother, and when the day comes I will wield the blade.'

'I am sorry that I was not here.'

'We cannot change what has been done,' she said, and leaned her head against his. Never before had she shown such intimacy, for Minura was a woman of few words and stern character. 'We must face the truth and continue along our path. Is that not what we were taught?'

'Yet, I long to wipe the smirk from that pig's face.'

'The day will come, but we were sent by the queen and

must finish the task she set us.' Her fingers tightened hard around his. 'If I can bear to wait, then it should be a smaller deed for you.'

Minura stood, the blanket opening a little to show that she was naked underneath. At any other time Bran would have thrilled at the sight, but now he looked away. When he turned back she was covered and smiling.

'There is a stream not far away,' she said, 'and I need to be clean. Stay here.'

Sosius got the captive down from his horse and told him to sit and not be a nuisance. While Bran brought in the horses and saw to them, the Freedman dragged the corpses away and then got the fire going again.

'When she gets back you can fetch some water,' he said to Bran. 'Believe it or not, I started out in the kitchens and haven't lost the touch. A hot meal will do us all good.' The boy's hatred was obvious. 'Look, sonny, I'm sorry how things worked out, but I can't change them. If you'd ever lived as a slave you'd know that life is a bastard and that no one is safe. She's strong and brave, and she'll learn to live with it because I don't reckon she is the sort to give in. So we'll all have a good meal and then decide what to do.'

Sosius was a good cook, his stew a rare treat, making Bran wonder why the slave had got either him or Minura to cook for them on all the other days. She was more herself when she returned, dressed again and skin clean, and if she sat apart and said little that was nothing unusual.

After they had eaten, Sosius told them that he must ride to see the local chieftain at his farmstead. 'Chrauttius and the others were his cousins. Distant ones, but blood is blood and I'll have to pay him in gold to make things right.

'In the meantime, you take him,' he jabbed a finger towards the captive, 'back to the province and then south to the queen. Guess she'll be in Moesia by then, probably the Upper province. Maybe Viminiacum, but I don't know. The letters you have will see you through. No one will question those seals. I ought to have joined you long before then. If I can, it will be in a day or two, but it is hard to be sure.'

Sosius had ridden away almost immediately, even though night was falling.

'Doubt that we will see that slave again,' Bran said after he had gone.

'We will, on the day we find him and I kill him. And he is a free man now, no longer a slave.'

They kept the prisoner tied hand and foot at night, and only released his legs when he needed to ride, and did the same on the days that followed.

'I'm just a merchant,' the man kept on insisting. 'What do I know that really matters?'

Sosius had told them that the man worked for Decebalus, and that his main business was recruiting allies for the king to help him against Rome. Such great affairs did not matter to them, so they ignored him, and spoke little and then only in the language of the tribes of Britannia. If the merchant understood, he showed no sign. Their job was to take him to the queen and that was what they would do. Bran had made it clear to the man that his head would do almost as well as the rest of him, if the task proved difficult.

Sosius did not return and they were glad of that, especially as the journey was easy. They saw few people, and fewer still who wished to speak, so perhaps Sosius had cleared their path for them by speaking to the chieftain and others.

On the third night Minura came to Bran as he was swilling their pan and plates in a brook. The merchant was tied up, and fastened to a tree trunk, so did not need to be watched.

'Am I fair to look upon?' Minura asked.

'You are beautiful,' he said and it was not flattery for he did consider her among the fairest of women he had seen. 'If it were not for our oaths…' A brother and sister who had learned the craft of war as they had done were not supposed to lie with one another.

'My oath means little now that my honour has been taken,' she said.

Bran wondered when he would wake from this dream. She was taller than he was, and he had to reach up to lay his hands on her cheeks. 'May I kiss you?' he asked.

'I should like that.'

He felt the cut on her lip and tried to be gentle, but she pushed her mouth closer to his.

'I know little of the way of these things,' Bran said, wondering that he admitted to his ignorance, but unable to boast or posture with her.

'Nor I,' Minura said and she ran her fingers through his short hair. 'Perhaps we can learn together?'

X

On the Ister between Dobreta and Pontes
Fifth day before the Ides of April

I T WAS A wonder without any doubt. If he had not had
good reason to be here, simply seeing this would have
made the long journey worthwhile. From down here
on the waters of the Ister, the long southern stretch of the
Danube, the pillars reared up like man-made cliffs. There
were twenty of them, each 170 feet apart, the foundations
great piers of stone, curving like the prows of ships into
cutwaters so that the river's force was spread and guided
around them without pressing its full weight; functional
and elegant, like all good architecture. The stonework rose
to a flat top, carefully levelled off, and above that was the
wooden supports, five great beams supporting a regular
lattice pattern like a spider's web or even a parade of isosceles
triangles. From those rose the arches, curving up, each arch
identical to the next, rearing high above them. As promised,
the helmsman took them between two of the pillars so that
he could see the design properly and stare up at the joists on
top of which were planks of the roadway itself, unfinished
here, since they were at the centre of the bridge.

'Be finished in a month at the latest,' the architect's

assistant told him. The great man himself had claimed that he was too busy to accompany them and had sent an underling.

'Ephippus here will be your guide. I am sure that he will be able to answer whatever you feel inclined to ask,' Apollodorus of Damascus had assured Hadrian. The chief architect had an immensely high opinion of his own merit and little patience with others. His talent was obvious, as was the emperor's trust in his abilities, so that for the moment his conceit was understandable, if unfortunate. Hadrian was eager to learn, and it was so rare to encounter a man who had so much to teach. So the day before he had asked questions, when the architect had shown him the work from the Pontes' bank of the river, where the monumental arch spanning the approach road was already complete, apart from the statues to be mounted on top. There was a matching arch on the far, Dobreta shore, which was making quicker process now that the soldiers who had built the other one had joined the workers there. Hadrian was pleased to see that some of his legionaries were involved, and spent time meeting them and praising their efforts.

This was only part of the great projects undertaken to help the army secure the region, and the last to be completed. For several years now barges were able to bypass the long stretch of rapids on the Danube by using the new canal, aided by the road which for miles ran along the river, often cut out of the living rock. All of that had been completed while Hadrian was last in the area some three years ago, when the bridge was little more than plans and a bold idea. Now, it was almost finished, conceived by genius and turned into stone and timber reality by the labour of many soldiers, including the contingent from Legio I Minervia.

It was natural for a commander to take an interest in work done by his troops, and equally natural that when officers visited the site they asked the presiding architect about the project. Hadrian had put great thought into his questions, wishing to demonstrate that he was no ignorant aristocrat, showing interest for form's sake and caring little for the answers. So he had asked about the details of the design, of the forces in play, of weight of material and current. They were good questions, useful questions, but Apollodorus' answers were the same vague platitudes designed for the ignorant. Hadrian pressed him, trying to show that he was different, and even anticipated part of the answer in his question.

'Apelles to Alexander,' the architect had told Hadrian, not bothering to explain the allusion. Piso, who had up to this point shown no deep interest, sniffed as if he understood.

Hadrian struggled to control his anger, aware that his face had reddened. It was an old story, and like so many about Alexander the Great, hard to know whether or not it was true. While sitting for a portrait at Ephesus, the Macedonian king had chattered away to the artist and his assistants, asking about composition and colours, and often making suggestions. Eventually Apelles, already famous and soon to win even greater reputation when Alexander declared that only he would be allowed to paint the royal image, told the king to stop talking, because even the lowest apprentices were laughing at his ignorance. The rebuke was a sharp one, arrogant because for all his great skill Apollodorus was speaking to a *vir clarissimus*, a member of the Senate, let alone kin to the princeps. It was also unfair, for engineering and architecture were among Hadrian's great passions, and his interest was as informed as it was genuine. He would let the Syrian have his moment, but still wanted to learn all that he could. So he had asked to see some of the plans and said that he wished to take a tour around the bridge from the river. Apollodorus had agreed – it would have been hard to refuse – and delegated this underling to the job.

Ephippus was a Greek from Syracuse in Sicily, who stuttered and twitched in the presence of the distinguished guests, but tried his best. His nervousness was not helped when Hadrian requested that an engineer come with him on his tour of the garrisons to provide technical advice, prompting Apollodorus to say in front of the Sicilian that he was sure he could spare him. By now Hadrian was satisfied with the choice. He had been patient with Ephippus, encouraged him with his smile and by gradually moving from simple to complex matters as he asked about the bridge. The man struck him as thoroughly competent, with extensive knowledge, if lacking in the spark of inspiration or any real appreciation of the aesthetic as more than just theory.

For the tour, the garrison of Pontes supplied and manned one of the slim boats used for patrolling the river. Hadrian and Ephippus stayed in the stern, so that they could direct the helmsman to take them where they wanted to go. Piso hovered nearby, while an equestrian tribune and the two more surprising guests went up by the prow. Most of the rowers were more interested in them than anyone else, and Hadrian could see them twisting their heads at every opportunity to peer back over their shoulders. That was when they had effort to spare, because often the views he wanted meant rowing hard against the current. They muttered, as soldiers will, each time he had the helmsman turn about and head back upstream under yet another of the great arches. As far as he was concerned it was worth it.

'Quite beautiful,' Hadrian said softly as they came out into the open air again. He had to admit that Apollodorus had done a good job.

'Not bad,' Piso smirked, mistaking his meaning and instead staring at the two ladies standing in the prow, the wind rippling their dresses and outlining their figures. Hadrian's senatorial tribune could be both vulgar and tiresomely direct. He tended to frown when he was thinking, head slightly bowed, so that he almost stared up as he fixed his gaze on whomever he was addressing at the time. Perhaps Piso believed this made him appear earnest, but the impression was of a halfwit, although Hadrian was coming to believe that it was a false one. Now he was almost leering at the women as blatantly as the soldiers, whenever they got a chance.

They were both married to officers, on the way to join their husbands and would travel with Hadrian on the first stage of his journey beyond the river. Apart from his own escort, there were several hundred troops marching with them on their way to garrisons, so they had asked to come with him and he had been happy to grant the request. The older of the two, Sulpicia Lepidina, was a senator's daughter, so a *clarissima femina*, even if she had married a mere equestrian. Her own family was impoverished, from a mixture of excess and poor management, which did much to explain the choice of husband, who had money if not high birth, and was by all accounts a decent enough fellow, well thought of by the emperor – at least when Trajan remembered to think of him at all. Lepidina's uncle by marriage was Neratius Marcellus, just coming to the end of his term as governor of Britannia, and his brother was in charge of Pannonia. There were six hundred or so senators, and Hadrian always felt that it was like living in some rustic village, where everyone knew each other, and husbands were the neighbours' cousins or brothers, wives their sisters, and all old kindnesses were remembered just as long as the old squabbles. Doing a favour was always wise, as long as it did not come at too high a price, and he had willingly granted the request when the ladies called on him, having arranged the matter with a courteous letter. When to his surprise they asked to accompany him on his trip on the river, Hadrian readily assented again. Curiosity was impressive in a woman, if not carried to excess.

Hadrian guessed that Lepidina was in her thirties, yet her pale skin was flawless, her hair thick and golden, tied back in a simple bun. She was a beautiful woman, a rare intelligence in her eyes, her pale blue dress, like her hairstyle and modest jewellery, in contrast to the opulence of many fashionable ladies and far more elegant. He liked her, wondered whether she might be interesting company, and regretted that she was not even better connected for he suspected that she might have a formidable instinct for politics. That was a guess, for the lady was also reserved and he had not yet had the time to see whether this could be broken down. If she were ten years older he was sure that he could soon make her laugh enough for the walls to drop and for her to take him into her confidence.

There was a little shriek as the rowers drove the boat against the current and the prow dipped, sending a spray of water over the ladies and the tribune escorting them. The cry was from the second lady, the younger one, Claudia Enica. She was laughing, flirting with the tribune and soon she was talking again, as she had jabbered away from the start. Claudia was green eyed, her flaming red hair rolled and piled high in a style more suited for a dinner than a boat trip. A number of red strands had worked loose of the pins and blew around her. She was younger than Lepidina, perhaps twenty-five, with an expensive green silk dress, almost too much make-up and almost too much jewellery that almost took away her own beauty.

Hadrian was beginning to think that Claudia was not quite what she seemed, and was no longer so ready to dismiss her as an empty headed nobody. She was an equestrian, a third-generation citizen, from the royal family of the biggest tribe in Britannia, claiming to be their queen, although not formally recognised, at least so far. There were plenty of would-be kings and queens throughout the empire, most of little account except locally. The red hair was a distraction, contrasting with the would-be fashionable Roman lady, and reminding the world that a barbarian lurked underneath. Hadrian could not help thinking that this was deliberate, for surely someone wanting to pose as fully Roman would have dyed it some unexceptional shade.

The tribune offered Claudia his cloak, apologising to Lepidina that he only had one. The redhead refused, very politely, as did the older lady when the embarrassed officer proffered the garment to her. So different in so many ways, the close bond between the two women was obvious, which in itself hinted that Claudia was play-acting the part of a frivolous young woman. There was something else, although Hadrian struggled to pin it down. Claudia moved well, almost like a dancer, and yet not like a dancer, and for all her good looks there was almost something boyish about her.

As the boat turned to head back under the bridge a final time the wind shifted, gusting stronger. The tribune almost fell as the boat lurched, and Claudia squealed and Lepidina gasped with surprise as the wind struck them, their dresses ballooning up over their knees for an all too brief instant.

'Lovely the virgin seemed as the soft wind exposed her limbs, and as the zephyrs fond fluttered amid her garments, and the breeze fanned lightly in her flowing hair,' Piso intoned.

'She seemed most lovely to his fancy in her flight,' Hadrian continued the quote. 'And mad with love he followed in her steps.'

'Quite,' Piso said.

'They're married, you know, else they would not be here.' Like the mention of Apelles, having his broad stripe tribune quoting Ovid was another sign that the man was not without learning or wit.

'Since when did that matter?' Piso said hungrily, and he smiled at the ladies' embarrassment, becoming once again the crude, feckless young aristocrat. 'The chase makes it worthwhile.'

'You ought to be careful,' Hadrian told him. Whatever his feelings for this man, what Piso did during his time with the legion would reflect on his own reputation. Hadrian needed to make the man useful, and if there was a mistake or worse, show to the world that he was not to blame for his tribune's folly. 'Daphne was turned into a tree to save her from Apollo's lust.'

'That'd be her problem not mine. Still, the blonde might be easier to run down. Less speed on her by the look of it.'

'If you must be a fool, do not get caught while you are with my legion,' Hadrian kept his voice low, so that even Ephippus could not hear, but made his tone as menacing as possible. Piso was not required to like him, and what mattered was that he obeyed.

'My lord,' Piso said, giving that familiar frown of earnest concentration.

Ephippus was drawing his attention to the breakwaters once again, explaining matters Hadrian already understood, but it was better to turn to this. Yet something Piso had said had let him see clearer than before, and a name for Claudia came to mind and would not go, seeming less absurd with every moment – amazon. He laughed at the thought, and still it was there, like the red hair, utterly absurd if all someone saw was the chattering, rather silly young woman.

After heading back under another arch they were to row to the far bank and stay in the fort at Dobreta for the night. The troops who were to accompany him had been ferried across the Ister during the day, along with the baggage, and all the impedimenta brought by the ladies. He could see the last load being carried across. As they came out from under the bridge, he saw the top of Dobreta's new amphitheatre. Pontes already had one, and it was surprising how swiftly these garrisons were developing into substantial towns. When the bridge was finished they were bound to grow even more.

'Soon be ashore now, sir,' the helmsman told them, and pointed at the jetty.

Hadrian turned around because he wanted to take a last long look at the great bridge. He doubted that there would ever be anything else like it built in his lifetime, and part of him hoped that it never would. Like all works of genius, Apollodorus' creation was dangerous as well as miraculous.

'Big, isn't it?' Piso said.

'You do not see it, do you?' Hadrian said. 'None of them do.'

Piso stared at the line of great arches. How could he not see it – the thing was vast! His commander was a strange fellow, but after the telling off, there was no harm in trying to win favour. 'I see a wonder of engineering.'

Hadrian glanced back, saw the frowning forehead again, so turned his eyes to the bridge. 'Have you noticed that it points both ways?'

'Shouldn't it?' Piso's confusion was obvious.

'I mean that it can be crossed from either side.'

'It's a bridge.' There was a hint of contempt in the voice.

'Of course it is, silly me,' Hadrian said. 'Well, now that is sorted out, I rather think I ought to go forward and have a word with our charming guests. You stay and supervise the landing.'

Piso shook his head as the legatus of his legion and cousin of the emperor made his way carefully along the narrow strip of deck between the rowers.

XI

Near the road, twenty miles south west of Piroboridava
The day before the Ides of April

THE HORSEMAN WAS silhouetted on the top of the hill, watching them. He had his arms folded, a common gesture among his kin, and the horse, its mane and tail braided with colourful ribbons, simply stood there, now and again leaning down to crop the grass. The man wore loose trousers, a long sleeved, long hemmed tunic and boots, all of them a deep grey, and had an orange-brown cloak.

Ferox had halted the column. 'Where there's one, there's always more,' he said. They had caught up with the scouts he sent ahead, pleased that they had obeyed his orders and waited after bumping into anything strange. Not that this was all that unexpected, for the spring was properly here now and this was a good place for grazing and hunting. Seeing the warrior brought back a lot of memories.

'He's a Sarmatian,' Sabinus said.

'A Red Alan,' corrected the decurion in charge of the twenty auxiliary horsemen who had joined the fifty Carvetii and Brigantes on this ride.

Ferox gave a slight nod. He was one of the Roxolani, of the Stag clan, unless he was mistaken, although in truth it was hard to be sure when warriors often moved their tents from one band to the next. Unless the sun had stopped rising and setting, they were a tough bunch, good friends and really bad enemies, and you never quite knew which way they would go.

Vindex was less impressed. 'Ugly beast he's got.' The Roxolani, like most Sarmatians, liked small horses, thick legged, rather snub nosed, but strong and able to run for hours.

'Bet your horse says the same about you,' the decurion suggested.

'Cheeky bugger.'

Sabinus ignored them. 'He doesn't look out for trouble.'

'They're all thieves,' the decurion said.

'Aren't we all,' Vindex muttered. 'Although the Romans do it in style and steal the world.'

'Nonsense, we spread peace and enlightenment,' Sabinus snapped, then scanned the horizon. 'Cannot see any others, sir. Shall we press on?'

'Yes, take the column on for another two hours and then camp – and keep a close watch, especially on the horses. We should meet the legatus and his men tomorrow. I will re-join you as soon as I can, but until then you are in charge. If I am not back by the time you meet the legatus, then offer him my sincere apologies and say that I will return within three days if I am able, if not... Ah, told you there would be more.' A second rider appeared beside the first one, with a third hovering behind.

'If not, sir?' Sabinus asked.

'What? Oh, if I'm not back in three days then I'm dead. They don't torture anyone longer than that.'

'Sir?' Sabinus said, but Ferox was already walking his horse away. 'Are you sure about this, sir?'

Ferox glanced back at Vindex. 'Coming?'

'Oh bugger,' the scout said, and followed. Sabinus watched them go, saw the three Sarmatians turn and canter out of sight, but Ferox and Vindex did not check and followed them over the brow of the hill.

'Better go, sir,' the decurion said after a while.

'Yes, I suppose we should.' Sabinus had seventy men under his command and had rarely felt so alone.

Ferox and Vindex rode for a few miles. The valley was wide, the fields open, rolling up and down with little hills, and they gave the horses their heads, letting them run. There were farms dotted around, wheat and barley growing well and they avoided the cultivated patches. Now and then they saw the three Roxolani. From one of the higher hills they could see the road and the little figures of Sabinus and his men trotting along, before they dipped down again. Up ahead was a longer, higher ridge and one of the horsemen had stopped on the crest.

'That's where they'll be,' he called to Vindex and pointed. 'They like to surprise you.'

'How big a surprise?'

'Well, some of them hate me.'

'I like 'em already.'

Their horses surged as they reached the ridge, racing up

the slope, hoofs pounding on the turf. The lone rider waited until they were almost there before spinning his mount and galloping away.

'Keep going!' Ferox shouted as he saw Vindex begin to rein in. They reached the top, wide and empty and suddenly it was filling with riders, spilling up over the crest ahead, cantering around them. There were about twenty, and all had bows or javelins in hand.

'Now we stop,' Ferox said as the Roxolani formed a circle around them. 'And don't worry.'

'Really.'

'No point, it wouldn't do any good.'

The riders had weapons, but the javelins were held upright and none had placed an arrow on their bows. Many were of strange design, held not in the middle as usual, but two-thirds of the way down so that the lower arc was much smaller than the one above their hand. They were horseman's weapons, awkward until a man trained himself to use one, but then far more powerful at short range than an ordinary bow.

Ferox placed his right hand, palm flat, against his left shoulder, and kicked his horse while holding the reins tight, so that its hind legs stayed where they were and the front made the beast turn a full circle.

The riders watched, saying nothing. To Vindex's surprise, one was a young woman, her face decorated with tattoos, but dressed like a man and carrying a bow.

There was a man beside her, his beard dyed bright red, but showing grey hairs where drink had washed the colouring away. He lowered his bow back into the case fastened to the rear of his saddle, made the same gesture as Ferox and walked his horse forward. He came close, saying nothing, face impassive. Ferox took off his centurion's helmet with its tall crest – a replacement for the one he had broken on his first day at the fort.

The rider stared at him. No one said anything, and even Vindex had the sense not to crack any jokes, although he did wink at the young woman. She ignored him, and all of the warriors had the same impassive stare. For a long while they sat on their horses.

'It is you,' the bearded man said at last, using strongly accented Greek.

'Yes,' Ferox replied.

'Flavios Kakos.'

'Yes.'

'We thought you dead.'

There was not really an answer to that, so Ferox said nothing.

'Then come.' The warrior turned and raised a hand to the others. A moment later they were streaking away down the far side of the ridge.

Vindex was puzzled.

'He said to follow,' Ferox called, forgetting that Vindex spoke no Greek, and then set off in pursuit. The scout followed and caught up after a few hundred paces.

'Talkative buggers, aren't they?'

'When they are riding they only speak when they have something worth saying.'

'Oh aye,' the scout said, 'that could take some folk a lifetime. And what's this about cack.'

'It's what they call me.'

Vindex roared with laughter, and said no more. The path

was easy to follow, and more riders appeared to look at them before riding off. None came close enough to speak, although now and again they called out 'Kakos!' Vindex laughed a lot.

The camp was not a large one, with about a dozen waggons, some tents, and a few hundred horses and ponies, with half that number of goats, the bells on their collars tinkling as they moved. There was a great fire burning in the centre of the main ring of waggons and tents, and at the head a canopy beneath which rugs were spread and three people sat in high-backed chairs.

'Do as I do,' Ferox said and put his helmet back on. This one had been made in the workshop at the fort and had crosspieces over the bowl and the crest holder above that. He dismounted, so Vindex copied. A servant, clad in simple tunic and trousers and barefoot, appeared and led the animals away. A lot of people stood in their path, mainly warriors, but women and children as well, all with the same rigid stare.

Ferox walked straight towards the canopy. Men, and one or two young women, barred his path, sometimes sticking out their tongues, but he did not check or slow. At the last moment they moved out of the way, apart from one fair-haired youth, and the centurion barged him out of the way with his shoulder, and pressed on.

Two men and a woman sat under the canopy. All three were in armour, the men a shirt of bronze scales and the woman in mail, there were swords at their sides and conical helmets resting on their laps. The woman looked about forty, black hair streaked grey, skin lined, jaw firm and grey blue eyes clear and cold as the sea. The man on her right was older, bald apart from a fringe of grey hair, but with a thick beard dyed red, and the one on the left was younger, with fair hair and beard. None of them smiled.

'It is true then,' the older man said, again using Greek. 'I did not believe it when I was told.'

'I did.' The woman had a deep voice. 'I saw it in the stars.' She changed to Latin. 'The Bad Flavius has returned.' Like the young woman, her face was dotted with little markings, as were the backs of her hands.

Ferox could almost feel Vindex stifling a laugh.

'I do not come in vengeance or anger,' Ferox said, using Greek since it was more likely that they understood enough. Since arriving here he had started to use the language more than for many years, but his speech was slow and careful, matching his hosts. 'I leave to you whether there is anger or vengeance in your hearts. If there is, then I will face it, but this man is my friend,' he indicated Vindex, who understood not a word, 'and I ask that he be allowed to do what is necessary afterwards.'

'That is for the dawn after next,' the older man said and the other two nodded. 'Now you are our guest.'

The feast was already in preparation, the smell of roast meat growing as carcases were roasted over the fire – sheep, goats and cattle. There were blankets on the ground around the long fire, and guests came and went, sitting for a while, talking, eating and drinking. Few spoke to Vindex in any language he could understand, but laughter and gesture made him welcome. Ferox was with the leaders, sitting on a stool only a little lower than theirs and whenever Vindex glanced in that direction they were deep in talk.

'It is fitting,' a man said to him in Latin, and flashed a

broad grin, the whiteness of his teeth all the brighter because his skin was a deep shade of brown unlike any of the others in the camp. 'Chieftains talk and tell stories and will ask the Bad Flavius where he has been and what he has done.'

'Why the bad?' Vindex asked, but the man had already gone, called away by a scowling warrior. Another warrior, his sword belt and scabbard a deep red colour, matching his long tunic, offered the scout a bowl filled to the brim with milk, so he took it and drank, before passing it back and smiling in thanks. The young woman appeared and held out a smaller cup, this time filled with a bitter wine. Vindex drank deeply, for this was a welcome change, only handing it back when the giver must have begun to worry that none would be left. He gave the girl a big wink and she ignored him, heading off. A servant brought a platter of cheese and cuts of meat, so he took some and ate for a while. He began to pick up a few of the words for food, but otherwise the talk flowed past him. As the sun set and the stars filled the sky, there was more wine as well as mead and beer and as far as he could tell little of the conversation made much sense anymore. He saw the dark warrior a few times, but never close enough to speak. Ferox was still with the chieftains, and if they had drank as much as the rest it did not seem to have fuddled their wits for they talked on and on.

Vindex must have passed out like so many of the warriors, for he woke the next morning inside a tent. His head throbbed and he had no great urge to get up, so he lay there for some time until Ferox appeared.

'Time to go,' he said. 'There is to be a hunt and we are invited as guests.'

Vindex groaned.

To his relief, the hunt began at a leisurely pace, and seemed more about taking a ride than pursuing game, as forty or so set off. The warriors rode horses decorated with ribbons, and many had donned their armour and wore swords on their hips. All had bows, and some carried quivering spears ten foot or so long.

They went south and west, heading away from the road and saw no sign of Romans. There were plenty of farmers, but none challenged the riders as they crossed over their land. Ferox rode at the head of the party, with the chieftains, while Vindex was gently led to the rear, where he was pleased to see the dark-skinned warrior.

'How are you feeling?' the man said, with another broad grin. 'My head's like thunder and I ought to be used to it by now.'

Vindex groaned, prompting a big laugh. Two other warriors, one with a golden beard and the other with a long brown moustache joined in, as did Vindex, rubbing his forehead in mock pain.

'You are honoured, I think,' the man said.

'No, I'm Vindex,' the scout replied, blinking as if still half drunk and confused. The warrior translated and the others roared with laughter once again.

'My name is Ardaros,' he said.

'You don't look as if you are from around these parts?'

'This is my home and these are my people. I would not now exchange them for any in the wide world. I have horses and children, a wife and my own tent. And I have brothers and sisters of my clan and they have me.' Some of the phrases came with difficulty, and Vindex guessed that Ardaros rarely spoke Latin and struggled for the right words.

'Then you are a fortunate man,' Vindex said, sensing the pride with which the man had spoken. 'But I take it that it was not always so.'

Ardaros sighed. 'The past has faded. Once I was a child and had another family who loved me. The Garamantine slavers came and took me and many others. They sold me to a Roman who sold me to a Greek, who sold me to another Roman – or at least a man who claimed that he was. He sold trinkets to fools, and his path led him – and me – to Moesia and his death. Warriors of the Golden Ox clan were on a raid and they killed him and took me as a slave. My new master was the best I had ever known and one day his tent was attacked while he was away and I fought off the enemies, killing two, though I took great hurt in the deed. My master helped me heal and made me free and his brother, and so Ardaros was born and lives as one of the truly free. The stars have blessed my path and the wind guided me.'

'Aye,' Vindex said. The Latin was awkward, though probably this time because there were not the right words. 'Freedom and courage are great things.'

Shouts interrupted them. They had come over the brow and scattered a herd of pigs. The man and boy watching them showed no surprise or fear and merely watched as ponies reared or bolted away from the sudden burst of squeals.

The moustached warrior was carrying one of the tall spears and took it now in both hands, driving his mount into a canter, forcing it towards the scattering herd. He lowered the spear, point reaching out ahead and down, closing fast with one of the smaller pigs which fled in front of him. The horse balked, tried to pull away, but he checked it and went forward again, leaning to the right in his saddle as he drove the spearhead straight through the beast and then lifted his prize into the air and galloped on. All of the Roxolani whooped with delight, and the herdsmen just watched.

'Do you want to try?' Ardaros asked, as the fair-haired warrior offered his lance to Vindex.

'Fonder of mutton really,' he said, and was pleased when the translation prompted more merriment. He reached out for the spear and was surprised at its lightness. The shaft was slim, wobbling a little as he held it, and he tried to remember how the other man had done it. His mare was not keen, but Vindex had had her for years and they knew each other well, so that it did not take much tightness on her bit or more than a few taps with his heels to push her on. For the moment he had the spear upright in his right hand and kept the left for the reins. Singling out one of the larger pigs, which was slower than the rest and a big target, he swerved towards it, lowering the spear. One-handed it was awkward and end heavy, but with great effort he managed to hold it, arm bent at the elbow.

The pig was gathering pace, squealing in alarm, but he was close now. Vindex looped the end of the reins over one of his saddle horns and grasped the spear with his left hand as well. The mare was steady, keeping straight, and he lowered the spearhead, knowing that it would need less of a thrust than a steady hand to let the speed drive the iron into the beast.

The pig swerved to the right. Vindex reached, point chasing it, then his mare stuttered in her run, he felt his legs slipping from the grip of the saddle horns, and the point of the spear rammed into the ground. The shock flung him off and to the side to crash onto the soft turf.

There were more whoops of delight and amusement. Ferox passed him, a pig neatly skewered on the lance he held up.

'Having fun?' the centurion asked and then trotted away.

'Bastard.'

Ardaros and the man whose lance he had taken appeared.

'I told you I prefer mutton,' Vindex said, and when the warrior translated his words the nearest riders cheered. The scout rose, sore, but nothing broken.

'That's a good horse,' Ardaros said, for the mare had gone no more than a few yards and stopped, waiting for him.

'That's one mean pig.' Vindex reached the mare and jumped up. The herdsman and his boy remained where they were, watching and saying nothing.

'Do we pay them for these?' he asked.

'We do,' Ardaros said. 'For we do not kill them or plunder their homes. None will starve because of what we take.'

Vindex did not bother to say anything. These were not his people or his lands, and soon they were riding again, leaving the pigs and their owners far behind, apart from the bloody carcases slung behind a few saddles. 'So tell me why they call the centurion Flavius the Bad?' Vindex asked after they had ridden for some time.

Ardaros shrugged. 'Because there was already a good Flavius when he arrived.'

'Makes sense.'

'And he is a life-taker. A taker of many lives.'

'He's a proper bastard all right,' Vindex conceded. 'But he's a warrior and we all must kill to live.'

'There are stories. Most must have happened when I was a slave, if they happened.'

'Knowing the centurion they probably happened.'

'One day five warriors swore an oath to avenge the death of their cousin and kill Flavius or die in the attempt. This was far to the east, near the mouths of the great river.'

'I'm guessing it didn't work out for them.'

'Flavius was alone, and they thought they caught him unaware, sitting by his fire at night. He killed two when they attacked. The third he killed the next morning and the fourth that night, and each time he cut off the man's head. The head of the fifth man was found within bowshot of his people's encampment on top of a stake driven into the ground.'

Vindex nodded. It was easy enough to believe. The Silures were skilled at using the night, and Ferox was good even by their standards. The moustached warrior asked Ardaros what they were talking about, and as he explained the fair-haired one joined in the discussion and a couple of others rode over to join them.

'He says that there were six of them – and another man says that he heard that there were eight,' Ardaros said after a while. 'Many tell the tale and much changes in the telling.'

'Except that they all died.'

'Yes.'

'So,' Vindex said, 'your folk don't have much cause to love him, do they?'

'We used to know him. Some hate, some trust and all fear him. That is how it is and how it should be. Tomorrow morning any with a grudge may challenge him to fight and kill him if they are able. That is our way. If they do not challenge, then none may attack him for one moon after he leaves as our guest. The same applies to him. Flavius must challenge anyone or leave us in peace for the same time.'

'What about me?'

'What about you?' For the first time there was impatience in Ardaros' voice. 'You are his sworn brother. You must fight if he refuses, do what is necessary if he dies, and then decide whether or not to avenge him.'

'Just me?'

'That is the duty of a friend.'

Vindex did not have more to say and nor did the others. They chased some deer, shooting several down, and soon after noon stopped to eat. The older chieftain drew his sword, shouting something as he spun around, arms wide, and then drove the blade into the earth. All of the warriors went in turn to the sword and bowed.

'It is the symbol of their god of war, the greatest of their gods,' Ferox said, appearing at Vindex's side. 'They revere the wind which blows wherever it wills as the breath of life in all living things. The air gives life and the iron sword rips it away, so they offer to both for good fortune.'

Already the pigs were cooking, the smell rich and making Vindex hungry.

'Is this what you planned?' he asked the centurion.

'More or less. We'll see in the morning. There might be trouble, so be wary, although you should not be at much risk. Should be fine as long as no one really wants to kill me.'

'Oh shit,' Vindex whispered. He was about to introduce Ardaros, until the man saw that Ferox was beside him and turned away.

'He's one of theirs, but still wary lest they think he is a spy of the empire,' Ferox said, as if he knew or guessed who the dark warrior was. 'No one is sure whose side anyone is on these days.'

'Is that good?'

'It's how it is.' Ferox clapped him on the shoulder, making Vindex wince from the pain. The aches were growing now that they had stopped. 'I'll see you in the morning. Probably anyway.'

XII

Piroboridava
The sixteenth day before the Kalends of May

PHILO WORRIED BECAUSE never before had he been responsible for entertaining such a prestigious guest and everything had had to be done in such a hurry. Ferox had not returned, and from what the Lord Sabinus had said, this was also worrying, although Philo had waited too long and too often for his master to return to give the matter much thought. Even if the centurion had been here, the real work would have fallen to him, for Ferox had little sense of what was proper and had far too casual an approach to food, furnishings and those little touches that showed true respect for the guests and reflected honour to the host. In some ways, the centurion's absence was for the best.

The ladies had helped, and it was fine to see them both, and even more the staff they had brought with them. Privatus, the chamberlain of the noble Sulpicia Lepidina and her husband Cerialis, was an old friend from Vindolanda, and had been a wonderful and very practical help, as well as having the sense to step back and assist rather than try to take charge. In haste they had unpacked some of their finest tableware, to add to the items produced by the queen. To the three new slaves purchased by his master were added his pick of the other households – or at least those travelling with their mistresses.

The legatus had naturally occupied a number of rooms in the praetorium, just as Ferox had ordered. His stay was to be a short one, perhaps no more than a single night, and the modest number of slaves and freedmen travelling with the noble senator were under strict instructions to make no fuss or demands and to obey Philo's orders on domestic matters. It was courteous and a great condescension, since even Philo had to admit that his own master was of minor importance compared to a former praetor and relation of the emperor himself. It also made it easier to ignore the thinly veiled arrogance of the legatus' staff, especially his bald freedman, Sosius.

Sulpicia Lepidina supplied the clue to one of the guest's favourite foods, while Privatus had heard of this from one of the legatus' staff and was able to offer the recipe. Thus, Philo was able to watch as the slaves carried a tray to place in front of each couch. Apparently it was called tetrafarmacum, and he prayed that they had put in the right mix of ham, pheasant and sows udders and baked the pastry as it should be. The whole mixture was outlandish and the name had puzzled Privatus until Philo wondered whether it was meant as a joke at the expense of the Epicureans, and Sulpicia Lepidina had nodded in approval.

Philo stood apart from the diners, and part of him enjoyed the sheer responsibility of presiding over the occasion, directing the slaves and arranging every detail like a general with an army. Once Indike passed him, carrying a small jug of sauce to garnish the meats, and as she passed she pressed his hand for a moment and smiled. It was going well, but the 'battle' was not yet won and the 'enemy' willing to acknowledge that they had been well entertained.

They had lamps on high brass stands, but not too many. Overzealous efforts to clean the walls on the part of one of the new slaves had smeared the paintings and broken off whole pieces of plaster. As a result, one nymph had only one leg left to her, while in the scene where a shepherd surprised another group of nymphs bathing, he no longer had a head, which may have helped to explain their distress. Nearby a city appeared to have suffered an earthquake, so much had fallen away. The shadows offered some protection, and only one of the guests had commented so far. For a timber fort this was a decent enough dining room, even if it could not compare to some of the ones in the stone houses in forts they had visited on the long journey from Britannia. This room was a good size, had a flagstone floor, plaster walls, and just one high window, the window closed and shutters drawn to keep out the noises and odours of the fort. Yet it had not been well maintained, and the painted walls were cracked and had damp patches even before they were attacked in an effort to clean. Nor was the place ideal, for the ceiling was lower than it should be, so that the music of the lyre player and even the diners' conversations echoed uncomfortably.

There were eight guests, for the ninth place was reserved for Ferox, should he have appeared in time. Philo was relieved that he had not arrived at the last moment, no doubt filthy from travel and truculent in his refusal to be made acceptable for the occasion. The two ladies sat, one on either side of Hadrian, for one was a senator's daughter and the other in a sense their hostess. Apart from that, Hadrian appeared to enjoy their conversation, no doubt because both were well able to make themselves entertaining. Sabinus, Dionysius and the senior decurion were on one couch, and Piso and an equestrian tribune from I Minervia on the third. Hadrian had sent word that this was to be the seating order, and this had been his only intervention. Piso was the one who had seen the headless shepherd and pointed it out to the other diners.

All in all, Philo was pleased so far, while remaining intensely nervous. He watched every step taken by the girls as they carried the pies to the table, his mind racing with nightmares of someone slipping and dropping their precious cargoes. Thankfully, they arrived safely, were placed without fuss, but in the most convenient places, and then their carriers gave the slightest bow and retired.

Hadrian was in mid flow, speaking of the genius of poets and slipping easily between Latin and Greek and back again as he quoted. Now and again the ladies said a line or two, and Philo noted that Claudia Enica tended to get the words slightly wrong, no doubt deliberately for this permitted the legatus to correct her. This was always done with good humour and better manners – or almost always. Piso tried to take the lady's side more than once, saying that her change was an improvement. The others said little, and if Philo had not been so occupied he would dearly have loved to listen to the legatus, for he seemed a man of immense learning and considerable insight. He was also obviously fond of all things Greek, unlike so many Roman lords who privately were Hellenes, but paraded in public a boorish disdain.

The conversation seemed to be nearing a natural break,

for they had moved on to descriptions of food, with Sulpicia Lepidina saying that at last they were eating their tables, which Philo remembered as an allusion to Virgil, when Privatus came to his side and whispered a message.

Philo sighed, but orders were orders and he did not feel that he could ignore them. Privatus waved a questioning hand, indicating that he was willing to do the fell deed, but Philo stilled him.

He tapped his staff – another item borrowed for the night – on the flagstone floor. 'Noble lords and great ladies,' he said. 'Please beg my pardon for interrupting.'

'Not at all, Philo,' Hadrian said. 'Do go on.' There were not many senior officers – or junior for that matter – who would have learned his name and used it, and Philo was impressed.

'I am pleased to announce that Flavius Ferox, *praepositus* of the *numerus Brittanorum* and *curator* of the praesidium has returned. He apologises profusely for his absence on duty at the time of your arrival and thus for his inability to greet you in a fitting manner.' Ferox had never apologised profusely for anything in his entire life, but Philo was not about to let the truth get in the way of fitting words.

'He also apologises for the limitations imposed on his hospitality in this desolate outpost, but hopes that the humble hospitality his household was able to offer such distinguished guests did at least do a little to refresh them after the rigours of their journey.' Philo considered this to contain the essence of his master's 'I bet the mongrels are complaining.'

'It has indeed, dear Philo,' Sulpicia Lepidina replied.

'Quite so,' Hadrian added. 'And tetrafarmacum, if I am

not very much mistaken. My four-fold medicine never disappoints. You must try it, dear ladies, you really must. But where is the centurion? Surely he will join us.'

'My lord Ferox begs to excuse himself from attending on his esteemed guests. Stained as he is from a long ride.' Philo's tone implied a level of unutterable filth. 'He does not wish to interrupt or spoil his guests' enjoyment of their meal. He will refresh himself and bathe.' Philo almost regretted not being able to supervise and chivvy his master into performing these tasks properly. 'And will then be ready to wait upon the noble legatus later tonight or in the morning, as most suits my lord.'

'He should come,' Hadrian said mildly.

'My lord,' Philo said, surprised by his own boldness, 'my master fears that he is scarcely presentable.'

'He rarely is,' Claudia Enica commented. Philo saw Lepidina's lips purse in disapproval, although since Hadrian reclined between the two ladies, Claudia did not notice.

Hadrian smiled. 'This is the praetorium, not a villa in Baiae. I do not think anyone would be offended by the honest sweat of a good soldier doing his duty.'

'We are not all soldiers,' Lepidina suggested.

'And you have not smelled my husband.' Claudia wrinkled her nose in exaggerated disgust.

'Indeed we are not,' Piso said, speaking loudly, his voice a little slurred from wine. 'And may Venus and all the nymphs be praised that there is beauty among us.'

Julius Dionysius wriggled his shoulders and moved his head from side to side, as if preening. 'Well it's nice of someone to notice.'

'Send for the centurion,' Hadrian ordered.

'Are you sure, my lord?' Philo said before he had time to think.

'My husband is not the finest companion at a table,' Claudia said quickly to cover the freedman's embarrassment at having doubted so distinguished a guest. 'His manners are…' she paused in thought, 'at times a little rough. And apart from that I…' She trailed off into silence, dropped her head and blushed.

'They have been apart for a long time,' Sulpicia Lepidina whispered into Hadrian's ear. Less discreet, and just audible was Piso's muttered, 'Don't worry, he can rape you later.'

'Please ask the centurion to join us as soon as possible, and not to worry about his appearance.' Hadrian reached over to pat Claudia on the hand. 'I am sorry, my dear, but this is a matter of duty and the good of the res publica. You may have a proper reunion later.' Hadrian caught Piso's smirk and glared at him.

'My lord,' Philo said and bowed his head in obedience. Privatus caught his eye, nodded and left the room to seek Ferox.

Hadrian reached for the plate with the pies. 'Let me offer you some, dear ladies? Four-fold medicine,' he said happily, 'is the cure for all ills and every woe.'

'Is it filling?' Claudia asked. 'I have eaten a good deal.'

'You need have no fear – not least because your figure is that of a goddess.'

'Well yes,' she conceded. 'However, dear Lepidina, do you not realise the implication of that compliment.'

'Dear Claudia, I am sure that Aelius was not in any way contrasting us.'

Hadrian's smile broadened. 'Tis as well you two are not generals, for I am already outmanoeuvred. But have a taste, I beg you both.'

Philo's nervousness returned as Hadrian cut small slices to serve each of the ladies. On the other tables, the guests were devouring the pie, but that was only to be expected when it was known to be a favourite of so senior an officer, who might notice their reaction. Only Piso remained disinterested, picking at his food with no sign of emotion just as he had done with every course. Philo jerked his head to Indike, who now had an amphora of wine, which she took over to refill the senior tribune's cup. Piso made no effort to hide his scrutiny of the young woman, especially as she leaned forward.

Hadrian did not watch as the ladies nibbled, instead focusing on the whole pie he had served himself. Philo could barely breathe as the legatus cut into it and began spooning up the contents. The first mouthful was chewed and swallowed and the legatus paused and looked straight at Philo, his face rigid.

'This is good,' Hadrian said at long last and smiled. 'My compliments to your chef.'

Philo breathed out. 'I will pass them on, my lord.'

Privatus returned, walking quickly to pass on the message.

'Well, what's this?' Hadrian said, his tone sharp. 'Where is Ferox?'

'The centurion regrets that he is unable to join his guests,' Philo began.

'Hercules' balls, he'd better have a damned good excuse,' Hadrian cut in.

'Yes, my lord, he feels that he has.'

'Well?'

'My master begs to report that the fort is on fire.'

The granary was blazing furiously, and all was chaos, with alarm bells ringing and men shouting. Ferox felt his skin scorching with the heat and coughed as smoke blew towards him. That was at least a consolation, for it was blowing away from the other buildings and towards the *intervallum*, the wide road running around the camp inside the rampart. Hopefully, that would give them a little time.

'Keep moving! Keep moving!' he yelled at the men carrying all that they could from the granary beside the one on fire. There was barely a yard between the two buildings and it was amazing that the flames had not already spread.

'What's this lot?' Vindex and another of the Carvetii staggered as they carried a big amphora.

'Olive oil.'

'Shit!' They hurried away to add their burden to the piles of stores a hundred yards away.

'*Optio*!' Ferox shouted as he saw one of the men from I Minervia. 'Where are those tools and ropes?'

'Coming, sir!'

'Get a move on!' More men were arriving, summoned by the bells and the noise, and he was pleased to see a group of men with a long ladder because he had not thought to ask for one. 'Up on the roof,' he called, pointing at the third granary, which was separated from the first pair by a wider alley. 'Use anything you can to prise off the shingles. As many as you can as quick as you can.'

The soldier, who looked like one of the auxiliaries, nodded in understanding. Before he left, Ferox put his hand on the man's shoulders. 'Do what you can, but no silly heroics, eh?' The response was a grin, and then the man started shouting at the others.

At last the tools were arriving from the workshops, and he saw axe blades and saws gleaming red in the firelight. He needed them, but most of all he needed heavy hammers, and then he saw Naso with a group of bearded veterans coming with half a dozen. Ferox's voice was hoarse, the smoke thicker than ever and carrying with it odd scents of roasts from the barrels of salted meat and the rancid smell of burning oil, but he kept on shouting and chasing. Dividing the men with tools into two groups, he sent Naso with one to start pulling down the barrack block on the far side of the burning building, while the rest were to work on the third granary. There was not the slightest hope of water dousing these flames, even if they had had a good supply and pumps and hoses, which meant that the only way to stop the whole fort from going up was to make a firebreak on either side of the blaze – and to pray.

Any Brigantes he saw went to the walls if they were carrying weapons, and to help saving anything they could from the second granary if they were not. Ferox doubted that there was much risk of a surprise attack under cover of night and the confusion, but there was no sense in taking the chance, so Cunicius was at the main gate and told to keep a good watch. Many men he half knew or did not recognise at all had arrived with the legatus and most of these had their arms handy as they had not yet settled down to barrack life. There was another centurion with them and Ferox had told him to take all the men he could find and obey Cunicius, whoever was the senior. At a time like this, it was better to have someone who knew the layout of the fort.

'Oh bugger,' Vindex said, and pulled the wheel of Taranis he wore around his neck up to his lips to kiss it. The wind had shifted, and gusts were blowing the flames against the second granary. 'Won't be long now.'

'Hurry!' Ferox yelled at the men carrying sacks out of the building. One swayed as he watched, eyes gleaming in the red light, and then passed out, falling off the platform. The sack burst, grain spilling out. Ferox darted forward, starting to lift the man and then Vindex was with him and they dragged the soldier away. It was Vepoc. 'Get some water!' Ferox told another of the Britons.

'Can I help?' A man appeared, wearing an unbelted tunic which hung down past his knees. Ferox did not recognise him, but he spoke in Latin and had a beard and thick mop of hair so must be one of the veterans of I Minervia.

'Take that axe.' Ferox had spotted the tool lying a few yards away. 'And go and help chopping down that granary!' He pointed at the third one in the line, just visible. As he looked he saw a man prising a wooden shingle off the roof and throwing it down. If they were falling into the alley then they might burn there and spread the flames, so he turned to find someone to organise a party and make sure they were moved.

'What?' the man stared open mouthed.

'That humping great building over there!' Vindex shouted angrily, realising that the centurion was not listening. 'The one we don't want to burn down.' He grabbed the axe and placed it in the man's hand. 'Well you take your chopper like a good little boy and chop the humping thing down!'

'I am Aelius Hadrianus, *legatus legionis*.'

'Oh shit.'

'Quite.' Hadrian was shouting over the roaring of the flames. 'Is that Ferox?'

Ferox had heard. 'My lord!' He raised his arm in salute. 'Now if you would be so good, please take charge of the men working to pull down the granary. It's our best chance of stopping the fire spreading that way.'

Hadrian stared for a moment, then his beard split as he grinned. 'Right.' The grin widened. 'And I'll take my little chopper.'

'*Omnes ad stercus*,' Ferox whispered, knowing the sound would be lost with all the other noise.

'Oh double shit!' Vindex yelled as flames leapt up from the shingles on the roof of the second granary.

'Get them out!' Ferox screamed as he ran towards the loading platform of the building. Brigantes came tumbling out of the open double doors, some with sacks and some with barrels. Three men passed him, then two more. 'Quickly!' The heat was appalling, stinging his eyes so sharply that he struggled to keep them open. Another man appeared, panting hard and dropping an amphora to shatter on the planks. 'You the last?'

The man shook his head, then shrugged. Ferox helped him out. 'Take him!' he ordered Vindex. 'Forget it!' he called past the scout to a handful of men, including a recovered Vepoc, who were coming to save more of the stores. 'Help with pulling the buildings down!'

Ferox went to the doorway and looked in, crouching and

trying to shield his eyes from the savage heat. He started to shout, but could only cough until he managed to spit. 'Anyone left?'

There were dozens of amphorae of olive oil stacked at the far end of the building. Some had been brought out, and another dropped so that it shattered and the thick liquid spread. As the roof caught fire, sparks and bits of burning wood dropped down, setting off the oil. Inside the amphorae the oil began to bubble as it heated up.

Ferox saw the silhouette of a man against the sudden flame and then the blaze exploded and a wave of air flung him back out to fall flat on the platform. Someone lifted him, and he recognised Dionysius.

'You all right, sir?'

Ferox gasped for breath and nodded as he was helped away. Sabinus was there, and more men milling around. 'Get them to work,' he just managed to say. 'Sabinus, take a dozen more men and all the equipment you have and tear down that barrack block. Julius, you help the legatus with the granary.' He stood up, pulling free and waving them away. 'I'm fine. Now go!'

He doubled up, panting for breath, and heard the roaring as the second granary was devoured and some of the roof collapsed in a great flurry of sparks. Looking past it, he could see a wide stretch of bare rafters where the men were yanking off as many of the shingles as they could. That reminded him and he headed off to make sure that they were not simply building a bridge for the flames. He was relieved when he reached the alleyway to see that men were already clearing it of the tiles and other debris pushed out as men hammered and hacked at the side wall. There were great gaps in this already, and another team was fastening hooks around one of the timber uprights, while a dozen others waited at the ropes to pull it down.

'All clear,' a deep voice shouted from inside.

'All clear,' a man answered.

'Then one, two, three, pull!'

Ferox joined the men on the ropes as they hauled. The rope took the strain, and men grunted as they used all their strength without shifting the timber again.

'Again! One, two, three!' Two more men added their weight and at last there was the slightest of movements.

'Nearly there, boys.' Hadrian joined them, and Ferox realised that he had been the one giving the orders. 'One more time. One, two, three, heave!' The timber cracked and with a jerk they almost fell as the top half pulled away from the rest.

'Come on, we're winning.' They dragged again and pulled the timber free. 'Get the axes.' The legatus of I Minervia seemed to be enjoying himself, and Ferox noticed for the first time that he was wearing delicate sandals, suitable for dining, but not for demolition. 'We'll be fine,' Hadrian told the centurion. 'You check on the others.'

'Sir.' The alley was fiercely hot as the fire spread throughout the second granary and he wondered whether the firebreak would work. The third building was one of the ones packed with artillery, which meant plenty of wood, ropes and grease to burn if the fire got a hold. He was pleased to see that they had already started to pull down the end of the barrack block opposite the second granary, while the one opposite the first was now a ruin. Barracks always tended to be less sturdily built than the towering granaries, whose raised floors only seemed to fuel the fires once they started.

Something fell onto the top of his head. He stared up at the clouds and another drop of rainwater splashed onto his chin. More came, pattering all around him.

'We're winning,' he said as the downpour grew heavier.

Some sense, some glimpse of movement from the corner of his eye warned him, and he threw himself down as something small whizzed through the air and banged into the wall behind him. He struggled to get up, exhaustion swamping him, so he pushed on his hands to force himself and just caught a glimpse of a figure running far down one of the alleys.

'Centurion?' It was Dionysius' voice. 'Can you get me more men?'

The rain was still driving down and if it kept on they should be safe as long as they could all keep working. 'I'll do my best,' he said and lurched into a run to find them. Turning a corner, Ferox tripped and fell headlong, landing with a grunt as the air was knocked from him. He pushed himself up and saw that he had tripped over a body.

'Dionysius!' he shouted, hoping that the auxiliary centurion was close enough to hear him over the noise. It was a man's body, well dressed with fancy shoes, although the once-bright white tunic was smudged with ash and grime. He was not dead, for there was the faintest gasp when he pulled the man by the shoulders out of the shadows. Ferox stopped, worrying that he had done the poor fellow additional harm, so started to search for signs of injury. The rain was still falling, although the nearest roof gave a little shelter and there was more light from the fires here. The man was a stranger. Ferox tried lifting the head slightly and at once his hand was sticky with blood.

'Sir?' Dionysius appeared and then saw the body. 'Holy Isis, it's Piso.'

B RASUS SAW THE clouds to the north east glowing a deep red and was glad. The gold had done its work, and the one who had taken it proved true to his word for himself and his men – at least so far. Rain was already falling steadily, and it was bound to reach Piroboridava before very long. That would help the Romans put out the fire and that was a shame. The forts these people built were so densely packed that a strong wind and a dry day could easily sweep flames through if the fire got a grip. No matter – the Romans would be hurt and would lose many of their stores. That would make them weaker, and unless this Ferox turned out to be a fool after all he would realise that he had traitors in his midst.

'Tell me about the bridge?' Brasus asked his companion as they walked their horses through the night.

The other rider shrugged. 'It is very big.'

'Is it finished?'

Another shrug. 'There is a piece missing, but maybe they only put it in place when they want to cross.' The Sarmatian did not hide his people's contempt for the waste of effort when a boat sufficed for the journey.

Brasus was not surprised by the warrior's lack of interest. He would have to get word to the merchant to find out more

or to look himself when he went back that way. It would
be nice to know when the Romans' great project would be
complete, but it was not crucial for the king's plan.

'Tell me about this Roman?' he asked instead.

'The Bad Flavios? He came, he rode with us and feasted.
None challenged him for his life, so he left us.'

The clipped manner of speaking of the Roxolani and
their kin could be irritating at times, and he had to work to
find out what he wanted to know. The centurion had ridden
willingly to meet the hunting party, bringing just a single
warrior. He had talked to the chiefs for hours and they had
judged that he was the same man some of them had known
almost twenty years ago. He had not asked for anything,
which was surprising, nor had he raised the question of the
clans' alliances with Rome.

'He is a warrior,' the Sarmatian said. 'A bad man as his
name proclaims. His friend is also a man.'

'Some of the Romanoi are worthy foes, but enemies still.'

'They are not us,' the Sarmatian conceded.

Brasus did not bother to point out that neither were
the Dacians. The Roxolani cleaved to their brothers, their
families, their kin and their clan, and their chiefs commanded
because warriors chose to obey. They were brave, wild,
greedy, fickle and great liars, but they could be useful. 'Will
your people answer when my king calls for them?'

'Maybe.'

'The Getae and Celtoi will follow the king, and the
Bastarnae, as well as many peoples in distant lands. And
once Rome has gone you may live as you will.'

The warrior sniffed. 'To be a Roxolan is to live as each
man wills. No one can give us that or take it away.'

'So what will your chieftains do when the time comes? What will they and each warrior choose to do?'

'As it pleases them, and as it pleases each man. We have no love for Rome.'

That was encouraging. 'The Romans have few shepherds to guard many sheep, and the sheep are fat and rich. This will be a good war.'

'Then it will please us to fight with your king and his warriors.'

'Good. That will please my king, just as it warms my own heart.' He raised his hand to his shoulder. 'Ride as free as the wind, my friend. And soon let us ride side by side and hear the terror of our enemies.'

'Until that time.'

Brasus rode alone through the night and was pleased that it took a long while for the glow off the clouds to fade altogether. He had met with many of the clan leaders in recent months, even visiting the same group just days before Ferox arrived, and there were friends of the king in many bands. He was encouraged and hopeful, if not fool enough to place absolute trust in any Sarmatian. At the very least there was little sign that they would join the Romans, so the Romans would worry that the Roxolani might ride with Decebalus or might just attack on their own while the empire was facing the bigger challenge of Dacia. Either way it should help, pinning garrisons in place and keeping the enemy spread out so that their defences were weak.

The time was drawing close, and a summons to return to Sarmizegethusa surely meant that they were about to strike. Timing was the key, and in the end this was all about time, for the king needed as long as possible to grow strong. In the past he had attacked to throw the enemy off balance, and this is what he would do once again. There would be more than one force, but this could be the main one for it threatened the enemy where he least expected danger. In the past, armies of Dacians and their allies had swept across the plains further south, especially in winter when the Danube froze and they could rush into Moesia, burning forts and plundering towns. The Romans knew this and had stationed more men in that area than ever before just in case. Soon an army would mass to strike there and they would see this and fix their eyes there. At this season the attackers would have to cross the river in boats, but there were plenty to be found and the winding river was long so that they would not be sure where the blow would fall. While this was happening, there would be attacks in the north, through the lands of the Iazyges, and far beyond them by the Suebi against Pannonia.

The Romans should not expect the sudden outbreak of war, but when the storm broke upon them they would see what they expected to see and shift their weight to meet it. Then, while their eyes were elsewhere, an army would cross the mountains and come down this valley. They would be strong in warriors and bring supplies and siege engines. The only fort in their path was Piroboridava, and once past that the way was clear right down to Dobreta and the Romans' bridge. This army would storm the fort, cross the bridge and sack the fort on the other side if they could, but, if they could not, at the least tear up and burn the Romans' monument to their arrogance.

None of this would win the war. Brasus knew that the Romans did not give in easily. In time their legions would mass and the army would be driven back – or better yet

XIII

Piroboridava
The fifteenth day before the kalends of May,
the fourth hour

P ISO WAS NOT dead, at least not yet, but his breathing
was faint and he would not wake. The medicus had
examined him, found no other injury apart from
the wound to the head. It was slighter than Ferox had
suspected, for head wounds always bled like stuck pigs, but
the medicus' opinion was that more severe was the force of
the blow.

'Will he live?' Hadrian had asked when he visited the
hospital early the next morning.

The medicus shrugged. 'Perhaps? Perhaps not? And
perhaps he will have some life, some of his wits, but not all.'

'When will you know?'

Another shrug. 'I cannot say, my lord.' The medicus added
the title, because even the authority of his rank in his hospital
ought to defer a little to a senator and senior officer. 'I have
attended to the wound and bound it. He sleeps without the
need of poppy seed or any other comfort, so he does not
feel any pain. The tribune may sleep for hours or many days
and he may never wake. At the moment there is no more

that can be done for him apart from keeping him warm and comfortable and making an offering to the gods.'

'See to it.'

The other casualty, a Brigantian struck so hard that the back of his skull had collapsed, was most certainly dead. Found under a pile of debris from one of the buildings when the fire was well under control, the death might have been an accident, but Ferox had not had the energy to investigate in any more detail as yet for there had been so much to do. Hadrian had not slept until the fire was extinguished, by which time the night was more than half spent. Ferox had kept awake even longer, and finally got a little sleep on the cot kept in the hut behind the main gates. Even then, he only gave in to exhaustion on the promise that he be woken at the slightest sign of trouble inside or outside the fort.

An hour before dawn, Philo appeared with fresh clothes, and managed his old trick of shaving Ferox while the centurion slept. With less than half an hour to spare he had shaken his master awake.

'Mongrel,' Ferox had croaked at him, but the freedman was persistent and the centurion knew the signs.

'The legatus, the noble Aelius Hadrianus, wishes to see you, so you must look your best.'

Ferox grunted his opinion of that, but knew how the army worked and also how relentless Philo was bound to be. By his own standards, if not the much higher ones of his servant, he was smartly turned out by the time he stood waiting in the main office of the principia. Hadrian appeared just as the trumpets sounded the end of the night and the first watch of the day, and looked as if he had slept twelve hours on a feather mattress, before bathing and taking a leisurely breakfast.

They talked for an hour, just the two of them, or rather Hadrian asked a lot of questions and each answer prompted even more queries. Then they toured the fort, talking all the time, but now attended by several officers and clerks. Apart from the hospital, Hadrian watched as the guards were replaced at the gates, before visiting the debris from the fire.

'We were lucky,' the legatus told them. 'Without the rain…'

They paused while the legatus had a light breakfast served in the principia, during which he issued orders for his escort and essential staff to prepare. After that he spoke to all the men from I Minervia not on other duties and, after dismissing the others, ordered Ferox to come with him and inspect the ground outside the rampart. They looked at the ditches, the pits and obstacles, wandered through the canabae past the bath house and down to the river. The questions kept coming, and they always were apposite. Ferox had met plenty of senior officers, and the senators even more than the equestrians liked to hear their own voices, but with Hadrian there was a grasp of detail that was unusual. It was a considerable relief to have undertaken so much work on the defences, for he suspected that the criticism would have been far harsher if the inspection had occurred when Ferox had only just arrived. Even so, there were suggestions that were effectively orders to do more, and Ferox could not really resent them. On the whole, the legatus was right.

'This is not an easy task,' Hadrian said as he strode across the planks of the bridge. His escort was still waiting inside the fort, and only two troopers had accompanied them and they sat their horses well out of earshot, for he wished to speak to Ferox alone. 'That blaze was deliberate, no doubt about it. Do you think it was some of your Britons?'

'No, my lord. I don't see what they would gain. The sling shot lobbed at me most likely was, unless it was whoever attacked the noble tribune.'

'Not much noble about that sod. No restraint or wisdom, little honesty and randy as a stoat.'

Ferox forbore to suggest that this was surely fairly typical of Rome's ancient families.

'Cannot say that I'll miss him,' Hadrian said. 'Saw him slide his hand onto your wife's arse more than once.'

'He would regret that,' Ferox said without thinking and did not explain, just in case Hadrian decided that Enica or her people had anything to do with the attack.

Hadrian's brow furrowed, as if trying and failing to read the centurion's thoughts. 'Have you seen your wife yet?'

Ferox shook his head.

'My apologies, for I have kept you too busy. She has travelled a long way to be with you.'

The tone implied surprise at such determination for so small a prize, or perhaps that was Ferox's imagination. He was no longer sure whether he and Claudia Enica were married and was still wondering what her appearance meant.

'I am truly sorry,' Hadrian said, 'but let us talk instead of the assault on Piso. Any idea who might have done it?'

'No, my lord.' Ferox suspected that the legatus was more likely to guess what had been behind the attack. 'I had never heard his name until last night. Perhaps there is someone with a grudge against the family, but it seems improbable.

And I cannot help wondering whether the dead soldier was killed by whoever attacked the tribune.'

'Unless that Briton had a go at Piso, and then had a roof fall on him...' Hadrian hesitated, and that was striking in so suspicious a man. 'Or he was the one who tried to kill our tribune, and some pious citizen saw it, stopped him from finishing the job and then made sure that the would-be assassin would not have the chance to make any more trouble?'

'Perhaps, my lord.'

'Well, it would fit the facts, would it not? Robbery, hatred of Rome or even mistaken identity. If he was also the incendiary, then disposing of an officer would be an added treat for his Dacian paymasters.'

'I shall see what I can find out,' Ferox said, although he could sense that the legate knew a good deal more about the whole affair.

'As you wish,' Hadrian said. 'See what you can discover, but some sense tells me that something very much like that happened. As long as there is no one else here in the pay of the Dacians, the danger may be over.'

Like hell, thought Ferox, but said nothing. He would investigate even though he suspected that only Hadrian or someone working for him knew what had happened and had no intention of telling him.

Hadrian grinned, his neat teeth very white. 'Well if Piso wakes up he will be your problem and there is nothing I can do about that. But what can I do for you?'

'I could do with more men,' the centurion said, 'more food to replace what we have lost, and assurance that help will come.'

Hadrian walked to the far rail and tossed a pebble into the flowing water. 'A legatus of a legion scattered in dribs and drabs in several provinces cannot command much. I shall do my best for you – and for my men serving here. But I cannot command and dispose as I will. And perhaps we are starting at shadows and seeing enemies where there are none? What do we have – rumours, suspicions, disgruntled men in an outpost. And the thought that Decebalus wants a new war and will attack as he has done before, and that he might attack here because then he could drive on unmolested, take our own bridge, damn his impudence, and invade our provinces while we do not have enough to stop him. In Rome that would all sound very wild.'

Ferox said nothing.

Hadrian stared down at the river, surging beneath them and almost bursting its banks from the snow melting on the far mountain tops, and waited. 'Just a little river,' he said after a while, 'and just a little road leading to a great river and a wonderful bridge. What would the enemy gain – that is if they are the enemy? But if they are not the enemy then why does Decebalus send his men among the Roxolani?' Ferox had told him what he had learned from his visit to their camp. 'And I hear on good authority he has sent men and gold among many peoples and tribes, and why does he keep luring over our deserters to serve him? And why does a well-built and kept granary in our only fort on this route get set on fire?'

And why send Ferox and the troublesome Brigantes as its main garrison in the first place? Ferox thought, but did not say.

'It cannot all be chance,' Hadrian resumed. 'There is

too much to be a false trail, so somewhere the wild boar is lurking, waiting to charge. Then again what would he gain? We would win in the end. You were there weren't you when Oppius Sabinus was killed?'

Ferox nodded, surprised that the legatus knew this for it had happened twenty years ago, when the Dacians plundered Moesia, and he had been a newly minted centurion.

'And with Fuscus, and then with *XXI Rapax*?'

'I was.'

'That's three big disasters, and yet here you stand as large as life – and as miserly with your words as Atilius Crispinus warned. Yes, yes, I know him, and he is much recovered in case you are interested. There is even talk of fresh offices in due course.'

That explained some of the knowledge, for Crispinus had been a tribune in Britannia and spent a lot of time in the north. A clever young aristocrat, perhaps too clever, life had become complicated and dangerous whenever the tribune had appeared – indeed it had been quite a surprise that he had not turned up at Piroboridava. Still, during the rebellion of the Brigantes, Crispinus had played a dangerous game and presumably lost, for he had ended up a prisoner of the rebels, paraded in chains like an animal, beaten and brutalized. Ferox had never learned the truth of all that had happened and where Crispinus' true loyalties had lain. Hadrian was enough of a friend to know about this and speak of his recovery, although not enough of a friend to avoid mentioning it at all. From what Ferox had heard, the former tribune's family had done their best to cast a veil over his 'illness'.

'So I know something about you, centurion, much more

than you guess, and since no one else up to now has bothered to have you dismissed from the army, I will believe that the good things are true and that gives me hope. You are a hard man to kill, and you have the knack of winning against the odds. ... And please don't try to make a joke of this and assure me that you are still young and can easily make a fresh start.'

'Wouldn't dream of it, sir.'

Hadrian glared at the rigid face for a long while. Then he stared over Ferox's shoulder, but the centurion remained at attention and did not follow his gaze.

'Very well,' the legatus said at long last. 'We will all have to do our best.'

'Can I tear up the bridge, sir?'

'Why?'

'The fort is here to guard the road, and especially the bridge. It's the route that matters, nothing else. Let's say they come with an army. With luck, the fort may hold out – at least for a while. If it does, what's to stop them leaving a couple of thousand men to keep us honest and sending the rest off to Dobreta. They could be there before the alarm has been raised, and certainly before a decent force can be concentrated. But without the bridge—'

'Nothing big can get through,' Hadrian cut in. 'Not much in the way of supplies, no artillery – at least not decent sized stuff – and without those they're not well placed to take Dobreta or anywhere else by storm or siege.'

'So if we pull up the bridge they might not come at all, unless they're looking for a cheap victory by taking one of our most vulnerable posts, stuck out on its own and unsupported.'

It was Hadrian's turn to lapse into silence for a while, before shaking his head. 'No,' he said at long last. 'It won't do. Not proper for a Roman officer to flinch at rumours. And if you rip it up and they change their plans and do not come then that's what it will seem – a nervous officer who cannot even control his own soldiers panicking and destroying a perfectly innocent bridge.'

'We'd be alive though,' Ferox suggested.

'Still,' Hadrian went on, clearly giving little weight to that point, 'have a word with the Greek and see if he has any ideas of how to make their life difficult if they do come.' Ephippus was to stay at the fort, as were all but the legatus' most important staff – and now Sulpicia Lepidina and her household, at least until Hadrian had seen the lady's husband and found out his situation and whether or not it was safe for her to join him.

Hadrian shaded his eyes from the sunlight as he stared up the slope at the fort as if measuring the distance. 'Have you thought of reaching this spot with a ballista on top of the gate towers?'

'They say it is too far, sir.'

'Talk to Ephippus. He's been trained by one of the best there is and strikes me as thorough. Maybe an extra storey to one of the towers would give more height and a longer range? There's usually a way if only you can find it.'

'My lord,' Ferox said flatly so that the words could mean anything.

'Yes, Crispinus told me you were insolent. Let us hope he was right in his other judgements.' Hadrian whistled to attract the attention of one of the two cavalrymen and then gestured at the fort. The man rode away to summon the escort, while the other brought over the legatus' horse. Hadrian nuzzled its face with great fondness. 'I must leave,' he said.

'Are you sure that you do not want a larger escort, my lord? It is a long way to Sarmizegethusa.'

'Then better to travel fast. If they kill a Roman senator in time of peace then the princeps would be implacable and destroy Decebalus and his kingdom.' Hadrian snorted. 'He might even thank me for the chance! But I don't think any harm will come to thirty well-armed soldiers. Not yet at least.' He swung himself easily up into the saddle. 'And I do love a hard ride. Reminds me of when I was a tribune and...' He seemed to decide that Ferox was not a worthwhile audience for the story. 'No matter.' The escort were trooping out of the main gateway. 'Time to leave. Good fortune to you, Flavius Ferox. Let us hope we meet again, eh!'

'Sir.' Ferox saluted and Hadrian gave a wave in return as he put his horse into a trot.

'Come on, lad, they can catch us up!' he called to the other cavalryman and headed away up the valley. Ferox stood on the bridge and watched them pass – twenty-nine troopers, half a dozen mules, and five civilians, one of them the surly freedman, Sosius. He stared at Ferox, eyes cold and confident. If anyone on Hadrian's staff knew more about the fire, the dead Brigantian and unconscious tribune it was surely him, but he was going and Ferox suspected that it would take a lot of coercion to break a man like that even if he had the chance.

Once across the bridge they broke into a canter to catch up with the already distant legatus. Ferox stared at the little column as the figures grew smaller, revelling in a solitude that was unlikely to be repeated for a long time. When he was young he might have thought of riding away in the opposite direction, although he would not have done it. Now, not even the thought occurred because he knew that he had to go wherever the army sent him, for he had no other life or home. Finding a pebble, he tossed it into the water. Then he took a deep breath and prepared for the first great battle.

A wood-gathering party passed him on his way up the slope, with forty men and three waggons, making him wonder whether he needed to increase the size of such detachments, or at least the proportion fully equipped to fight if necessary. Probably this was too soon, but it might do no harm to err on the side of caution. Ephippus already had plans, and most would require more timber. There was also the question of repairing the demolished ends of the barracks and finding space for all the stores they had saved.

Sabinus was waiting for him behind the gateway, as was Petrullus, the centurion who had come up with the newly arrived contingent of Brigantes. He was tall and slim like most Brigantes, with a lean, sneering face, and hair and moustache so blond that they were almost white. He was the eldest son of an important chief, head of a clan which had stayed loyal to Rome and to Claudia Enica, and he was said to be brave and capable. Ferox had met the man for the first time that morning and already found him irritating. Therefore it was no surprise that Petrullus had come to complain, for he had done as much and more to Hadrian, then complaining about the billeting of men and horses in the belief that the existing garrison held more than its fair share of the barracks and stables.

'There are no servants,' Petrullus said. 'My warriors were promised servants when they arrived at the garrison.'

'Not by me,' Ferox said flatly. There was no sense in letting his anger spill out. 'Nor at any time to my knowledge. They can keep anyone that they have brought with them, but otherwise no slaves to be brought or purchased while they are here.' He just stopped himself from adding families to the restriction, not because it was not also true, but because Enica was now here. While it was unlikely that any sane woman would travel all the way from northern Britannia to drag herself and her children to be with her man, you never knew. If any appeared, then they would deal with the problem at the time. 'No more slaves. And while you are here and under my command, everyone works – everyone.'

'My men are warriors not labourers.'

'They'll be dead warriors if we don't all work our hands to the bone.' He sighed. 'I will meet with your warriors as soon as I am able, but know that they must train as hard as the rest of us for the fight that is to come.' Ferox noticed Sabinus' doubt, but could deal with that later. 'Tell them that this is now their dun. Here we will live or die, but I have no doubt that the blue shields of the Brigantes will ring with new honours whichever it is.'

'We will serve the queen,' Petrullus said, apparently sincere.

'And she will be proud and generous,' Ferox replied, knowing that the first was certainly true and wondering about the second. He left them and pressed on down the via praetoria. Ephippus was taking a reading from a *groma*, the staff resting on the road and one of the four arms with its lead plumb weights pointing at the left-hand tower of the gateway. He wondered what the Syracusan was up to, but there was no time for that. He nodded affably, and asked the engineer to see him in two hours' time.

'Yes, my lord.'

Ferox was a little early reaching the praetorium. It still did not feel like his house, but at least now it felt and sounded like a home as he caught the excited shouts of the children, no doubt playing in the open garden in the centre. Philo was waiting for him, with that predatory look that suggested he was poised to brush at his clothes and make a fuss.

'She's seen me before,' Ferox barked. 'She isn't about to be fooled if I'm clean.'

'It cannot do any harm, my lord,' Philo replied, and as expected raised a little brush.

'No. And you do not have to call me, my lord. Sir will do, and none too often.'

'It will not, my lord.' Ferox had long since grown used to the boy's disappointment in him. 'The queen will see you in the afternoon room. You are a little early.'

'This is my house – or was anyway. And I know the way, so be about your business.' Ferox went through the porch, continued through the reception room and out into the garden. It was a glorious afternoon, the sun already warming up, so that the shade was welcome.

An arrow whizzed noisily past his head. A second followed, wobbling in the air because it had a blunt tip and flights made deliberately too heavy. Ferox snatched it as it passed and pressed it to his chest before reeling in mock agony. A deluge of children swamped him, screeching with excitement. There were three boys, the youngest a dark-haired and blue-eyed ruffian, and all three grabbed him around the waist. Ferox staggered, taking them all with him and then let himself be borne down onto the ground.

'You are a shockingly bad influence, Flavius Ferox, as I have said many times before.' Sulpicia Lepidina had her hands on her hips, but was smiling. They had been lovers, briefly and secretly, years before and the dark-haired boy was her child and his, unlike the other step-children, although she loved them all. She was a senator's daughter, beautiful and intelligent, as well as another man's wife, so they had never had any future, and then later she had sent him to what could easily have been his death. None of that seemed to matter, and he felt her to be a true friend as well as the devoted mother to his son.

'Better not linger,' she said. 'So you must all let him go until later!' With some reluctance, the children broke free.

Ferox stood up, brushing himself down and glad that Philo could not see. He looked at Lepidina, her hair gleaming in the sunlight and wearing one of the pale blue dresses she favoured. 'What do you think are my chances?' he asked.

The clarissima femina held up her right arm, thumb outstretched and wavering like the president at the games deciding the fate of a fallen gladiator and trying to gauge the crowd's mood. After a moment she spread fingers and thumb wide and smiled. 'What do you think?'

Ferox did not know, so with a mock scowl back at the children to make them giggle, he walked to the far side, under the veranda and found the room. Two low stools were in it as well as a little round table, and he was not sure whether or not this was an encouraging sign. This was one of the better decorated rooms, although the painter shared the obsession with fauns and nymphs and the rooftops of distant towns.

The note passed to him by Philo that morning had said the fifth hour of the day and he knew that he was a little early, so he sat on one of the stools, finding it too low for comfort. There were two doors in this room, one leading to the garden and the other to a corridor and he guessed that she would come that way. He also guessed that she would be late and make him wait, so he waited and wondered whether being treated in this way was another unexpected aspect of commanding a garrison. After a long while, he stood up, and studied the paintings as there was nothing else to do. He had never looked that closely before, and noticed for the first time that wherever there was a nymph or group of such beauties exercising, playing or bathing, they were always watched from cover by a satyr, just visible from his horns or hoof as he hid behind a bush, tree or wall.

She came from the garden and at first he did not turn, wondering whether she would cough or speak, but she did not. Was this a test? He waited and the silence stretched on and on. The Silures raised a boy to cherish silence, but he doubted that his grandfather and the other elders had ever anticipated a situation like this one. Probably they would despise him for creating it.

'You know,' Ferox said at last and started to turn, 'I'd never noticed...' He stopped.

Claudia Enica stood like the statue of a goddess. Memory is a fragile thing, often vague, and if he had known that she was beautiful that was not the same as seeing her just a few feet away. Her dress was green silk, shimmering in the light of the open door behind her and just hinting at the elegant lines of her legs and body. She liked green, feeling it set off the vivid red of her hair, which today was piled high and dotted with tiny pearls in what was no doubt her own adaptation of a current fashion. It suited her, as did the rouge on her lips and the gentle make-up. This was Claudia, the Roman lady, well educated, teasing and dignified as an equestrian should be. At other times this same woman became Enica, granddaughter of Cartimandua, the witch queen of the Brigantes, surrounded with the same awe. That person was wilder, a warrior trained to a high pitch, who killed readily if she felt the need and was as out of place at a sophisticated dinner party as a tiger.

Ferox knew what it was like to have two souls in one body, with the prince of the Silures, the wolf people, living alongside the Roman centurion. Claudia Enica was so much younger and yet seemed to find the dual life more natural, perhaps through some magic inherited from her grandmother.

The door closed, and he caught a glimpse of the dwarf Achilles, Claudia's 'whisperer' when she was acting the part of the frivolous and fashionable lady. Still she stood, without a trace of a smile so that she was more than ever the perfect goddess, as cold as she was lovely.

Ferox took a pace forward. 'I am...' The words trailed away and he stopped. What was there to say that would do any good? 'You are so beautiful,' he managed at last, and although he meant it the words sounded false, just what any man would say in flattery.

Claudia moved quickly, one step, then another, the built-up heels of her light shoes tapping on the wooden floor boards. Her hand moved even faster and she slapped his left cheek, so hard that it stung. Still her face was rigid.

Ferox flexed his jaw. Although tall like many Brigantes, she was shorter than him by a good few inches in spite of the extra height from her shoes. That meant staring up at him, her green eyes hard as flint. The last time they had met those eyes had blazed with anger.

Claudia's hand swept back and slammed into his other cheek so hard that his head jerked to the side. Ferox straightened up and stood absolutely still. He knew he deserved this and far more. Almost four years ago the army had given him six months furlough to be with his wife. She was busy, working as queen of the Brigantes to rule her people, and working even harder to persuade the Romans to make official and final acknowledgement that she was indeed queen, recognised forever by the empire. There was not a lot for him to do and idleness never suited him. The fiery Enica was frustrated and short tempered, not helped by a difficult pregnancy, the result of a leave he had spent with her a few months earlier. He was bored and started to drink, and when she snapped at him once or twice he had snapped back, which led to fights. There was a little scar next to his eyebrow from where he had been hit by a nicely decorated Samian cup. Whether he was patient or argued back it only seemed to rile her all the more, but he had to admit that he might have done better had he found things to do rather than drink. As Vindex had so aptly put it, he had buggered it all up.

She hit him a third time and then stepped back.

'You look older,' she said.

'You do not.' Ferox meant it. Claudia smoothed her hands down her silk dress past her waist. Her figure was as lithe as it had ever been. 'You truly do not.' Years ago, when he had first started to learn about this strange young woman she had told him with absolute assurance that he was hers. Whether or not it was true then, it had become true. He belonged to her, to do with as she wished. 'How are the children?' he asked.

'How should I know?' Her head was slightly on one side, and Claudia was in charge, always ready to mock. 'They are at home.' She sighed as if in disappointment. 'You have received the letters?'

'Yes.' Every month Claudia had one of her servants write to him to say that their twin girls were well, and list accomplishments such as the times they had learned to crawl and then walk.

'I would guess that they are squealing and dirty, demanding food and attention and anything else that takes their fancy. That is how they usually behave.'

'Would a mother's guidance—'

'Silures!' Claudia interrupted. 'They make their women work like slaves, whether they will or not. Brigantes and Romans alike are more enlightened.' Her hands were on her hips now, and she snorted. 'Huh! Your children are well, no thanks to you, that much I sense even from so far away. They are cared for and loved by women and a few men utterly devoted to them, rather than a mother who finds their bawling and self-absorption tiresome. That is a good deal more than most children get!'

'How do they look?' Ferox asked.

Claudia smiled. 'They take after their mother, thank the gods for great mercies. And so alike that I for one cannot tell the little mice apart. No wonder the Romans call them both Flavia.' Her head went back on one side. 'You are grinning like a halfwit, Flavius Ferox,' she said. 'They have each sent you a snail shell, and you can have them later. Why snail shells? Why indeed, but I understand the choice was between that and some leaves. They are as half-witted as their father, but at least have the excuse of being infants and may learn in time.'

'Thank you,' he said, and on instinct put his hands on her arms. She did not flinch, but did not respond either.

'Your gifts for conversation have not improved, have they.'

'Why are you here, my queen?'

There was another smile. 'At least you know your place, even if you speak like a surly brute and maul me about. Well, I could be here as the dutiful little wife, to help her husband in his many onerous tasks, could I not? Just as dear Lepidina follows her Cerialis half way across the empire.'

'It seems unlikely.'

'Pig.' She pulled one arm free and reached up to her forehead as if wiping away tears. 'I have missed you,' she added, serious once again.

'Not every time, but I am pretty good at ducking.'

'Brute.'

She did not pull free from his other hand and her skin was soft and warm. Her scent was all around him, and brought back memories of better times.

'I am here to help,' she said, and brushed his chin with her fingers. 'Philo still does a good job, and more remarkably yet manages to restrain himself from slicing the razor through your throat. Remarkable fellow that.'

'And I am here because I am queen and my people are going to war.'

'We are still at peace.'

Another snort. 'War is coming. You know it as well as I unless you have truly become a fool. So the commander's wife has joined her husband as far as the Romans are concerned for there is much that they could not or would not understand. My warriors will know that their queen is here, her sword as sharp as any of theirs.'

'Speaking of swords...' Ferox pulled her towards him and kissed her. Her lips were soft, and her arms gripped onto him pressing their mouths ever closer. He was not thinking, not worrying, for the moment all that mattered was to be with her. She moaned very softly, and their bodies started to blend into one. Ferox reached for the shoulder of her dress, feeling the silk and trying to find the catch of the little brooch.

Claudia Enica's knee jerked up sharply and Ferox groaned with the pain, doubling up as she pulled away.

'You have to earn more,' his wife told him, her eyes bright. 'Now sort yourself out and be off with you. I shall see you tomorrow, but not before. Still, it is good to see you, husband.'

Ferox's thoughts came slowly as he left the praetorium, for part of him was happy and the fears that now almost all that he cared for in the world had come to this place of danger could not yet drive the happiness away.

'Did she hit you?' Vindex was waiting for him.

Ferox nodded.

'Good lass. Kick in the balls?'

'Used her knee.'

'Aye, well enough. She's a queen and no mistake.'

XIV

Sarmizegethusa
The tenth day before the Kalends of May

T HE STRONGHOLD OF the Dacian king was a
remarkable place, and not for the first time on this
journey Hadrian had thought of all those mountain
cities stormed by Alexander and his men on their long road to
India. As he understood it, those were made from mud brick,
as brown as the land around them, whereas the Dacians
built mainly in stone, and built well. In one sense it was a
pity that he had left Ephippus behind, for he had wanted
the engineer to examine the towers, walls and temples, and
sketch as many as he could. There was never any harm in
learning from others, and indeed the Romans boasted of
their willingness to copy even from enemies, which was one
of the few ways they showed themselves more rational than
the Greeks.

Whoever had built this fortress had understood how to
use the land itself, for its walls dipped and rose over the
ridges, so that slopes added to the height of the defences.
Merely approaching it would be hard for a tower or ram, the
assault ramps having to be made very large or precariously
steep, and then there were the walls themselves. Hadrian

had been told – and had glimpsed in a small outpost – of the timber boxes within the stone, stronger even than the Gallic framing that had so impressed Julius Caesar. The Dacians were no simple barbarians, and they were not afraid to learn from others any more than the Romans. Greek influence was plain, most of all in the well-cut masonry and the square towers, but here and there the curve of an arch or the tiled roof of a turret showed the work of an army engineer, whether a renegade deserter or one of the men sent by Domitian at the time of the treaty. The same was true of the artillery, well maintained and cleaned – and indeed of the soldiers, all in mail, with bronze helmets, matching oval shields and spears, guarding the fortress. At any distance they were hard to tell apart from regular auxiliaries, and only closer did the untamed beards, cloaks of all shades and patterns, and long trousers stand out.

The Roman garrison was separate, uphill of the main royal compound, not that this advantage would make any difference if there was trouble. There were just under six hundred men in the garrison, more than a third of them from I Minervia and the rest picked men from equally good units. Yet they were stale. Hadrian could tell that from the first glance and nothing he learned subsequently did anything to change his mind. By army standards the fort was crowded, partly so that it was entirely on the hillock above the royal fortress. Even though from the rampart and towers the Romans could look down on the Dacians as they went about their business, somehow this only reinforced the sense of being isolated and surrounded. Beyond the fortress there was peak after peak, some with smaller Dacian towers and forts, and the nearest help was a long way away. There was nowhere to drill or train, unless the garrison commander sought permission from the king and that always took a long time to be granted. When permission finally came it meant a long march to find a decently open and level patch of ground among all these rugged slopes and deep valleys.

By all accounts the winter had been savage up here, so bad that legionaries lost fingers and noses after standing guard on some of the worst nights and several had died. That had meant even more time inside the barracks, huddled around their fires to fight the chill in their bones. Decebalus had been generous in sending up plenty of wood to burn, as well as food and drink, even arranging with traders to buy wine that neither he nor many of his aristocrats were willing to drink. They had managed, but all the while it was a reminder that they were dependent on the king's goodwill. There was no well or spring in the Roman fort, and little space in the modest granary. They lived at the king's pleasure, and if ever he chose he could snuff them as easily as a slave doing the rounds of a house at night extinguishing all the lamps and torches. The men of the garrison all knew this and all lived with the knowledge and with the dullest of routines even by army standards, so that it was not surprising if they lacked spirit. They were a symbol of peace and nothing more.

'Decebalus does not want more trouble,' the narrow stripe tribune in command had assured him. The man was from *Legio VII Claudia pia fidelis*, and was supposed to be junior to a senatorial tribune from his legion, but that man had done a year and departed for home. Piso was supposed to have replaced him in the job, but now Piso was not coming and that left the equestrian tribune all the more nervous because not only had Hadrian arrived, but so had the legatus Augusti in charge of all forces in Dacia.

Cnaeus Pompeius Longinus was surprised to see Hadrian and did not bother to hide his resentment.

'Crowded enough here already without sightseers turning up.' Longinus was a former consul, had governed Moesia Superior under Domitian and Pannonia under Nerva and was not about to be impressed by a distant relation of the princeps. He had a high, heavily creased forehead, slightly milky eyes and the thin face of a scholar, all of which appeared to inspire him to be gruff and aggressive in speech, as if worried that no one would take him seriously as a commander.

'The king is always happy to give rooms to distinguished visitors in one of his halls,' the tribune suggested.

'Sod that,' Longinus barked. 'Not eating meat for days and having the pious little bastards sniffing as their slaves pour you wine. You can go if you like,' he added, gesturing at Hadrian. There was not a lot of room in the praetorium in the fort.

'I should like to stay with my men,' Hadrian replied mildly. 'That is why I am here, so that I can inspect every detachment of my legion and make sure that they are ready to do their duty.'

'Their duty is to remind Decebalus that he had better keep his word or ten thousand more just like them will turn up and drag his royal arse over the coals until he squeals – that's their job, and they do that simply by being here, no matter whether you come to gawp at them or not. And thanks be to Jupiter, Juno and all the rest he is a smart enough barbarian to understand threats and won't make any trouble. Oh, he will stamp his foot and have little tantrums, but in the end knows we have the bigger club and can pound him into the dust.' Longinus sniffed. 'Still, while you are here you may as well come along to the audience tomorrow so that we can use the language of diplomacy to lie to each other while making clear the power that lies behind us. No harm in saying that you are Trajan's cousin either – family is important to them.'

The audience did not happen the next morning as planned, nor the one after that, for on each day a message arrived soon after dawn to say that the king was indisposed by illness. On the third morning the messenger informed them that the royal diviner had observed the stars and concluded that this was a day for fasting and prayer rather than business.

'Impudent rogue,' Longinus declared, after sending a formal message saying that he quite understood and would look forward to meeting the king tomorrow. 'Mucking us about just to show that he can. Pity the princeps is not keen on a new war at the moment otherwise I could soon teach the king a lesson.'

As the days passed Hadrian began to feel the true claustrophobia of the place, but there was nothing to do but wait, now that he was here. An attempt to raise his concerns with Longinus prompted amused scorn.

'Might want to spend more than a few days in the area before jumping to conclusions. Decebalus is irritating, but not a threat. As I say he's bright and no mere barbarian. He knows just how big the empire is and how small Dacia is by comparison, so understands that he cannot go too far. If we ever decide to do it, then we can bring enough force to crush him like a beetle. Might take time to muster, but the end will never be in doubt. The little cuss will never risk bringing that on himself. He knows that Trajan will fight if he has to, and won't give up like Domitian.'

Hadrian remained unconvinced. For all his many faults, Hadrian reckoned that the last of the Flavians had not been that bad an emperor, nor his campaigns against the Dacians the humiliation that everyone – not least Trajan – liked to claim. Domitian had done enough to cow Decebalus, but then had to shift the weight of his forces to meet other threats from the Sarmatians and the Suebi. True enough, the empire was strong, with thirty legions now that Trajan had added a couple, and even more auxiliaries, but it could not be strong everywhere all the time. Now that he had seen Decebalus' stronghold, its strength and good order, his last doubts that he was wrong were fading away. He wanted to leave this place, leave Longinus with his fool's confidence, and start to see what he could do to prepare.

'His fortress is strong, equipped with siege engines he isn't supposed to have anymore, and it's not the only one,' Hadrian said, in a last effort to persuade Longinus. 'And he is welcoming deserters as readily as ever.'

'Worthless scum the lot of them. If they've betrayed us, they're not likely to prove loyal to him. No, no, my boy, you worry too much because you don't know these people.' The boy was insulting to a former praetor, but Hadrian let it pass. Longinus was sure of himself, so let the man plough on with this furrow and see where it took him. Defeats were coming, probably a crisis, and with them would come opportunity.

At long last the king's health and his diviner's opinion

both agreed that the day was a good one, so the Roman party marched out of the gate, through the bigger gates into the royal compound, and along a circuitous route through several compounds until they came down to a wide terrace.

'We're honoured,' Longinus said, his irony heavy. 'These are some of their shrines.' Hadrian glanced at a great circle of pillars and another beyond it. Neither had roofs, and he remembered reading somewhere that the Getae and Daci worshipped the stars and made their temples open. He wished that there was time to take a closer look and ask questions, for he was sure that there was a pattern and purpose to the designs.

Decebalus was waiting for them, sitting on a chair that resembled the ones used by Roman magistrates. This stood on a wooden platform and over this was a canopy striped in many colours. There were noblemen around him, all of them *pileati*, the cap wearers, and beyond the platform at least fifty warriors, wearing brightly polished scale cuirasses and carrying the curved swords of their people. By convention, the Romans brought only a dozen legionaries as escort, as well as Longinus, Hadrian, a prefect from the garrison and a centurion from the governor's staff.

As they approached a shout went up and a man who had been kneeling in front of the king was dragged away by two men, followed by another who carried a stout club.

'Oh, justice time,' Longinus whispered to Hadrian.

The victim was made to kneel again, this time with his head resting on a flat stone. There was no signal, no last glance back to receive the order, for the clubman simply swung with all his force, producing an audible crack when it hit the man's head, as his limbs jerked. The executioner raised it high and struck again, and this time the weapon came up bloody, but he hit four more times before wiping the tip of his club on the grass. There was little left of the victim's head as the others dragged the corpse away.

'Don't notice it,' Longinus said in a low voice. 'They always lay an execution on for our arrival. Sometimes it's the club and sometimes a beheading with a falx. Always wondered what would happen if the king did not have a criminal handy to execute.'

'There's always someone,' Hadrian whispered.

'True enough.'

Decebalus was smaller than Hadrian had expected, for without really thinking he had assumed that any barbarian king must be large – Polyphemus, but with two eyes. The king had two, both blue and both alive with intelligence. His beard and hair had plenty of grey, and he must have been in his forties at least and probably older, but he showed every sign of vigour. Longinus had told him that Decebalus spoke Greek well and more than a little Latin, but that he tended to speak via an interpreter most of the time.

'Just do not say anything tactless,' the governor commanded. 'Leave that to me, if it is necessary.'

The prefect accompanying them had said little, although Hadrian had met him before back when Trajan had been adopted by Nerva. Petilius Cerialis was a Batavian from the Rhineland, an eques, and coming to the end of a long spell as commander of a cohort of his own people. He was handsome, clever and ambitious, although by now Hadrian suspected that he might be wondering just how far the emperor's old promises of favour would translate into reality now that there was a whole empire to satisfy. Well, he was not alone in that.

The king asked politely about the health of Cerialis' dog, which had been sick, and smiled at the news that the animal had quite recovered.

'And are your family well?' the interpreter asked on the king's behalf.

'I am pleased to say that I have recent news of them and all are flourishing,' Cerialis answered. His delight at Hadrian's news of Sulpicia Lepidina and the four children was still fresh after several days, during which he had no doubt read and re-read the letter he had brought many times.

'I hope to meet them,' Decebalus said, using Latin and not waiting for the interpreter. 'A man should have children.'

'I regret that they are unable to join me for some time, lord king,' Cerialis said. Hadrian had been tempted to warn him, but had been relieved when the prefect had been adamant that his family stay away from Sarmizegethusa and wait until he received his posting as narrow stripe tribune to a legion, which must come soon. With any luck that ought to mean a decent sized base somewhere with a good house for them all. Hadrian had already requested that Cerialis be appointed to I Minervia when a post became vacant at the end of May and was gratified by the man's delight when he told him of this.

After children and dogs, the king showed concern for the garrison's horses and the welfare of the soldiers stationed at other spots in his kingdom. This went on for some time, before Longinus was invited to ask what he wished. His questions were equally banal, and when once or twice they approached a sensitive subject, the answers were vague and were not challenged. Hadrian had hoped to learn from the audience, but it did no more than confirm his impressions of both the king and of Longinus.

XV

Piroboridava
The Kalends of May

THE DAY BEGAN with excitement, Ephippus almost bouncing as he supervised the trial. This was the culmination of many long days of work since he had first rushed into the principia shouting, 'I've worked it out, I've worked it out!'

Ferox had never seen the man so animated before, or indeed so ready to chatter. Sabinus and Dionysius had exchanged glances, while the nearby soldiers had adopted the wooden expressions that suggested they were trying not to laugh.

'It's a *monâkon*,' the Syracusan had shouted so loud that his voice echoed round the courtyard. Heads appeared at several windows. 'A monâkon! Just think of that.'

'One-armed?' Dionysius at least reassured Ferox that his guess was right. 'I fear that I am still at a loss, my dear fellow.'

Ephippus regained some control as he realised that he was now the centre of attention and his nervousness tried to reassert itself. 'My apologies. It is an engine. Philon of Byzantium writes of them, as do others, though no one for hundreds of years. I've never seen one, nor even a picture, but that is surely what it is. Thank you once again for the loan of Philon's book.'

'Did not even know I had it,' Sabinus assured him. 'Did you notice, sir?'

'Geometry has always given me a headache,' Ferox replied. He had read a fair few of the scrolls from Sabinus' little library, but had struggled with anything talking about measures and ratios and set those aside. Thankfully it seemed that Ephippus had discovered something useful – or at least that was what he must hope, while he waited for the engineer to get to the point.

'Geometry.' The Syracusan was shaking his head. 'Not geometry, my lord...' He seemed genuinely puzzled to encounter someone so lacking in basic understanding and yet given a post of authority. 'You must come and see!' he shouted again and scurried away.

Ferox chuckled. 'Well, I suppose if we must, we must.'

They followed the engineer to the granaries. In the best traditions of the army, the shells of the two that had burned and the remnants of the third had been thoroughly demolished, leaving an odd patch of open ground in the fort. Ephippus' wonder was in the remaining building given over to Dacian engines. Ferox had not been there for some time, and was impressed at how much more space there was. Naso and his men had done well, aided since he arrived by Ephippus, and had managed to get a fair few of the ballistae working again. The Sicilian was now standing with great pride by one of the tall cranes.

'So that's what it is,' Sabinus said, voicing the words before Ferox had a chance.

'You see it is really a lot like one of the old staff slings. A one-arm engine rather than a two-armed like all the others. Isis knows how the Dacians knew how to make it. Advice from one of the cities on the inner sea, I suppose. I really wonder who and what plans they used. As you can see, this cranks down and is held under tension of the sinew and ropes, and you can adjust the washers so that it lobs high or low. Of course, it is not easy to aim, for you have to move the whole frame and cannot pivot at all, but then the force produced…' It was a while before Ephippus realised that his audience had ceased to follow him.

'Apart from its historical interest, I take it there is a reason for bringing us here,' Ferox asked as patiently as he could.

Ephippus blinked at him, mouth hanging open and giving his face a fish-like quality. 'You told me that you wanted something that could shoot as far as the bridge. I think that this may be the answer.' He smiled as he saw their renewed interest. 'That is if I can get them to work. They are in a bit of a state.'

That had been ten days ago and since then they had been busy. On several nights it had taken a direct order to send the engineer to his bed, for if he was not in the workshops, he was outside measuring and surveying, or indoors with the beads of his abacus clicking back and forth and his stylus scratching away on writing tablets. One of the machines was in a dreadful state, the other only a little better, and it was soon decided to strip all that was useful from the first. Other parts had to be made, which in turn required exact measurement and more than a little guesswork for the manual was vague on many points. After a few days Sabinus took charge of a work party building a platform extending back from the rampart about twenty paces to the left of the porta praetoria, because Ephippus informed them that the machine would need to be raised up.

'How about a tower?' Dionysius had suggested.

Ephippus dismissed the idea. 'No. We could not build one that was high enough and strong enough.'

When the machine was pronounced ready, Ferox could understand why. It was bulkier than any ballista he had ever seen, with a rectangular frame of big, squared off beams as its base. About a third of a way back from the front was a solid upright, heavily padded and with supports joining on to the front of the frame to give it more strength, and just behind it the great metal washers. Now that he had looked – and had it explained to him plenty of times – Ferox could see that this was like one side of an ordinary ballista, whether a light scorpio or one of the big stone throwers. The only difference was that this was on its side, running between the two long sides of the frame. From it sprouted the high beam to which Ephippus had fitted what for all the world was just like a giant sling. A heavy rope hooked onto a catch on the beam, allowing it to be cranked down and held by a second cross-beam near the back, turned by a big wooden windlass worked by levers. A rachet prevented this from spinning back as the levers were lifted out and moved to the next socket.

'You really wouldn't want that lot going off without warning,' Naso assured him. Like many others he had taken more and more interest in the machine as the days passed.

'Some men just like machines,' Ferox told Claudia when she asked why so many kept wandering down to see what was happening and whether they could help. 'Machines are straightforward and do not get mad at you.'

'Huh!'

Eventually Ephippus tested the mechanism under a low tension and was satisfied, so that they could begin the major task of moving the monâkon to the rampart. The engineer had designed a cart with a wide, flat platform, and cranes to help lift the engine onto it, but even so fifty men were needed to haul on the ropes. 'I wondered about fitting the thing with wheels of its own, but am worried that it might roll back when we shoot.'

Five pairs of oxen pulled the cart, and men pushed and made sure that the wheels did not bog down as the weight pushed them into the packed grit on the road surface. Sabinus sighed at the sight of the deep trails ruining the previously flat surface. 'I guess we have another task for a work party,' Ferox told him.

'The men will be delighted,' Sabinus replied with heavy sarcasm. 'Let's just hope this demonic device actually works.'

'We'll soon see.'

Ephippus had ordered that the platform end in a ramp, and had made the slope as gentle as was possible while still permitting people to pass this section of the intervallum. Ferox had refused the engineer's eager request to knock down a couple of barrack blocks to make more room. Posts were driven deep into the rampart so that an array of blocks, ropes and pulleys could be secured, with rollers prepared to ease the catapult as it was drawn upwards.

It took half a day to get the monâkon to the base of the ramp, and night had fallen by the time that they were done, so that men with torches lit the way. Ferox had been surprised at how slowly the engineer raised the great machine, inching it up the slope, then stopping and having men thrust in levers as brakes to hold it in place while pulleys were adjusted. He did not stay to watch the whole thing, because he wanted to show trust and also had a lot of other things to do. Yet he made sure to pass by every half hour or so and sometimes the thing had barely moved.

'Sure this is a good idea?' Vindex asked time after time.

'No,' Ferox replied, prompting Claudia Enica to shake her head in dismay. She was dressed in high Thracian boots, a short, belted tunic under a mail shirt, with a sica, a curved sword of the type common in this area and used by Thracian gladiators on one hip and a gladius on the other. Today she was not wearing a helmet, and her long hair was braided and coiled on top of her head. This had been her garb each day, sometimes with a different cuirass, sometimes with a plumed helmet, and very occasionally adding a cloak if the morning was cold.

'I am queen,' she had told him when she appeared at morning orders the first time. 'These are my warriors, so I must lead them.'

Sabinus had gulped nervously, for the skirt of the queen's tunic showed most of her legs and he was not accustomed to seeing an equestrian lady display herself in this way, let alone such an attractive one. However, the army was the army and things ought to be done properly. 'The numerus is under the care of your husband.' He swallowed again, for like everyone else he knew that the marriage between Ferox and Claudia was scarcely orthodox. 'That is Flavius Ferox. It is not the Roman custom to let ladies serve as soldiers.'

Claudia gave him a look of the sort Ferox had always

felt she reserved for him alone, mingling disappointment with weary contempt at the stubborn idiocy of a small boy. Having already had this conversation with her, and realised that she was absolutely determined and quite possibly right, he let it play out.

'I am queen, and we are Brigantes.'

'You are Roman, my lady,' Sabinus said, surprising Ferox by his determination. 'This is not proper.' Then he made a huge mistake as his lips curled into a smile. 'I admire your bravery, but war is grim work and best left to men.'

Enica nodded thoughtfully as if seeing the wisdom, prompting Sabinus to smile, but before he could say another word she started to turn. Her hand gripped the sica, which slid from the scabbard in one fluid motion and flicked up, the curved edge stopping a whisker short of the centurion's throat. It was all so sudden, but then Dionysius jumped back in surprise and a guard was shouting, hefting his *pilum* to use as a spear.

Ferox waved at the man to stand fast. 'You will discover that the queen has considerable skill at arms,' he said gently. Sabinus was gulping again and again, eyes wide, still struggling to believe what was happening. 'And the Brigantes will fight all the better – if the time comes – for the queen's presence. But,' Ferox raised his voice. 'This is a principia of the army, and more than that the principia where I command and not some tavern suited for brawls. You will sheath your sword, your highness, and do it now.'

Enica glanced at him, then did as she was told. Then she gave Sabinus a flirtatious smile that was pure Claudia, leaving the centurion even more confused than before.

Ferox stood up behind his desk. 'I command here. If

anyone draws a weapon here again, they will be in chains before the day is out. Is that understood?' He saw that his wife was fighting the urge to make a lewd joke – or at least a statement easy to interpret more than one way – and was pleased that she controlled it. This was not the time.

'You command and I will lead my people to serve you,' she said.

'Good enough,' he replied. 'Have it added to today's orders that the queen is to command the Brigantes, second only to me, and that she is to be treated by all with the respect due to a centurion and an eques.'

So from then on the queen attended morning orders, and did the rounds with Ferox and the others, openly supervising the training of the Brigantes and riding out once or twice with patrols, when she added silk Parthian trousers to her attire. As the days passed the officers all became used to it, not least because she was attractive and charming and very positive when she gave orders. The contingent of Brigantes she had brought to the fort came equipped with a *vexillum* standard, the blue flag painted with what most Romans must have assumed was the figure of Victory. To the tribesmen the woman was Brigantia, the goddess of their people, who lived on earth in the women of the royal line. Ferox had not been surprised to see that the painted figure had red hair and a short tunic. Some of the legionaries and auxiliaries had scoffed when they saw it installed in the *aedes*, the shrine for the standards in the principia. This was almost empty for a fort this size, for none of the men at the fort had brought a *signa*, and otherwise there were just two other *vexilla*, one for I Minervia and one for cohors I Hispanorum veterana.

The Brigantes showed no surprise as their queen took charge of them.

'She's the queen,' Vindex explained to Sabinus. 'And they don't hate her like they do Ferox.'

The rest of the garrison displayed shock, amusement, and then surprisingly swiftly became used to the sight of a woman wearing armour and giving orders. That was the charm again, and helped because this was a fort full of men largely deprived of the sight, let alone the company of women, so that such a pretty one was a treat. Ferox quickly noticed that there were always more men around than usual whenever they were carrying out an inspection and began to climb one of the towers. Even when he tried to vary the route, there they were, off-duty soldiers and sentries arriving early or lingering late for this shift, talking among themselves or apparently busy, but ready to cluster as close to the bottom of each ladder as they dared when it came time for the queen to climb.

'I wish you would wear a cloak, at the very least,' he whispered to her as she followed him up onto the top platform at the *porta decumana* at the back of the fort.

Claudia Enica's expression was one of supreme innocence. 'Some of the men have no breeches under their tunics.'

'It's not the same,' he hissed, as Sabinus appeared through the open trap door, his face somewhat red.

After that Ferox made sure that she went first up any ladder in front of him and came down last. There would still be plenty of interested bystanders, but at least he spared his senior staff both embarrassment and enjoyment. Vindex was not impressed whenever he joined the party.

'Jealous, eh?' he leered. 'Or just desperate?'

Ferox ignored him, for in truth the repeated views up his wife's tunic as she climbed were reminders of his failure as a husband and his surging desire. Having her here, but still unreachable, was a lot harder to bear than when she had been so far away, especially when he tried and failed to stop himself from staring up at her wondrous rear and the little pants she favoured. She knew it too, and Ferox was sure that she was deliberately stopping part way up and even wriggling more than necessary each time she got onto a platform. Yet still he slept alone, in one of the smallest rooms in the praetorium.

Sulpicia Lepidina was sympathetic, at least to a point. 'Claudia will come around. Be patient and play her games. It is all your fault in the first place for losing her. Sometimes you are too much the barbarian, aren't you?' Her face had a wistful look, and he wondered whether she was thinking back to their own affair. 'I would like you both to be happy,' she said. 'And while I wonder about Claudia's talk of magic and fate, I do suspect that you are meant for each other, while also guessing that it will be the rockiest of roads.'

Although she had been disappointed when the letter arrived from Cerialis telling her to stay at Piroboridava for the moment, Sulpicia Lepidina had got on with things as she always did, running the household since Claudia had little interest in such matters when there were warriors to supervise. Remarkably, she took over without making Philo resent the new, far tighter oversight. The praetorium bustled, and often echoed to the cries of the children. Ferox remembered reading that Cicero felt his new villa had gained a soul when a library was created, but nothing made a place a home faster than children. It was all so comfortable that he wondered whether he was ready for a quiet life, even a dull life, if only Claudia would take him back. Then he would remember where they were, and think of Dacians swarming over the ramparts of the fort. They were ruthless in war and could be cruel to captives. He had heard too many stories of what the local women had done to captured Romans in past wars to doubt that there was a lot of truth in them, and the allies in any Dacian army could be even less predictable. If his fears were right then that meant captivity or death for everyone here, perhaps with many cruelties along the way and such thoughts chilled him to the very bone.

On the morning when all was ready to test the monâkon, it was easier to live with such fears. The day was glorious, with the sky an almost unbroken field of pale blue and hardly a breath of wind. Almost the entire fort was watching, with the ramparts lined wherever there was a decent view of the canabae and bridge beyond. On top of the right-hand tower of the porta praetoria was a place reserved for the ladies and the children, the latter especially eager when told that this mighty machine flung vast rocks to smash all in its path. To Ferox's relief, Claudia Enica was as elegant and proper in her attire as Sulpicia Lepidina, both adding broad-brimmed felt hats to guard against the sun. They still attracted plenty of sidelong glances, as did their maids, both of whom were pretty. A man would struggle to peek up a long dress when they climbed or through the gaps in the planking, but Ferox knew that plenty would still try.

The mood of celebration was helped because this was genuinely a festival day for the Brigantes, and later several cows were to be sacrificed and form the basis for a feast.

'Is it safe, do you think?' Vindex said with great suspicion.

'Bet it doesn't work,' Sabinus told Dionysius.

'I reckon it'll either tear itself apart or work so well that it knocks the bridge down,' the auxiliary centurion replied.

'No, it'll hit the tavern,' Vindex suggested. 'Accidents always happen to the most important things.'

Ferox had thought the same thoughts, which was one reason why he had ensured that the ladies and the children would watch from this tower, rather than the left one which was closer to the catapult. They should all be well out of reach of any unexpected event up here. He walked over to the rear of the tower. Below him, Naso stood with a *cornicen*.

'Signal that we are ready,' he shouted.

'Sir!' Naso replied and a moment later the trumpeter sounded a deep note on his curved *cornu*.

Ephippus waved, but was still making final adjustments. Ferox stayed at the rear of the tower, for he felt that luck was more likely to be with them if he did not watch the first shot land. Apart from that, only from here could he see the machine properly. Two men loaded the stone into the sling which had already been cranked down. Ephippus was confident that the engine would be capable of hurling something twice the weight, but had agreed that a cautious approach was best. The men stepped back, the engineer checked that all were safely away from the frame and then took the cord ready to pull. Ferox wondered which gods the Greek prayed to as he hesitated, and then yanked it free, releasing the arm. Even at this distance Ferox flinched at the force as the arm sprang forward, banging into the padded upright with more noise than he had expected, and at its tip the sling whipped over the top and released the stone. The whole frame shook with the action, and he knew that it was at a pretty low tension.

'Bugger me, it works.' That was Vindex, but anything else was lost in a great gasp from the crowd that turned into a cheer. He pushed his way back to the front. There was a faint puff of dust where the stone had landed and broken apart. It was still well short of the bridge by a good hundred paces, but about the longest range for any of their other engines.

The second shot bounced thirty paces nearer, the stone cracking into two big pieces, one of which kept going straight. They were using soft limestone for the trials. Partly that was to avoid smashing the bridge or – if it went wild, a building – and partly because Ephippus had suggested that the fall of each missile would be that much more obvious and easier to measure afterwards. The third was closer still, the thump as it was loosed the loudest by far. After that Ephippus began to adjust the tension on the main washers, lobbing the missile higher if slower. Within a few shots, a stone splashed into the river beside the bridge.

'Tell him if he breaks it, then he'll have to pay for it,' Sabinus said cheerfully.

'Riders!' Vindex interrupted, pointing to the south, where three horsemen were coming up the track.

Claudia Enica pulled the brim of her hat down as she stared for a long moment. 'They're mine. We must warn them.'

'I am sure they will work out the danger for themselves, dear lady,' Sabinus suggested.

'Depends how daft they are,' Vindex muttered.

Claudia turned to Ferox. 'Either send someone to ride out and warn them or I will do it.'

He glanced down, taking in her long dress.

'I can ride in this,' she said, and he hoped there was more amusement than anger in her eyes, 'or take it off.'

Ferox went to the rear of the tower and shouted down to Naso. Before the cornu sounded there was another dull thump. He heard the murmur of the crowd, softer now than at the start, but still excited and then it turned into shouting.

'Oh bugger,' Vindex said. By the time Ferox could see there was a plume of dust beyond the bridge and the three horses were bolting in all directions. Two of the riders stayed on, while the third was down and not moving.

'I hope that is not Bran,' Claudia Enica said quietly.

'Bran?' Ferox had almost forgotten the boy he had not seen for six years, and struggled to accept that the lad – a man now presumably – was over there.

Claudia nodded.

'Oh shit,' Vindex muttered.

XVI

The valley to the north west of Piroboridava
One day after the Kalends of May

'I T REALLY IS good to see you,' Ferox said and meant it.

'Oh yes,' Vindex added, but he was not looking at Bran. He winked at Bran's companion, who continued to ignore him.

'I took an oath,' Bran said.

'Yes, and I am all the more glad that you gave it,' Ferox told him.

The five of them were riding a hundred paces ahead of the main force with the line of outriders ahead of them. At the moment the woods were more than half a mile away, and otherwise the ground too open to hide many enemies. Soon, they would have to be far more careful. They were higher up the valley, some twelve miles from the fort, looking for the missing half of a patrol. The remainder had split away to follow a different path as they returned to Piroboridava and ought to have met up when they were almost home. There had been no sign of them, and still they had not returned, so Ferox had decided to go and look. Sabinus had argued, saying that they ought to wait or send someone else, but Ferox used his rank to make it an order. Apart from anything else, he was hoping for a little time to speak to the new arrivals when the grip of the army did not hold them all so tight. Bran and the other warrior were from a world beyond Rome.

Bran must be about sixteen by now, and it was an effort to see in the confident young warrior much trace of the boy they had captured on that desolate beach almost six years ago. He had grown, not so much in size or breadth, for he was still small even by the standards of the Selgovae. His tribe were not large people, but they were slim and much stronger than they looked in both spirit and strength. The Selgovae thought highly of themselves and did not bother to hide it, and he saw some of that in the boy, but far more, for his assurance was as much the mark of knowing his own skill. Bran moved like a cat, always careful, always balanced, his eyes steady and unblinking. If the lad drew the gladius on his belt then Ferox had no doubt that it would move as an extension of his hand, every cut and thrust fluid and practised. That was the training he had received in the last few years, taught by the Mother, that head of the strange cult living on one of the smallest islands far to the north west of Britannia. She taught a select few, boys and young women from the tribes, who passed her tests and survived the hardships of getting there and winning her respect, showing them how to use sword, spear or whatever came to hand as a weapon.

'The Mother is pleased with my brother,' Enica said, giving Bran a smile. Interrupting her education as a good little Roman, her parents had sent her to the island to become a warrior. 'As she is of my sister.' Bran had come with a woman a few years older than him, a Hibernian whose family had all been slaughtered in a power struggle within her tribe so that she had no home left to her. She had raven black hair, today coiled under a bronze helmet, and a beguiling, pale face utterly misleading in its softness. Her name was Minura and she did not say much, or at least had not done so far in Ferox's hearing. There was a hardness in her eyes and the hint of great sorrow.

Vindex gave the woman another encouraging smile. 'Aye, bound to be proud of you both.'

'So am I,' Enica continued, for once not indulging the scout. Minura and Bran both touched their chests, where Ferox knew the members of the cult had a tiny scar given by a blade. Enica had the same mark between her breasts and a moment later she pressed her fingers against the mail rings above it.

'We have travelled and we have fought,' she added, and it sounded like a quote, but Ferox did not recognise it so wondered whether it was from a song of the Brigantes or verses special to the Mother and her children. So far the queen had said little about their activities in the last few months. He suspected that it was all part of her scheme to secure the rule of her tribe once and for all. As things were, there was little point in prying, for they had little time alone and then she was not forthcoming in any way. He hoped that the knowledge was not dangerous, or that if it was she would tell him in time. That it involved death he did not doubt. The Mother taught remarkable skill at arms, but her children did not kill during their time with her and some never managed to do that well. A mere glance at Bran and Minura revealed to eyes willing to see that they had already walked that path. There was simply an extra edge to their bearing.

The man with them, whose horse had bucked when the missile struck nearby had fallen, was not helped by having his hands tied. Landing badly, his neck had snapped and he had been dead before anyone reached him. Neither Bran nor Minura would say much about him, apart from the obvious fact that he was their prisoner, and that they were bringing him here as instructed.

'Later,' was all that Enica would tell him, for she clearly knew all about it, but later had not yet arrived. Ferox had looked at the body, seen the hair dyed red and tied into a knot on the right-hand side of the man's head, the thick beard and the pale grey eyes and the little tattoo on his left wrist. With his dark, almost black trousers and the striped tunic, he was clearly one of the Quadi from across the Danube near Pannonia. Yet he wasn't just that, for there was the look of a soldier about him, something hard to pin down, but obvious even before he pulled up the man's sleeve and saw another tattoo, this one of the she-wolf suckling the twins on his arm. That was the relic of some drunken furlough outside an army base. Too young to have served his full stipendia and too hale to have been invalided out, this one was surely a deserter turned bandit or trader or both. Whether originally one of the Quadi who had crossed into the army and stayed as long as it suited him or a soldier who had gone over the rampart and found a new life among the tribes was hard to say. He thought of the former slave they had met with the Roxolani. People ended up in odd places – like a good Silurian boy turned Roman centurion and stuck out here in charge of a fort, he thought grimly. Bran and Minura had not chosen this captive by chance, that was for sure, and must have been sent to fetch him and bring him here. Ferox had overheard the young warriors asking Enica whether 'he' was here, seen her shake her head and say, 'Ah well, it does not matter now.'

There were mysteries aplenty, but for the moment the dangers they might pose were distant, and there could well be a real enemy waiting for them up ahead, so there was no sense in thinking about anything else.

'Is Brigita well?' Ferox asked. He had fought alongside the children and seen one Mother die to protect her pupils. She had been succeeded by Brigita, once queen of an Irish tribe, who had trained on the island in her youth.

'The Mother cares for her children,' Bran replied.

'Sister, have you given the Lord Ferox the Mother's message?'

Minura shook her head just slightly, and for the first time seemed abashed.

'Come, it is what she asked of you.'

Minura kicked her horse so that she caught up with Ferox and rode alongside, staring straight at him, reins loose.

'The Mother asks you to remember,' she said, still gazing into his eyes. Then her left hand shot out and grabbed his shoulder, her right went to his chest, and for all his surprise his arms moved to grab her, until she kissed him full on the lips. Ferox pulled her body towards him, as he kept his mouth pressed to hers.

Minura started to pull away. Ferox held her for a little longer before letting her slip free. Her cheeks were red, although he doubted with passion so much as embarrassment.

'The Mother said that I might be curious. Now I am curious no longer.'

Vindex roared with laughter, and Ferox smiled as he remembered Brigita saying much the same to him all those years ago. He was relieved to see that Enica was as amused as the rest.

'Does that mean you're going to hit me again?' he asked, grinning.

'I probably shall not waste the energy,' Enica replied. 'One of the soldiers can do it for me when it becomes necessary.'

'Always happy to oblige, lady,' Vindex announced. 'Want him beaten up, just say the word.'

Ferox hissed for silence and raised his hand. One of the outriders was holding his spear above his head as a signal.

'Wait here!' Ferox told them and urged his gelding into a canter. He heard the hoofs coming up behind him as Vindex came up on one side and Enica on another. The bright green silk of her trousers shimmered in the sunlight.

'You should not be here,' he told her.

'Neither should you, husband.'

'It is too much of a risk,' he said, 'and it is unnecessary.'

'No more than the commander of the garrison galloping headlong into trouble.'

'Want me to rough him up, lady?' Vindex asked cheerfully. 'Wouldn't be any trouble.'

'There you are, I told you it was dangerous,' she said, and the scout laughed so much that when they reached the man who had signalled to them he was obviously baffled.

'Ignore them,' Ferox said as he shaded his eyes to see better. 'I see them,' he added. It was not difficult. There were nine dark shapes in the grass a few hundred paces away. Smaller than the dead horses and mules, but standing out because they were so pale were the white corpses of the men. Ferox counted. 'Looks like all of them,' he said and was not surprised. 'You,' he said to the cavalryman who had signalled. 'Ride back to the main force and tell them to come up and wait here, just where you have been. Tell the decurion not to do anything else unless I signal.'

'My lord,' the Brigantian said and trotted away. Ferox could not get used to soldiers calling him lord, but so far it was proving difficult to persuade the Brigantes to call him plain sir.

'Suppose there is no point in asking you to wait?' he said to Enica, who responded by walking her horse forward. 'Didn't think so,' he added and joined her. 'But nice and easy, all of us.' He waved his arm for the other outriders to keep level with them.

His senses told him that the enemy had long gone, but sometimes feelings were wrong and there was no gain in taking a chance. He walked his horse steadily, scanning the ground ahead and especially the treeline only a hundred paces away. That was the obvious place if there was an ambush – and was clearly where the attackers had been earlier. Still, doing the obvious was something the best leaders would avoid whenever they could. He remembered that there was a little gulley up ahead, just beyond the furthest of the dead horses. It was only a few feet deep, with a tiny stream in the bottom rushing down to join the main river, but if a man did not mind getting a bit wet and was good at keeping still, then there could be a dozen or more in there, already within bowshot. Vindex was staring at the same place, so he must have remembered the ground as well. They were half a mile from where Vepoc and his men had been attacked and on that day they had come past this patch as well.

If they were waiting then they were good. There were carrion fowl picking at the dead men and beasts, and they flapped noisily into the air, voices harsh when Ferox suddenly put his horse into a run, wanting to rush at the gulley and spring any ambush if it was there.

Nothing happened. The birds complained and the wind hissed through the grass, but no warriors appeared and no arrows sped towards him. Ferox sighed before dismounting to take a better look.

'What was that little gallop in aid of?' Vindex asked as he and Enica rode up. Ferox was crouching, ignoring the nearest corpse and instead studying the ground. 'Trying to be a hero?'

Ferox stood and shouted at the outriders to keep going and form a line nearer the wood. 'From this distance they could drop every one of us as quick as boiled asparagus.'

Vindex frowned. 'What?'

'Don't show off, husband,' Claudia Enica said. 'The divine Augustus could get away with using vulgar expressions, but you are not granted the same licence.'

'Vulgar? Didn't sound very vulgar to me. Not like…' Vindex chuckled. 'No, not in front of the queen.'

'She's probably heard it already,' Ferox said automatically, without really paying attention.

The pommel of a sword bounced hard on the top of his helmet. 'Next time I'll use the blade,' Enica assured him.

'Next time I wish you would stay back,' Ferox said. 'I mean it.'

'I am sure some fool will rush ahead to distract the enemy,' she said, but there was a warmer smile than he had seen for a while. She was so close that he brushed against her silk-clad leg without Vindex seeing.

'He's right, my queen,' Vindex said. 'Be a shame for the lassies to grow up without a mother.'

'If that mother is daft enough to let herself be killed they will feel no great loss.' Enica edged her horse on, and this time tapped Ferox's shoulder playfully with the flat of her sword. 'My story does not end here or for a long time yet. This much I know.' There was neither humour nor a trace of doubt in her tone.

'Wonder if these poor souls thought the same,' Ferox said, gesturing at the corpses, their places and the marks in the earth and flattened grass telling him of the story of what had happened as clearly as if he had been watching. There were seven Brigantes, one of Vindex's Carvetii and an auxiliary duplicarius who had been in charge. The little fight had not lasted long as fifteen or more archers shot from the trees. Horses and men fell, as one flight of arrows followed another before the first had struck home.

The patrol had been careless as soldiers often were when nothing had happened on all the other long patrols. Half the horses were down and the rest wounded when warriors had come from the gulley and the archers had followed from the wood to hack down the survivors. Only two of the Brigantes had no arrows in them, and the rest were dead or staggering and bleeding as the little charge swept over them. One of the unwounded men had his whole chest opened by a savage cut. He cannot have been wearing armour, which would have taken some of the force from the blow, and Ferox made a note to check that all the Brigantes had been issued with a cuirass and that all wore it, whether it was uncomfortable or not. The other had a hole in the top of his skull, fairly small and neat, which probably killed him outright after punching through his helmet, which lay broken and discarded a few yards away. Ferox sighed, for he had seen wounds like that before, many years ago and knew what caused them.

'Why not steal the horses?' Vindex asked.

'Too easy for us to track,' Ferox said. 'And they didn't want anyone to get away.'

'They took the clothes though. Stripped the poor buggers bare.'

'We will probably find most of it dumped nearby. They will only take what they need.' Ferox did not bother to explain that pieces of the men's clothing would help some of their killers purify their bodies. Instead he went over to his own gelding. 'We need to take care of them. Perhaps you two can deal with that and I'll take a couple of men and see where the trail leads.'

Enica was by him now, holding his bridle. 'That is not your job. Not anymore.'

'It's mine,' Vindex said. 'I am supposed to be in charge of the scouts.'

Ferox did not bother to argue. They were right, much as he regretted the days when he could head off alone or with just a handful of companions. 'Don't go far and don't take any risks.'

'Always sensible, me.'

'Take Bran and Minura,' Enica commanded. 'And be careful.'

Vindex, already grinning at the mention of the young woman warrior, beamed. 'For you, my queen, anything.'

After he had called the others, the scout headed towards the trees, the tracks that far very obvious.

'Why can't you be like that?' Claudia Enica asked Ferox.

'I am of the Silures,' he said. 'And I do not understand women – at least not the ones worth understanding.'

She treated him to another smile. 'Your folk are all liars.'

They did their best for the bodies, by which time Vindex and the others returned. The trail was clear, heading through the woods. Bran gave a terse report. 'About thirty or so, going up the valley, heading for the old tower or the pass. Weren't trying to hide anything, so did not push our luck.'

Ferox patted him on the shoulder and praised Bran which for a moment made him seem like the happy little boy instead of the stern warrior. The ride back was easy, helped by the lengthening days, although Ferox missed the far longer spring evenings of Britannia and suspected many of the others did as well. It was two hours into the night by the time they rode back through the porta praetoria. Sabinus was waiting anxiously for their safe return and carrying news. Piso was awake.

A cave near the pass
Just before dawn, five days later

B RASUS SAT AND *tried to keep his mind clear of everything.*
That was never a good sign and he knew it, for the
emptiness should come naturally and not be forced.
Wise men and old, the truly pure were said to be able to sit
or lie and almost at once be empty of worldly thoughts, a
vessel waiting to be filled with enlightenment. Once or twice,
such peace had come to him, or he thought later that it had,
but only when he was weary and a treacherous part of him
wondered if that had simply been fatigue.

He opened his eyes and could see the faintest hints of the
rocky chamber around him. Dawn was coming outside, the
light seeping in from the distant mouth of the cave and soon
it would be time to leave this place and take food and drink.
His fast had begun two dawns ago, a day before he came to
the cavern.

A drip of water plinked into a puddle. He had not seen it
when he entered the holy place at sunset yesterday, but all
through the long hours of the night the noise had gone on
and on. Brasus had not slept, that much he knew, and had
only shifted his posture a few times as he sat cross-legged or
squatted on the bare stone. He had felt the cold of the rock,
his limbs going stiff and then numb, and he had listened
to the dripping water while outside the moon rose and the

stars turned in the Heavens. Several times he had thought of them and tried to work out how far into the night it was. Some men were said to be transported by their visions into the Heavens themselves and spoke of walking among the stars. His was no vision, but yet more of the thoughts he could not prevent.

Brasus wondered whether he was different, but that was surely vanity, and instead once again wondered whether he was a fraud, pretending to be pure so that others would treat him with honour. The king had been very kind in his words when Brasus had gone to his stronghold, and also in his gestures. He had been permitted to meet his bride to be, the king's youngest daughter, who had presented him with a tress of her deep brown hair, neatly plaited and tied with a ribbon. One day soon he would learn her name – her real name not the one that was used by others in daily speech – and he would know one of life's great mysteries. A woman's path was a different one, but in marriage he would glimpse a little of her world and hope to learn from it.

Thoughts of marriage, of a girl, round-faced with the wide nose and mouth of her family, had come into his mind often, and especially during the night. Brasus was not quite sure whether he had seen fear as well as anticipation in her eyes, and wondered about his own feelings. His father had once said that the best of wives made a man relish this life and cease to long for death and the transformation it gave to the pure. A mean-spirited part of him sometimes made Brasus wonder whether his mother's death from fever months before the last war had done as much to inspire his father's stubborn fight and the taking of his own life as his quest for a pure life.

Thoughts were treacherous, and brought doubt and suspicion. Brasus wondered whether the men who claimed to find emptiness lied and had spent the hours pondering one thing or another or whether he was the liar for pretending to be faithful and pure. So the night passed, with the water dripping and Brasus worrying about so many things.

Oddly enough, Brasus had spent less time wondering about the trial to come than other things. He was worried by some of the king's choices. It was an honour to be tasked with leading the advance guard, the men who were to storm the fort and seize the bridge by surprise. Yet he wondered why the king had chosen Diegis and Rholes to command the main army that would follow. Diegis was said to be a man of great piety, rigorous in thought and life, but was also widely known as a fool who struggled to make up his mind and was sometimes timid and sometimes reckless in battle. Rholes was rare among the king's advisors, one of the Getae rather than the Daci and a man who wore his hair long and piled into a ball on top of his head so that the cap he wore was tall, like a bag. He drank wine like a Thracian, ate all meats like a Roman, was crude of speech and an open whoremonger. Rholes was also a great warrior and an even greater leader, shrewd in thought and cunning in action.

Brasus wished that Rholes was in sole command and knew that this was wrong, for Zalmoxis would surely guide only the pure to serve his purpose, but Rholes won battles and Diegis led men to needless deaths, puffed up by his royal name. The court of the king was not a comfortable place, for all that most of his noblemen were held to be of the pure. Brasus had overheard some of them talking after the plan was announced, and saying that Decebalus was too wise to trust an army to one man's command, lest a new hero emerge, just as Decebalus had once made his name in war and been able to supplant the old king. Another surprise had been Diegis' interest in Ivonercus the Briton, which surely can only have come from the king, since how else would he have heard of the deserter and known his name.

The night had seemed long, even endless, for he felt that every moment had been filled with ideas and confusion. He wondered about marriage, about his bride to be, for he knew that the lust was growing, and he thought of kings and nobles, wars and lies, but most of all he felt hungry, while the dripping water was a torment for reminding him of his desperate thirst.

Far and faint, there came the notes of a horn greeting the rising sun. That was one good practice copied from the Romans, rousing soldiers to be ready. Brasus now had some six hundred warriors, almost a third of the force he was promised, and the latest band were camped just below the pass. Today he would lead them to a hidden place within the woods on the south side of the valley, for until the last moment he wanted to conceal his strength from the Romans. First he would sting them, like the ambush of their patrol several days ago. Ivonercus had helped with that and shown no reluctance to slay his own kin. Deserters could be useful, as could their ideas, although Brasus still felt that this was an unclean way of making war.

Getting up was painful, his body and especially his legs hurting with the movement, and he doubted that he could have stood upright even if the roof of the cavern had been higher. The fast was done, the time of waiting in the bowels of the earth complete. There had been no emptiness, no real *peace during the long night, although he wondered whether he would lie if anyone asked him about his experience. Stumbling up the passage, he also wondered whether men had lied to him of their visions and insights. He had been alone and he had thought long and hard and that was all there was to it.*

Brasus blinked as he turned around a bend in the cave and saw its mouth, the red light of the dawn appallingly bright to his eyes. The horn sounded again, oddly fainter this time, and it was even more strange that he did not think about anything apart from forcing life back into his painful feet and legs as he tried not to fall or trip. He felt chilled, and draping the cloak he had left near the entrance did little to warm his naked body. His other clothes were outside, and he fumbled with buckles and brooches as he drew them on. The climb down the little cliff was not hard, and by this time he was shaking off the stiffness. After that the walk to the camp was easy and by the time he reached it he felt invigorated. Men stared at him, some nervous, some showing their awe of what he had done and others with no interest. Half these men were deserters, who understood nothing. Brasus did not speak for it was only as he saw these faces that he realised that his mind had truly been clear from the moment he left the cave. This was how it had always been for him, after the long hours of vigil and the jumble of thoughts, ideas and doubts. Afterwards his mind felt stronger and fresher and everything he set his hand to do went well. Whether or not others felt the same he could not tell and it no longer seemed to matter.

Brasus smiled at one of the younger warriors, a nervous lad whose wisps of beard made him look even more childlike. 'Soon,' he said.

XVII

I T DID LOOK odd, no matter how many times he saw it, but this was the first festival day of the standards, so it was to be draped with roses like the other vexilla and that was an end to it. Ferox had already crowned the flag of the vexillation of Legio I Minervia as the senior unit, the standard-bearer lowering it so that he could place the wreath of flowers. The flag was an old one that had seen a fair bit of service, so that its original red had faded to a paler pink, on which the golden boar of the legion charged. After that came the lone banner for the largest contingent of auxiliaries since they were next in seniority even if far fewer in number than the Brigantes. All of the garrison who could be spared were on parade, the regulars immaculately turned out and the Brigantes putting on a decent enough show when it came to polished helmets, armour and metalwork.

Their vexillum dipped, pendants jingling, so that Ferox could place a wreath over the spearhead on top and that meant that he did not have to see the banner itself. He lingered, hoping that the choice of mainly blue flowers would please the warriors because their tribe was fond of the colour and saw it as lucky. Then he was done, and the standard-bearer nodded and raised the pole just as the wind stirred so that the flag hanging from it flapped, almost waving in his face.

Ferox sighed, and kept a straight face, for he was the commander and must act as priest, but it was hard. The painted goddess stared back at him, unsmiling with its flowing red hair. Back on the night of the Brigantes' festival, when all of them were drunk and their generosity with wine and beer meant that so was almost the entire garrison, someone had got into the aedes and tampered with the flag. Gone was most of the figure's dress, and the painter had given the goddess bare and very large breasts.

'I doubt that she would be able to stand up straight,' Claudia Enica had said when she was shown the damage.

'You manage, my queen,' Vindex suggested.

'The Carvetii are an insolent folk,' she had said, shaking her head in mock reproof, 'and vile of tongue.' She had also refused to have the additions painted over. 'We don't want to weigh the poor girl down with layer after layer.'

So the bare-breasted goddess stayed, although Ferox had never seen any other unit in the army with such a standard. Piso had almost choked in surprise when he saw it after demanding to inspect the entire base.

The tribune had woken with a raging temper, perhaps in part because of his sore head. He had no memory of how it had happened, and indeed had to have it explained why he was in hospital at all. More surprisingly he seemed to have little interest in investigating the matter. Snarling at the medicus, Piso had insisted that he was fine and got up that first day. Since the effort did not kill him, perhaps he was right, and by the next morning he was demanding an escort to take him to Sarmizegethusa as intended. Ferox argued, although not with great passion. Perhaps once or twice he had wished to have a superior officer present so that the responsibility passed to someone else, but the mood had not lasted. For all the dangers – in fact because of all the dangers and all that was at risk – he was determined to be in charge. Added to that, the little he had heard about the tribune made him eager to be rid of the man.

That opinion was confirmed on the next day, when Ferox led out a hundred and fifteen horsemen in addition to the twenty allotted to escort Piso all the way to the garrison at Decebalus' stronghold. If the tribune was to be killed, Ferox preferred to make clear that it was not through any lack of care or precaution on his part. Enica did not come, although the bulk of the men he led were her Brigantes, and he gathered that she had no enthusiasm for the tribune's company.

Piso said little during the long ride up the valley, and Ferox got the distinct impression that the man had no interest in anything that a mere centurion could say. Sabinus was with them, and tried to engage the tribune in conversation, most often talking about I Minervia, but the responses were brief and surly so that after a while he lapsed into silence and found plenty of reasons to ride back down the column to check on the men. Unlike many aristocrats, Piso did not enjoy the sound of his own voice sufficiently to crave any audience at all. He expressed surprise at the size of the whole force.

'They're just barbarians, and we are at peace,' he said, and was unimpressed when Ferox spoke of the ambush of his patrol and of the suspicions that he and Hadrian shared. Piso's lip curled at the mention of his commander, but his scepticism was obvious. 'The war here was won three years ago and there won't be another. They may be barbarians, but they know the might of Rome. Behind every man who rides with us today, they will see the hundred or a thousand who would follow if there is trouble.' He grinned, and was the most affable he had been all day. 'If you wish to rise in the army, centurion, you must see the bigger picture. We represent the full empire and majesty of Rome, even when we have a rabble of our own barbarians and not legionaries with us today.' His voice was loud and he obviously did not care who heard his opinion.

'What does an attack on a small patrol mean?' he went on. 'Only that there are bandits here as there are in so many lands, especially in the mountains. Your men were unlucky to be caught, and poorly trained to be caught so easily, but there is no more to it than that. Bandits are desperate men, living without gods or laws, and they murder and steal because that is all they know and trust to their very unimportance for safety. Why should we send men to hunt a few scum like that when there are so many things for us to do? Decebalus is different and his people are barbarians but live under laws of their own. They know that the empire can crush them any time it wishes – and you need to show that you know it too by your bearing and every act. So you must be audacious, centurion, always audacious for in your small way you are Rome.'

'Thank you, sir,' Ferox said, doing his best to sound sycophantic. 'I had not perceived that truth.'

Piso gave him an odd look, and soon they stretched

the horses' legs with a gallop which ended any need for conversation.

Ferox led them to within sight of the high pass. They had set out before dawn and gone at a steady pace, so that there were almost three hours of daylight left. He suggested that they camp, and that the tribune set out first thing the next morning.

'Nonsense – a pure waste of time. I'm going now, and will see whether we can get across before we camp.'

'Sir.' If the tribune wished to be audacious then that was his business. They had seen no enemies or anything suspicious during the day, but nor had they seen as many herdsmen and travellers as he would expect at this season.

Ferox made the most of the remaining light to take his men a few miles back so that they could camp on a low hillock, out of bowshot of the forests on either side of the valley. Still he had not seen anyone, and if a hundred or so men was enough to make the enemy wary then that was a good sign. Their caution was unlikely to be so great in the darkness.

'No fires,' he ordered, and was rewarded with a chorus of moans. They had nothing to cook anyway, and only rations of bread and salted meat. The camp had to be big, given all their horses, and they had brought blankets but no tents for the men, but the high ground was large enough for them all to have space, animals in the middle, hobbled or tethered and the men in a circle around them.

'I want one in three men awake at all times,' he told Sabinus, Vindex and the two decurions. 'Patrols one hundred paces out every half hour. On horseback so you can ride down anyone unwise enough to come close. You organise that, Vindex. There's no moon, so it won't be too light. Keep your eyes open. There are five of us, so first and last ones on watch do a three-hour shift and the rest two hours. I'll take the middle one, Sabinus the first and Vindex the last because he will be out a couple of times on patrol. All understood?' They nodded. 'And don't worry if I clear off for a bit.'

Vindex sucked in his breath. 'One of those nights, is it? Or are you going over the rampart?'

'Might be an idea. Wonder how much Decebalus would pay for a good centurion these days?'

'A good one, plenty,' Vindex suggested. 'But you...' He patted Sabinus on the shoulder, and now more used to the Britons and their rough ways, the officer only started a little. 'The centurion here likes playing games at night, my lord. Silures are all like that. Ugly buggers you see, that's why they go out at night when they can hide.' Sabinus did not seem reassured.

The first arrow hissed into the camp part way through the second watch, flicking a sentry's cloak without doing any more harm. He turned towards the direction from which it had come before pitching forward, a second arrow in the small of his back. His companion was shouting the alarm, as another flew high overhead and grazed one of the horses.

'Keep down!' the decurion screamed. 'Use your shields!'

Sabinus had leapt up from his blankets, jerked from sleep that had come late and with difficulty. A man pushed into him, then there was a dull smack and the Brigantian fell, the shaft of an arrow sticking from his eye. Someone else screamed in pain, and a horse whinnied and broke free of its tether. The others were stirring, panicking.

'Get them under control!' Sabinus shouted and ran to grab the mane of one of the nearest. 'Whoa, boy, whoa!' he cooed to the animal.

One more arrow whipped through the air above him, but order was coming to the little camp.

'Wait for 'em, boys,' Vindex shouted.

'Stay together,' called one of the decurions.

There was silence.

'Where have the bastards gone?' someone asked.

'Quiet!' snapped the decurion.

A man screamed, some way away in the darkness. There was a grunt, a clash of blade ringing on blade and then a yell so unearthly that Sabinus shuddered and feared that the horse would bolt, so he patted it and ran his hand through its mane. The cry went on, longer and longer until he prayed that it would stop.

'Taranis!' came a voice from close by. 'The poor sod.'

'Shut up, you stupid bastard,' snapped the decurion, obviously unnerved by the sound.

No more arrows came and the silence enveloped them again. They waited. Sabinus felt that the horses were calm now, and knew that it was his duty to see what was happening. He stumbled over the corpse with the arrow in its eye, recovered and then went where he thought that he had last heard one of the decurions.

'Best keep down, sir, or find a shield,' the decurion said from the shadows.

'Looks like you are in charge,' Vindex added, his teeth white in the dim starlight.

'Where is Ferox?' Sabinus asked, forgetting to call him the Lord Ferox after the fashion of these folk.

'Is he down?' The decurion was still nervous.

'You in the camp!' The shout came from outside. 'I am coming in. Don't do anything daft!'

'There he is,' Vindex said cheerfully.

A darker shape appeared against the night, turning into a man as he walked closer. He had something bulky in each hand and when he came close Sabinus smelled the blood.

'One got away,' Ferox said as he dropped three severed heads onto the grass.

'You're getting slow, old man,' Vindex told him.

Ferox grunted. 'No harm in letting one tell the story. Might make them cautious next time. He won't be back tonight and there is no one else around. Still, be prudent to keep a good watch. Did we lose anyone?'

One man was dead, the sentry wounded badly and there were a few scratches to men and horses, but it could have been worse. Ferox wished that he had a few dozen Silures to stalk the nights and make the enemy fear the darkness. Still, if they had faced thirty or forty of his fellow tribesmen then they would have lost many men, and most if not all of the horses would have been dead, crippled or stolen, leaving them with a long march to the fort, and at least one more night of murder, so that few if any would have made it back.

The next morning the sentry was feverish, but clinging on and they rigged up a blanket on a couple of poles which could be dragged along by a horse. There was no sign of the enemy, apart from the three headless corpses of the men Ferox had killed. He had tied the heads to the front horns of his saddle, so that they dangled there as he rode, just like the heroes in the songs of the tribes. The Brigantes liked that, and he suspected that Vindex was feeding the stories about the skill and savagery of the Silures in the darkness, and most of all the centurion.

Sabinus was fascinated by the sight of the heads bouncing as Ferox's horse walked along. One had a truly ghastly wound that had destroyed the right eye. It was unlike anything he had ever seen, even in the arenas, but he had not had the courage to ask how it had been inflicted and wondered whether that had provoked the appalling cry of pain they had all heard. Ferox had scrubbed his hands when they came to a stream, without removing that much of the dark blood engrained in the nails of his right hand.

'Daci,' Ferox had said when Sabinus managed to ask about the man who had lost his eye. The head was bearded and had shaggy, but quite short fair hair. 'Getae,' Ferox had told him, lifting another with longer hair and a network of tiny dots tattooed on his forehead. 'Probably Piephigi as they are face painters.'

'What about him?' Sabinus asked. The third head was older, thickly bearded and with long black hair.

Ferox shrugged. 'One of ours, once. Who knows? Maybe a Gaul or a German. Probably had a Dacian wife and children by now, and his own few fields to till.'

'Poor fellow.'

'Depends on your point of view,' Ferox said. 'But these were no bandits or even the warriors of a local chief – they were king's men and that can only mean trouble for us.'

'What about the tribune?'

'What indeed? We could not catch him even if we wanted.'

They saw no enemy for the first few hours, until Vindex and another of the Carvetii who had been riding as rearguard came up to join them.

'I've seen them,' Ferox said. 'Three horsemen, sometimes a mile back, sometimes a little further.'

'Shall we scrag 'em?'

'Wouldn't get close in the open. No, they're showing themselves to us.'

'Why?' Sabinus asked. 'Up to now they have been careful.'

'They want us to believe that they are not afraid of us,' Ferox spoke loudly.

'And they are?' Vindex sounded dubious.

'Of course, we are Brigantes. If they do not fear that name now then they soon will,' Ferox said and hoped that he could make it come true.

That had been six days ago and ever since then he had worked them even harder than before. More obstacles were dug in front of the ditches, and under Ephippus' supervision they added to the ramparts and towers, mounting as many more ballistae as could be made to work, and protecting the positions around them. A high timber wall was made in front of the monâkon, so that it could lob missiles over, but would be hard for the enemy to hit. Ephippus experimented, painting markers to allow the engine to shoot without seeing the target as long as someone called orders down from the tower.

The fort was stronger that it had been, and with more men to defend the long walls they had a better chance of holding on for a while. Yet unless Hadrian or someone else sent a big column, marching hard and quickly as soon as news reached the Danube of any attack, then it would not matter in the long run.

Desertions, which had sunk to a trickle since Enica arrived, died away altogether in the days after they came back from escorting the tribune.

'They like the tits on the flag,' Vindex claimed. 'And on the…' He gave a big and obvious wink. 'Never mind.'

Ferox had to admit that through magic or charm the queen had changed the spirit of the Brigantes and even the other soldiers. Bran and Minura were her shadows, following her everywhere, their swords ready, and that gave him comfort. They both stood, with helmets and armour of polished scales, at the parade to wreath the standards. Claudia Enica for once was not armed, but while she wore the dress of a fine Roman lady she had her long hair unbound and falling around her shoulders. Ferox had to admit that it suited her. Seeing him staring at the vexillum with its bare-breasted goddess, she had for a moment glared in feigned disapproval.

The parade was followed by sacrifices and a day of light duties, for there was no sense in exhausting the men too soon. A few patrols went out, but since the tribune had left and the night attack on their camp, he had changed the pattern. Unless they went wholly by a route in the open, then detachments going up the valley did not go as far as before. He did not have the strength to challenge the enemy too far from the fort and did not want to lose men here and there, or have the rest depressed by casualties. The price was not knowing so much about the enemy or what they were doing, and that bothered him, but he could see no other way.

It was not a long parade, and the mood was good when he gave the order to dismiss, after small escorts of ten men from each contingent had marched the wreathed standards back to the principia.

'Husband,' Claudia Enica called to him as the men filed away. Bran and Minura waited a few paces behind the queen, the girl attracting a fair few admiring glances as men trudged away.

'My lady?'

'We would be pleased if you would dine with us in the praetorium this evening – Sulpicia Lepidina and I.'

'It is my house, you know,' he said.

'Whatever has that got to do with it? I own you, so everything that is yours is mine.'

'Then I shall be delighted.'

'Yes, you will, otherwise I will sell you, although I doubt that I shall get much in return.'

'Much obliged, I am sure, my queen.'

Claudia Enica cocked her head to one side. 'Do you know, I do not believe that you have ever called me that since I arrived.'

'I only just recognised you from the flag.'

Her green eyes flashed. 'Huh!' The sound was pure Brigantian, pure Enica. 'Since there is no time for Vindex or anyone else to kill you and I cannot be bothered, you had better still come to dinner.'

Ferox bowed. He let the queen and her guards pass and stood for a while, staring up the valley and wondering who the Dacian leader was and what he was thinking.

Finally, he strolled back towards the fort, knowing that the responsibility was his and his alone for this place and all these people. The three heads he had taken were on spikes above the porta praetoria, their skins already tinged with green. Guards looked down at him from the towers. Few commanders ever wandered on their own as he sometimes did, but they were getting used to his peculiar ways. Knowing that Philo was bound to be waiting and ready to fuss, he did not hurry, but went to the principia for a while. There were reports and returns to read and some to write as there always were. If he liked some of the numbers more than he had a month or more ago they still were surely not enough. Even so he felt happier than he had for some time.

XVIII

Dobreta
The day before the Ides of May

HADRIAN LET THE masseur do his work, for this was one of his own slaves, and not one of the butchers you tended to find around army bases. He was in the praetorium at Dobreta, on the west bank of the river, and sharing the house with an equestrian tribune from I Minervia. The fellow had offered to vacate altogether, but Hadrian had insisted that he and his family stay and keep the lion's share of the rooms. Word would spread, and it was easier to lead happy officers than sullen ones. Apart from that he did not intend to be here very long, so could put up with the tribune's noisy and badly behaved children, and unctuous attentions of his plump little wife, who was a freedman's daughter and absurdly excited to have a senator and relative of the emperor in her house. Thankfully she fell into mumbling incoherence whenever they met, so did not chatter away in useless flattery or irritate him too much.

An hour earlier she had come upon the legate wrestling in the courtyard garden in the middle of the house, facing off against Ajax, a former professional now in his service. They were naked and oiled, as men should be, sparring on a patch of sand set down for the purpose, and the woman had appeared from nowhere, two maids behind her with baskets of purchases from the market. The mistress had shrieked, the slaves dropped their baskets, but Ajax had not been distracted and they had held the lock until they broke apart, honours even. Hadrian had stood up straight, and greeted the woman, who was now blushing crimson. Perhaps he was cruel, although when the story spread through the ranks of the legion – as it surely would – he had little doubt that men would laugh at her rather than him. For all the mistress' shock and embarrassment, she had lingered long enough to take a good look, and that would surely become part of the story as well. Her husband was a slight, rather weedy little man, and the sight of Hadrian's tall, well-proportioned and highly trained body was probably a treat for her. He smiled as he lay on the table and the masseur moved on to his thighs.

The bout and the massage made him feel well, for he was getting back into a better routine than had been possible during his travels. He had told Ajax not to go easy on him, and the man knew his master well enough to do as he was told. The first few bouts had been painful, for a man lost his edge so quickly without practise, but this morning he felt that he was getting back to his peak, as muscles loosened and toned. Soon there would be no time for training, so he wanted to make the most of the chance and revel in that sense of being a fit and civilized man.

The war was coming soon. All that he had seen confirmed his suspicions, and made him realise that there was less time than he had thought. No one else of high rank seemed to see what he saw, but that was all to the good for Dacia was a bonfire waiting for the torch to ignite it. The image reminded him of the fire at Piroboridava, of those desperate hours as they brought it under control. Once it was raging you had to channel and starve a blaze, which meant sacrificing some buildings to save others, tearing them down so that there was no fuel for the flames. Now it was a question of controlling, slowing and preserving what mattered. A mere legatus legionis like Hadrian could not extinguish the inferno that was soon to erupt – nor would the emperor thank him for doing so. Dacia had been Trajan's victory three years ago and making that success final was his task and his alone. Hadrian's task was to prevent the start of the war being too much of a disaster.

Men would die whatever he did, probably many of them, for the garrisons across the Danube were scattered and vulnerable and nothing could be done about that. A few small disasters were both inevitable and useful to prove the seriousness of the situation to those far away. What he needed to do was make sure that the losses served a purpose, channelling the blaze and giving him the chance to slow it and then stop it, while making sure that all could see what he had done.

A slave entered and coughed, in case his arrival had gone unnoticed.

'What is it?' Hadrian asked. The masseur continued his work, knowing his master's preferences.

'The noble Lucius Marcius wishes to see you, my lord.'

'Let him come in,' Hadrian said, suspecting that the tribune had come on business.

If Marcius was surprised to see his commander naked and being rubbed by a slave, he did not show it. 'Half of the waggons are now across the river, my lord. The remainder will have to wait for tomorrow as the ferry is needed for a caravan of merchants who have the permission of the legatus Augusti to cross.'

Hadrian sniffed.

'Once the rest are across there will be forty-seven waggons and two hundred pack mules, carrying a mix of wheat, flour, salted bacon and wine,' Marcius said. 'The detailed list is here.' He passed a writing tablet to the slave who had ushered him in. 'It is a great deal, and I cannot help wondering whether they have the space for it at Piroboridava.'

'They will make the space, my dear fellow. I doubt that they have rebuilt any of the lost granaries, but I am sure that they can find somewhere for everything to go.'

'Yes, my lord.'

'You still appear troubled, my dear Lucius.'

Marcius gulped nervously, but to his credit persisted. 'It is the escort, my lord. Fifty infantrymen and a dozen cavalrymen all under a mere duplicarius and from a ragbag of different units. It seems too few for such a large convoy.'

'There are the galearii – they will double the numbers.'

The struggle not to point out that the army slaves were poorly trained and unprepared for any serious fighting was plain on the tribune's face.

'We are not at war, are we?' Hadrian asked.

'No, sir, but the Roxolani tend to be thick on the ground at this time of year. They are thieves, my lord, and utterly brazen when they are tempted and believe the pickings to be easy.'

Well done, for seeing the threat, Hadrian thought to himself, his opinion of Marcius steadily improving. 'But I cannot spare you to go,' he said out loud and enjoyed the shock on the man's face. 'Nor an escort commensurate with your rank. Nor can I spare even a centurion and a couple of hundred legionaries. The bridge is what matters more than anything else and we must get it finished.' That was an excuse he was using a lot, for he had taken it upon himself to see that the work was done. Apollodorus resented his involvement, but was glad of the fresh impetus and increase in the labour force. Hadrian had even persuaded the governor to send more troops, including half of the men from Legio I Minervia currently at Viminiacum.

'Still,' Hadrian went on. 'I am pleased with your diligence and willingness to speak up. Find a reliable cavalryman to carry a message to Piroboridava with all haste. I shall order Ferox to lead a strong force out so that they can meet the convoy half way and protect it on the rest of the journey. Does that satisfy you?'

'Of course, my lord,' Marcius said, lying reasonably convincingly in the circumstances. It was no real solution, for the convoy would be on its own for two or three days given the slow plod of the draft oxen.

'Risks sometimes cannot be avoided, and unless we could find several hundred spare soldiers we could not make them absolutely safe. We have not the men available, and even if we had they would need to eat on the journey, which would mean adding another twenty mules or a couple of carts because they would all need to come back.' Hadrian was exaggerating, but only a little. 'The more men we add the slower they will all go and the more food is wasted on the journey. And if we add a handful it will not make any real difference should there be an attack. ... But I do not think there will be any attack, for the Roxolani would not take the risk of punishment. They will know that Ferox has a fair few cavalrymen, and that it would be hard to make off with waggons and not be caught.'

'Yes, sir.' Marcius' face was wooden, and Hadrian could not blame the man at all. The flaws in all that he had said were obvious to anyone with a little sense and experience, and the tribune had both.

'It is a risk, but soldiering has a lot of risks,' Hadrian said blandly, and knew he must sound like a fool. This was a gamble and a deliberate one, based on how he felt people behaved, and especially barbarians. Added to that was Ferox's account of his visit to the Roxolani and his comments on where their loyalty lay. The convoy and its escort might well be one of the houses he had to pull down to stop the fire from spreading, a prize too tempting and too weak for the Sarmatians to resist. If not, then the food would reach Piroboridava and give the garrison a greater chance of holding out for a long time if there was a siege. 'But make sure that the trooper who takes the letter to Ferox understands how important it is that he gets there quickly. That ought to give them time to put together a column and meet the convoy in plenty of time.'

'Sir.' Marcius left, and Hadrian turned his mind to the letter he was writing to Trajan. The wording was delicate, and at the same time had to appeal to the princeps' preference for direct, soldierly reports. In it Hadrian spoke of his certainty that war was coming:

Decebalus is preparing and breaking every part of the treaty. Apart from his attack on the Iazges, his envoys go about the tribes of the whole area, bribing with gold and promising more. His forts are being rebuilt, his army trained and deserters welcomed with rich reward. It is only a question of when he will strike rather than if, and at present our garrisons are spread out and weaker than they should be, with so many men detached from the standards on other duties.

That was a nice touch, for it was an obsession of the emperor that units were depleted by the demands of communities and officials for officers and men as escorts or to police roads and cities.

In the past, Decebalus and other Dacians have launched unprovoked surprise attacks on our provinces and allies, and it is surely most likely that they will do the same once again. An attack using one of the mountain passes – or by the king's allies across the plains against Moesia Inferior – could get across the Danube and lay waste a wide area before sufficient soldiers can be gathered to stop it.

Hadrian wondered whether that was quite right. He wanted to show a rare insight without too accurate a prediction, which might raise questions as to why he had not done more or spoken up sooner.

I have arranged to revictual the garrison at Piroboridava, which included veterans from Legio I Minervia and a strong force of Britons recruited in the wake of the troubles in that province several years ago. The post is commanded by Flavius Ferox, centurion of II Augusta on

detached service, and in spite of his humble origins he
appears to be a capable officer. Yet this fort is isolated,
and the only one guarding the road leading directly to
Dobreta and the works there.

Was that all too specific? By the time the letter arrived
in Rome Hadrian had little doubt that the war would have
begun, and he was sure that he was right and one of the
main attacks would strike first at Piroboridava heading for
the great bridge. Perhaps there was a way of hinting at all
this and he would need to think about it.

Timing was the key. Hadrian wanted Trajan to receive
and read the letter only a few days before the first news of
the outbreak of the war reached Rome. That way it would
do little to change the emperor's plans, but should stand out
fresh in Trajan's memory as a lone voice of clarity and sense
in all the shock and confusion.

Decebalus has grown strong once more and will soon
reveal himself as the enemy of the res publica. I humbly
suggest that strong forces be concentrated here on the
Danube under your personal supervision to deliver the
much deserved – and I am sure final – punishment.

There was rarely harm in recommending what someone
was planning to do in the first place. This was Trajan's war
and he would win it.

The masseur had stopped and Hadrian pushed himself up
from the table. He gave the man a smile. The slave was one
of the ugliest people Hadrian had ever seen, but also one of
the finest at his trade.

'Thank you, Sextus,' Hadrian said. 'That feels much better.'

Hadrian made up his mind. The letter would be sent in three days, which ought to mean that with luck it would reach the emperor by the end of the month. Trajan was always restless at this time of year, like anyone else with sense, itching to get away from Rome before the hot and muggy weather set in. When this emperor thought of travel, his mind went first to thoughts of camps and marching armies.

Yes, three days should be just right. That also gave time to consider every phrase to make sure that it was perfect.

XIX

Piroboridava
Thirteenth day before the Kalends of June

'I DO WISH that you would reconsider,' Ferox said.

'You are persistent,' Sulpicia Lepidina told him, before prising an oyster from its shell. Ferox had learned by long practice not to wince at the sight. The Silures did not eat anything that came from the sea, lest it pollute their souls.

'He is,' Claudia Enica said. 'Like a dog with a bone. So tiresome.' Tonight she was once again the Roman lady, in a smooth silk dress so thin that it was like the drapes on a statue as she lay, propped up on her elbow. There was no one else on the couch, for with just the three of them dining each reclined alone.

'There is unlikely to be another opportunity,' he said. 'You could come with us to meet the supply train, and then you and your whole household travel straight back with the escort to Dobreta.'

'Take care that persistence does not stray into discourtesy,' Sulpicia Lepidina told him. 'As the wife of an officer it is my duty to stay.'

'But you are not my wife, lady.'

'Really,' Claudia purred, 'you used not to be so sure.'

Lepidina shot a glance at her friend. 'Now, now, children, behave nicely.' Until then, Ferox had almost been able to forget that he was dining with a former lover and a wife who still kept her distance.

'I am no stranger to hardship or danger,' Lepidina went on. 'You of all people must know that. But the children and I have come this far to be with my husband. Soon either Cerialis will send for us to join him where he is or he will go to join his legion and either collect us on the way or send word. Until then, I should prefer to be here. The air is healthy for the children, although the soldiers spoil them, and I have the company of my dearest friend. That is a good deal more pleasant than the boredom of a town like Dobreta, filled with gossip and lonely officers on the prowl for any unaccompanied lady. I feel safe here.'

'But I fear that is not true,' Ferox said.

'It had better be, husband!' Claudia Enica toyed with a small table knife.

'That was not my meaning,' Ferox said, making a final effort with his last lever. 'This fort is a long way from any help if we are attacked. The risk is too great for the children.'

Claudia Enica screwed up her face. 'So we ladies no longer concern you? Callous man!'

Lepidina raised her voice as she ignored her friend. 'The answer remains no. We – that is I – appreciate your concern, knowing it to be genuine and from the highest of motives. But I ask you to consider this as a soldier.

'We are here, and have been for some time now. There are only three of my husband's Batavians with us, the ones who came with our escort, but they talk with the others. Thanks in no small part to Claudia here…'

'It's always down to me,' her friend preened like one of Lepidina's cats.

'As I was saying, thanks in some small part to my dear and immodest friend and her strange fascination with swords and killing, your men here are in good spirits.'

'Trying to look up my skirt, that's what it is – and that wretched flag. We all know where men do their thinking…' came the muttered commentary from the other couch.

Sulpicia Lepidina waved an arm to hush her. 'Sometimes your wit can be too dazzling, my dear! And sometimes you think that you are the only one with eyes and ears, Flavius Ferox. I have followed the standards for more than six years now, and I believe I have learned something about soldiers. These men may not like you, but they have come to trust you and they all sense that something is going to happen. That business with the catapult made plain to anyone that you expect trouble – bad trouble and soon. With you – and with this little spoiled school girl at your side – they reckon that they can win, or at least survive. If the trouble is as bad as you suspect, and I have little doubt that it is, for trouble seems to find you wherever you are, then you need every advantage you can find.

'They've heard some of the stories about you. I've told several of the officers about an island far away, and a tower, and you and Vindex and that handful of men holding off hundreds of savages.'

'There was a woman too, among those fighters,' Claudia Enica added, respectful this time, for Brigita had fought at Ferox's side.

'Indeed there was – and now he has you at his side to distract him and poor little me to protect!' Lepidina threw back her head in a great laugh that always came as a surprise from so poised a lady. 'My point is that you give them hope. A thin, fragile hope perhaps, but hope still and that is a greater weapon than any one-armed catapult. You told me as much long ago.'

Ferox did not remember, but perhaps he had said something like that.

'If I leave now, and take my children with me – even if I leave a silly girl behind to play soldiers – then what does that say?' She stared at him, her blue eyes looking very dark in the lamplight. 'It will tell them that you do not really believe after all, and that perhaps they are doomed and then that slender thread of hope snaps and cannot be repaired. What are all our chances then? Like it or not, you need us here. And I know my duty.' Lepidina sighed. 'There is something about you Flavius Ferox that always makes me sound like a schoolmaster lecturing a thick-headed boy.'

'Sounds about right,' Claudia said. 'But even the dullest must see wisdom in the end when so patient a teacher explains. And you once told me, husband, that men without spirit will never win.'

'I never realised I talked so much,' he said, knowing that he had lost because they were right.

'You do,' Claudia Enica said. 'When you are not sunk in sullen silence you prattle away like… well like a certain beautiful young queen.'

'Hardly that, my dear,' Lepidina said fondly. 'Hardly that.'

Privatus interrupted them. 'Excuse me, my lady, but you

did ask me to interrupt. Young Marcus is not sleeping and the girl is worried about him.'

'He had a fever earlier,' Lepidina explained, seeing Ferox's concern. She was already on her feet. 'Not a great worry, but I had better take a look and see what I can do. You will excuse me, won't you?'

Ferox stood up out of respect. 'Of course, lady.'

'She is right, husband, as she usually is,' Claudia said when they were alone again. The food was long since finished and although the slaves would appear soon enough to clear away once they called, none waited inside the room.

'I know, wife. Or should it be queen?' Ferox remained on his feet. Claudia Enica stretched out on her couch, the silk dress spreading over her like liquid as her legs moved.

'It should be both.' She rested her chin on her hands to watch him. 'And it should be my lady, and my love and my mistress. Or to put that in the silver-tongued speech of the prince of the Silures turned centurion of Rome, something like this.' She grunted loudly. 'Does that sound about right?'

Ferox shrugged. 'I have always thought my voice a little sweeter than that, but close enough.' He went over to her couch and sat beside her. 'Words have never come easily, not when I am with you.'

Claudia Enica turned to lie on her side facing him, one elbow on the raised end of the couch to support her head.

'Oh, it's my fault, is it?'

'In a way, yes. You overwhelm me – you always have.'

'You sound like Caesar – "And the Belgae attacked their country, laying waste to the tribe's lands."'

'Sorry. Huh!' he grunted. 'Is that better?'

'More familiar at least.'

'It's just that you are beautiful, so very perfectly beautiful. Your skin is softer than the silk you wear, whiter than the snows, and your eyes seem to see right through me. Makes me feel naked and helpless.'

'Hmm, getting better. But you have not yet spoken of my hair. Surely even you remember that you must always tell a woman that she has the loveliest hair.'

'Well, it's not blonde!'

'Pig.' Claudia Enica rolled so that she was on her back and gave him a smile that was almost shy.

Ferox reached over to touch her hair, drawing out one of the many pins fastening it into place. 'Your hair is magnificent, the hair of a queen or a nymph.' He eased himself up onto the couch properly.

'Not a goddess? There is divine blood in my family – perhaps Caesar's as well if my poor fool of a brother was not mistaken.'

'I worry about impiety,' he said, close to her now, but still sitting up. His hand found her leg, just below the knee, touching lightly as if she was made of the most fragile glass. Memories were coming back, yet after all this time there was nervousness as well. She was beautiful as he had said, and he had always wondered why she had ever wanted to be with him.

'We are becoming bold, centurion.'

'That is why they pay me, my queen.' He smoothed his fingers, feeling her beneath the thin dress. Royal family or not, her clothes and finery were always very expensive and sometimes he wondered how she could afford so many.

Claudia Enica did not react or move, her eyes still staring up at him.

'Tell you the truth, I'm a bit worried about this.' His hand clasped her knee through the silk.

She laughed at that, but still did not move into him. Ferox leaned down and kissed her and at last they came together, murmuring without words as their lips pressed together. His hands were on her, hers on him and they lingered on each kiss. After a while he pulled slightly away.

'Here or the bedroom?'

'Why not both?'

Ferox's fingers felt down her leg and grasped at the dress. Slowly he began to pull the silk of her skirt upwards. Her stockings had a different texture, until above them he found bare skin.

Someone coughed. 'My lord!'

Claudia Enica did not hear or did not care.

'My Lord Ferox!' It was Philo, shouting now. 'It is important, my lord. There is news.'

It was a pity that the law forbade having a freedman whipped as you might a slave. Claudia had heard and was pushing him away.

'I am sorry, my lord, but they say that it is urgent.'

'Who says?' Ferox had sat up, although his hand was still high on his wife's thigh.

'The Lords Sabinus and Dionysius. They are at the principia.'

Claudia laughed and lay back on the couch, and when she looked at him she laughed all the more. She was still helpless with laughter when he left the room, trying to straighten his tunic and the toga Philo had insisted that he wear.

The man sitting on a stool and clasping a cup of wine as if his life depended on it did not look up when he entered.

His shoulders were hunched, and not from the weight of his mail shirt with its shoulder doubling, for it was clear that the burden was as natural to him as his own skin after many years with the legions. His head was bare, a well-polished iron helmet covered in dust on the table beside him. His face was grey with dust as well, save where the lines of sweat had run down it. There was stubble on his chin, several days' worth with plenty of grey amid the black, but he was one of those dark-headed men who went grey early. Ferox recognised something about the way he sat and held his head, before the memories flooded back and he knew the man.

'Here is the commander,' Sabinus said, his tone gentle. 'Tell him your news.'

The soldier raised his head, frowned and then drained the rest of the cup. 'Oh shit,' he said, 'it would have to be you.'

Ferox went to the table and offered him some more wine. 'How are you Tiberius?'

'Alive, sir.'

'Well that's something. Are you still with the Seventh?'

'Aye, *vexillarius* in the legion's cavalry.' He drained a second cup. 'That's good,' he said and held the cup out again.

'This is Tiberius Claudius Maximus, who claims to be a Macedonian and is one of the toughest legionaries in VII Claudia pia fidelis. He served with me as *explorator* when he was a young tiro – what would it be, eighteen years ago?'

'About that, sir. Sometimes feels like a hundred years.'

'So what has happened?'

Maximus had come from Sarmizegethusa. 'Three of us when we started, but the others did not make it. It was all so sudden, and the legate, sir, well he was caught by surprise, begging your pardon.' Longinus had returned to Decebalus' stronghold to see the king, but all he found was thousands of warriors surrounding the little Roman fort. The men up there were getting no more food, no more water, and the enemy were all around, watching, but not attacking. The Dacians kept Longinus as a hostage.

'They asked to talk, and there was not much choice really, was there? Some young broad stripe tribune…'

'Calpurnius Piso and a lot of other names.'

'That's him. He was senior, so he went to see what they offered and came back with good news. They wanted us out, but were willing to let us march away, keeping the Legate Longinus as surety for our behaviour.

'The tribune agreed. It was that or die of thirst up there unless we fancied attacking their whole army. We were humped and no two ways about it, so that was a way out. So the next day – the day after the Ides, it was, out we trooped, between lines of the king's men and plenty of the other wild buggers as well. Ugly lot and they were jeering as we passed. Then there was trouble and a bit of fighting before some of the king's chiefs rode up and yelled at them. The tribune and most of the officers were summoned to see the king – summoned if you please. I was riding escort, and heard them argue. One of the prefects – handsome lad from the Batavians.'

'Flavius Cerialis?'

'You know him? Good soldier, even if he did put on airs. Sorry, sirs, not my place to say.'

'We'll let it pass,' Sabinus said, his face concerned.

'Well he said that they should tell the king to piss off,

or words to that effect, and that Romans should not obey a barbarian's demands. And him a Batavian, if you please, talking about barbarians. He said that we should press on, and if they wanted a fight, give it to them, for they would not find it as easy as all that. There's some good lads in that garrison, who wouldn't die that easily.

'But the tribune says no, they must be sensible, and orders the prefect and seven or eight of the other senior officers to go with him and see the king. As escort, that meant me as well, although they only took a dozen of us. I did not dismount, but acted as horse-holder for a couple of men who did, otherwise I wouldn't be here now.' He paused to take another long drink.

'Were they killed?' Ferox asked.

'No, sir, not that I saw, but at a signal warriors swarmed all around them, yelling their heads off, pinning them all by the arms and grabbing their swords. Reckon the king wanted more hostages or something. I managed to gallop off, knocked one sod out of my path, but did not use blade or spearpoint and maybe that was why they did not press too close. There was only one centurion left in charge and he led the whole column on. Now and then there were spears or arrows, or some warrior too wild or too pissed to stop himself from charging in, slashing at us with his falx. We killed a few and kept going. Lost a few too, but the centurion drove us and there was no big attack. Bit later a rider came close enough to shout that it was all a mistake and the king had punished the men responsible, but we just kept going. Late in the day, the centurion wanted to send riders out to warn all the garrisons. Been on the road ever since. Got chased a few times and they got the others. Saw a lot of men about ten miles away, marching along as if they owned the place. All armed and singing, but praise Herakles all on foot. You might be having a bit of trouble soon.'

'You have done well, Maximus,' Ferox said. 'Now get some food and rest.'

'And more wine?'

'That too.' Ferox beckoned to Sabinus. 'Send a man to the praetorium and tell Philo to pass my apologies to the ladies, but I shall not be able to return to them until the night is well spent.'

'Shall I have the alarm sounded?' Sabinus asked.

'No, not yet. I want to do the rounds of the sentries. It probably won't be tonight, but we cannot take chances. *Consilium* for all officers in one hour's time. In the meantime, I want you, Dionysius, to write a summary of all that the vexillarius has told us and have it copied and the first copy sent as soon as that is done. Send a couple of men each with a spare mount. They need news of this at Dobreta.'

Maximus rose stiffly to his feet. '*Omnes ad stercus*, sir?'

'*Omnes ad stercus.*'

Maximus grinned. 'Yes, thought so as soon as I saw you here. Just seemed natural after all that had happened. Had a feeling that you would turn up. Like old times.'

'Good luck to you, Maximus.'

'And you, sir.'

'Odd chance running into an old comrade like that,' Sabinus said after Maximus had gone.

'Does seem like a small army sometimes,' Ferox said.

'Perhaps it is an omen.'

'Perhaps. The last time we served together a legion died.'

XX

Piroboridava
Close to dawn on the eleventh day before
the Kalends of June

FEROX SILENTLY CURSED the mist and himself for having been so certain. The mist had appeared soon after sunset and thickened, as it had several times in the last month. The bright moon was no more than a vague presence, lending the mist a faint glow, while leaving it hard to see very far. The picket of half a dozen soldiers stood as darker shapes in the gloom where the road passed between the front ditch. That was an uncomfortable job at the best of times, and a long, slow nightmare when there was little chance of seeing an enemy until they were almost on top of them. All they could do was stand and wait, staring out into nothing and wondering when the attack would start. Ferox had been sure that the Dacians would attack, making the most of the night and the even heavier veil provided by the fog.

So the garrison was on alert, with half the men on the walls and the rest waiting in the closest barracks, sleeping in armour with helmets, shields and weapons to hand. That is if they could sleep. Some probably could, Ferox thought, for there were always those few who were able to close their eyes and be snoring in moments. More would pretend to sleep, eyes closed, but minds racing. Others talked, and that included some of the handful actually asleep. He had heard the murmurs of low conversation and the sudden shouts and screams of nightmares whenever he had taken a walk around to see how everyone was.

Yet most of the time he had stayed here, on the tower above the porta praetoria. Without the mist, a man up here on the gate tower would see glints from the river and could just about make out the dim shape of the bridge. Instead, during this long night there was nothing much visible beyond the shivering picket and the outer ditch, while even the closest buildings in the canabae were no more than vague shadows. If they survived this night, then he would have to see about tearing them down. Their occupants were inside the fort, on that much he had insisted, and as far as he could tell all had been brought in. If the enemy had been watching they would have seen this, or the unnatural quiet and absence of activity outside the fort earlier that evening, and guess that the garrison was wary and on the alert.

Maximus had spoken of a large force marching towards them, and if the Dacians were true to character what was visible would only be a part of their true strength. There was no good reason for them to wait, especially if they knew – as they surely would, that two hundred cavalry had ridden out before dawn and headed down the valley. Ferox did not hold out much hope for the supply convoy, but wanted to give its escort a chance and give the garrison any chance at all of getting the supplies it was bringing. In the official orders, the centurion Cunicius was in charge, but Claudia

Enica and Vindex had also gone, with Bran and Minura to ride on either side of the queen, and he was confident that they would behave with sense and caution. That was almost all his cavalry. They should have a good chance unless they met a very large force, and perhaps they would be the only ones to escape if things went badly here. Yet it was odd that no word had come from them, since they had to camp out for at least one night

The night was almost spent, the moonlight long gone, but the pale, thin light of the dawn not far off. The enemy had not come and had not attacked, nor even shown the slightest sign that they were out there at all. Ferox glanced at the other men on the tower, at the legionaries and Vepoc with three more Brigantes. Their nervousness was fading as exhaustion washed over them, and even though he could not make out their faces he knew that all the men on the rampart top and in the other towers would be in the same state. These were the ones who had rested for the first half of the night, before coming to relieve the others, and then they had waited, staring into emptiness, fearful and swinging between boredom and excitement depending on each character. The enemy had not come, and all he had achieved was to deprive the garrison of rest and what might be the last good night's sleep they would get for some time.

There was the sound of creaking wood as someone came up the ladder to the top of the tower, and he did not turn because he suspected it was Sabinus or one of the other officers and that he would have to admit that he had been wrong. There was a simple water clock under a little roof on the back corner of the tower, but he did not need to check to know that there was little more than a quarter of an hour until dawn. Ferox could feel it, and then heard the first chirrups of the birds waking to the new day.

Someone coughed to attract his attention, but it was a gentle clearing of the throat, not only unmilitary, but distinctly feminine.

'Good morning, centurion,' Sulpicia Lepidina said. Her hair was in her usual bun, for the hood of her cloak had fallen back to show her pale face. 'Or nearly morning, at least. I thought that you all must be cold and tired, so have brought soup.' She held up a small, lidded cauldron. 'I am afraid that there are no bowls, so you must all share the same ladle.'

'That is kind, lady, but...'

'If the "but" is to say that I should have provided for all,' she interrupted with mock severity, 'then I am disappointed to face such doubts.'

Ferox heard low voices and the clink of metal on metal and realised that someone was walking along the rampart to his left, stopping at each man.

'There is plenty for all,' Lepidina went on, 'and if you show surprise then I am disappointed that you have such a low opinion of a senator's daughter. Supervising a meal for five hundred is straightforward compared to seating guests at a dinner.' She laughed, not her wild bray when she let herself go, but a gentle chuckle.

'Thank you, my lady,' Ferox said and gestured at the others, 'but an officer should always eat last.'

'Of course,' she said approvingly, before the laugh returned. 'Dear Claudia has been saying that you are getting fat!'

Ferox could smell the hot soup as Lepidina removed the

lid and each man went up and spooned out a few mouthfuls. He wondered why he had not thought of ordering food to be brought. That he expected there to have been a hard fight long before now was beside the point.

'The children are well – all of them,' Lepidina said, coming over to him now that the others had finished. They had all moved to the far side of the tower, grinning and bowing their heads to thank the lady for her kindness. Ferox had seen it before, how just a little hot food could lift a man's spirits and breathe new life into him. 'And she will be fine. She is a survivor that one, and has good folk with her. They will come back.'

In truth Ferox had not been worrying about the cavalry – or at least it was no more than one amid many worries. They ought to be able to handle themselves, although it would be much harder if the Dacians had bypassed the fort in the darkness and fog and pressed on down the valley. They must be mostly on foot, judging from what Maximus had said, for it was unlikely that too many horsemen would have travelled hidden through the woods at the side of the valley. Still, if some of the Roxolani were back and they had arranged to join forces... That was not a comforting thought, although quite a likely one. At least the Brigantes were well mounted and knew how to ride if they had to flee, and even the handful of auxiliaries sent with the column were the pick of the bunch as regards men and their mounts.

'They have a good chance,' he conceded.

Sulpicia Lepidina patted his hand where it held the parapet. 'You will see us all through – as you always do.'

Ferox hoped that was true, then panicked in case saying

something like that was bad luck. 'Well, I seem to have given us all a sleepless night for nothing,' he said. 'And they didn't like me much before!'

A horn blew, faint and distant, followed after a moment by the rasp of a cornu, much closer and louder.

'East gate,' Ferox said, as much to himself as anything else. 'Excuse me.' He loped past Lepidina to the back of the tower and shouted down. 'Sound the alarm!'

The three tubicines on the level below had already spat to moisten their lips and now raised the long trumpets and started the fanfare ending in a peal of three notes, repeated again and again.

'That's enough!' Ferox called down. He could see movement around the nearest barracks as men ran out. Anyone who had not woken by now was unlikely to be roused by more blasts and he wanted to be able to hear any signals from the rest of the fort. Down below a horse was waiting in case he needed it to get quickly from one side of the fort to the other. There were no more trumpet calls, nor sound of ox horns from outside, and the only shouts came as the woken men were formed up. On the ramparts and towers – at least to the little distance he could see – everyone was alert and expectant, staring out into the mist. There was no sign of any threat here, and no noise of heavy fighting from the east gate.

The gates were the weak spots as was bound to be the case. If this was a full assault with rams and other engines, then it was easier to knock down a gate than a section of timber and turf rampart. More likely, the enemy would hope to rush the fort and bring nothing more sophisticated than ladders and ropes, but even so they would attack near the gates because only in front of these were there easy paths through the obstacles and over the ditches. The porta praetoria was the most vulnerable of all, for even without this mist the houses of the canabae gave any attacker plenty of hiding places at night.

'I suppose that I had better go,' Lepidina said. 'And get all the slaves to shelter so that we are not in your way.' If she was nervous then there was no trace of it in her voice or manner.

'It would be best, lady,' Ferox said. 'But thank you for the food.'

Ferox was itching to run to the east gate, but that was not his job, not yet at least, and he had to stay here and wait for reports. This was where he had told all the officers that he would be and they all had instructions. In the intervallum behind him, some thirty men had formed in six ranks as reserve under an optio from I Minervia. Similar parties were ordered to wait at intervals around the fort, while Tiberius Claudius Maximus ought to be getting all the remaining mounted men in the garrison ready to ride at a moment's notice. Their station was outside the principia, for the horses had been kept in its courtyard, which would no doubt need thorough cleaning when all this was over, at least if anyone was left to do fatigues.

'Lady!' Vepoc's shout was harsh. 'Stop, lady!'

Ferox turned, fearing some treachery, only to see that the Brigantian was pointing to where the lady's cloak had snagged on the upright top of the ladder. He bounded over and freed the material, for she was carrying her cauldron, had the ladle tucked under one arm and was using the other to hold the ladder.

'Thank you,' she said, giving him a dazzling smile and then vanishing down through the open trapdoor.

Vepoc nodded. 'We thank you, noble lady,' he said softly, even though Lepidina had already gone.

'Well done,' Ferox said, but the Brigantian ignored him and simply went back to his place at the front of the tower.

There was still no sign of anyone apart from the picket to their front. Light was growing, giving the mist something of a milky quality, but it remained so thick that he could not see far. Inside the fort the shouting had died away as everyone got into position, and Ferox could hear nothing from the east gate. That ought to be a good sign, for a real attack ought to make a lot of noise if the defenders put up even the mildest of struggles. Still, it was hard to wait, unable to see and not knowing what was happening.

A horse came pounding across the grit pressed into the earth of the intervallum and skidded to a halt below the tower. One mounted messenger was stationed at each gate for this purpose.

'Bolanus' compliments, sir!' the rider shouted up when Ferox appeared at the rail above him. 'Dacians have shot arrows at us. One of the picket is wounded, but they have all come in. Still shooting at us, but no sign of any more.' The man spoke the words as one well rehearsed. Bolanus was the other optio from I Minervia and a solid, very thorough soldier, which was why Ferox had put him in charge at the gate.

'Tell Bolanus well done, and to keep me informed!' Ferox called, and in a moment the cavalryman galloped back the way he had come.

There was some puffing and Sabinus appeared through

the trapdoor. 'Phew, what a climb. Must be getting old, eh, Julius,' he said to one of the veterans from his legion who was on the platform.

'I've got a son as old as you, sir,' Julius replied with only a little exaggeration.

'Tell him not to join the army,' the centurion said, 'it's too much like hard work.'

'Too late for that, sir. Hear he's building some great bridge.'

'That's what I said, hard work.' Sabinus came across to join Ferox.

'You heard the report?' Ferox asked.

'Yes. You were right then – about the attack.'

'We'll see. It's not a real attack yet.'

'Dacians shot at them, sir?'

'Yes, although I doubt that they saw any of them well enough to know who they were. Might have been naked nymphs and cupids for all they could tell in this damned mist.'

'Think the lads would notice nymphs, sir,' Julius asserted from a few paces away.

The light was growing. Ferox could see almost all of the closest building in the canabae and the dim shape of the inn beyond it stood out in the white fog. He felt a breath of breeze on his face and wisps of the mist swirled across the grass in front of him. Then the wind died and the movement faded, but not before he saw something low scuttling between the buildings.

'Bring in the picket,' Ferox said. 'Quietly though. Send someone out to bring them in.'

'Sir?' Sabinus was dubious, and Ferox had no energy to

explain that he thought or sensed that he had seen someone in the canabae.

'Now. And send men along the walls to get the scorpiones ready.' During the night artillery was of little use because it was so hard to aim and there was no sense wasting bolts. Better to keep the engines covered up to protect them from the damp, but if an attack came now, it was clear enough to make a difference, and at least worth using the smaller machines. 'Tell the men they'll be coming soon – and send a runner to each of the other gates to alert them as well.'

'Sir?'

'Just do it, centurion.'

Sabinus went off. The fog seemed to glow brighter without making it any easier to see. Ferox squinted, out of habit rather than expecting it to make any difference. He saw the soldier walk out and call to the picket that they were relieved. That was good, for there was no sense in telling any enemies that they were waiting and ready. After the horn and trumpet calls, anyone with sense would know that the Romans were not asleep, but they would not be able to tell just how alert and prepared the defenders were.

The picket turned, each of them stiff as decayed old men from standing nearly still for so long, until the senior soldier remembered that so many eyes were watching and barked at them to look smart. They started to march back up the path.

Ox horns blasted, close and oddly loud as if echoing in the mist. There was a great shout, splitting into many individual cries as hundreds of dark figures came streaming up the slope towards the fort.

'Oh shit!' Julius gasped.

'Run!' Ferox shouted down at the picket. 'Inside now!' The soldiers stumbled into a lurching run, one at the rear dropping a spear. 'Leave it! Get inside, now!' The men broke into a sprint. Just one of the gates was open a few feet, with a team ready to close it the moment they were through.

'Wait for the order!' Ferox shouted, arm raised to signal even if few would be able to see it. The dark shadows of the enemy were becoming clearer, faint glints coming from spear points and the bosses of shields. Most were oval, not at all unlike the ones used by the auxilia and he could see plenty of men with helmets and probably armour. A dense knot of fifty or more were pelting up the road, closing with the picket and the open gate. Ferox never quite understood how time seemed to go fast or slow in a battle, but found himself imagining being put on trial for misconduct, with a stony-faced accuser throwing question after question. So when the enemy attacked you gave the order to run away? The order to leave a weapon behind? And it was you who had left the gate open so that the enemy could just run in?

He laughed at the absurdity of the thought.

'Sir?' Julius asked.

'Silures are all mad,' Vepoc said. 'Every one of them.'

'Wait, lads!' Ferox shouted.

Warriors were at the edge of the obstacles and some started running onwards. Ferox heard the first scream as a man crashed through the thin layer of sticks covering one *lillia* and the stake drove into his thigh. Other men stopped where they were, raising their bows. Arrows hissed as they flew, arching high over the attackers towards the ramparts and towers. One struck the parapet just below Ferox with a dull thunk. He heard a hiss of pain, probably from someone on the floor below them.

'Arrows and javelins, wait for the command. Aim for the ones on the road!' Ferox shouted. There were barely a dozen archers on the walls in this sector and as always he wished he had far more, but he wanted them to wait until they were very close so that the volley would be strengthened by the thrown javelins.

The picket was almost in, with the first man already through the gate, but twenty paces behind them the dense mass of warriors was coming on and another band of much the same size was not far behind. A few men were at the outer ditch, scattered and going carefully as they tried to thread their way through the pits, stakes and caltrops. More arrows came from the archers, one whipping past not far over Ferox's head.

'Loose!' Ferox bellowed.

It was hard to run fast and keep a shield upright, let alone present a wall of shields to the enemy. The knot of men staggered, seeming almost to jump back as arrows struck, closely followed by twice as many javelins. Half a dozen of the Dacians were down, others screaming in pain.

'Scorpiones!' Ferox called. His orders for the engines was to wait for his command for the first shot, but after that to use their own discretion.

No shield would stop the bolt of even a light engine like the scorpio, least of all at this range. There were two on the lower floor of the tower, one more up here on the top platform and a couple in each of the neighbouring towers. All of these crews could see the attackers in front of the gate without any trouble and at this range it would be hard to miss.

Ferox saw a man flung bodily by the strike of a bolt to knock down two of his comrades, and another whose head snapped back with the impact.

'Got the bastard!' Julius said with deep satisfaction as he began to crank the slider of the scorpio back for the next shot.

Ferox heard the gate slam shut beneath him. Of the leading group of Dacians, almost a half were down, whether moaning or quite still, and the rest fled.

'Stones!' he shouted. 'Pick your targets! Make each one count and kill them! Kill them!'

Men were in the outer ditch, a few spilling over the top and charging at the next one, and far more working their way through the obstacles to get to it, and some of these were carrying ladders. On the road the second band was pushing on steadily, shields up and locked together. Ferox saw a flicker of movement and one of the shields shake as an arrow struck it and stuck fast. Then a scorpio stung, its bolt driving clean through to pin the shield to the man holding it. He fell and the wall of shields quivered, but the gap was there for just an instant before another took the dying man's place.

The air seemed full of arrows. Ferox leaned to one side to see down and felt the air snap as one flicked by where he had been a moment before. Another buried itself deep into the rail of the parapet, flinging up a big splinter. It was shorter than most, and he remembered facing such bows before. They were almost like little ballistae, from some old design he had heard was Greek, making it possible for one man to carry and shoot, but delivering more force over a short range than any ordinary bow.

Ferox reached for the shield he had brought and left leaning against the parapet. Yet he needed to see and could not simply cover himself. The Romans were sending back as many or more missiles than came in, so that there was a storm of arrows, spears and stones of the sort poets described even if few of them had ever seen such a thing.

The scorpio beside him slammed forward again, spitting a bolt which created another gap in the shields.

'Got the bastard!' Julius said again.

Without needing to be ordered, the defenders were lobbing stones or shooting arrows at whoever came closest. There were a few bodies at the foot of the wall, and more on the lip of the inner ditch, but still the Dacians came and still they screamed. Four carrying a long ladder were at the outer ditch when an arrow hit one on the leg. The three staggered on, down into the ditch, slipping and dropping the ladder, but others ran to them and they were hauling it up the other bank and down into the second ditch. A volley of stones and javelins hit them as they came up again, leaving the ladder dropped just at the foot of the rampart, with two dead or dying men around it and the rest, bruised and bloodied, back in the shelter of the ditch.

'Got the bastard!' Julius started cranking the slide back ready to shoot again.

Ferox saw or sensed something coming and lifted his shield in time to cover his face as a point burst through the layers of wood and calfskin on both sides. It stuck there, lacking the force to go further, even though he had swayed back with the impact. He guessed that it was from one of the special bows, and wondered whether to try and spot the men with these and use the scorpiones to pick each man off one by one.

For the moment, the raw power of the engines' bolts had shattered the column coming up the road, leaving a debris of dead men as the rest retreated, like seaweed thrown onto a beach by the waves. Yet a third group was mustering on the edge of the canabae, swollen by the survivors of the earlier attacks. Someone was blowing a carnyx, one of the high bronze trumpets used by many tribes in many lands including Britannia and beside him there was a warrior who was surely a leader shouting and gesturing at the men.

'Julius?'

'Sir.'

'Look down the road. See the column massing and the active little fellow egging them on?'

The veteran squinted and then grinned. 'Yes, sir.'

'Kill him for me.'

'Pleasure, sir, I—'

Ferox heard the dull thump of the blow and suddenly where the veteran's left eye had been was a thick shaft with leather flights. Julius' head had snapped back, and then he sighed as he dropped to the plank floor. The veteran who had been loading gaped at him, mouth hanging open. Ferox rushed over. It was years since he had used a scorpio, and the machine felt odd and awkward in his hands as he raised the end and tried to aim.

'Come on, lad, load for me,' he said to the soldier who was older than he was. Snapped from his shock, the man laid the bolt onto the slide. Ferox was searching for the leader, but could see no sign of him, and as the column was starting to lumber forward he aimed at that and pulled the release. The slide slammed, somehow seeming slower from this angle than from the side, but he could see no sign that he had hit.

'You, Flavius isn't it?' Half the army seemed to be called Flavius these days, but the name struck a chord.

'Sir.'

'Know how to shoot this?'

'Yes, sir.'

'Then take over. Vepoc, you load for him, you've seen it done even if you've never done it. Just keep your fingers out of the way when it goes off!'

'Centurion!' A voice that had been on the edge of his hearing for a while now sank in. 'Centurion!'

Ferox ran to the back of the tower and looked down to see two riders below.

'Centurion Dionysius reports that the porta decumana is under heavy attack, but that he and his men are holding,' the first said.

'Bolanus' compliments,' the second began and then coughed for a while. It was the same rider who had come the first time. 'Sorry, sir. His compliments and says that there are a lot of archers shooting at them, and a strong force of soldiers hanging back, but no sign of an assault yet.'

'Do either need support?'

'No, sir. The lads are holding well.'

'Good, tell them we're winning here as well.'

For a moment the cheering and chanting of the enemy slackened as trumpets blared out the alarm and then followed with another signal. Ferox ran and almost jumped down the ladder to the next floor. Sabinus' head was just through the trapdoor coming up from the lower floor.

'The west gate?' he shouted.

'And a break-in!' Ferox was far enough down to leap the rest of the way, his boots banging onto the floor. 'Out the way!' he said to Sabinus. 'Stay here and take charge while I find out what is happening.'

'I should go,' the centurion had to shout because the Dacians were surging forward again and their battle cries had redoubled.

'You've got enough to do,' Ferox said and almost hauled the man up and off the ladder before rushing down. He no longer had the shield and could not remember dropping it, and then he was out on the rampart top. A Dacian appeared beyond the parapet, his helmet tall with a thin metal crest in the centre, and a curved sica sword raised behind his shield. A Brigantian was there and rammed a spear against the warrior's shield so hard that although it did not break through the wood the force pitched the Dacian off the ladder and he fell screaming. Ferox was close enough to see the top of the ladder and he pushed, trying to topple it, but there was weight from the climbing men.

'Help me, lad!'

He had wanted the Brigantian to add his weight but instead the lad, for he was little more than that, leaned through the gap in the parapet and flung his spear down. The weight was suddenly less, as the falling warrior knocked another off on his way down and with a grunt Ferox was able to tip the ladder back.

'Well done, boy!' Ferox said and rushed down the steps cut into the rampart. His horse was there, waiting for him, held by a *galearius*. The mist seemed clearer down here or perhaps more time had passed than he thought. Ferox turned his run into a leap, landing hard in the saddle, so that the mare protested and bucked until he had calmed her.

The light was changing again, and he saw that there was a red glow from behind the dim shape of the praetorium. Ferox kicked the horse hard and cantered down the road, terrified that he had made the worst mistake of all.

leading his own column and he got lost early in the night. He still could not understand how this had happened, but somehow they arrived at the river where the banks were steep and hard to cross. He knew the spot at once and that it was a mile or more from where he was supposed to be. Men stared at him, wondering, and then before he could make up his mind the first scrambled down the banks and waded across. It took a lot longer than it would have done at the ford, and left them all soaking and muddy, with more than a few lost shoes, but they were across and he tried to judge as best as he could the right direction to take him where they were supposed to go. The moon had not yet risen and clouds were low and getting lower, with thin tendrils of mist so close a man could almost think that he could grab them.

Brasus was walking near the front, with just a few of his own band of warriors a little ahead as scouts. Suddenly they stopped and word came hissing back that there were people ahead of them. Cautiously, Brasus went forward just in time to see one of the guides coming back towards him. He was at the head of the second column and they were hopelessly lost, which meant shouts and anger and trying to sort everyone out. Eventually they started going once again, and he kept the other column moving within bowshot of his men and parallel to them. Soon after that they all walked into a mist that became a thick fog and the true chaos began.

By the end of the night Brasus felt that he had walked three or four times as far as the distance he was supposed to have travelled, even allowing for his earlier mistake. Men got lost and confused and now and again there were shouts as they tried to find each other. Then as suddenly as all the other surprises he found that he was walking on the

*planks of the bridge below the fort and had no real idea of
how he had got there. There were barely fifty men with him
and he guessed that it was two hours before dawn, long
after he had meant to attack.*

*Brasus told his men to wait and walked to where the
others were supposed to be. There were a couple of dozen
men from the first column sheltering behind the building
where the Romans performed their ritual bathing, but as yet
no sign of the second or fourth columns. The fifth was to
threaten the east gate and there were more than a hundred
of them where they should be, joined by a score or so more
almost as soon as he turned up. Resisting the temptation to
take some of these to reinforce the rest, Brasus trusted to
faith and the guidance of the Lord Zalmoxis and told the
chieftain in charge here to wait for the signal for the attack
would still go ahead before dawn. By the time that he was
back by the river things were more encouraging. More than
two hundred men from the first column had arrived and a
few score men for his own force, including thirty Bastarnae,
wild folk as cruel as they were brave and unpredictable since
they were either loyal to the death or lightly treacherous.*

*Brasus waited and more men came in, and if all were weary
at least they were here. Three-quarters of the first column
were just where they should be, although barely a third of
his own men. Then a panting runner arrived to say that the
second column was on its way and ought to be in place
before very long with a good half of their numbers. Brasus
stood on the bridge, hearing the water flow underneath and
stared at where he knew the fort was, even though he could
not see it. Fate was strange, and the guidance of Zalmoxis a
mystery for now the fog that had confused them was in their*

favour because it would hide them from the Romans just as well as the veil of night. There was still time.

Dawn was close when the horns blew and Brasus realised that the chieftain must have thought that he wanted the east gate attacked whatever else happened. His own men were on their way to the west of the fort, with, as far as he knew, no sign of the men who were supposed to lead the way. No matter, the plan was still sound and the faithful would prevail over the unclean. Brasus jogged over to the chieftains in charge of the first column.

'Go!' he shouted. It was enough for they knew what to do. As Brasus ran to join his own men he heard a great shout challenging the night and his blood thrilled to the sound. Before he reached his own men there were more trumpets and cries from the far side of the fort.

'My lord!' a voice called from out of the white mist. 'We are here!'

Brasus took his time because this was the key to it all. The attacks on the two main gates would keep the enemy busy, but unless the god was truly kind to them they would not break through, not on their own. The west gate was the key, because he reckoned that it was the least vulnerable to be rushed and that because of this the Romans would not watch it as carefully.

Brasus chose fifty men to make a charge at the west gate, with the Bastarnae and a dozen others to follow them. Of the remainder, sixteen were to start crawling across the field, their backs covered in dark cloaks, and the other five came with him. They also had drab clothes and cloaks, although the black paste they had smeared on their faces was of less use now. They began by crawling until they reached the outer ditch, where they headed to the left, towards the corner of the fort. No arrows came and no sentries shouted. Brasus was trusting to the darkness and fog, and most of all to the instinct of the Romans in the corner tower and on the rampart to watch the big attack unfolding and pay little heed to quiet and empty fields. They went slowly, and one by one slipped out of the first ditch and into the second.

The noise of battle ebbed and flowed and the light slowly grew, although the mist did not thin or rise and made it hard to tell which direction sounds came from. His own men attacking the west gate were close enough to be sure and he heard them shout and then scream as they were hit by arrows or javelins. There had been no ladders left over for them to use, which meant that the assault was little more than a sham, but it sounded as if they were giving their lives willingly by pressing close.

Brasus slid over the edge of the ditch, saw no one on the rampart above when he glanced up and dashed to reach the foot. Another warrior followed him, then another, while the next man was stringing the bow he had carried on his back. Brasus had his falx, the great curved sword that took skill and strength to use, in a scabbard slung on his back, along with a coil of rope, and two straight daggers in his hands. One of the men crouched down so that Brasus could stand on his back and start to climb, thrusting the knives into the piled earth to help.

A shout from above, then the twang of a bow and the Roman dropped back from the parapet with an arrow in his face. Another Roman appeared, then gasped as the men who had been crawling forward sprang up, hurling aside their *cloaks. The pause gave the chance for the archer to string and lose another arrow, which hit this Roman in the throat. Brasus was almost at the top and jabbed the knives in just below the wooden parapet so that he could stand on them as he hauled himself up.*

There was no one in front of him and he got onto the top of the parapet and then jumped onto the walkway. A man was coming at him, but the archer loosed again and the Roman hissed as the arrowhead punched through the palm of his hand. Brasus crouched, drawing his blade two-handed and slicing a chunk out of the plume on his captured Roman helmet with the same fluid motion.

Another Roman pushed the wounded one aside. This one had an oval shield, a gladius held low and was protected by an old bronze helmet with flat neck guard mail armour and. He had a moustache and Brasus wondered whether he was one of the Britons. A trumpet was blowing as the men attacked the gates and there was shouting and the heavy thumps as the Romans shot their engines.

Brasus stood, his falx raised high above his head. Behind him, one of his warriors was scrambling onto the walkway. The Briton twitched his blade and shield, feinting, but Brasus was not to be drawn and waited. With a roar the Briton rushed at him, shield up and jabbing forward to punch with the boss. Brasus was quicker. He shifted slightly to the left, so that he was on the edge of the walkway and swung down hard. The falx was end heavy, its tip like a spearpoint and there was a hollow ring like a cracked bell as it went through the bronze of the Briton's helmet. The man jerked convulsively, pushed his shield feebly at Brasus before dropping it and his sword. Brasus staggered for a moment on the brink and then jerked the blade free. He grinned, the power of the god filling him.

'Come on!' he shouted to the men behind him and ran towards the gateway. The wounded Roman, perhaps another Briton, screamed in terror and flung himself from the walkway, bouncing and rolling down the slope into the fort. Brasus ignored him and went on. A legionary with a rectangular shield stood in his path, holding a stubby spear, until an arrow sprouted from his ear, having found one of the few vulnerable spots in the side of his helmet, and Brasus would have thought such a thing remarkable luck if he had not known better. The Roman dropped, and a Dacian appeared above the parapet.

Brasus ran on. A Briton appeared, and the downward swing of the falx smashed through his upraised shield and beat the man to his knees. Brasus yanked it free, struck again and the shield broke apart as the Briton gaped because his severed hand was still holding its grip as it fell away. A third cut went through the mail armour, through the ribs and into the wounded man's chest. Brasus had to put his foot on the dying man to draw his blade free.

'The gates!' he shouted. 'Down here!' Perhaps five men were following him and he saw a score or more of Romans waiting on the road some fifty paces behind the gateway, but they were not moving. Two auxiliaries appeared in front of him, and then the one on the right took a spear in the face and there was a yell of triumph from one of his own warriors who must have thrown it from up on the wall. Brasus ran at the other, dodged the thrust from the man's javelin and this time scythed a great horizontal blow. The man's head flew through the air as his neck jetted blood high like a fountain.

'The gate!' Brasus shouted again, and had to spit because there was his enemy's blood on his lips and face. 'Open it!' Three of his men rushed at the nearest, cutting down a Roman who stood in their path. There was shouting, commands in Latin and one of the Romans' trumpets blowing, but no one else was trying to stop them and in a moment they were lifting the bar.

Brasus turned to watch the Romans on the road. They were coming on, clashing their spear shafts against their shields, but there was something weak and unconvincing about the sound.

'Fight me!' Brasus shouted in Latin. 'Or are you a coward?' He brandished his falx, trying to provoke one of them, ideally their leader, to face him in single combat and give his men more time to get the gate open.

It worked. A tall, broad-shouldered warrior stepped forward, holding up his hand to stop the rest.

'Pig, whoreson, I will feed you to the dogs!' the man yelled in a voice sounding a lot like Ivonercus. The Brigantian had got lost in the fog, and Brasus wondered whether or not he had caught up by now.

Brasus let the man come to him, bringing the falx back up into a high guard.

'I am Bellicus of the Brigantes and I spit upon you.' The man turned back to face his men and waved his shield and sword high. They cheered and Brasus let them, still waiting for the Briton to come at him. He heard a creaking and guessed that the gate was opening. A Roman trumpet from up on the tower blasted a signal out.

The Briton came forward carefully, step by step, always balanced, his shield out and sword back ready to thrust.

'You will die, scum,' he said and only his chatter made him seem nervous, but perhaps that was the way of his people.

There was a roar, a wonderful Dacian roar, as the first wave of attackers rushed through the gate, but the warrior was still coming on and Brasus did not let his gaze leave his opponent for an instant. Instead he sprang forward, feinted left and then went right, the Briton turning his shield to face. Brasus swung down, not to strike the man, for he was still too far away, but hooked the top of the shield and pulled, gambling that the Briton would never have seen such a move before. The man gasped and let the shield go. Then he turned and ran as feet pounded past Brasus and a couple of dozen of his warriors charged forward. The Roman formation broke apart as the men panicked and fled.

Brasus let the rush pass him as he panted for breath. An older man appeared, followed by two more carrying packs.

'You know what to do?'

'Yes, lord.' The old warrior had lost all his front teeth in some ancient battle so that his grin was a strange one. There was no sign of the deserter who should have been with them to show the way.

'Then go!'

Brasus ran back to the gateway as the Bastarnae came through, yelping their strange cries and grinning like devils. He let them go, trusting that they would create plenty of chaos on their own and doubting that they would follow orders even if he gave them. Half a dozen of his men were clustered around the gate, smiling at what they had done. For the moment the Romans were hanging back or had fled, but he knew that there were still some on the tower above them.

The track outside the fort was empty. The mist was starting to rise so that he could see a little further in the pale light, but apart from a handful of his archers there was no one there. Brasus stared into the mist, longing to see shadows take shape and a rush of warriors surge out of the fog. He stared out, as if willpower and faith could make it happen just as it had led him up and over the wall. Give him two hundred more warriors and the fort was his. With one hundred he might just be able to take one of the other gates from the rear and let another column inside. The odds would still be against them, but with faith and courage it might just work,

No one came. The archers were trading shots with the Romans on the tower, keeping them busy for the moment, but as he watched one of them was pitched over by the bolt of an engine.

'My lord!' One of his warriors was calling and pointing excitedly. There was the red of flames coming from a building ahead of them, which showed that the old man was doing his job. Then there was the thunder of horses and he saw a line of Roman cavalry charging into the score or so of warriors who had gone down the road. A Roman was shouting and he saw a big man with a centurion's crest coming in against the flank of his men in a lone attack.

It would not be long now. There was no sign of any break-in from the front gate, and while he could not see the rear gate from here, surely there would have been some sign by this time if they had succeeded.

Brasus rested his falx on the ground and touched one of his warriors on the shoulder to attract his attention. The man carried an ox horn trumpet slung over his shoulder.

'Blow the signal!' Brasus told him. 'We're going!' He could sense their disappointment, but knew that they would obey. If they waited much longer there would be no chance of escape and he wanted to win, so he would return and take this fort another day. 'Don't run straight. There is an engine up on the tower, so dodge as you go. All of you first, and I shall follow!'

The plan had failed in spite of all he had done, so Brasus ran.

XXI

Piroboridava
Later the same day

FLAVIUS FEROX ACHED and was so tired that he knew that if he sat, let alone lay down, he would be asleep in moments. There was too much to be done while they had the chance and not enough time or pairs of hands to do it. Everyone was exhausted, so he had divided the fit men into four groups, and each would get two hours' rest while the others worked. It was not much, and might even mean that they woke even more weary than before, but it was the best he could manage for the moment. He had to order the officers to try to sleep when their turn came, because as soon as they realised that he planned to keep going they were eager to do the same.

'We did it, sir, we did it!' Sabinus' exhaustion manifested itself in an unceasing flow of chatter. This was the first time that he had been in any sort of serious fight, and all the fear and exhilaration combined with the sheer relief at still being alive left him elated. Ferox had allocated the centurion to sleep with the last group, the men he judged to be freshest because he doubted that the man would be able to sleep at the moment. So together they toured the fort, smiling, encouraging whenever they could, telling the men that they had fought well, and sometimes also yelling at them to work harder and faster.

'We've won, sir!' Sabinus repeated. 'Well done, boys, well done!' he added as they passed a group of soldiers carrying baskets full of stones picked up from outside the walls. They were one of several teams scouring the ditches and ground in front of the rampart, recovering any missile that could be used again.

'We have won for the moment,' Ferox said after the men had gone on back into the fort. 'They'll be back.'

'Won't be so keen next time though, will they, sir?' Sabinus spread his arms to indicate the enemy dead. 'Over two hundred of the beggars – apart from the ones we caught inside. Make 'em think twice, won't it?'

Ferox reckoned that something like a thousand enemies had attacked them, which meant that, with the fifty-one corpses that had been picked up inside the walls and then carried out to where they would be burned, around a quarter of the Dacians were dead. That was a heavy price for a failed attack, but it had not been easy. The ones charged by Maximus and his cavalry died quickly even though they fought hard. One, a stocky bare-chested warrior with a falx, had sliced away the front legs of Ferox's horse, as he was bearing down on him, pitching the centurion far and high and giving him his worst bruises of the night, He was lucky that nothing was broken, and luckier still that Maximus had appeared and hacked down before the staggering warrior recovered himself and came for Ferox.

Thirty more men had got inside the fort and they had died hard, fighting until each one had to be killed. They were

Bastarnae, that odd, half-German, half-the-gods-knew-what race, with their hair tied into knots at the side of the heads, and their fondness for falxes and long spears. Ferox had almost forgotten the ferocity with which they fought, as they charged like wild animals. Dacians, especially the aristocrats following the code of their stern religion, fought as if they despised life and willingly sacrificed it, but they also fought with skill and cunning. Bastarnae fought as if violence itself was a joy to them and there was no tomorrow, no gods judging the deeds of men.

When Sabinus had seen what the thirty Bastarnae had done in the hospital he had vomited again and again until there was nothing left to come out. Plenty of others had done the same, for the warriors had not simply killed, but mutilated everyone they found. There had been thirty-seven patients in the rooms, a couple of them men just brought in from the ramparts. One had survived by hiding in a big box used to store blankets, but all of the others were dead, hacked into pieces where they lay, hands and arms severed as they tried to protect their heads. Most of the staff were dead as well, along with some slaves and two wives who had been visiting sick husbands. The women's bodies were barely recognisable, just like the men's, left in pools of their own blood with more spattered up on the walls.

'I wonder if they...' Sabinus could not finish the sentence as he started to gag.

'There was no time,' Ferox told him. He had not been sick, even when he saw this and the reek filled his nostrils, and wondered what this said about him, but was too tired to think and too frightened of what he might learn. Perhaps it was the nightmare thoughts of what could have happened if the Bastarnae had broken into the praetorium instead of the hospital and he had found Lepidina like this, or her son, or Philo and his wife or any of the others.

A thousand had attacked and a quarter died, with more wounded who had been able to walk or had been carried away. There were no prisoners, wounded or whole. Ferox had been stunned by his fall and it took a while for his wits to recover. By then word of what had happened in the hospital had spread and no one was in the mood to take captives. He did not blame his men for sparing not a single Dacian and finishing off even the direly wounded with a quick thrust. There did not seem to have been any other Bastarnae in the attacking force, but to most of his men all the attackers were simply a murderous enemy to be killed like a mad dog. Ferox might even have given the order to execute any prisoners they had taken and kill all the wounded because such men would be a burden, needing to be guarded and fed. Still, it would have been useful to interrogate a few beforehand.

One thing that puzzled him was why there had been so few attackers, given the force Maximus had seen. The Dacians must have had a pretty good idea of the size of his garrison, and known that the cavalry had ridden away, yet had attacked with barely double his strength. It made little sense for them to launch the attack on the west gate without anyone to exploit it. If they had had a couple of thousand, Ferox suspected that the fort would have fallen and he and all the rest of them would now be dead or captive. He had left the west gate too weakly defended, since it seemed least threatened, and the men he had sent there were not his best.

By all accounts Bellicus had made a fool of himself and his men had hesitated for too long and then broken. There could not have been many more men attacking the gate and rampart than defending it, which meant the way that the Dacians had got in was even more remarkable. There was talk of a tall warrior with a great falx scything through men as if they were wheat as he charged along the wall. He did not seem to be among the dead.

Apart from the massacre at the hospital, the garrison had lost fourteen dead, and three or four more who would most likely soon join them, and thirty-nine wounded more or less seriously.

Sabinus had been pleased with the numbers. 'We killed fifteen or more of theirs for every one of ours – more than four if you count our wounded as well, and most of them aren't too bad.'

The centurion's calculations were loose to say the least, and did not allow for the other damage. A small number of Dacians had brought torches and little barrels of pitch, and had set light to a granary and two more buildings before they were caught and killed. Ferox was thankful there had been so few of them and that they had not had enough fuel to get the blazes burning more quickly. As soon as the attack was repulsed and even before he was back on his feet, Dionysius had set men to fighting the fires. They saved half the granary and its contents, helped by the new way of storage Ephippus had suggested to them after the last fire. This meant that there were wide lanes left at regular intervals between the stores and a wall of mud bricks half way down the floor, broken only by a doorway. The other buildings, a barrack block and a storeroom, had been gutted, the latter taking the bulk of their straw for feed and bedding with it.

Yet everything could have been so much worse, and the fears that thought brought to his mind helped Ferox to drive himself and the men to work. The mist had cleared, which was a comfort and although they saw a few Dacians watching from a mile or so away on the far bank, none came any closer and that left the Romans to labour with only a small number of pickets to keep an eye on the enemy.

Ephippus was supervising gangs of men tearing down the buildings of the canabae, taking all the material that could be useful. The engineer had an idea that Ferox thought was a good one, and although he was not yet ready to start work on it for a while, he wanted the man to have what he needed ready and waiting. Once they had all the useful timbers and stone they could get, the buildings were to be burned. The only exception was the bath house, which was too far away to be much use to the enemy as cover and because it would have broken the legionaries' hearts if they had had to set a torch to its roof.

'Sir!' A shout interrupted Ferox's train of thought.

'I see them,' he said, shading his eyes. His helmet had lost a cheek piece in the fall and was being repaired, so he went bare headed because Philo had insisted that he was unable to find either of his battered old wide-brimmed hats. Ferox suspected that this was deliberate, and that the boy disapproved of what he considered to be undignified headgear.

'Oh, sweet Diana, no,' Sabinus gasped as he realised where the others were looking. Higher up the valley an army was advancing. The closest were half a mile away, a vanguard of perhaps a thousand unless they were some of the survivors of the night's attack. Behind them, another mile or more, was a dark shadow like the ones made by clouds, but there were no clouds on this sunny day.

Ferox glanced around him. It was the sixth hour of the day and by this time they had gathered in all the spent missiles that he could see. The enemy dead still lay scattered everywhere, apart from in the ditches, and from a few dozen already burning on a pyre. He had lost his temper earlier when the man in charge of a work party had suggested tipping them all in and covering them with a bit of earth. As far as had been possible, the *lilliae* and other spiked obstacles had been cleared and repaired.

'Start getting the men back inside,' Ferox told Sabinus. 'There is no great hurry, but let's not leave it until the last minute.' He jogged over to see Ephippus.

'Have you got all you need?'

'Pretty much, my lord.'

'Then finish and put a torch to the lot of them.' Ephippus seemed shocked, but behind him several of the veterans grinned happily. Soldiers always liked burning and breaking things.

'Serve 'em right,' one of them said as he carried a torch over to the fire to light. He covered his mouth with his other arm to block the sweet smell of roasting meat. 'They always cheated you if they could.'

His comrade lacked sympathy. 'Nah, you just can't add up, you daft old sod.' They lit more torches from the first and walked purposefully over to the inn.

'I am not used to destroying,' Ephippus said sadly.

'You get used to it,' Ferox told him, 'and it's a lot easier than making things.'

An hour later Ferox was once again up on the tower over the porta praetoria. The scars on the parapet seemed a lot smaller than they had during the fight, when the enemy arrows had been coming at them. Someone had spread sand out on the floor to cover the bloodstains, and it crunched under his boots.

The enemy kept on coming. Through the black smoke from the burning houses he could see some five hundred men around the bath house and bridge. No one was coming closer than a long bowshot, after the first to try was spitted by the bolt from a scorpio and the man next to him narrowly missed by a second shot. Another large band had moved over the bridge and now stood or sat in the fields either side of the track leading down the valley. A dozen riders were within half a mile, and he suspected that they were leaders for some way behind were eighty or so cavalry, and behind them a lot of infantry, some marching in more or less neat columns and some straggling like a crowd coming out of an amphitheatre after the games. Beyond were waggons, lots of them, and mules or other pack animals and more soldiers on foot.

'There's a lot of them,' Sabinus said. The arrival of the enemy army had taken much away from his earlier good spirits.

'About eight or nine thousand, so far,' Ferox said, 'near as I can judge, but more coming.'

'How can you tell? Looks more like twice that to me. Almost too many to count.'

'A wise old primus pilus once taught me a trick – you count their legs and divide by two.'

'Ah, a wise man indeed.'

Ferox stared down the valley and still saw nothing moving. The cavalry ought to have been back before now, that is if they were coming on their own. The convoy probably had ox carts and oxen were slow and stupid and could not be rushed. If they had found the supply convoy then it could be another day, which meant that they had not the slightest chance of getting past the Dacian army and must then abandon them or die. That the enemy had bothered to send men across the river to wait made him think that they might have word that someone was on the way, or could just be a commander taking sensible precautions. Most Dacian leaders were not fools, as they had shown time and time again. Ferox had let the men use the bridge unmolested, wanting to keep the monâkon a secret for as long as possible. That's if the enemy did not already know about it. After all, they'd built the thing in the first place and they seemed to know far more about the fort and its garrison than he would like. Spies inside these walls were likely enough, whether some of the civilians or still disgruntled Brigantes willing to send word to Ivonercus and the other deserters. Ferox wondered whether the man was out there amid that host.

'Send for me if anything exciting happens,' Ferox told the sentries. 'And you, centurion, get some rest. No arguments this time.' He headed back to the principia where the innkeeper and several others were waiting to receive signed statements that their property had been destroyed on army orders according to military needs. The odds were that the statements would not do them much good. Legal rights for anyone living in the canabae were pretty loose at the best of times, until the garrison had been there for many years and the civilians organised themselves and were granted the communal status of a vicus.

Half way through the last hour of the day, Ferox was called back to the gate tower. There were thousands of Dacians now, close enough for him to see bands of king's men, chieftains and their kin and tenants, some groups that were surely deserters, and more than a few warbands of Bastarnae, but none of this was why he had been summoned.

'There, sir! It's them,' the sentry was excited as he pointed at horsemen coming over the rise to the south west. They had a blue vexillum standard at their head, and there was a smaller figure riding a grey in the lead.

Well done, wife, or Vindex or whoever had made the decision, thought Ferox. They must have forded the river lower down, so that they did not need the bridge. That helped explain why they had taken so long to get here, for the only crossing places were half a day away and even then could only be done a couple of horses at a time because the banks were broken in just a few places allowing the animals through.

There was not any sign of waggons or pack animals, but Ferox had never really expected that. What mattered was that the horsemen kept coming over the crest and across the field towards the west gate and as far as he could see they had lost no one.

'Scorpiones!' Ferox shouted. He did not want Dacian archers moving to shoot at the cavalry. That was the most that the enemy could do, because they were in the wrong positions to block the horsemen and would have to move closer to the fort to get at them. If they did, then he would make them pay a high price.

Julius Dionysius appeared through the trapdoor.

'Sorry, but would you mind going to the west gate to see them in.'

Dionysius gave a wry smile and hurried down the ladder. Ferox just heard one of the auxiliaries with him muttering, 'Up, down, up, down, can't the bugger make up his mind.'

The Dacians had archers with the men over the river and these ran forward to the bank. It was a long shot, but as the riders urged their weary mounts to a last great effort arrows began to loop high in the air. One of the horses stumbled and fell, throwing its rider. Another man dropped from his saddle and lay still in the grass. There was nothing Ferox could do, for the range was too great. Someone went back for the fallen man and scooped him up to ride behind his saddle. The horse took an arrow, making it kick, but both men stayed on somehow.

'Sir!'

Ferox turned and saw the Dacians carrying a scorpio forward from behind the bath house. 'Kill them!' he ordered the crew on the engine next to him. Vepoc was loading again to his surprise, but then it was odd how some men took to machines. Ferox went to the trapdoor and shouted down to the crews below. 'I want all the men with that ballista dead!' The scorpio behind him slammed forward while he had his back turned.

'Too low,' Vepoc said.

'Then get another arrow, you mongrel,' the legionary said as he cranked the slide back.

Cracking like whips, the engines on the lower level spat their bolts. Men on the ramparts cheered as one of the Dacians was flung down. Another followed as engines in the next tower joined in. The Dacians managed a single shot, which slammed into one of the last riders in the column. He shook in the saddle and the horse arched away from the terrible blow, shaking its head, but somehow they kept going and made it through the gate. All the men on the walls and towers were shouting now, and hardly noticed that the half dozen Dacians lay dead around their scorpio.

XXII

Piroboridava
Ninth day before the Kalends of June

IT WAS THE birthday of Germanicus Caesar, grandson of the divine Augustus, and a man dead some eighty-six years who had never been emperor, yet who was fondly remembered by the army. In morning orders, Ferox gave instructions for the supplication in honour of the long dead hero, although he doubted that it would be as lavish a celebration as usual.

'Anyone too drunk to do his duty will get sent out to sober up among the Dacians, is that clear?'

'No chance of that, sir,' Dionysius said. All of the centurions except Petrullus were present and he was doing the rounds of the walls. 'I can maybe squeeze a double ration of wine to issue today, but that is the most if you want it to last for a month.'

'There's always someone with amphorae stashed away,' Ferox said. 'Always.' Dionysius was in charge of the food and was doing the job with thoroughness and ingenuity, although the picture was not good, in spite of having saved some of what was in the burned granary.

'A month?' Claudia Enica said. Since riding back in she

was more inclined to speak up in these briefings and it no longer seemed odd in any way.

Ferox doubted that they would last that long if no help came, but had set it as a target. 'Thirty days. You said that we can manage that, Dionysius?'

'Yes, sir. Fifteen days on near enough full rations and then another fifteen on half and we might just make it. The animals won't though.' There was fodder for the horses and the few pack animals in the fort for barely six days. As Ferox had expected, the cavalry had found only the debris of the convoy, the men slaughtered, animals dead or gone, waggons broken or burned, and their contents stolen or ruined. That meant that there was no more food or fodder, nor any chance of getting any more.

'We'll deal with that when what we have runs out. If we have to slaughter them then may as well have the meat as fresh as possible.'

'Eat horse?' The queen's face was screwed up in distaste.

'It's not bad,' Ferox said. 'If you get it tender and cook it well.'

'Barbarian.' Claudia Enica shook her head. 'But then we all knew that already.'

'Is there enough salt?' Ferox asked Dionysius.

'Plenty.'

'Well, *commilitones*,' Ferox began, only to be interrupted by a cough from Claudia Enica, 'and honoured royal leaders who like dressing up as men.' That got a laugh, especially when she cuffed his head. 'Do you want to be on a charge, girl?' The queen held up her hands as if pleading for mercy, which made them laugh all the more.

'Well, as I said, yesterday we upset the enemy's plans.'

There were more grins. The Dacians had rested on the night of their arrival, the ox carts only arriving slowly. They camped in front of the fort, filling much of the valley with camp fires and songs. Ferox had wished that he had a few score of his fellow tribesmen to prowl the night and slit throats, but did not trust any of the still weary garrison to do such things. At dawn the enemy camp had stirred, and he had let several thousand warriors march across the bridge unmolested. Hundreds more, mainly archers, stood just out of range on all sides of the fort, but it was clear that the Dacian leaders planned to screen the garrison and march on with the bulk of their army.

When the first cart was nearing the bridge, Ferox signalled for the monâkon to be made ready. Ephippus was with them, the machine aligned by marks painted on the timber rampart that they had built in front of it. Neither he nor his crew could see the bridge, but they all knew just how to tighten the washers and crank the tension on the springs.

'Now!' Ferox shouted as the leading yoke of oxen plodded onto the timber of the bridge. He watched as Ephippus made a sign to ward off the evil eye, shut his eyes and then pulled the cable to release the catch. The arm slammed forward and the stone flew high. Ferox was sure that he could hear the enemy gasp, but knew it must be his imagination. He followed the arc of the pale grey stone as it went higher, seemed to slow and then was going down, faster and faster until it struck the leading ox on the head, smashing it into bloody ruin, and took the front legs off the animal alongside it.

'Beautiful!' he had shouted down. 'Another one!'

The second hit the rail of the bridge, breaking the wood

apart and sent big splinters slashing into the men trying to cut the dead ox and its mutilated companion free from the yoke. Ten more shots followed, and a couple splashed into the river, but the rest slammed onto the bridge itself, shattering the cart and killing men. After that they stopped shooting.

'Tell Ephippus that he could not have done better,' Ferox said to Sabinus. 'And tell him that I will do what he wants.'

Claudia Enica arched an eyebrow at him as the centurion left. 'Please tell me that you are not changing your inclinations, husband? Not after all this time.'

'Such vulgarity would be more becoming from Achilles,' he said. 'You have spent too much time with him.' Claudia's dwarf was also a fine book-keeper, and was now helping Dionysius manage the provisions. With Sulpicia Lepidina 'assisting' – which meant taking over, but doing it politely – the sole surviving medicus ran the hospital; this was becoming a truly unorthodox garrison.

'One needs intelligent conversation sometimes,' the queen said. 'But tell me then, if it is not shameful, what is it our Greek engineer desires?'

'He wants to build an acropolis.'

'Typical Greek. It will be a gymnasium next, have no doubt, and then a theatre.'

Ferox explained that Ephippus believed he could build them an inner stronghold, based around the stone buildings where they could hold out for at least a while if the enemy came over or through the walls.

'Seems wise,' she allowed.

'Yes, it is. But I do not want to start planning for retreat too early. Not good for the men's spirits.'

'I see, although I am not sure that you are right. Their spirits are high, all of them, and from what I hear of the hospital none will want to give up. You should trust them more.'

'And you should wear trousers when you climb up here.'

'It's good for the men's spirits,' Claudia Enica said dismissively. 'You should trust me. Have I ever been wrong in the past?'

'Well that could just be fluke.'

'It is the blood in my veins and the souls reborn in mine. We will win and that is all there is to it.'

'Yes, my queen. Now, let us take a tour round the walls – and I am going first down the ladder and you follow me.'

'Lecher.'

A few hours later the Dacians had cleared the debris and tried again to cross the bridge, this time with pack mules. Six shots maimed several beasts, made one jump into the river and scattered the rest. That was the end of it for the day, but Ferox was pretty sure that they would try again overnight and was absolutely certain when he heard the Dacians chanting, no doubt to cover the noise. The mist had risen again, the first time since the attack, so that they could not see anything, but Ephippus aligned the frame with the paint marks, made the same adjustments to the machine, and then lobbed a stone.

'Four more!' Ferox told him as the chanting broke down and they heard screams.

Throughout the rest of the night, he had them shoot the monâkon every half hour or so and sometimes there were screams and sometimes the distant thud of the stone landing. During the course of the day and night they used a third of the rocks prepared as ammunition, but Ferox reckoned that if he could convince the enemy that the defenders could always pound the bridge whether or not they could see it, then they would believe that trying to cross was hopeless until the monâkon was destroyed. They used ten more stones at dawn, before the mist cleared and by the time he had gathered the others for his morning orders Ferox was convinced that they had frightened the enemy.

'We've made them angry, so it's just a question of when they attack,' he told them. 'They'll want to get on and not waste time here. In the bigger scheme of things, we don't matter, but we are stopping them and the longer we can do that the more secure Dobreta becomes and the more chance there is that they will gather a relief force. The noble Hadrian promised to do everything in his power – and he is a capable and influential man.

'So that means we have to hold and keep on holding until help comes. The more they hurry the more likely they are to make a mistake. I'd love them to attack today, but I don't think they are that stupid. Instead they'll start digging and building cover, so that they can bring up their own engines and maybe build some more. All the while they use their archers to nibble at us, but we must not waste all our arrows and bolts chasing them away. Unless they are covering an assault party or workers doing something we don't like, then ignore them. Tell the men to keep their heads down and let the fools waste their arrows – which we can collect and shoot back at them when it matters. Understood?'

'Yes, sir.'

As predicted, the Dacians sent several hundred archers, some on each side of the fort, but at first they did not shoot.

At noon trumpets blared and three horsemen rode slowly up the track to the porta praetoria. One carried a vexillum, with an image of a galloping horseman on it barely visible because it was draped in ivy. Beside him was a man with an ox horn trumpet and in the lead a young warrior, wearing a scale cuirass, but with a high red cap instead of a helmet, marking him out as a nobleman.

'They want to talk,' Ferox said, waving down the crew itching to shoot the scorpio. 'No shooting!' he shouted. If the enemy wanted to waste time, then that was no concern of his. 'No shooting! Let them come on.'

'I suppose they're giving in,' Claudia Enica said quietly as she stood beside him. For some reason she had one of the Brigantes carrying their vexillum standing behind her.

'Bet the goddess has 'em terrified,' Ferox whispered.

'Pig.'

The Dacian nobleman was either new to his horse or not the best of riders, for the animal shied, turned half sideways and took the last few steps crabwise. Then it tried to turn away and he had to drag it back with the reins. Ferox watched, not wanting to interrupt.

'In the name of Decebalus, King of Dacia, Lord of these lands, the god's prophet on this earth and master of the pure.' The nobleman managed well, speaking decent Latin, until the horse spun around so he was facing away from them.

Claudia Enica laughed, an oddly light and feminine sound in such a place. Finally, with brutal use of the animal's bit, the Dacian brought himself and his horse back around. Even at this distance Ferox saw the man's eyes widen when he saw a woman standing above the gateway, her polished armour glinting in the sun. Then his gaze went higher and his mouth fell open when he saw the flag, with its bare-breasted goddess. He stared, as if mesmerised.

'Was there more?' Ferox called down.

Snapping out of his surprise, the man coughed and then resumed. 'The king wishes to avoid war and needless bloodshed. Although he can no longer permit the pollution of our lands by the presence of unbelievers, he wishes for peace with Rome and its emperor. If all the Roman soldiers leave our lands they may go free and safe and we shall have peace.' The words sounded rehearsed, and probably those of someone more senior for the young aristocrat did not look or sound stupid enough to be so tactless in negotiation. 'You may all go free and march away with your pride and honour intact, taking all your possessions. That is the promise of the king.'

Ferox stared down, saying nothing. The Dacian waited, his horse now happy to stand where it was. There was muttering behind him, and he caught a 'Tell him and his king to go hump themselves,' no doubt from Vindex.

'Your commander, Longinus, is a prisoner of our king as are all his officers. They are surety for the good behaviour of their men as they retire. The men who were at the king's stronghold have marched away and soon all the others will follow. You are the only garrison still to accept the king's mercy. Why delay?'

Liar, thought Ferox, but still said nothing.

'What is your answer?' the Dacian shouted after a long silence. 'Yes or no.'

'Can we think about it for a few days?' Someone behind him laughed nervously.

'What?'

'It's a big decision.'

Vindex sniggered.

'Yes or no!' The aristocrat was growing angry. 'If you refuse you will all die here.'

'Ah well, you did not say that. But are not men born to die?'

'Well they're born stupid, at least,' Claudia said, prompting more laughter.

The Dacian moved to say something and then stopped. His face was growing redder.

'And when you say we can take everything with us – how about the buildings?' Ferox was doing his best to sound serious.

The Dacian's temper erupted. 'So be it! You will not accept the king's mercy so you will all die! The whore as well!'

'Think he means you,' Claudia told Ferox. 'He must have heard the stories.'

Vindex doubled up as he laughed, and the mirth was infectious as the herald and his escort rode away. As they galloped past the foremost archers, the nobleman waved his hand and the first arrows took flight. The range was long, but most struck the parapet or lower down on the rampart. No one was hit. At this range there was plenty of time to see each one coming and either duck or raise a shield.

'Remember we do not waste bolts or arrows,' Ferox told Sabinus and the other officers once again. 'One arrow, one dead Dacian. Anything else is a waste. Have one of the scorpiones knock one or two of them on the head every hour or so to keep them honest but that's all.'

The men obeyed, and as the archers realised that no

missiles were coming back at them they cautiously edged
a little closer over the next few hours. The scorpio on the
top level of the main gate spitted two archers and grazed
another during the course of the day, but the few others
to shoot missed as many times as they hit and Ferox sent
word for the crews to calm down and wait. Instead a small
number of men did duty on the walls and took care to
dodge the arrows. Any looping high and coming over the
top were collected and kept if they were good enough to
use again. Those stuck in the timber of the ramparts and
towers could wait for nightfall when it would be safer to
salvage what they could. They could see the Dacians lifting
artillery down from carts and working on other engines, but
they were too far away to reach with anything apart from
the monâkon and Ferox did not want it shifted lest they lose
the concentration on the bridge, so they let the enemy work.
Now and again the sound of hammering drifted over the
walls. Only when some Dacians started setting up a timber
palisade not far from the burnt out remains of the inn did he
order the two bigger ballistae they had on the lower levels
of the corner towers to lob some stones and shatter the still
flimsy barricade.

Ephippus began work on his acropolis, starting with a
turret in the alley behind the principia that was to be as
high as the towers on the wall. He was also exercised by the
thought of preparing plenty of boiling oil.

'The fire would be dangerous, though, if we had braziers
in the towers of the gates,' he admitted.

'If by dangerous, you mean we could easily burn ourselves
to the ground, then yes,' Claudia said.

'Boiling water?' Sabinus suggested.

'Still the problem of heating it,' Ephippus said. 'I can rig up pulleys and ropes to haul cauldrons full of it onto the tower after it has been heated, but it will be delicate and easy to spill, so that those hauling the ropes will have to be careful. Or you could have men carry it in smaller vessels, either to pour on their own or add to a bigger one. It will lose heat all the time though.'

'Some oil or tar to be flung down would be useful,' Ferox said. 'A flaming arrow would set it alight when we are ready. There is just about room for a small brazier on the walkway. If that falls back there is only turf to singe and not wood to roast.'

Ephippus snapped his fingers. 'Hot sand!'

'Sounds like the sort of treatment that doctors recommend for invalids,' Claudia said. 'Might hurt a bit, but surely would not kill.'

'The Tyrians used it against Alexander's men,' Sabinus told them. He shrugged with embarrassment. 'I do read sometimes. They say it got down tunics and inside armour, scorching men, so that they either fought on in pain or took off the armour and were vulnerable.'

'See what you can do,' Ferox told them. It was late, and although the arrows still thudded into the ramparts, there was no sign of an attack, and thankfully no sign of the fog that might cover one. 'I reckon they'll throw up some works tonight and prepare their engines, then attack tomorrow or the next day.' He ordered most of the men to rest, but everyone knew the alarm calls and where to take their place. After going through everything one more time to make sure that all was clear, he made a final tour of the ramparts and then headed for the principia. The children were asleep,

Sulpicia Lepidina visiting the hospital once again, and no sign of Claudia Enica, so Ferox asked Philo for some cold food and told the man then to get to bed. For once, Philo obeyed without prolonged resistance, leaving him to eat in silence.

'On your own again,' Claudia had changed from her tunic, boots and armour into one of her silken dresses.

'I was hoping that I would not be, my queen.'

The alarm bell rang, faint, but unmistakable.

Ferox bounded to his feet, taking a bite of meat as he ran for the door.

'I was going to be gentle,' Claudia Enica said as he passed, and then yelped because he slapped her on the behind. 'Pig!' she called and then followed, hitching up her dress.

By the time Ferox was out in the street the bell had stopped, but he could see torches and activity at the east gate, not far away to his right. There was no sound, no roar of attackers, but a soldier was running towards him.

'Wait,' he said to the queen as she came outside.

'Sir!' The soldier saw him. It was one of the veterans of I Minervia, his arms pumping and legs pounding yet still moving at a slow, almost stately pace. 'There's a peasant turned up at the gate. Says he's a freedman of the legatus and has news.'

'Sosius?' Claudia asked.

'That's right, lady. What he says he's called anyroad. Says he was here before as well. Sneaked up to the gate and then called out bold as brass. Weren't going to let him in, but he knew your name, sir, and by that time there were arrows flying, but no one too close, so we let him in.'

Sosius was filthy, unshaven and had a wild glint in his

eyes. His left leg was bound up and he limped as he walked. Wine steadied him, and some food restored him, although it was still a while before he was willing to talk. Ferox sensed the veils coming back down across the man's soul.

'The Legatus Longinus is dead,' he told them at last, as they sat in the principia. 'He drank poison rather than let himself be used as a hostage.' Ferox did not ask the obvious question of how a prisoner had obtained the means of killing himself, or voice his suspicion that there was more to it than simple suicide. 'I got the draught for him,' Sosius went on. 'That was one more reason for slipping away, but Decebalus also had me carry a letter for Trajan in which he sets out peace terms, so I was able to ride out openly. That is until the legatus was dead and the king got angry.'

'And the other officers?' Ferox asked.

'Safe. Prisoners, but the big prize was always Longinus. The Lord Trajan might have pause if the life of a distinguished senator was threatened – but some young sprig of a tribune, let alone equestrians...'

'They are ten to a *denarius*,' Claudia agreed, her fingers feeling the ring marking her own membership of the order. Women did not usually wear this badge of rank. 'But the rest are safe?'

'Were when I left, and Decebalus isn't vicious for the sake of it. Especially when he is hoping to win back some land and then talk.'

Ferox glanced at Claudia, who nodded. 'I shall see whether the Lady Sulpicia is still awake and give her the news.'

'Why did you come here?' Ferox asked after the lady had gone.

Sosius sniffed. 'Nowhere else to go. My horse went lame,

then some warriors found me and chased me. Got as far as the forest before the beast gave out altogether. Managed to deal with the two lads who followed, but they stuck me in the leg and I'd lost all my food. Your fort was the only sanctuary in reach. I can't see Decebalus being too pleased with me.

'But look, I could not get too close, but I came around the edge of their camp. Heard them talking about a big attack tomorrow.'

'Then you are just in time,' Ferox told him.

*B*RASUS NEVER TRUSTED *a servant to sharpen his weapons, so had spent a long while sitting in his tent and honing the falx and his sica with a whetstone. The noise of scraping, and low murmurs of conversation were all that could be heard in this part of the sprawling camp, although now and then there came drunken singing from the Bastarnae. Working on the blades was a simple task, and his mind wandered less than when he had spent all those hours in the cave. For a while at least, he had forgotten the humiliations of the last few days.*

Diegis and Rholes had said little as he told them of the failure of his attack on the fort. Neither had criticised him openly, but they had made him report in the presence of dozens of others, and not simply pileati and men of worth, but whoever happened to be riding in their train when he had gone to meet the advancing army. Many sneered, and he heard mockery that was spoken in a low voice, but not hidden, nor reprimanded by the commanders. Brasus had failed, and he knew it, but only by a whisker and they had managed to burn more of the enemy stores.

Brasus had told them that the Romans had an engine capable of reaching the bridge, for his scouts had seen the defenders practising with it some days before. No one had believed him, and everyone seemed to blame him when the stones came slamming down around the bridge, smashing the waggons as they crossed, shattering men and beasts as if they were clay toys. He had suggested that they try going during the hours of darkness and he had been wrong about that. Who could ever have guessed that the enemy was able to guide their missiles with such uncanny precision? Yet he still felt that the leaders had given in too easily and ought to have sent the mules one at a time and then the carts slowly. A few might have perished, but the Romans surely would not realise what was happening every time? In two or three nights, they might have got enough of the essential food and equipment across and the bulk of the army could have pressed on.

Diegis would not hear of such a plan, and Rholes was willing to agree. The older warrior was paler than Brasus remembered, slower of speech, and seemed far older and less well than he remembered.

'The Roman filth have defied us,' Diegis declared at the great council. 'So they must surrender or be crushed. Now that they have seen the greatness of our numbers, they will surely give in.'

Brasus had thought that Rholes was about to say something, but after a moment the old warlord simply waved his hand, a sign of agreement among his folk. A woman mopped his brow, leaning against the chair on which he sat. She was at least thirty, a pleasant face fading with the rigours of the years, and her manner almost maternal as she fussed over Rholes. She was also the only woman he had brought with him, a far cry from his troop of companions in past campaigns. Brasus knew that he should not hope for such things, but he could not help feeling that it would have been better if Rholes still had the vigour to require more entertainment.

The commanders chose him to summon the Romans to surrender.

'Because you know more about these people and this place than any of us,' Diegis said to him, and then also told him precisely what he should say. 'If they come out we can always decide then whether or not to kill them,' the commander had added. Neither in speech nor actions did he seem to belong to the pure. 'Now run along, and redeem yourself.'

That first direct reproof stung, all the more because it came across as casual disdain rather than based on any thought. Brasus had not expected the Romans to surrender, yet felt that the army was watching, disapproving and judging him instead of the enemy as he rode forward on that dog of a horse. The Romans mocked and laughed, and he could not help wondering whether they realised that he was the man who had attacked them. He remembered the centurion's voice from that day in the forest when he had hidden from them. He had at least expected more respect from Ferox, if indeed his enemy knew that Brasus was the man who had almost taken his fort. Then there had been the filthy banner, and that pale, flame-haired and remarkably beautiful woman staring down, armed as if for war. Ivonercus had spoken of the queen in words of hate and fear, yet never of her loveliness. Brasus was shocked to see her because he had dreamed of that face many times, since he was a child and did not understand why. She was perfect and she was terrifying like some spirit or demon of the air. He had lost his temper, less from the mockery for all its sting, but because this was a vision and he did not know what it meant as wild desire fought with cold fear.

Diegis was not welcoming, asking whether he had said the words as instructed, and then whether he would fight as well as he had raged.

'You will lead your warriors in an attack to distract the enemy,' he said. 'Against the same gate where you broke in last time. At least you can find that. Draw their eyes to you, even if you have no chance of getting in a second time.'

'If it please my noble lord, let none think in that way.' Rholes' voice was louder and firmer than before. 'What is meant as a diversion can win the day. And I feel it better that Brasus take men against the east gate. The west is strongest in daylight, and we shall need the sun's smile to guide us and let us use our numbers. If we are to serve the king, this place must fall swiftly.'

Diegis breathed in deeply, his small eyes flicking from side to side, never looking directly at his fellow commander. 'Do you have something in mind?'

'I do, my lord, I do.'

Brasus listened as the plan was explained and felt his spirits rising. Almost in front of his very eyes life stirred inside Rholes, so that when he stood, shaking off the arm of his woman, he stood taller and straighter.

'We will attack at noon,' he declared in a voice that would have required a bolder man than Diegis to contradict. 'But we must not let them realise that. We will form half the army ready before dawn and show every sign of attacking, for we want them on their walls so that we can kill them. Our engines and our archers will already be in place.' He turned to Brasus. 'It will be hard, but you must get one of the three mina stone throwers in place within reach of your gateway during the night. You may have as many men as you need. Its task will be to smash the gate down if it can – or at least make the Romans fear that this will happen.'

'My lord, it shall be done.'

'Good,' Rholes said. 'Throughout the morning we will shoot at the enemy, pressing forward ever closer, so that he must reveal himself or let our work parties tear up his stakes and fill in his ditches. When they reveal themselves we kill them or wound them or at the very least tire them.

'The men who face them first will not lead the attack. Instead, the rest of the army, rested and fed, will take their place. That will require close supervision to prevent a shambles, so I would suggest that you, my Lord Diegis, and I supervise. The main attack will be at their front gate, using ladders and the ram. The second attack on the east gate led by Brasus – I fear you will get no rest, my boy, but I need you – with more ladders. At the other gates we will hold back, for the Romans are fond of sallying out and if they do I want men ready to smash them into pieces.'

The plan was longer, each chieftain told where to be and what to do, and Brasus felt much better as he listened to Rholes filling them all with confidence. Yet the woman's face kept coming into his mind, and sometimes she transformed into the naked goddess of that flag, beckoning to him, enticing and mocking at the same time. The Roxolani and other Sarmatians had women leaders, he knew that, and he had encountered one or two, always finding them strange creatures, neither man nor woman. He had heard that there was one with the fifty or so Roxolani who had come to join the army, less than a tenth or twentieth of the number hoped for. The rest had gone off with their loot and had no interest in more fighting, at least for a while.

'Are you listening, boy?' Rholes asked.

'Yes, my lord.' Brasus' wandering thoughts had not quite taken over his mind. 'You were asking how many men I will need to move the catapult. I should guess at least one hundred, with yokes of oxen and an engineer skilled in such things.'

'Sounds about right.'

Brasus wondered whether a ballista, even a large one, could smash through a well-built gate. He could not set it up within easy reach of a bow, and could only protect its crew a little. 'I should like any sacks we have or can make,' he said. 'Filled with earth we can pile them in front of the machine.'

'Good idea.'

The queen's face came back to haunt him, although she was not his queen or anyone of note, merely a Roman lapdog of a faraway and unimportant tribe. Like all her kind she was a drinker of wine, impure of thought and body. Yet she had power, a strange power that was trying to reach him. Ivonercus had spoken of her as a user of magic, and all his doubts had now fallen away. A witch queen from a dark tale and yet so fair of face.

Brasus knew the strength of their army and the vulnerability of the fort, so frail compared to a proper stone-built fortress on a high peak. The plan was good, Rholes filling them all with certainty of victory. Yet in his heart he doubted.

XXIII

Piroboridava
Eighth day before the Kalends of June

MEN WERE STARTING to die. Ferox leaned hard against the parapet as two Brigantes carried a third in a blanket along to where the steps led down. The warrior had the broken stump of a ballista bolt sticking from his chest. It had pierced his mail shirt, and Ferox suspected that the wound would claim his life because each breath came as a desperate gasp.

'Watch out!'

Ferox ducked at the warning and felt an arrow flick through the crest of his helmet. It was another new one, hastily repaired from pieces in the *fabricae*, so that there was one bare bronze and one tinned cheek piece on the iron bowl. It was a little small, leaving a clear line on his forehead because his wool hat kept slipping up.

'Thanks,' he said to the auxiliary who had shouted out. The man grinned, then bobbed down when another arrow hissed by.

There was still no sign of the main assault, but all around the fort archers and a few slingers were pressing ever closer. Some worked in pairs, with one using a shield to shelter the one who did the shooting. Others crouched in the ditches, although their V-shape meant that they only got some protection. That did not matter much for the men with the belly-bows – the name Ephippus used for the handheld ballista-like weapons used by some of the Dacians. Further back, there were more archers, many lobbing arrows high without worrying much about aim because chance was bound to find them a few victims, and the artillery. All told, Ferox had counted at least a score of engines, more than half scorpiones or of a similar size. The rest were bigger, of a far greater range of sizes than the army normally used. At first the shooting was wild, and there were ironic cheers when some stones and bolts struck the ground short of the walls, and even more when an archer had to scuttle aside, dropping his bow and scattering the arrows from his bag as he avoided a bouncing stone. Ferox guessed that the crews did not get much practise, but as the morning passed they were getting plenty and learning all the time.

Ferox pressed on.

'Hot work, sir,' a veteran of I Minervia said as yet another arrow thunked into his big, rectangular scutum. There must have been at least twenty shafts sticking out from its front already, as the soldier hefted a rock in his hand, waited and then flung. 'That'll learn him!' Two more arrows struck the shield so that it quivered, but the three layers of wood encased in leather let only the merest tip of one poke through.

'Keep it up,' Ferox told him and went on. Another veteran had a shield almost as covered in broken stumps and shafts. He stood up in the gap between the raised sections of the parapet, took aim and sent a light javelin thrumming down.

An arrow's point rang as it struck the iron boss and bounced away. Then a bigger, much faster bolt slammed into the scutum, ripping it from the veteran's grip so that it fell away and slid down the bank at the back of the rampart. The man ducked, wringing his left hand.

'You all right?' Ferox asked.

The veteran was bearded like many older soldiers. He clicked his tongue against his teeth. 'No. Bet the army will charge me for that!'

'Typical army. They'd charge you for your own spit if they could.'

'And make you get a receipt each time you go to the latrine!' The jokes were old, very old, but there was a comfort in the familiar. 'Yes, it's those bastard officers that cause all the trouble.'

'I know,' Ferox said. 'Can't trust any of them.'

There was a savage crack as the top of the parapet above the man was struck by a great stone, breaking the wood and throwing up splinters.

Ferox winced. 'I think we've upset them.'

'Any chance of a month's leave, sir?'

Ferox crouched as he went past. 'Sorry, lad, you know the army, put it in writing or bribe some centurion.'

Ahead of him, a Brigantian rose to throw a javelin just in time to meet another great stone, ripping his head from his shoulders as missile and head kept going to land down in the intervallum. The rest of the body stood for what seemed an age, blood jetting high to spray over the other men sheltering around him, until slowly the corpse fell.

'When are they coming, lord?' asked another Brigantian, as he wiped blood from his lined face. He was one of the men from the mines, and that had aged him. He was wearing a helmet today, but underneath his head was wholly bald, which made him stand out for he was the only bald man among the Brigantes. 'When are they coming?'

'Soon,' Ferox said. 'Just wait and we will all be avenged.'

'Good.' In the past the man had done little to conceal his hatred of Ferox and Vindex, but there was no trace of that now, only anger at the enemy outside.

If bolt or stone from an engine struck a defender then the man had little chance, even if he did not die instantly. Arrows flew with less force, but because his soldiers stood behind a parapet, the odds were high that whenever they were hit it would be in the head or chest. A lot of the wounds were bad, and as the morning wore on dozens were carried down from the walls. The centurion Dionysius had been hit in the eye, fortunately by an arrow that was almost spent, and he was not the only one. Helmets gave decent protection, but always left the face and ears vulnerable, for the army wanted its soldiers to be able to see what was going on and listen for orders. There were few orders to give at the moment, only encouragement, so Ferox toured the walls, smiling, praising and sharing the danger. He began to wonder whether he ought to relieve the men on the walls with some of the ones sitting in groups down in the intervallum and streets. It was a risk, because he wanted and needed reserves who were fresh to take any breakthrough head on and drive the Dacians back. On the other hand, it would not do to have all the men on the ramparts exhausted before the attack came. Ferox spotted Sabinus, walking up and down in front of one party of reserves and saw him look up expectantly.

'Another hour, maybe less!' Ferox shouted down loud

enough for everyone nearby to hear. 'They'll come by then and then we'll slaughter them like sheep!'

Sabinus did not look convinced, and was obviously eager to do something, and at least to see more of what was happening. It was tough for the reserves to watch men being flung from the ramparts by the missiles from ballistae or be carried down wounded. Waiting was harder on the mind than doing, but that was just as true for the enemy as well. So far the Dacians were doing what he would have done in their place, wearing the defenders down, weakening them, always knowing that they could send plenty of fresh men forward whenever they wanted. It was about a half hour to noon, and Ferox knew that the enemy would be nervous. Attacking a rampart, any rampart, even one like this built by an army who always expected to fight on the fields outside, was hard. No doubt there were warriors waiting away from the fighting, ready to come up and launch the attack. You could not stop them thinking and worrying, and there was the danger that they would drink too much or just lose the edge to their courage as the hours passed.

Ferox was approaching the east gate when he heard the singing.

'Oh the raven, oh the wolf, come to me and I will give you flesh.'

Ferox smiled. It was the old war song of the Brigantes and it was good to hear the verses rising as more and more men took them up and the singing spread along the ramparts. Well done, Petrullus, he thought, for it was a good way to lift spirits.

As he reached the gate tower and began to climb, he heard a familiar laugh.

'Hello, husband.' Claudia Enica was dressed for riding, with loose Parthian trousers tucked into the top of her boots. Bran and Minura were with her, and he had insisted that they stay at her side, even though the boy had wished to serve as his personal guard. 'I doubt that the Silures can sing, but you can always mime the words.'

'You should be at your post, my queen,' Ferox spoke mildly. Outside the principia, Maximus was in charge of the remaining auxiliary horsemen and the queen had a band of thirty Brigantes with their horses ready. Their job was to rush to any weak spot, especially if the enemy made it through one of the gates. Vindex was in charge of a score of Carvetii stationed so that they could cover the rear gate, which it was hard for the rest to reach. Ferox missed having his old friend beside him, but wanted someone he could rely upon to do the job.

As he glanced away to smile at the other men, the queen stuck her tongue out at him like a little girl. Men sniggered, especially when he turned back and she took on a look of studied innocence.

'Shall we all go and sleep, while those cowards outside pluck up the courage to attack us?' she asked.

'Soon, lads, they are coming soon,' Ferox happened to look as the big engine the Dacians had placed behind a mound of sacks some two hundred paces away loosed with a sharp crack. After a moment there was a pounding thump below them and the boards underneath his feet quivered.

'They are shooting at the gate,' the queen told him. 'Have been at it for an hour. There are cracks, but for the moment it is holding.'

Petrullus shook his head. 'The Romans should learn

from the Brigantes. Even your people would not build a fort whose gate could be approached – or be shot at – in a straight line. The army would do the same in a marching camp, so why not here?'

The answer was that the Romans never expected to defend a fort like this, least of all against an enemy with artillery and some knowledge of siege craft. That was why the towers were set back and did not project outwards and no one worried too much about defending gateways.

'Send men to bring up the carts from the fabricae,' Ferox said. 'And anything else to make a barricade in case they do smash the gates.'

There was silence and Petrullus broke into a grin. 'The queen has already given the orders.'

Enica made a show of preening. 'I do have my uses, you know.' She paused. 'Of course, I had forgotten that Vindex was not with us.'

Ferox was not listening. As he watched, some of the Dacians around the ballista turned and ambled away. Others appeared to take their place.

'Lady.' Ferox bowed his head. 'It is time. I ask you to return to your men and wait. If you see the men bringing the waggons then tell them to hurry.'

For once she did not say anything, and just inclined her head slightly.

'Petrullus, they will come soon. First they will blow all their horns and trumpets and raise a great shout. The gate still holds, but they may have a ram. Get your men to carry up the oil and he ready to use it.' Several small cauldrons and buckets were boiling over a fire down below them. 'Watch out for ladders as well. I shall be at the porta praetoria, so send word if you need anything. The supports know what to do.'

The men in the tower were a mixture of warriors loyal to the queen and those who had fought for her brother. Ferox tried to think of anything he might say to make them all trust him and trust that they would live through this and win. A true Roman would no doubt have made a great speech and perhaps the honeyed words would have moved spirits.

'Good fortune. For Brigantia, for the queen, for our oaths.' He feared this was too much and might seem false. 'Let's make some food for the ravens!'

Petrullus raised his arm in salute. The rest grunted. As Ferox went down through the trapdoor he just caught another inspiring cry. 'For the tits!'

A lot of Brigantes were like Vindex, for they were still cheering and laughing as he made his way along the intervallum, warning the commander of each group of reserves that the attack was coming soon. There was no way of controlling them, so he patted each one on the shoulder.

'Use your judgement, and when you hit, hit 'em hard.' Half the reserves were veterani because they were the best suited to heavy fighting, and ought to be confident. Bronzed and lined faces, beards flecked with grey, they waited, making the most of rest as old soldiers could. They would be nervous like everyone else, some because they had done this many times before and knew what was coming, and a fair few because in decades of service they had never gone toe to toe with an enemy.

As Ferox reached the porta praetoria, he heard men up on the wall talking and realised that there was an uncanny silence, with no more arrows hissing through the air. Then the trumpets and horns blared out, far more of them than the enemy had sounded before, and the Dacians raised a great cheer. He dashed up the stairs onto the rampart and headed for the tower.

'They're coming, boys. Time to butcher them all!' Men were following him, carrying boiling oil with great care and buckets of the heated sand almost as warily.

Sabinus was at the top of the tower, waiting for him. 'It's a ram,' he said, pointing at a wheeled shed being pushed up the track towards them. 'Just as you said.' He jumped back to dodge an arrow that flew between them. In moments the air was filled with clouds of missiles.

'Down!' Ferox shouted. 'Wait for the order!' Men crouched behind the parapet. There were baskets of stones to throw every few paces, and heavy siege spears leaning beside them. Crews knelt beside their engines. He and Sabinus moved either side of one of the gaps in the parapet so that they could shelter while still seeing out. Arrows thudded into wood or rattled off when they did not strike squarely.

'Wait!' The ram in its wheeled shell was coming on steadily.

'Wait!' It was at the gap between the outer ditch. Behind the ones pushing it were several hundred king's men, all with red shields decorated in a pattern of rosettes. Another unit followed and on either side there were bands of warriors, still blasting their horns and chanting.

'Ballistae!' Ferox shouted. 'Archers!' There were a dozen archers detached from a specialist cohort and a similar number of men who had some idea how to use a bow. They bobbed up, drew and loosed at the first target they saw. A few arrows struck the hides on top of the moving shed, but most were better aimed and warriors began to fall or stopped as they hunched behind shields. Scorpiones spat their darts, and the bigger ballistae in the corner towers had the sense to aim at the ram while they still could. The side of the shed shook as a stone slammed into it, but after only a slight pause – no doubt with their heads ringing – the men pushing it went forward again.

The chanting of the warbands turned into a mass of individual cries as they split up, some dashing on through the remaining obstacles and others going more gingerly. Ferox saw one man trying to leap the ditch only be struck in mid-air by the bolt from a scorpio and flung backwards. An auxiliary archer spun away as a similar dart shot by the enemy drove through his teeth and mouth with such force that the point erupted from the back of his helmet. Beside him, a comrade ducked and was sprayed with splinters and fragments of wood as a stone hit the parapet.

The ram was closer, but luck was with the Dacians and, just as the crew levelled the ballista in the right-hand corner tower to shoot, it was hit squarely by a great stone. The missile shattered the frame, releasing the tension in a whirl of flailing cables and fragments of timber and iron, scything down the men serving it and half of the rest of the soldiers on that lower level.

'Hercules' balls!' Sabinus gasped.

Fortuna was as fickle as ever, because the ballista in the other tower aimed too low with its shot, so that the stone pitched a pace short of the ram, only to skim under the sides of the shed, ripping the legs off two of the men pushing from inside. Ferox could see a great pool of blood spreading from underneath.

'Up!' he shouted. 'And kill the bastards!' Men rose all along the parapet and began lobbing stones, javelins and siege spears into the mass of tribesmen flooding up to the walls. Some had ladders and they were vulnerable, for it was hard to carry one of those and use a shield. Warriors fell around them, but each time a ladder was dropped more men appeared to lift it again. The ram was lurching forward once more, and soon was safe from the remaining ballista, which with its next stone cut a lane through the king's men following behind, sending up a spray of blood and fragments of shields and men. Bolts from scorpiones slammed in to knock down others so that the whole column seemed to shudder.

Ferox went to the back of the tower. There was no sign of a big attack at either the back gate or the west, but he could see men all along the ramparts by the east gate as they hurled missiles at the attackers. In front of the principia the cavalrymen stood beside their horses, and as far as Ferox could see none of the other reserves had so far committed themselves. Enica was the only one mounted, and he could see her and her grey quite distinctly, her standard-bearer beside her along with Bran and Minura.

'Sir!' Sabinus called. 'The ram!'

Ferox dashed over to the front, first picking up an oval shield like the ones the auxiliaries used. As he reached the parapet he raised it to block an arrow, then angled it so that he could see out. The roof of the shed, a patchwork of soaked hides, was beneath them.

'Oil!' Ferox shouted to the men on the level below. 'And bring the torches!'

The ram swung and struck the timber gate with a great

boom. Ladders were being raised all along the wall. A chieftain in gilded helmet and bright bronze scales climbed one of the first, shield held up. On the wall a little to the side, a veteran raised a *pilum muralis* – one of the siege spears made by twisting back the stem of a broken pilum and sharpening it into a point. It was clumsy and heavy, but he timed it well and struck the chief in the side, and whether or not it broke through the scales of his armour he was knocked from the ladder onto the men clustered below. He screamed as he was impaled on their spears. The veteran lingered too long to watch his success, and his head snapped to the side as the bolt from one of the belly-bows drove through the cheek piece on his helmet. He staggered and fell, rolling down the grassy slope into the intervallum.

The ram struck again and a third time. Amphorae full of olive oil were flung down to shatter on the roof of the shed, spreading the thick liquid. An auxiliary was raising another one to throw when the bolt from a ballista drove into his chest, easily snapping the rings of his mail. He was flung back, dropping the little amphorae which broke and seeped onto the boards. Three soldiers appeared carrying burning torches.

'Stop!' Ferox shouted, but the one in the lead had already slipped on the oil and was falling. One torch went out as it dropped, but the other landed in the pool and surged into a great yellow flame. Some of the oil was on the man's arm and he screamed as it burned. Ferox dropped his shield and bounded over, ripping free the brooch holding his cloak to beat with it at the flames. 'Sabinus, help this man! You and you, over there!' He pointed to the front of the tower.

Ferox managed to smother most of the flames, helped

because a lot of the oil had seeped through the cracks between the boards. The screaming auxiliary suddenly stopped, and he turned to see Vepoc, wrapping something around the scorched arm. Then he noticed that the Brigantian had no trousers.

'This'll frighten them!' Vepoc told him.

Sabinus had frozen, and was still behind the parapet when the men with the torches reached him. Beneath them, the ram pounded against the gate and the sound snapped him out of his shock. He took one of the burning torches, leaned through the gap and let it fall. A curse showed that he had missed, but he jerked back out of the way in time to let another arrow pass. 'Another!' Taking the second, he swung it gently to rouse the flames. 'And you throw another from the side!' he told the second auxiliary. 'Now!' Both men lobbed the torches down and Ferox heard the fire flare. 'One more for luck!' Sabinus said and the soldier threw the last torch down. There was black smoke, reeking of oil, rising in front of the tower.

The ram slammed into the gate. Vepoc, his backside barely covered by his mail shirt, went back to loading the scorpio. Sabinus reached down to lift one of the big stones they had brought up to the top. Trusting to the cover of the smoke, he stood between the crenulations, hefting it and then flinging it down with all his strength. There was a crack as it hit the roof of the ram's shell.

'Come on!' he called to the auxiliaries. 'The rest of them.'

The ram banged again.

'I'm going down!' Ferox shouted. On the lower level he saw men lifting the heated oil to tip onto the roof. It fell in a yellowish stream and the flames surged, the smoke growing thicker so that men started to cough as it blew back into the tower.

Out of the tower and onto the rampart, Ferox saw a few warriors fighting with his men, but the only ones up on the walkway were all dead, so he kept running, scooped up a scutum lying on the ground, tried not to think about its former owner and hurried down the steps.

Just as he arrived, the blunt head of the ram smashed through, shattering a plank and leaving a gaping hole just above the bar holding the two gates shut. Thick smoke came through the hole, but then he heard the screams from outside as the crew of the ram started to burn. Yet men must have been running past it, in spite of the scalding heat, for an axe head chopped down onto the bar and he could see the gates straining as they were pushed, inching inwards.

Ferox drew his sword. The ram had attacked the gates on the right, and the pair on the left, separated by a narrow arch, were not under threat. He waved at the reserves to advance, saw the commander, one of the *optiones*, wave back, and some way behind him could see the cavalry mounting up. 'Come with me, all of you,' he said to three soldiers who had been tending the fires where they had heated the oil and sand. 'This way.' He led them into the shadows behind the far gates.

The bar snapped as the other gates pushed inwards and open, and with a yell king's men came pouring through the gap. They ran forward, and the optio shouted to his men so that the front rank of three hurled their pila into the mass. The heavy javelins punched through shields as if they were glass, the slim shank sliding on to drive their pyramid-shaped heads through mail, bone and flesh. Half a dozen men were down, and more fell as the second rank threw their javelins. There was a stutter, but so many men were pressing from behind that the leaders could not retreat and found themselves almost pushed forwards.

The optio and his men charged, drawing their swords, and the Dacians ran to meet them until both sides stopped barely a pace apart. They hesitated, arms raised, swords or spears ready, until one or two went that last pace and struck at the enemy. There were some sixty or seventy Dacians to thirty legionaries and in time they would realise this and start to spread out around their flanks, but for the moment the rough lines faced each other, men probing and jabbing from behind their shields as they searched for openings. Ferox's job was to make sure that no more of the enemy came in. There was the sound of roaring flames and he guessed that the ram and its shed were truly ablaze, for he could feel the heat even from where he was. That ought to make it harder for the enemy to flood into the fort.

Ferox gestured with his sword and walked towards the open gateway. Another dozen Dacians ran through and turned to the left, away from the fight, but someone else would have to deal with them. A man who looked like a leader was standing with his back to Ferox yelling to the men outside. Another was beside him, and he gaped when he saw the centurion and his men creeping out of the shadows. Ferox took another step and then stamped forward, lunging with his gladius beneath the neck guard of the leader and into his spine. An auxiliary came past and hacked at the other man, who parried with his shield high and Ferox had just enough time to rip his own blade free and stab underneath the shield into the warrior's thigh. He fell, blood pulsing from the wound.

A man appeared, his clothes and body aflame from oil, and he staggered through the gateway. As Ferox stepped into the opening the heat was appalling and it was amazing how much the fire had spread. More men were screaming as they burned, some rolling on the ground trying to beat out the flames. A bare-chested warrior came at him, falx held high and two-handed, and there was barely time to raise his shield before the weapon sliced down, breaking the bronze trim on the top edge of his shield and cutting down three inches into the wood. Ferox was swinging away and used the motion to stab forward into the warrior's belly. He glanced back over his shoulder.

'The gates! We need to close the gates.' He took a step back, struggling to free his scutum from the falx as the warrior doubled over, clutching his stomach and trying to hold in his innards.

Another step back and Ferox was between the gates. The falx at last dropped away and he had time to lift the shield which shook as a spear struck it. A warrior came at him, sword drawn, and this was one of the king's men, but as he charged he ran into a spray of sand poured from above and yelped with surprise. Ferox stepped back one more time, trusting that his soldiers were covering his retreat and he hoped that no more sand would come in case it helped to put out the flames.

Screaming, whether in rage or pain, the king's man came on again, slamming the boss of his shield against Ferox's scutum. The centurion staggered, but saw the man's arm raised for a downward cut and jabbed forward at eye level.

The Dacian went back, still screaming, and tripped over the legs of the warrior wounded in the belly.

'Out the way, sir!' a soldier yelled and Ferox moved to let them close the gates behind him.

'The bar, quick!' One of the others called as Ferox and the first man put their weight on the gates to hold them closed. Something struck the outside and Ferox jerked back, almost losing his balance, but his feet got a grip again and he leaned with all his weight. The other two had the longer section of the bar and lifted it towards the brackets.

'Push, lad! Push!' Ferox called as much to himself as the other man, and he turned his back against the wooden gate, feeling every muscle strain. The bar came down into one bracket, then the other and the pressure was gone.

'Shields!' he shouted, for the men with the bar had dropped theirs. 'Get behind us!' He and the other man went forward, for Dacians were turning, realising what had happened. Above the helmets and clashing weapons of the two lines, cavalrymen were walking their horses, lobbing javelins over the heads of the legionaries.

Dacians were turning to face him, and one or two were coming towards him, until a deep voice shouted out a command. The enemy bunched together forming a rough circle. Maximus and five of his men came trotting up from the right, kicking their horses into a canter, and the circle was not yet ready and some of the king's men flinched as the cavalry bore down. The Dacians opened up gaps wide enough to let them through, or were barged out of the way if they did not move fast enough. Maximus ran a man through with his spear, let the weapon fall with the dying warrior, and had time to draw his sword and hack down into a neck before he was through and out the other side. Another cavalryman darted his spear back and forth in quick, well-judged attacks, wounding three as he passed. The last horse in the group balked as a warrior stood firm. It reared, front hoofs kicking the Dacian and knocking him down, but the rider lost his seat and fell, screaming briefly as swords cut down.

The Dacians stepped away from the legionaries, who let them go and panted as they struggled for breath. The deep voice was shouting again, and the warriors made a circle of shields facing outwards, two or three ranks deep. For the first time Ferox noticed that they carried a *draco* standard, like the ones some of the Roman cavalry had copied. Its bronze head was shaped like the gaping maw of a dragon and behind it hung a long red sock that would hiss and ripple in the wind when they ran. Now, it hung limp, but the leader was urging his men on and the shields were level and steady.

Reserves were coming up on either side, and Ferox had to hope that there was no danger to the ramparts.

'Come on!' he shouted. 'Let's kill these bastards!'

XXIV

Piroboridava
Fourth day before the Kalends of June

ISO STILL HAD a bandage around his head, but otherwise appeared unscathed. Ferox had watched the tribune ride slowly towards the fort, a warrior on either side of him and standard-bearer and man sounding an ox horn behind them. The young aristocrat kept his hands together close behind his horse's neck, suggesting that they were tied.

Sabinus was nervous. 'It is not unknown for besiegers to execute or torture a captive in sight of the walls to persuade the defenders to surrender.'

Ferox did not need to be told that, for he had seen Roman armies do the same thing more than once. He had not particularly liked Piso, and doubted that anyone would wish to give in merely to save the tribune from torment, but hoped that they would not have to watch. Sosius had hinted that there were doubts over the aristocrat's loyalty and Lepidina told him the story of the father's incompetent plot and exile. The family sounded more like a poor joke than a real threat to the emperor.

'I do not like it,' Claudia said. 'And see the rider on the left?'

Ferox had already recognised Ivonercus. 'If they are talking, then they are not attacking,' he said. It was four days after the big assault and during those days the archers and engines had continued to nibble away at the defenders. Twenty-three men had died during the assault, almost half in killing the Dacians surrounded and shut inside the fort when Ferox and the others had closed the gates. Half a dozen more had been killed by missiles or succumbed to their wounds in the last few days. Four times as many were wounded, not counting the flesh wounds and scratches that many more had taken. Sulpicia Lepidina had run out of bandages and begun cutting up spare clothes, including some of her own.

'If it was good enough for the Lord Trajan, then it is good enough for me,' she said, referring to a much trumpeted incident in the first war when the emperor had given spare cloaks and tunics to the surgeons to help them cope with a deluge of wounded. The Dacian skill with bows, and their fondness for cutting swords like the sica and the great falx always meant that there were plenty of wounded. As usual the lady had made no fuss, but simply got on with the task at hand, but the story had spread nevertheless. Ferox heard men joking that they should all stick their legs up over the parapet and take wounds, because that way Lepidina, Claudia and all the other women might end up naked.

Spirits remained high, buoyed by the victory, and managed to cope with the slaughter of half the horses, which were butchered and the meat either cooked for issue or salted.

With more than a hundred animals that was a big task, and at the same time work parties laboured to build Ephippus' acropolis, and to clear up after the fighting, whether gathering arrows and other usable material, or lifting the dead Dacians and tipping them over the ramparts to join the hundreds of corpses left by the attack. The enemy made no request for a truce to gather up their fallen, so most of the bodies lay where they were, faces changing from the odd, wax-like pallor of the newly dead into a deep red brown as they bloated and the stomachs started to burst open. The stench was awful, clawing at the throat like something physical, but at least it was outside and from the enemy.

They had burned their own corpses, using a patch of open ground where one of the granaries had once stood, and a pyre carefully planned by Ephippus to produce the most heat. Claudia Enica told her tribesmen that although this was not their way, this was what must be done, but before the thing was done relatives or someone from their clan snipped hair and cut the little finger from each body, so these could be kept and taken back to their homeland when all this was over. Ferox admired their optimism, and at times like this was glad that his wife was here, for she inspired them in a way he knew he could not. Like a family, the Brigantes seemed to forget their grievances with each other as they united against the bigger enemy. Even the gruffest and most hostile now grinned when Ferox appeared, for he was the queen's consort and he was their war chief for the moment. She had proven her courage as well as her right to rule, leading a charge that killed or chased out all Dacians who managed to come through a hole knocked in one of the east gates. Whatever Rome said, she was their queen, descendant of Cartimandua, and Ferox was her chosen husband. So they would serve him and fight by his side, at least until this was over.

Ferox wished he knew whether Hadrian or anyone else was mustering a force to relieve them, but in his heart he doubted that help would ever come. Strangely, such thoughts did not depress him, for there was always so much to do.

'You're enjoying this, aren't you?' Vindex said whenever they met, while Claudia would shake her head on the rare times that they were alone and say much the same thing. In truth there was a simplicity about it all, and trying to outwit the enemy, anticipating and blocking his next move, kept his mind far too busy to brood.

Ferox did his best to give the garrison some rest, but there were always too many things to do. Clearing up took time and effort, preparing the pyre and the corpses for cremation took more, and all had to be done before they started slaughtering horses and mules because he did not want the smell of bodies and of cooking meat to mingle in the air and stick in men's minds. The live horses still needed grooming and care, and they would only live for as long as there was fodder and no need for their meat. Weapons needed cleaning, blades needed sharpening, armour and helmets to be greased or repaired, as did the engines, and as many new missiles made as they could. Some fatigues could not be abandoned, so men were tasked with cleaning the latrines, replacing the sponges and water. Sickness would come in time, as it always did, for the evil spirits that caused it could sense weakness in a man, but he would do his best to delay the inevitable. All of these things needed to be done, and all the while the enemy needed to be fought. Apart from the near constant deluge of missiles, now and then a few score would rush forward with ladders, so men needed to be on the walls all the time, and although they had not yet tried it, he feared another night attack, so kept strong detachments on duty throughout the hours of darkness. If the men were worked hard, then he had to work harder still, so there was little rest and when he took a break he tended to fall asleep as soon as he lay down. Queen's consort or not, there had been no opportunity for consorting.

'What are you smirking at?' Claudia Enica's sharp tone snapped him back to the present.

'Sorry, miles away.' He was getting tired and he knew it, sensing the same in all those around him. That was the problem. With all their numbers the enemy could rest and the garrison could not, so it would be worn away like a cliff by the sea. The only consolation was that they were doing the job and holding the Dacian army here. Ferox was surprised that they had not tried to sneak heavy supplies over the bridge, or taken the bulk across under cover of their attack. For the last two days he had not even ordered the monâkon to lob an occasional stone as reminder of what they could do, half fearing that he might remind the enemy leaders of why they had come here. He wondered whether the fort had become a challenge for them in its own right, rather than a distraction.

The riders were close now.

'May we approach?' The Dacian leading them called out. It was a different herald to last time, a little older and more slightly built.

'I would speak with you, Flavius Ferox?' Piso shouted out. 'Will you come down so that you can see my face and know that I speak the truth – no more, no less?' The Dacian seemed surprised at this, but said nothing.

'Can we not speak from here?'

'I am your senior, centurion, by birth and in the army. It is not fitting that I look up at you.'

'Don't be a fool,' Claudia whispered.

'I thought that was why you married me,' he replied, before raising his voice. 'Sabinus, make sure the scorpio is ready. If there is the slightest sign of treachery then don't let anyone escape.'

Vepoc winked. 'Even you, lord?'

'Use your judgement.' There were archers lurking in the outer ditch, although none that close to the road or the heralds. Ferox could not see any sign of an impending attack. Still, it was difficult to be sure. Over the last few nights the Dacians had thrown up a rampart less than a hundred paces from the wall, just beyond the remnants of the lilliae, all of which they had filled in. There could be men lurking behind this shelter, ready to pour out of the gaps left in the wall as soon as the gate was opened. If so, then they were unlikely to get there before it was closed again, whatever happened to him.

By the time the gate opened and Ferox walked out, the tribune had dismounted. After some uncertainty, the Dacian and Ivonercus did the same. Piso was wearing a cuirass and the rest of his uniform apart from his helmet, but the scabbard on his left hip was empty.

'It is good to see you well, my lord,' Ferox said. After all this was diplomacy, so the truth was neither here nor there. 'I trust your wound is healing?'

'It is.' The young aristocrat coughed nervously. 'I am sent

to ask you to yield the fort and march away with all your men.' The words were precise and obviously rehearsed. As obvious was the tone of sarcasm. 'I am informed that you have already refused these generous terms, but am to ask you to reconsider. There is no need for anyone else to die in this place.

'There, that is done,' Piso said, 'and I have kept my word to my charming hosts. Now, give me your sword.'

'Sir?'

'Trust me, this is necessary. Your fellows up there can kill me with ease if that is what they want.' He glanced up. 'Jupiter's holy toga, there's a woman up there. It is true then? Such a pretty little thing too. Your sword, man.'

'I will not yield, sir.'

'It is an order. You, Briton, obey me!' Piso barked the words and Ferox thought that they were directed at him until Ivonercus drew his slim *spatha*.

'This is a parley!' the Dacian said, stepping in front of Ferox, and then grunted as Ivonercus drove the sword into his stomach, the sharp point going between the scales and thrusting up. On the gate the scorpio cracked and its bolt whipped through the air, just missing the top of the Brigantian's helmet and burying itself in the chest of the standard-bearer's horse. The beast screamed, and rolled over, throwing its rider.

'Come on!' Piso was already running for the gate. There were Dacian shouts, anger mixed with shock, and arrows came, but struck the riderless horses instead of their targets. Ivonercus twisted his blade free and then stabbed the writhing Dacian in the throat.

Ferox dashed back to the gate. Piso was hit beneath the

knee by an arrow and fell in a heap. Ferox was close behind, so close that he jumped over the tribune rather than trying to stop. He kept going, the narrowly open gate just a few paces away.

'Centurion!' Piso screamed at him. 'Help me!'

Ferox hesitated, the temptation strong to leave them both to the Dacians. Horns were blowing and men shouting as hundreds of warriors streamed through the gaps in their wall. Breaking a truce was a great impiety. Silures respected few things, and liked nothing better than to deceive an enemy and hurt him without him realising what was happening, but even they felt that a curse would fall on anyone breaking a truce.

Ivonercus spun around as an arrow from a belly bow snapped the rings on his mail and dug into his shoulder. He dropped his sword and staggered on.

The habit of duty was too strong and Ferox turned around, lifted the tribune and swung him onto his back.

'I'm not your shield, you bastard!' the tribune snarled, but though arrows came close none touched them and the only one to hit Ivonercus bounced back from his armour. Then they were through the gate and it was slamming shut behind them. Ferox dropped the tribune, none too gently, and ran for the stairs leading onto the rampart. 'Sound the alarm,' he shouted.

It was not a planned attack, well thought out and hitting the fort from several directions, but a simple outpouring of rage. Hundreds and then thousands of warriors rushed from cover or came from the camp and hurled themselves at the walls. There were fewer ladders than in the last attack, but every time the men around them were shot down more appeared and soon half a dozen rose against the front rampart. Ferox cut down one warrior who had pushed back the defenders and managed to leap onto the walkway, but few others made it that far. The Dacians died, well over a hundred of them, and many more moaned as they crawled or were carried back when the fury at last was spent. Seven of the garrison were killed to inflict this carnage and thirty more wounded, while they threw or shot far more missiles than usual, for there was a frenzy about the fighting on both sides.

Piso tried to make light of it all, when Ferox went to visit him in the hospital. 'If I had known that I would be ministered to by such a fair doctor, then I believe I would have stayed here rather than going to Sarmizegethusa,' he said, beaming at Sulpicia Lepidina, before taking her hand and kissing it. 'Hygaia herself could hardly be more kind.

'And I would not have gone, nor trusted to those Dacian bastards – oh, my apologies, lady – if I had known what they were like. Decebalus took me prisoner during a truce, so I wanted to repay the compliment. Oh, and as I have said, that noble fellow, your husband, was quite well when last I saw him. A hostage it is true, but that means that he and the others will be treated well.' He shook his head. 'Poor Longinus, but then I suppose you have not heard that he is dead by poison. Did not want the emperor to worry on his behalf, so they say.'

'We have heard, my lord.'

'Then perhaps you had better tell me about your situation. Be a few days before this leg heals and I am fit for dancing, so you must command until then, but it is good if I know what has happened.'

Ferox told him, and sensed the tribune's disappointment as he spoke of their meagre supplies, growing losses, and rapid depletion of missiles.

'But help will be on its way, no doubt,' Piso said, as if trying to convince himself.

'It is to be hoped, my lord, but as long as we hold on here, we protect the route down to the Ister and the great bridge. We are doing our duty.'

'Yes,' Piso sounded unsure. 'Yes, that is good. I saw them working on a couple of siege towers, so that is what you can expect next. Struck me as rickety affairs, so more than likely fall down on their own, but I would judge that they will be finished in a day or two.

'By the way, I'll not take up space here that might be needed by those in a worse state. I will take a room or two in the praetorium. Won't need much, but I'd be obliged if you could spare a boy and maybe a girl or two to see to my needs.'

'I will see what I can do.' Sulpicia Lepidina was behind Piso and gave Ferox a look that made clear that no female slave or anyone other than the oldest of the men would be let anywhere near the tribune on their own. 'Of course we can oblige.'

Enica as queen had already spoken to Ivonercus, but Ferox wanted to see the man before the medicus tried to cut out the head of the arrow lodged in the bone.

'I want to be with my own folk,' the Brigantian said. 'And if they are fighting, then I want to be at their side not against them. I have sworn to the queen and I will not break my word. My quarrel with you is over – for the moment.'

Ivonercus appeared sincere, which did not mean that

he was not lying. Ferox put a couple of guards outside the hospital and doubled the sentries at the gates and protecting the monâkon just in case he had been sent into the fort for a reason, or still had friends among the Brigantians who might help him. That meant an extra burden on his ever-diminishing garrison, although a score of men with lighter wounds had asked to return to duty.

The day passed visiting the walls and work parties, issuing orders, encouraging, praising and now and again chasing weary men to work harder. The mood had changed, and he suspected the arrival of Piso and his breaking the truce was making men wonder whether he would bring down ill fortune on them all. No one seemed pleased to see him, and Sosius, who was working hard and showing a deal of skill in fletching arrows, hinted that the aristocrat was not to be trusted.

Half an hour before midnight, Ferox ate a little food and went to get a few hours' sleep before he needed to inspect the sentries and check that all was well. To his surprise there was a large wooden frame bed with its own roof and curtains somehow squeezed into his small chamber. It belonged to Lepidina and Cerialis, and had remained on the cart with the belongings the lady had not unpacked. In fact, Ferox had been wondering whether to ask for it and several other bulky pieces of furniture to help with the barricades needed for Ephippus' sanctuary.

Ferox blinked, wondering whether he had taken a wrong turn, then undressed mechanically, wishing that there was time for a bath, because he knew that the hot water would relax him. Still, sleep should not be a problem, for he ached in body and mind. He was half asleep already, otherwise he might have guessed.

'I had almost given up,' Claudia Enica said as he drew back the curtains. She smiled as he stood there, wholly naked, for the nights had grown sultry and oppressive.

'I am so tired, my love,' he stammered.

'We shall see about that,' she said, pulling back the blankets to show that she was as bare as he was.

R HOLES WAS DEAD. *The day after the grand attack on the fort, the old warrior had spoken in the morning of how they would win next time and of all that they must do to make this happen. He was pale, his eyes dark-rimmed, but his voice was steady and he filled all the council with confidence. Brasus cherished the praise he gave for his foresight in taking a tree trunk with him, so that he could batter at the gates once they were weakened by the stones from the catapult. That was what had got them in, only to find the way blocked by carts and barrels, javelins coming from all sides and horsemen galloping up in support.*

In the afternoon Rholes' bowels opened and would not stop for all that day and the night. When Brasus went to his tent the next morning the stench made him gag, even before he got a glimpse of the sick man through a gap in the tent flap. His skin was by then yellow, shrunken around his bones, and the eyes of his woman were glassy with tears on the verge of spilling out. If Rholes saw him at all he said nothing, and then he gasped and his face was wracked with pain as his muscles strained again. By the morning he was dead, along with a dozen others among the army, all of them with the same sickness.

An army camp meant filth and stink, and everyone knew

that. So many men and so many animals meant the reek of sweat and dirt, of urine and manure, both human and animal. The patches where the deserters pitched their tents were neater and cleaner than the rest, and one of their leaders kept urging Diegis to make the rest of the army copy.

'We are not Romans but free men,' was all that the man now in sole charge of the army would say. So the filth piled up, and men drank from the river downstream from where hundreds relieved themselves, and more and more were falling sick, adding to the piles of excrement and the appalling reek. By now the whole camp smelled like Rholes' tent and more men were bound to die. Brasus could not help wishing that Diegis would be one of them for the man was a dangerous fool.

The siege towers had been Rholes' idea, and two of them were rapidly taking shape, but it took constant prodding to remind Diegis that they would need the Roman ditches to be filled in and the earth well enough packed and supported to hold their weight.

'There will be time enough the night before we attack,' he declared. Brasus ignored him, and had some of the deserters and one of the Black Sea Greeks with the army making covered sheds and extending the attackers' rampart ever closer to the outer ditch so that it could be filled properly. Diegis mocked but did not stop him, and seemed uninterested in supervising the siege, and instead let each chieftain or leader act as he willed. Some did nothing, others were busy, but all too often did not speak to the rest so that they did not help or even hindered each other's efforts. Brasus managed to get a few to work with him, persuading because he could not order.

The army was restless, the animals' bellies swelling from eating too much grass as they were left to pasture all day, and more and more men began vomiting or spent half the day squatting over their own filth.

Diegis revived with the arrival of the captive Roman tribune and the news of the death of Longinus. He spoke openly of his hatred for the man, and the number of insults the Roman had directed at him in councils, and did not seem aware that the king's plan had been to use the man as a hostage.

'This will show them that it is hopeless to resist,' Diegis declared after an hour spent alone in his tent save for his bodyguards, one or two advisors, the captive Piso and – strangest of all – Ivonercus. 'We will send the tribune to speak in his own voice so that they know the truth.' There was much that Brasus did not understand and rumours passed through the camp that the Roman tribune had sworn an oath to Decebalus and was now his man. Someone else said that the tribune had murdered the Legatus Longinus, or had it arranged, for some dark scheme of the king's to outwit the enemy.

Brasus was relieved not to be sent with the envoys, for he feared seeing the queen again. She had been there when they broke through the gate, snatching his victory away as she rode behind her warriors, urging them on. Brasus and his men had had to fall back or be slaughtered for no purpose, but as they stepped back, shields facing the enemy, he had seen the queen throw a javelin which had struck the man beside him in the face. To see a woman kill like that was new to him and wholly disturbing.

Instead of Brasus, Diegis chose another chieftain, and it

was hard to know whether this was a mark of favour or punishment. Yet the commander had been as surprised as any at what had happened, and his rage stirred the anger of the men into that rash and futile attack. It did not seem feigned, but Brasus wondered whether the plan had always been to get Ivonercus or Piso or both inside the fort. Men whispered that they were spies and would open a gate during the night or murder the Roman centurion who led the defence. Brasus was more than ever convinced that Ferox was a great leader and warrior and part of him did not like the thought of such a man being murdered rather than falling in honourable combat. He also doubted that Ferox was the key to unlocking the fort, for he had seen a small figure with long red hair up on the tower when the envoy had been killed and the prisoner escaped, and he sensed her power everywhere.

Brasus was not sleeping well, unable to clear his mind, although so far he was healthy. He had always considered cleanliness a fitting accompaniment to purity of the soul. Yet all around him he saw pollution and he knew that his spirit was succumbing. Sleep had become harder, his mind refusing to empty of thoughts no matter how tired he was. When he did sleep he dreamed, and each night it seemed to be of the queen. Sometimes she stood over him, driving a spear deep into his naked flesh and sometimes she was naked too, as desirable as she was terrifying. Yet the other dreams were almost worse, when he pictured encounters, whether amid the crunching leaves of an autumn forest or a meadow rich with spring flowers, and she smiled at him, a little afraid, a little excited. Each time he woke up as he was undressing her and felt such bitter loss. For a man to take a woman as bride was right and natural, for the pure must father more souls to climb to purity of their own. Brasus should have longed and lusted for his bride to be, even though on the one occasion he had met the king's daughter she had struck him as insipid, albeit pretty enough. Now a spell had fallen on him, cast by the sorceress from Britannia and his soul was growing dark. Brasus worried that his mistrust of Diegis was fuelled by her magic.

The commander did not help. Brasus' men bridged both the ditches, supporting the sides of each hard-packed earth ramp with timber driven fast into the ground, so that one path wide enough for a tower led to the Roman rampart. It meant that the defenders knew where the attack would come, but at least ensured that the tower should reach their wall. At long last Diegis had realised the wisdom of this, and ordered a favoured chieftain to supervise the construction of another crossing, so that each tower could approach at different ends of the front rampart. Brasus doubted that the man put in charge understood what he was doing and his offers of advice were rejected, yet, perversely it seemed, Diegis ordered him to lead the column supporting the second tower. The whole business also meant a delay of another day before the attack was launched, as they worked on the second path. The towers had already been raised, clearly visible to the Romans even if Piso and Ivonercus had not already told them about the Dacian plan.

Brasus felt the power of the queen seeping into the camp like the mists that floated up from the river each night. Dark thoughts came and would not let themselves be pushed aside, *and he wondered whether her magic brought the sickness that was killing more and more and leaving others too weak to stand, while clouding the mind of Diegis. Brasus feared for the army as he feared for his own soul.*

XXV

Piroboridava
The day before the Kalends of June

FEROX HAD ORDERED the standards brought to the top of the tower over the porta praetoria. The carpenters had made a wooden block with grooves to take the three butt spikes so that the vexilla could stand in a row and be wreathed in garlands for this was the second day of the rose festival of the standards, twenty-one days after the first. He doubted that there would be much chance for a proper supplication, but had done what he could.

The enemy had taken longer to prepare their assault than Piso had predicted, even though the two siege towers had been ready the day before. Ferox had always wondered when the enemy planned to create routes across the ditches, as it seemed unlikely that they would try to come up the tracks leading to any of the gates, since the towers would merely be the same height as the ones over the gates and lower than the tall ones at the porta praetoria. The Romans had done their best to hinder the work, especially of the engineers toiling to the right of the track because those men seemed to know what they were doing. Perhaps a few had died from bolts and arrows, but the work had hardly slowed.

Piso had declared himself fit that morning, although he had sat in silence through the consilium after saying that he wanted to help and not take over. The arrow had come out cleanly and done little damage, so although he limped with his bandaged leg, he was sprightly enough when he climbed up to the top of the tower, shaking his head with amusement when he noticed the Brigantes' flag. His admiration for Claudia Enica's bare legs was as obvious, prompting her to leave and walk back to the road behind the gateway, where she was to command a score of her men, but for once not Bran and Minura, for they had another task. All save a handful of the horses had been killed in the last few days, so that the reserves were all stationed closer to the walls, with a unit behind each stretch of rampart facing the approach ramps for the towers. There were fewer reserves though, and fewer men on the walls, for although there had been no more major assaults, there had been plenty of smaller ones, and all the while the archers and engines shot at the slightest hint of a target. Plenty of men took their second, third or fourth light wound, so that barely a quarter of the garrison remained unscathed, and every day a few more died and others were hit badly. Petrullus was lucky not to have lost an eye, and would have a big scar on his cheek for the rest of his days, although he swore that he was fit for duty and remained at the east gate. Ferox had had to order his own men to save their missiles, for they were running low. The archers could shoot back any arrow they found in good enough condition, but the rest were to be saved for the next assault.

'They are coming!' someone shouted as the big towers lurched forward. Their timber fronts and sides were covered in hides, just as the ram had been, and they rolled on six big solid wheels.

'No rams,' Ephippus said after studying them for a moment. 'Just bridges to lower once they are close.'

'Good,' Ferox said. He had expected as much, for the softness of earth ramparts made them absorb a lot of the force of a ram and made them hard to undermine quickly.

'They should burn well.'

'If we get the chance,' Ferox agreed. There was little oil and tar left, so they had prepared torches and clay pots full of oil. Delivering them was another matter, and meant a big risk. 'Now get ready.'

'Are you sure, my lord?'

'Positive.'

Piso waited until the engineer had gone before he spoke. 'These Greeks need a firm hand, you know. Always want to argue, always have their own ideas.'

'The Lord Hadrian holds a high opinion of his talents, and in the last month I have come to share it.'

'Well, one would-be Greek is bound to like another,' Piso sneered. 'Better all offer *hetacombs* to Zeus, Aphrodite and Ares if we are relying on that bearded bugger to save us.'

Ferox felt it better not to be drawn. If this did not work, then he would have problems enough for the moment. 'I must go, my lord. The engines and archers will shoot when you give the order.'

'Good luck, Ferox,' Piso said, managing a smile.

'You too, sir.'

Ferox went down to the lower platform on the tower, waiting to be sure where the siege towers were heading.

They were getting close to the crossings, and he heard Ephippus shouting at the crew of the monâkon to shift the great machine just a little. Hopefully that would not take too long. The tower on his left was moving steadily until it stopped, and with some care and little pushes this way and that to turn it, the men lined it up with the ramp across the ditches. The one on that side was narrower and less well made than the other. On Ferox's right the second tower would move a few paces and then stop, but did not need to be turned and was pretty much squarely in the middle of the ramp.

Piso must have given the order, although Ferox did not hear it, for scorpiones cracked and bolts started to fly. Both towers quivered slightly when missiles hit them, but for the moment the archers on top were crouching behind cover. Some of the men pushing began to fall, for they were sheltered only from the front and vulnerable to missiles shot at an angle from the rest of the rampart and tower. Horns were blowing and men were cheering in the usual Dacian manner, and their own archers and engines kept up a steady barrage. A light-coloured stone came straight at them and men shouted to take cover, so that no one was hurt, but with a resounding clang it struck the bronze front piece of the scorpio over on the left, leaving it bent and one arm hanging down loose.

'Bugger's buggered,' Naso said ruefully, and went to help the crew of the remaining machine.

The monâkon's high arm slammed into the pad above its high frame and a great stone went high and straight towards the first tower, the one on the left. Ferox thought that it was going too high when at the last minute a figure popped up.

The stone shattered the man into fragments, flinging some high into the air.

'Daft sod,' an auxiliary said. 'Teach him to be nosey.'

'Shit! Look at that!' one of the Brigantians shouted. The first tower was on the causeway, coming across the outer ditch, when suddenly it lurched to a staggering halt, the front wheel sinking down into soft earth and the whole thing leaning sideways.

The monâkon lobbed a second stone, having reloaded faster than Ferox expected, and he wondered whether the line would be wrong now that the tower was at such a strange angle. Yet the stone hit with a great crash, shaking the whole thing so that he wondered whether it would topple over.

'Beautiful,' Naso said.

Ferox grinned and knew that he was not needed over here, so hurried down to the intervallum and went to where the second tower would reach the wall. Five veterans of I Minervia waited on the slope behind the rampart. All had helmets with upright bands welded to the top in a cross shape. They were strong enough to weaken the blow of a falx and save a man's life, even if he would still get the father of all headaches. Each also had his scutum, and apart from his cuirass, wore a laminated iron guard on his right arm. Ferox had wondered in the weeks before the siege about equipping all the men with the same added protection, but there had not been time and other preparations had mattered more.

'Ready, lads.'

'Aye,' one grunted. These were picked men, all of them highly decorated or in two cases the sort of men who would have won awards and promotion years ago if they had shown half the aptitude for the routines of soldiering that they had shown time and again in battle. They were killers, and they would lead alongside Ferox. Behind would come Bran and Minura, for if the fighting broke up and space was cramped he would trust their well-honed skills as much as those of anyone else in the fort, save Vindex and he could not be spared. Last there were two legionaries with torches and two more with pots of oil held in a string net.

Ferox led them up the slope and had them crouch just below the top, the veterans' shields in front as protection. There was no need to speak or remind them of the job, so they waited.

'Nearly here, sir,' a soldier called down from the ramparts and then a great cheer went up all along the wall. 'The tower, sir! The other one, it's smashed!' The man was grinning and then an arrow sprouted from his left eye and another drove through his mail into his chest. He fell, rolling down the slope past them. The arrows had come from above, which meant that the second tower was close, the archers on top beginning to do their job of clearing the rampart. Another man fell a moment later, and the rest were raising shields high and too busy to throw anything back. By this time, the tower was probably past the ground where any of the ballistae could reach it. He thought back to Ephippus cursing the Romans for their stubborn refusal to build towers that projected in front of the walls like any civilized folk.

'Soon, lads,' Ferox said softly. He heard the creaking of the great tower as it edged towards the wall and could see the archers sheltering behind wooden crenulations on the roof of the tower.

'Up!' he said. They stood, the legionaries in two ranks. Each one in front had his scutum level, as did Ferox who was on the right of the line, and behind them the man had his shield high. 'Forward slowly,' he said. They could not march easily on the grassy slope, so needed to be careful. Ferox's shield quivered as arrows struck the front, and he heard more missiles hitting the other shields beside him. 'Forward.' Their legs were covered by the slope and the parapet once they got up onto the walkway. That was a dangerous moment, because until the second rank came up behind them they could not reach up well with their shields. Ferox saw the arrow, pulled his head down and felt the point clang just above the brow-peak of his helmet, no doubt leaving a dent. The veteran next to him was slower and an arrow buried itself into the bridge of his nose. He sighed as he fell, and the man behind cursed because he tripped over the falling corpse.

'Swords!' Ferox commanded. They were all up, apart from the veteran who had had to get over the dead man and he joined them after a moment. The shields kept shaking as arrow after arrow hit them. Ferox saw the tips of two arrowheads sticking through the inner leather face of his scutum and other bulges, but none came further. Bran was holding a shield over his head as best he could and there were bangs as it was hit. The two other survivors in the second rank held their shields high and level, as if they were in a testudo.

There was another great creak and then a crash as the drawbridge came down and banged on the top of the parapet. Ferox had hoped that it would fall lower, level with the gaps between the crenulations, but as feet came stamping across the boards and men were screaming war cries he realised that this was better because the archers could not see them.

He stabbed upwards into the groin of a warrior, whose roar of defiance turned into a great squeal of agony. One of the veterans slashed, cutting right through another warrior's leg so that he fell sideways, taking another Dacian with him to fall screaming over the side of the bridge.

More warriors came, the one facing Ferox with a shield and a sica, and, before he realised the danger, his gladius was under the edge of the shield. The long triangular point drove into the inside of the Dacian's thigh before twisting free. Blood pumped out, spraying over Ferox and his shield. Someone had turned a scorpio from the next tower to the right and shot not at the archers, but at the crowd on the bridge, the bolt splitting the man on the side, hurling him over so that three more were knocked off their feet and two fell off altogether.

Ferox put his left foot up on the parapet and jumped up. It was narrow and precarious, but he felt Bran using his shield to steady him. An arrow skimmed past, missing his helmet by a thumb's breadth and he climbed again, getting a boot on the edge of the bridge. Another arrow slammed into his shield, almost making him fall back and he could hear the archers shouting. Men on the ramparts were throwing everything they could at the top of the tower and one archer fell back as a stone smacked into his mouth. The scorpio shot again, killing another and causing more chaos on the bridge just ahead of him. Warriors were hesitating, reluctant to leave the tower and step into that shambles of writhing bodies.

One of the veterans scrambled up to join Ferox. A second tried, until an arrow took him in the throat, but then the third man was up. Ferox punched forward with the boss of his shield, knocking a wounded man off the bridge. His sword was back, elbow bent, ready to lunge forward at eye level. Beside him the veteran took a low guard, ready to jab, and then thumped forward with his own shield. Each scutum was heavy, and Ferox and the veterans were powerful men, putting their weight behind each blow. They pounded the enemy with the shields, stabbed when there was an opening and kept going forward. The Dacians had not expected this, and several had falxes, far too unwieldy to use in the press of bodies, for the Romans drove hard against them. Those men died, stabbed in the stomach, through armour if they wore it, or tumbling off the sides of the bridge. Another warrior with a sica managed a slash at Ferox and he felt the blow fall on his shoulder, but the doubling of his mail armour held and he killed his opponent, driving his blade through the Dacian's teeth and out of the back of his head. He could not free the sword, so kept hold and grunted as he pushed the corpse into the men behind. Then he slammed the scutum forward again, knocking the dead man and the one behind him backwards. The two veterans from the second rank were up now, doing their best to fend off the arrows from above. One of the men in front had lost his helmet and his brow was bloody, but he stamped on his dying opponents, going over them. With Dacians trying to push forward and the men in front going backwards they could barely fight and the Roman swords stabbed again and again until the floor of the bridge was slick with blood. One desperate warrior grabbed the veteran on the right, leaping forward as the sword rammed into his stomach and both of them fell off the side.

The scorpio shot again, killing an archer. One of the rear rank men took the place of the one who had fallen, breaking a warrior's nose as he punched with the boss of his shield. Bran and Minura were on the bridge behind them, dodging or catching the few arrows still coming down, and the others doing their best to scramble up. Ferox's gladius at last yanked free and the corpse fell. He stamped onto the body, nearly tripped, and the lurch meant that the warrior in front mistimed his slash and overbalanced. Ferox punched forward, then twisted round, using the shield to tip the Dacian off the bridge. Behind the man, another lifted his falx one-handed, but the tip caught on the roof as he swung and before he realised, the centurion had recovered and slashed his neck open to the bone.

Suddenly the floor of the tower was empty, save for the dying, and Ferox just saw a head bob away as a man went down the ladder to the next level. They had a moment.

'Come on!' Ferox said to the remaining veterans and they went to the trapdoor to stop anyone from coming back up. The enemy were bound to recover soon, but it would be hard for them to fight their way up.

'You two!' he called in the language of the tribes. 'Up top.' There must have been half a dozen archers or even more up top and three or four at least must still be alive, so Ferox sent Bran and Minura to deal with them. It was hard not to lead them, but the aim was to destroy the tower and he had to make sure that they held on until that was done. The boy led up the ladder and his 'sister' followed, but none of the veterans paid attention as the pretty girl showed her long legs. A spear came jabbing up the trapdoor, but the veteran closest had greaves and the point threw off a spark without doing any damage. Another legionary slashed at the shaft, breaking it.

There were cries from the upper level, feet stamping on the floor and the clash of weapons. The two men brought the oil and Ferox pointed them to the left-hand side. 'There,' he told them, and they piled the rags against the solid side wall and then emptied the pots of oil all over them. Something thick and warm dripped onto Ferox and he realised that it was blood, coming from cracks in the ceiling.

'Time to go!' he shouted in Latin and then switched to the tongue of Britannia. 'Time to go!' Bran came down the ladder, face flushed and smeared with blood, but grinning from ear to ear. Minura's boots appeared after him.

'There were five,' Bran said. '*Thetatus*,' he added using army slang for dead. Vindex had taken to the word and the boy must have picked it up from him.

'Quick.' Ferox pointed his sword back towards the rampart. 'Go! Go!' The men who had prepared the fire ran. One stumbled as an arrow drove through the scales of his armour and almost tumbled off the bridge until the other caught him. Bran and Minura went next, leaping nimbly down onto the parapet.

One of the veterans hissed as a sica slashed up into the tip of his boot. 'Bastard!' He jabbed down, but could not reach his enemy.

'Get him out of here!' Ferox shouted to the others. 'I'll hold 'em back!'

The wounded veteran shrugged off the others and limped away.

'You sure, sir?' one asked.

'Yes, go!' Ferox glanced back at the men with the torches.

'Light it!' a Dacian yelled as he came up the ladder, sica ready. Ferox pushed the blade aside with the edge of his scutum and kicked the man in the face, stamping down again as he staggered. The warrior fell.

Already Ferox could feel the heat from the spreading flames. Everyone else had gone, so he ran back over the bridge and tried to vault across the parapet. His foot caught and he went sprawling headlong, shield and sword flying away before slamming onto the far edge of the walkway and sliding half way down the slope, his breath knocked out of him.

'Very pretty,' one of the veterans said. 'Like a salmon.'

Minura was beside him, helping him up as he panted. Her face was pitying, and then Bran appeared, still excited.

'It's burning!' he shouted, 'it's burning!' The wood inside must have been dry or the shape of the tower acted like a chimney because the fire was shooting upwards and black smoke rising high. Dacians were trying to beat at the flames with cloaks, but it was too late. Some ran across the bridge towards the wall, and the veterans stood up to meet them, striking at their legs. They fell and the ten men behind had nowhere to go because the tower itself was an inferno. Some burned and some jumped and the rest came forward only to be killed. The ropes burned through and the veterans managed to lever the edge of the bridge off the parapet with their swords until it flapped down against the front of the blazing tower.

The attack was not over, and many more men died before the Dacians gave in. They had plenty of ladders and a great deal of courage, and time and again men fought their way onto the parapet. Ferox led charge after charge to clear them off, and took a blow to the side that did not pierce his mail, but made a great bruise. Bran and Minura were always with him, and they worked as a pair, moving like dancers, each covering the other, dodging and cutting. The boy lost his helmet, took little cuts to arms and legs, but kept going until he was covered in the blood of the men he killed. The woman was untouched, and more than once she parried a blow that would have cut him down.

There was a moment when Ferox thought that the fort had fallen, and then his wife appeared at the head of her Brigantes, surging up the bank behind the rampart and killing all the Dacians who had broken through. He had not seen her fight for a long while and had forgotten her deadly grace, so that he marvelled even as he feared for her. Yet though tall and strong warriors fell on either side of her – several dying willingly as they used their bodies to protect her – she passed through unscathed, although her shield was left as little more than fragments by the end of the day.

The Dacians gave in just when he thought that the Romans could take no more, but the cost was dreadful. Sabinus was beheaded by a falx, Dionysius, returned to duty with a bandage over his ruined eye, lost his right leg and bled to death before he could be helped. Ephippus had his head torn off by a thrashing cable when the monâkon suddenly ripped itself apart as they were preparing to lob another stone into the mass of attacking warriors. Ferox did not know whether the repairs to the old machine had simply proved too weak or whether someone had tampered with it.

Thirty-nine more soldiers were dead, three times that so badly wounded that they might die and would certainly not walk for some time. There were hundreds more Dacians dead outside the walls and dozens inside to be tipped out when enough men had the strength to do the task. Piso was pale when he came down from the tower and for once said little and did not even leer at Claudia Enica when she passed. She was whole, and Ferox rejoiced because of that, but even she was subdued. Although she had fought and killed men many times, he knew that she had only ever been in one real battle before she came to the fort, and this was slaughter upon slaughter. The enemy were losing many more than the garrison, but since there were so many more of them still to attack it did not really matter. Ferox doubted that they could repulse another assault on that scale, because there were no longer enough men to man the walls and plug the gaps. Half of him wondered whether to let the Dacians know that the monâkon was ruined, so that they could go on their way. It probably did not matter anymore. After so much killing the enemy were bound to want revenge.

Ferox had less than two hundred and fifty men reasonably whole, and a few dozen more who could help if they were not required to move too much. That was far too few to hold walls as long as this against any real attack, especially as there were few missiles left. Apart from the hospital many of the rooms in the principia and praetorium were filled with wounded, mainly lying on the floor, on straw where it was available and on nothing where it was not. Ephippus had almost finished his acropolis and there ought just to be room for them all to squeeze in. He had already moved half the remaining food there. They might last a day or two more or they might not, depending on how determined the Dacians were to kill them. The trick was to delay the Dacians, hold the ramparts as long as they could and then pull back to the stronghold with as little loss as they could manage.

Claudia Enica came to him as he supervised the start of the clear up and she clung to him tightly. They had given up their room and bed to the injured, and now she slept with Sulpicia Lepidina and he bedded down in his office in the principia with Vindex and several others.

'You take risks, husband,' she told him.

'So do you. But I think now I have faith.' Ferox could not explain it, but he was no longer worried. He had rarely cared that much about his own fate, and more than once had come close to welcoming death. That had changed when he became a father and even more when he came to love this woman. He did not want her to die, not here, not for many years until she had seen their children grow. The fear should now have overwhelmed him, for it had preyed on his mind so often. Yet it was gone.

'We will be all right,' he said. 'I have faith in your magic.'

She stared at him, and he could not tell whether she was curious or worried. 'Now don't turn cheerful on me,' she said. 'I could not bear the shock.'

XXVI

Dobreta
The third day before the Nones of June

HADRIAN PACED BACK across the great bridge. It was complete at long last, although would not be formally opened until whenever the emperor chose to come to the province. He hoped that that would be soon, but it was too early to know what reaction his own letter and the other reports from Dacia would provoke. Trajan would come, that much was sure, but how soon and with what force was hard to say. If he moved fast, as he sometimes did, the emperor might leave Rome any day now, which meant that there could be very little time and yet everything was taking too long.

His staff knew enough to hang back and let the commander of I Minervia stride ahead of them. Why he chose to walk across the bridge and back after his evening meal each night they did not know, and had sense enough not to ask. The legatus could be friendly, even considerate, but he also had a temper and one or two outbursts had been enough warning. Rarely did he need them, but half a dozen soldiers had to escort him, along with the duty tribune and centurion and a gaggle of *cornicularii* and other functionaries, so Hadrian paced and thought and the rest trailed along, trying to appear as if they were enjoying themselves. Two of the escort were mounted, in case the legatus decided that he needed a horse.

The bridge drew Hadrian for its craft and its beauty and because it was so dangerous. Longinus was dead, that much was certain for the news had arrived from several sources, not least an angry letter dictated by Decebalus in which he demanded the return of Sosius. The king did not choose to state his reasons, but when pressed the envoy admitted that he blamed the freedman for the death of his chief hostage and hinted at murder. Sosius had fled, escaping his pursuers, but where he was and whether or not he still lived was anyone's guess, although Hadrian was confident that such a resourceful man would escape. Piso was alive, as far as they knew, and if Hadrian half regretted that, he was glad about the other hostages for they were decent enough men and might prove useful. So might Piso, and an idea was slowly taking shape with regard to the tribune. He would need Sosius, if the man could be found.

Hadrian had been right about the Dacians and their plans. Although they had harried the men fleeing from Sarmizegethusa and attacked most of the garrisons in lowland Dacia and those beyond the Danube, their main attack had been aimed at Dobreta and the bridge. Yet Ferox had stopped them, the gods alone knew how, and somehow he had held the fort against a great army. At least that was the latest news, admittedly days old. The centurion may even have been too successful, for if the Dacian army was stopped by the fort and never drove towards the Danube then in hindsight it might not seem to have posed a threat.

Lucius Herennius Saturninus, legatus Augusti of Moesia

Superior, was a crusty old man, set in his ways and almost as suspicious of clever men as Trajan himself, but Hadrian's reports had convinced him at last of the real threat to the bridge. Once convinced he had acted, and was busy now gathering more soldiers and riding further and faster than you would expect for a man of his age and considerable belly. He had put Hadrian in charge here, with orders worded to grant him considerable licence, while protecting Saturninus if anything went wrong.

Hadrian was almost ready, but the crucial word was almost. He had more than two thousand men from his own legion, formed into four strong cohorts, and another fifteen hundred legionaries from the other vexillations. Not all were in the best shape for campaigning after years of dull routine or building work, but even a few days in the field ought to rub off the edges. There was the bulk of three cohorts of auxiliary infantry already there, all *equitata* and one composed of archers. Two more, both infantry, were due to arrive within the next day or two. He also had most of an *ala milliaria* of cavalry and parts of two ordinary alae, as well as some irregulars, including a band of Numidians who were a nuisance in peacetime and a true blessing in any war.

That would give him a field force of six thousand men, a quarter mounted, even if he left a thousand at Dobreta and he was sorely tempted to cut the garrison to half that. Scouts reported that most of the Roxolani were far to the east, feasting and celebrating after their annihilation of the convoy. The bait had worked, and men who knew the clans well said that it would be a month or more before any chose to take the war path again. Perhaps a few score would join the Dacian army, but it was unlikely to be more and that should give him a clear advantage in cavalry. Still, he would be outnumbered by two or even three to one, so care would be needed. Roman armies had faced such odds often enough over the centuries, even here on the Danube, and they were not daunting in themselves as long as the commander knew what he was doing. Hadrian had no doubts about his own ability and was itching to be off, imagining in his mind arriving at Piroboridava having routed the enemy and hearing the cheers of the ragged garrison still clinging on to their battered ramparts.

The problem was food, as it always seemed to be in war, not so much possessing it as moving it. He had thousands of men, but only a few hundred mules, for none of the detachments had been prepared for a campaign, so lacked their own baggage trains. Again and again he ran through the figures, the weight of a daily ration for man and beast, in relation to the capacity of a pack mule. There were ox carts, but not enough of them, and taking the dumb plodding beasts along would slow him down for little substantial gain. A pair of mules or horses pulled more weight than they could carry and went far faster than oxen, so he had decided to change the teams around, only to find that there were no suitable harnesses in store. The fabricae were set to making them, which meant more time waiting. Saturninus might return any day and decide to take direct charge of the relief expedition or worse still might forbid it, reckoning that the fort must have fallen by now.

For Hadrian that did not matter. It was a good story to tell if he rode into the fort just in time to save the survivors. The presence of a senator's daughter and an equestrian lady

– both still young enough to be accounted beautiful, and one with four good Roman children beside her – would make the scene all the more uplifting. Yet if he was late, routing the enemy army only to discover the charred remains of the fort and the decaying corpses of its occupants, then it was time to speak of Mars Ultor and the need for Rome's avenging god to lead the legions on to fitting revenge on the savages who had done this. Even dead, the presence of the ladies and children could make it all far more poignant, if told well. They might even serve a purpose if they were captured alive, for the fear of their debasement, rape and torture gave the emperor even more justification for the utter destruction of Decebalus and his kingdom. Whatever happened could be made to help the emperor, and better still give him fresh esteem for Hadrian, but only if he could win a victory in battle or make the enemy retreat from him, and he could do neither unless the column was ready to move.

Hadrian turned to the tribune following three paces behind.

'How many carts are ready to move by dawn?'

'Tomorrow, sir?'

'Of course, tomorrow! What did you think, at the Saturnalia?'

The tribune balked at the anger. 'I, um, I think...' he stammered.

'Twenty two-wheeled carts drawn each by a pair of mules or horses,' the centurion snapped the report, trying to shield the senior officer. 'Twelve four-wheeled waggons with teams of four. Then twenty-seven carts carrying scorpiones and their ammunition and other equipment.'

Hadrian made up his mind. 'Men to carry four days

rations in their packs. Then empty all the artillery carts and strip them clean of anything that weighs. I want them packed with sacks of biscuit, grain and dried bacon.'

'Sir?'

'Do it. We carry food, only food, and men will fight with the weapons they carry.' The power of the bolt shooters was terrifying, but Dacians were less impressed than barbarians who did not understand such things, so this time they would do without artillery support. 'Half galearii to remain behind and senior officers may take one boy to serve them, but no more. That includes the legatus, so no one can complain that I deny others while enjoying my own comforts. Anyone disobeying will be flogged out of the camp, whatever their rank.'

The centurion's eyes widened a little, although he said nothing.

'When do we move, sir?' the tribune had managed to control his stammer.

'Form up at the start of the last watch of the night and march an hour before dawn. You'd better send a note to your wife that you will be going away for some time. There'll be no time to spare any of us from work tonight. You, man!' He pointed at one of the mounted soldiers. 'Give me your horse.' The man dismounted and Hadrian sprang into the saddle with his accustomed grace. He wished that there was time to unbuckle the girth and take the saddle off, for he felt like galloping bareback, but there was no time.

'Hurry everyone. We go before dawn.'

'Sir, what garrison do we leave here?'

'Five hundred men and no more. Drawn from all the

infantry in proportion. Tell them to select the oldest and least fit for marching hard and fast until we have enough.'

'Sir?' The centurion dared to hint at his doubts, but the legatus was not listening for he was already clattering away.

Hadrian felt the thrill before a hunt and urged the horse into a gallop, hoofs pounding on the planks of the bridge. The cavalryman was already yards behind him, struggling to keep up. This was a moment to cherish, as doubts faded and he faced the challenge of a hard task, but one that he knew would succeed. This was the moment. All of his stars were aligned in a way he had seen only two or three times before and always at a time when his life changed drastically for the better. He did not need a professional astrologer to tell him that the next nine days were his moment and that after that the heavenly bodies would move and all become uncertain again. He must win and he must win now.

The horse raced along, and Hadrian laughed with sheer joy as the wind rushed through his hair.

XXVII

Piroboridava
The Nones of June

THEY HELD OFF one more big attack, and Ferox never understood how they had managed it, shooting away the last bolts and stones for the artillery, the last arrows for the handful of archers still on their feet, and all the stones and javelins. The Dacians gave way before the Romans, and just maybe they were almost as tired. Enica led a charge along the top of one of the ramparts, the vexillum of the goddess behind her, and the enemy gave way. Even Piso fought well, clumping along on his bandaged leg and bawling out encouragement. Yet by the end they were almost spent, with about a hundred more men dead or too injured to fight anymore. As Ferox chivvied the men to gather whatever weapons they could find and to tip the enemy corpses over the walls, the men moved like sleepwalkers, unseeing, emotionless, and if ever a man stopped for a moment his eyes shut and he passed out.

The next attack came at night, as Ferox had feared, and for the first time in many days the mist rose again in the early hours, so that the attackers were very close before they were seen and the alarm sounded. All that meant was that the enemy swarmed up and over the walls even faster than they might have done if there had been men waiting to do their feeble best in repelling them.

Ephippus was dead, but his acropolis was finished in spite of Piso's scorn.

'If we can't stop them with high walls and ramparts,' he had said many times, 'how will low barricades help us? You cannot show fear to these people. If you do, they'll walk all over you. That's what Longinus let happen at Sarmizegethusa – only found his courage when it was too late, the silly old sod.'

The last stronghold was ready, even if it was no more than low barricades and the single tower joining up the praetorium, principia, hospital, a storeroom and barrack block. Ferox had wanted to move all the civilians and wounded inside days ago, along with as many of the men as could be bedded down within the compound. Piso refused, and as the days passed, he grew more and more assertive of his rights as senior officer. Fighting on the walls had invigorated him, so that he almost seemed to grow taller and bolder before their eyes.

'If we pull back it will tell everyone – including our men – that the fight is hopeless and they will give in. For all we know a relief column is on its way. That is what we must give the men – hope! Hope that after all this we will prevail. For the few hours, or if the gods love someone here a few days, longer we might last, it is not worth snatching that hope from them.'

Vindex suggested hitting the tribune on the head again, but Ferox was too accustomed to obey and was not sure whether the tribune was right or wrong. He drove himself hard, but he was so weary that he no longer had the energy to think about such big questions. There was just the next step and the next moment, trying to do each little thing to keep them in the fight.

Shrouded in mist, the Dacians crept up to the walls, newly made ladders at the ready. They came past the stinking corpses, many with bellies burst open, and most with eyes pecked away by the carrion fowl who never left the fort these days, growing fat on the flesh of men.

Sentries were tired, slow to see and slower still to react, and so the fort fell. The west gate was opened first, and hundreds of warriors poured inside, led by Bastarnae with falxes. Ferox, having taken a rare snatch of sleep wrapped in his cloak in the courtyard of the principia, woke to screaming and shouts of triumph and to Sulpicia Lepidina shaking him awake.

'They are coming,' she said.

There was little he could do except make sure that the acropolis held and that all those able to reach it were let inside. There were twenty or so men who had been sleeping in the courtyard and as many more of the wounded able to fight if not required to move too much, so he shouted orders and sent them to the weak spots. Fugitives were coming in already; Sosius was one of the first to slide over the improvised wall. About half the soldiers and even more of the few families, slaves and galearii made it in time, while all the rest died, for the Dacians were in no mood to take prisoners.

Piso again came to new life. He had been at the porta praetoria and he gathered as many men as he could and led then in a knot back towards the acropolis. He had almost fifty men when he rallied them near the gate, thirty by the time he reached the junction of the roads, and sixteen were left to run in through the small gap in the barricades. They were the last big group to make it through and they had drawn many of the enemies to them, giving others a chance to escape.

There were many heroes that night – and Ferox suspected a fair few whose deeds and names would never be known. Claudia Enica was in the praetorium, and he had had to hold her to stop her from running out to rally her warriors. She had bitten his arm before sleep faded, sense returned and she took charge of the far wall of the barricade. Vindex was at the rear gate with some of his Carvetii and some Brigantians and they met a much larger group of Bastarnae as they retreated. The fight was savage and swift, with half of the Britons cut down and dismembered where they lay. Vindex killed three of the enemy, until he took a bad cut to the shoulder even after the falx had shattered his shield, and a lighter cut to the leg. Ivonercus saved him, standing over his body to kill the warrior before he could strike again, and then kill another who came screaming out of the darkness. Vepoc lifted the scout onto his back, and they and five others made it to the acropolis. Maximus had similarly carried two men to safety, before a stone from a sling hit his ankle which had since swollen badly.

Some of the bravest were unlikely heroes. Privatus, the chamberlain of Sulpicia Lepidina, was away from the praetorium seeing to his owner's horses, some of the tiny handful left alive. Hearing the noise he found a group of three wives belonging to the veterans and persuaded them to come out from where they were hiding in the rafters above the horse boxes and got them back. Achilles, Claudia Enica's dwarf who served as both buffoon and accountant, somehow climbed onto the roof of the principia, prised off tiles and started lobbing them down at any warriors trying to attack one of the most vulnerable stretches of barricade where his mistress and some of her Brigantes stood guard. The Dacians flung javelins at him and the little man dodged. Then they brought up an archer, but even then he proved an elusive target and shaft after shaft bounced off the rooftop before he was finally hit and fell. He lived, at least for the moment, with broken legs, a broken arm and the arrow in his side, but the heavy clay tiles falling on the enemy had done a lot to keep them at bay.

There were piles of dead warriors in front of all the barricades before the Dacians gave up the attempt to overrun it and went off to rest or loot. Ferox guessed that they had seventy or so men able to fight, two or three times that many wounded, and thirty or forty civilians and others. He was not sure how to count Sosius as the freedman showed little enthusiasm for fighting for all his killer's eyes.

Bran wept, sitting with his back pressed against the wall of the praetorium. Ferox had never seen the boy like that, and it took a while before he learned what had happened. He had been with Vindex, but had broken away from the others to search for Minura, for he knew that the queen had sent her to carry a message to the east gate. The attack there was slower, and Cunicius had hesitated before ordering his men to retreat. By that time they were surrounded, and the centurion had to lead a charge to clear a path down one of the side alleys. They broke the Dacians, but the centurion lost both legs below the knee to a low sweeping falx and a fresh band of warriors were coming through the now opened gate and nearly upon them. Minura told the men to flee and stood beside Cunicius as his life blood flowed away. Bran was too far away to help, but close enough to see.

'She was like the Morrigan in her rage,' he told Ferox. 'Her armour gleaming like the sun, her shield a disc of fire and her sword like a bolt of lightning.' Ferox had never thought the boy capable of such poetry. 'I saw her behead one man and then spin to slice the arm off another coming at her from the other side. It was… beautiful. She put down seven at the very least, even when blood gushed from her own wounds. She had sworn that she would never let men take her. Never again.'

Claudia Enica had appeared and patted the boy on the shoulder. 'She kept her word, brother,' she said softly. 'Our sister is gone to join all the other brothers and sisters and all the Mothers since the world began. One day our souls shall join them. We must make sure that we live to be worthy of their company.'

Bran got to his feet. 'Aye,' he said. 'Fleeting though it be, there is vengeance to work.'

'Tomorrow,' Ferox said. 'I do not think they will come again tonight.' In truth the dawn was little more than an hour away, but as he watched the boy limp off, his left leg stiff from a wound taken several days ago, he did not envy the men who would meet him in battle.

As the sun was rising, they held a consilium in a side room of the principia.

'Well, it is not much,' Piso said, after Petrullus had read out a list of the men fit for action and all the other survivors. 'What about food?'

'Six days' worth if we are careful,' Sulpicia Lepidina told them. 'Ten if we take only the bare minimum needed for life, but the wounded and sick will be dead before that time has passed.'

'Six days, it is,' Piso decided. 'If no help has come by then, it will not matter and we may as well feast as long as we can. I take it that there is some wine left. Good. And thank you, lady, for all your efforts. I am so sorry that... Well, just take it that I am sorry. Now, Ferox and I will plan our strategies for holding this "acropolis" – or as Romans perhaps we should say our Capitol – and I think everyone else should get as much rest as they can. Thank you, all.

'The enemy will take most of their army and go,' Piso said after the others had gone. 'Today or tomorrow, but now that they can cross the bridge at will, they need only leave a thousand or so here to slaughter us and the rest can march for the river.'

'Perhaps, my lord.'

'If help is to come in time then an army must already be on its way.'

'Hadrian promised to do his best.'

Piso sniffed scornfully. 'I do not care to rely on the lisping *Graeculus*,' he said. 'Any fellow who sports a beard and is fonder of boys than women cannot be sound. Still, we have no choice, and my revered legatus is an ambitious man, there is no doubt of that. You have nothing to say, centurion?'

'Not my place, sir.' Ferox did not know that Hadrian was called the 'little Greek', although it did not surprise him. As far as he could tell, senators were as catty about each other as any group of fashionable young women.

'Is it not? I do wonder what your place – or mine for that

matter – is, given our circumstances. Well, it does not much matter. If somehow we can cling on here for a few days – I see no prospect of as many as six, but that is beside the point. We should not have lasted this long and Hadrian is a rational man, so he will surely expect us to be dead.'

'He probably does not know that you are here, lord.'

'Might be best that way. But he will balance the odds and judge that even the most heroic garrison must be dead by now. Which means that he will not hurry, and even if he is able to defeat the enemy army, he may not come to our aid in time.' Piso paused, leaning forward on the table. 'We need to send a message to him, so that he knows that we hold out and will hurry. He will not be able to resist the glory of saving the last remnant of the garrison, let alone two ladies, one of them well connected.'

Ferox knew what was coming, but was not about to volunteer.

'You are the man to go,' Piso said.

'Forgive me, my lord, but my place is here, trying to make sure that we are still alive if relief does come.'

'It is an order, not a request, centurion. The time for ingenuity in defence is gone, so I am sure that I can do whatever is needed almost as well as you could.' The tribune smiled at this false modesty. 'What I cannot do is creep through the night as quietly as a wolf. Is that not what they call your folk, the wolf people?'

'I am always told that my people are the Romans, my lord.'

'Don't be obtuse. You are one of the Silures and they take pride in fighting at night. Don't look so surprised. Even a tribune can read a book now and then or listen to the tales the soldiers tell of you here. You might get out of the fort, sneak past those enemy left behind and – when the time comes – their main army to reach Hadrian or whoever is coming to our rescue. Or if not get to Dobreta and at the very least take a report of what you and all the rest of us have done here. I'd rather my family know that I have done my duty for the Senate and People – and for the emperor, not that he likes us much.'

'But, my lord—'

'No buts. You go or I place you under arrest.' There was a hardness in his eyes and his right hand strayed to the bone handle of his sword. 'I doubt that anyone would question if I ordered your execution without trial – and the odds are strongly that I won't be alive to answer any questions they do raise. You are going, centurion, and if threats do not persuade, then think that this will give a chance to save your friends here. And your wife. If you don't want to save her then you are a fool. So you go tonight or you die. I have no time or patience for arrest.'

Ferox did not have his sword, for Vindex had offered to hone the edge and he had left the blade with the scout. There was a long stylus on the table, its point sharp enough to drive through the tribune's throat if he got the chance, and a heavy local bowl in which Piso had washed his hands at the start of the meeting, if he chose to take Vindex's suggestion and knock the aristocrat on the head. The problem was that he began to think that the fool might be right. Either way, this was not the moment. He relaxed.

'Yes, sir.'

'Good,' Piso said, taking this as acceptance. Then I shall write an account of the days since I left the hospital and you will write one of the siege up until that point. Apart from the message you carry in your head, these words will tell our story, so that the truth will be known even if we perish. So go away and write. There will be plenty of time for us to plan how you are to get out of the fort later on. I would suggest taking Ivonercus with you and perhaps some other Brigantes. If you run into trouble they can always pose as deserters and maybe you can all talk your way through. That rogue, Sosius, may be useful too. He is Hadrian's man, so his words will be all the stronger.

'And do not look so glum, Flavius Ferox. We may all be dead before nightfall!'

The Dacians did not attack, apart from sending arrows at anyone who moved in the open. With the ramparts and wall towers well above them, a man had to crouch close to the barricades to walk in any sort of safety. At noon the sentry on their own tower shouted down that large bands of Dacians were crossing the bridge, and in the hours that followed the flow continued, with waggons and mules as well as warriors.

Ferox had to admit that Piso was right about that, and the main army was continuing its advance, so he set to his task of writing a day-by-day account of the defence of the fort. The truth did matter, the tribune was also right about that, so he tried to remember every piece of bravery and name the men who had done it. Now and again he went back to read what he had written and struggled to believe that these things had happened.

Philo brought him food as the hours passed, and still he wrote, forcing his weary mind to concentrate and get it all right. He ate one-handed as he lifted one of the wooden tablets and read the tiny words. The door opened again, but he did not look up for it was surely Philo. Then it closed and he heard the key click in the lock. This was normally a storage room for records, and all such places had locks on the door. He was never sure why. Perhaps the army worried that a deranged soldier would break in and tamper with long forgotten duty rosters and reports.

Claudia Enica raised an eyebrow. 'I never took you for an author.' She was in her tunic and boots, with her hair loose around her shoulders. 'Sulpicia and I want you.'

Ferox did his best to mimic her fondness for arching an eyebrow in studied surprise.

'She would have come as well, but that would no doubt have prompted some lewd male humour.'

'You're thinking of Vindex, my lady.'

'Yes, well, if he did not have that unfortunate face and filthy mind and if he had those few virtues you possess, perhaps I would have been better off marrying him.

'You're going to sneak out. Don't look surprised. I am queen, it is my part in life to know as much as I can about what is happening. In this case it was simple. When we were all dismissed, I lingered at the door and listened. It is a method I have adopted since I was a small child and is often efficacious. There was a sentry, but he did not mind.'

'Dazzled by your beauty, of course.'

'Naturally. Well I know what Piso has ordered and I have spoken to Lepidina and Vindex and no one else. We all think that you should go. Am I right in thinking that you were wondering about bludgeoning our noble tribune over the head instead of going? You see, I know you better than you think. You must go because it is our best hope of coming through this. And along with everything else you will take two letters. One is from Lepidina in case it ever can reach Cerialis. The other is from me to our girls. No need to pull that face. I am not wholly uncaring whatever you may think.'

'I have never thought that.' He stood up, then hesitated. 'Why don't you come with me? You are not a Silure, but—'

'Thank the gods for that,' she interrupted.

'But you are a Sister and move well.'

Claudia Enica wiggled her hips and then became serious. 'We cannot all go, and I cannot leave the others behind while I am safe.'

'Safe? The odds are not good.'

'Yet you want me to come? What sort of husband are you?'

'A poor one,' he said, stepping forward so that he could put his hands on her waist. 'But I try my best.'

'Hmmm,' she murmured. 'And you have not asked why I have not written a message for you.'

'Because I rather hoped that you would...' He stopped because she stood on her toes and kissed him.

'That I would deliver it in person?' she said after a moment. 'Now there's an idea.'

Ferox was mildly surprised that the old and poorly made table took the strain. The chair was a bit sturdier and even that creaked a good deal. The afternoon passed and as far as he could tell the Dacians did not attack.

'We should get about our business,' she said, and giggled when he deliberately misunderstood and the table was tested again. Later still, she sat on his lap, bare save for her boots.

'Why do you like me to keep these on?' she asked.

'So you can always run away if you choose to,' he said, his mind blissfully hazy and unable to think of anything witty.

'If anyone has been listening to us they will be very jealous.'

'I know,' he said. 'Most of the men fancy me.' He dodged a slap.

'Take Vepoc as well as Ivonercus,' she said, once again the queen.

'Aren't they both sworn to kill me?' Even if Enica wanted to return to business, Ferox was determined to make the most of this moment and started to kiss her neck.

'Yes, but it will be a mark of faith and trust to take them with you.'

He pulled away. 'Lovely.'

'And do not trust Sosius.'

'I never have.'

'Then trust even less. He must go for he is Hadrian's man, but from what I have seen and from what Bran and poor Minura said, he is bad and a very dangerous man.'

'So I am going then.'

'You are going. The tribune says so, and much more importantly so do I.'

Ferox sighed. 'You have just given me a lot of good reasons to stay here with you.'

The queen freed herself from his grasp and stood up. 'Well you will not have any more of those reasons until you have saved us all.' She bent down to pick up her scattered clothes and Ferox bit his lip rather than risk a comment.

'Are you trying to get rid of me?'

'Yes,' she said. 'Go – but come back.'

'I do not trust Piso either.'

'Jealous, eh? Think I want you out the way for that reason?'

'Of course not.'

'So I am too old, too plain.' The old Claudia was back now. He still found it hard to cope with so many very different women all inside the same person. She laughed and took pity. 'I reckon he would try if he thought that he had a chance. Be the last thing he ever tried, and I suspect he knows that now.'

They finished dressing in silence and when they were done she again reached up and this time pecked him on the cheek.

'I did not think that it would be like this.'

The urge to say something flippant about a man trying his best died as he saw the emotion in her eyes.

'The fighting just goes on and on, and so many fall.' Sometimes the smoothness with which she killed made it easy to forget that she had seen little of war.

'It can be just hard work and butchery,' he said. 'And luck matters more than skill.'

'How have you stood it all these years?' she asked. 'I do not believe that I would ever again seek this out, save only to defend my own family and folk.'

Ferox was not sure what to say because he did not know what the answer was. Much of his life had been spent in fighting and killing and seeing friends die. It was not that he was used to it, but it was easier and he no longer really knew any other life. Somehow he kept surviving and then the next fight would come and he was still there at the end of that.

'Better to feel the sorrow than not be alive to feel it,' he said eventually, knowing it meant little. 'I just seem to keep on living.'

'That is because the souls in the Otherworld are in no hurry to have your gloomy face join them,' she said. 'Can't say I blame them, either. So you keep living, husband.' The seriousness had gone. 'Your children need a father.'

'And a mother.'

'Oh, I'll be all right. After all, you're the one going off in the company of men sworn to kill you!'

XXVIII

Piroboridava
Seventh day before the Ides of July

PISO WAS LUCKY that he was hit by a falx swung one-handed rather than brought down with full force. The blow dented the top of his borrowed helmet and knocked the tribune out cold and the Dacian bounded over his body, calling for the others to follow.

This was the second attack of the day at the line of barrels and filled sacks between the praetorium and principia and there was little space to fight. Bran was limping, and was knocked off his feet when the warrior swung his shield. He rolled as he landed, and slashed his gladius at the Dacian's ankle and felt the edge bite. The man screamed, dropping his shield and cutting down, but Bran rolled again out of the way, and Vindex chopped into the Dacian's neck.

'Up you get, lad. Between the two of us we've still got a pair of good legs.'

Another Dacian came at them, then hesitated as the two men spread as far apart as was possible in the alleyway. Vindex could see that the Brigantian and the legionary at the barricade were holding back the rest. He feinted to the right, drawing the man's gaze, but the warrior was quick and parried his real attack. Then Bran slashed behind the Dacian's right knee and he fell. Vindex stabbed down to finish the job. He was panting, his chest sore from a blow in the first attack that had not penetrated his mail, but had probably broken a rib or two.

The Dacians gave up for the moment, and judging from the quiet they had withdrawn everywhere else as well. An arrow zipped between Vindex and Bran and they did a lurching run to the shelter of the barricade. A slave and an auxiliary dragged the unconscious tribune away.

'Bastards,' Vindex said to no one in particular.

'You should not have let him go,' Bran said once again.

'Will you let up? They didn't ask me, did they, and wouldn't have listened even if they had.'

'Then we should have gone.'

'Hopped our way there, I suppose.'

Bran lowered his voice. 'I do not trust the tribune who sent him. He's a useless shit.' They were both peering over the top of the barricade, but could see no sign of any more warriors or of the archers.

Vindex guffawed. 'I'm rubbing off on you, aren't I? Well copy me, son, and you could end up a thousand miles from home on one leg and struggling to breathe! Oh bugger me, you already are.

'Come on, you know him well enough to know he didn't go because of that clown.' Vindex had switched to the language of the tribes in the unlikely event that the legionary might take offence. 'Herself told him to go. He'll always do what she tells him. ... Me too, for that matter. The queen said go, so he went. But he wouldn't have gone unless we were here to keep an eye on her.'

'You keep your eyes to yourself, Carvetian!' Enica had come up so softly in her felt boots that they had not heard her. 'I know what you're like.'

'You in charge now, my queen?' Vindex asked. 'With the tribune away with the fairies and Petrullus in the hospital.'

Enica kneeled beside them to shelter behind the barricade. 'I have always been in charge, you should know that by now. I just let those daft men believe that they are important.' She turned to the legionary. 'How goes it, Lucius?'

'Hanging on, lady. I'll make the bastard res publica pay me my bounty yet. Sorry, lady, forgetting myself.'

'When is your time up?'

'November, would you believe it?'

'Well drink one for me when the day comes.'

'I will, lady, I will.'

'Time for me to go,' the queen said. 'Now be good children, and don't talk to strangers!' She ran bent almost double, and either heard the swish of the arrow or guessed for she swung to the side to let it pass.

Vindex watched her go, his admiration obvious. 'That one's special and no doubt.'

Claudia Enica heard the compliment and let herself smile. She was going around the whole position, checking that all was well and doing her best to encourage. Ferox had once told her that an officer was often too busy to worry about the big things, because there was always so much to do and so many little things to worry about. Still, as she squatted behind barricades or climbed up to the rafters and peered cautiously through the holes they had made in the roofs, she could not help wondering whether her husband lived and where he was. A lookout spent the daylight hours on top of the tower, because the ladders leading up were exposed to archers on the ramparts and it was too risky to climb except at night. For all they could see there might be no more than four or five hundred Dacians left at the fort, but for the second day there was no sign of anyone else, whether the enemy's main army or any Roman relief force.

The buildings were vulnerable, because there were few windows and it was also hard to fight through small holes like that. Stone or not, the Dacians had tried to pile up timber and start fires against several walls. So far, it had not worked, mainly because they had ripped rafters and tiles away so that men could perch and follow Achilles' example by lobbing the tiles down at anyone who came close. The dwarf was doing well and might survive, assuming any of them did. Half the food would be gone by the end of this third day, and there was a steady trickle of losses each time the Dacians attacked. If they attacked on all sides at the same time, they would surely swamp the remnants of the garrison. The only reason she could think of why they had not done this was that they did not want to lose men when it was just a matter of days.

Claudia Enica kept herself busy and worried about all the little things. Now and again she wondered about all the little steps in life that had brought her to this place, and that led to thoughts of other days and other times, some good and some bad. She and Lepidina shared a light meal together, saying little, which was rare for them, and simply enjoying the other's company. Lepidina was worried about the games she could hear the children playing.

'"He's lost his head!" you hear them shout, and "That one's got an arrow in the lungs!" Even young Flavia waves

a stick as if it was a sword. That's your influence, no doubt!
… They seem less bothered than I would expect by all the
dying though.'

There was not much other news, apart from the fact that
Piso had woken up, but declared himself too hurt to do
anything other than go off to one of the last rooms with no
one else in it, taking an amphora of wine with him.

'It's dangerous after a blow to the head or at least I fear
that it is,' Lepidina told her friend. 'Although in truth I did
not argue too much. Angry and resentful man that – not
happy in himself and blaming everyone else for it.'

'Sosius had doubts about his loyalty, and I do wonder
whether…' Claudia hesitated, and would probably not have
said this to anyone else. 'I wonder whether it was Sosius
who attacked him on the night of the fire. Probably acting
on orders.'

Lepidina did not need to ask whose orders. 'Perhaps.
Sweet Minerva, that all seems an age ago. I just hope
concerns about him do not deter them coming to help us.'

The Dacians made no attacks throughout the afternoon,
although arrows flew now and again. Enica wondered
whether they would wait for darkness and decided to get
some rest before the sun went down, so that she would be
fresher if something did happen. Before trying to sleep, she
indulged herself with a wash down and a change of tunic
and undergarments, going to one of the little rooms in
the praetorium's bath suite. There was no one else there,
although the tribune was in a chamber off the same corridor.

Washing was a joy and she longed for a true bath and the
feeling of the steam cleansing all her skin. Yet just a simple
wash refreshed her so much that she wondered whether

she could sleep. She ran her fingers through the clean tunic. Philo had taken it upon himself to launder her spare clothes, devoting his energies to her improvement. There was a knock on the door.

'Lady?'

It was Indike, sent by her husband to collect the dirty clothes and take them away to where he could work his magic and restore them to life. She smiled as she came in. A slave was used to seeing nudity among the wealthy, just as Claudia gave little thought to the other woman's presence.

'Anything else, lady?'

'Thank you, no.'

Claudia lifted a small bronze-backed mirror she had brought and studied her face, bereft for days of any cosmetics. Were there lines around the eyes and mouth? She thought that she had seen them when she last looked, but washing off the dust and grime had reduced them to no more than hints. Sighing, she thought of her grandmother, the great Cartimandua, whose mirror had helped her to see the future. She had been a frightening old woman, usually stern until one of her rare moments of kindness. Enica sought in her own mind for the dead queen's voice, for her certainty and guidance.

Instead there was a man's voice from the hall outside, gruff and unclear.

'Girl!' the man was shouting now. 'Here, girl!'

Enica could not hear the response. She had already drawn on her boots, and might have smiled at this mark of the Mother's training. Shoes or boots first, each Mother told her pupils. 'You can fight naked if you have to, but a firm grip on muddy ground will often save your life.' Not worrying about undergarments, she pulled the fresh tunic over her head.

There was a scream, cut short in an instant.

'Come on, bitch!' The voice was Piso's, very slurred and unclear.

Enica drew her curved sica from its scabbard and unlocked the door. There was no one in the hall, but her old clothes were scattered on the floor where they had been dropped. Across the way, two doors were shut tight and only the one in between them had light showing around its edges and underneath. She wondered about kicking the door, then decided that calm might be better. Enica lowered her sword to her side, and opened it.

Indike was on the table, face-down amid the plates and scraps of the tribune's meal, her long dress bunched up over her bare buttocks. Piso was holding her down with one hand, while fumbling at his breeches with the other. The girl was sobbing, her whole body quivering with fear.

'Stop, lord tribune,' Claudia Enica said, doing her best to sound firm and level as her anger rose.

'Piss off, Ferox!' Piso mumbled without looking back. The broken fragments of the amphora showed that he had drunk the whole thing.

'Stop at once!' Claudia yelled at him. 'You're a disgrace, tribune, to your family and rank.'

'Jupiter's balls, at last.' Piso's breeches started to slide down. 'Go away, you fool. You cannot judge a noble.' Indike wriggled, trying to free herself, so the tribune slapped her hard across the bottom. 'Still, you slut! Still!'

Claudia Enica went forward and pressed the tip of her blade against Piso's throat.

'You dumb bastard, Ferox, what are you playing at? She's just a slave.'

'I said stop or I slit your throat,' Claudia told him. 'And I am not Ferox.'

Piso stood up, turning his head and focusing his bleary eyes. He shuffled back, breeches around his knees. Enica kept the blade close to his throat, but let him move away.

'Go, girl. Find your husband and stay with him – or if not him, the Lady Sulpicia Lepidina.' Indike was up, pulling her dress back down. She could not speak, but the gratitude showed in her eyes as she fled.

'Lady?' Piso blinked as he started. 'The Lady Claudia? Is that you?'

'It is, and come in time. That woman is free, so what you tried to do was rape. Still, I am sure that we can persuade her to forget this ever happened.'

He was very drunk and anger flashed into his face as his mind cleared a little. 'Slave or freedwoman, what's the difference? I have many consuls among my ancestors.'

'And wouldn't they be proud,' Claudia said before she could restrain herself. Piso had begun to pull up his breeches, but stopped. 'You have fought like a hero,' she went on, for a wildness was coming into his eyes. 'Worthy of your family and worthy of praise and reward and honours to come. Do not throw all that away in a moment of weakness.'

'You are right, lady.' Piso stood as straight and dignified as a man can when holding up his trousers with one hand. 'It is the drink. I must thank you for stopping me and beg for your discretion.'

Claudia smiled, feeling the tension fading. 'Of course, tribune.' She lowered her sword.

'In the old days men would have sung of you,' Piso told her. 'Warrior maiden, never having trained her woman's hands to Minerva's distaff or basket of wool, but hardy to bear the brunt of battle and in speed of foot to outstrip the winds.'

'Poor Camilla,' Claudia said, recognising the lines from the *Aenied* and remembering how, long ago, even Ferox had compared her to the Volscian heroine. 'But we are Romans and so destined to overcome the proud in war and not share her fate.'

'We are Romans...' Piso's face changed like cloud passing over the moon. The rational, educated aristocrat fell away and rage filled his eyes. His left hand shot forward and grabbed her wrist, squeezing and twisting with a strength she would not have guessed he possessed. Perhaps she was tired, for she should not have been surprised like this and the thought brought a moment of panic. She slapped him with her free hand.

'Bitch!' he hissed and punched, catching her on the cheek as she tried to twist out of the way. Her sword fell with a clatter that seemed loud. 'We're all dead,' he screamed and taking hold of her pushed with all his weight. 'All dead! So nothing matters, nothing!' She tried to strangle him, but his brute strength broke the lock and then he lifted her up onto the table. Her hand found a cup and she flung it at him, but missed and then he had both her arms and was pinning her down, his weight pressing onto her.

'You'll do better.' The words were soft, almost tender and so surprising that she stopped struggling, wondering whether this was all some perverse joke. 'You are so beautiful. A lady rather than some slut.' His breath reeked of wine, and pressing her down with one elbow she felt the other hand take the hem of her tunic. He stood beside her, and she kept her legs tight together, but could not work out how to kick him. 'Steady, girl, gently now,' he whispered as if soothing a nervous horse. 'It's all right, it's all right.'

Enica pulled her head away from his rank breath and the gaze of his mad eyes, and saw a chance. She relaxed, stopping her struggles.

'You're a hero,' she said softly. 'A great hero.'

Piso's head swayed as if struggling to understand the change. He glanced down. The tunic was tightly bunched under the woman, so he began to yank hard at the material until it started to tear. Anger and hate filled his eyes again as the tunic ripped open from hem to neck. 'And you're no lady,' he shouted, realising that she was wearing nothing underneath it.

'I'm a bitch,' she said, licking her lips. Piso started to drool, and the feel of it on her skin revolted her, but she had a plan and just one chance, so ignored it. He felt for her legs, and Enica helped him to lift her a little further onto the table top, and let her knees part.

The change in her mood for some reason made his eyes burn with new anger.

'Bitch!' he growled and hit her on the face again.

Enica's legs were in the air and the tribune was trying to wriggle so that his breeches would drop, but the trousers remained stubbornly in place so he felt for them, trying to work out what was wrong. Her right hand reached the bone-covered haft of a table knife on the plate beside her. Piso was staring down at his trousers, then grunted with satisfaction as the breeches at last dropped. Enica crossed her legs, grasping the tribune tightly and used that to lever her torso up, the knife in her hand. Piso's eyes widened and then the tip of the blade drove into his left eyeball with less force than she had hoped. He squealed, a noise more animal than human and reached up to his face. Enica clung on to him, ripped the blade free, dragging the remnants of the eye out of the socket, and plunging it into the man's neck. His arms flailed and she let go with her legs, slamming hard onto the table and losing her grip on the knife. Piso staggered, moaning, and when he pulled the blade free a jet of blood sprayed all over her bare skin. Yet the tribune would not die and came at her. Enica half rolled, half fell from the table, losing the rest of her tunic and the dying man dropped onto her. His face pressed against her and she was not sure whether he was trying to bite her or kiss her, and the blood was everywhere so that it was hard to take firm hold and lift him off. She had finally managed to shift the corpse and push herself away when the door opened.

'Bugger me!' Vindex said. Bran was behind him, face grim as if he had failed, but then Sulpicia Lepidina pushed past them. She took in the dead tribune, his mutilated face staring one-eyed at the ceiling, and Enica, standing up, naked save for her boots, her white skin half covered with blood. The tribune had fouled himself in his last moments, adding to the stench and the wreck of the room.

'Are you all right, my dear?' Lepidina asked.

Vindex undid the brooch on his cloak. Claudia Enica gasped for breath.

'Are you all right?' Lepidina's voice was eerily calm. Vindex held out his cloak and she took it and went over to her friend.

'I am,' Enica said, amazed that her words were level. She pulled the cloak around her. 'I am.'

'Did that bastard...?' Vindex could say no more. His fingers were clenching and unclenching in his fury.

'He tried.' Claudia Enica managed a thin smile. 'And failed. My honour is preserved – and he is dead.'

'Good,' Vindex said.

'Perhaps, but he is a tribune and the son of a senator.' Claudia looked over her shoulder at Lepidina. 'What should we do? And what should we say? He has fought well in the last few days and won the men's respect.'

'Sometimes the truth is not only the simplest idea, but the best,' Lepidina said, patting her friend on the shoulder. 'A bad blow to the head can change a man's character, sometimes forever, and wine does not help. Whatever respect he may have won, the men love you – all of them.'

'You too, lady,' Vindex said.

'Perhaps, but a blind man could see that you are the heart and the head of this defence. So we will say that he tried to rape you and that you killed him. They will hate him for this crime and admire you more for your strength and skill.

'As for later, his family is in disgrace and he was here to redeem himself and perhaps one day redeem his fool of a father. Whatever is said in public, I doubt that many will miss him.'

Claudia Enica had the odd feeling that what had happened was no more than a dream from which she had woken. 'I do wonder if he was sent here to die.'

'Perhaps. Which may mean that some will be grateful, although whether or not they can show it is harder to say. But those are problems for another day, if we live to see it. And to do that we need you fresh and restored. Go and wash again, and put on some clean clothes.'

'Yes, mother, right away, mother.' Enica did a little curtsey, making the cloak fall open. Vindex and Bran turned away and she thought how strange that was, especially for the scout.

After she had washed again and dressed in her last clean tunic, Claudia Enica fussed with her hair and then took another look in her mirror. The eyes that stared back at her were the eyes of Cartimandua. She did not smile, for her grandmother had rarely smiled, but she felt stronger.

XXIX

On the road
The same day, an hour later

'LET'S KILL HIM and get out of here,' the leader
jerked a thumb at Ferox. 'Bastard will only get in
the way and slow us down.' The centurion had his
hands tied behind his back and was astride a mule. Above
them the clouds were heavy with rain, and the air seemed
thick with the scent of flowers.

'The general wanted to see him,' Ivonercus insisted.
'That's my orders.'

'Orders!' The leader leaned to the side and spat, then
cursed his horse when it shied. 'Piss on orders! Didn't run
from the legion just to be ordered about by some ape of a
barbarian.'

'The Lord Diegis was very clear—'

'Diegis! That useless bastard!' The leader tried to spit
again, but his lips were too dry. 'Marcus, the wine!' he
called to one of the other riders, before taking the proffered
wine-sack and raising it high, spilling as much as he drank.
For all his long hair and beard the man still looked like the
legionary he had once been before deserting to the Dacians

almost a decade ago. For one thing, Ivonercus thought, he rode with all the grace of a sack tied up with string.

'Forget Diegis! Can't you use your eyes?' They were riding down the valley, and all the while passing warriors going the other way. Some were in groups and some on their own, and some still had weapons and shields, but many did not. All walked or rode, heads bowed, exhausted and silent. 'Or have you never seen an army in rout? That daft sod Diegis has fought the legions and taken a kicking.' There was almost pride in the man's voice. 'Diegis has lost, and from all I've seen old Decebalus doesn't take too kindly to chieftains who lose. What Diegis thinks about anything ain't going to matter.'

'I do what I'm told,' Ivonercus said stubbornly. 'The general said bring the prisoner to him, so that's what I'm doing. You don't have to come with us.'

'No, I don't,' the leader said dubiously. He and his five men had joined them late in the afternoon, carrying a message from Sarmizegethusa. 'Look, it's nearly dark. Let's stop and cook something to eat. The army's coming back this way so Diegis will be along sometime if he's still alive. How about it? I can't let you wander, mate, you know that. Not until I'm sure you are with us.'

'I'm in no hurry,' Ivonercus lied, nodding to Vepoc. The two Brigantians jumped down from their horses. 'No food for that bugger, though!' he said, pointing at Ferox.

'My thoughts exactly,' the leader agreed. He walked his mount over to the centurion and pushed him hard on the shoulders so that he slipped and thumped onto the grass. 'Bastard centurions.'

Ferox lay where he had fallen as the others made a fire and cooked a stew. Deserters or not, they still mixed biscuit, onions and salted bacon soldier fashion. The men passing now were more talkative, and he was surprised that they were not drawn by the scent of cooking.

'Best get a move on, boys,' they called. 'The Romans'll be here soon and spill your guts out, full belly or no.'

'Think we better go?' Ivonercus sounded nervous. The sun had appeared briefly as it set and the gloom gathered around them. They had settled down a few hundred yards from the main track, and could barely see the dark shapes of men retreating along it. A couple of oak trees spread their arms above them, and should give some shelter when the rain came.

'No hurry. Be a few more hours before any of the bastards turn up. You can trust me, because sure as Hercules' cock I don't intend to be taken.' The leader tried a sip of the stew and winced. 'Nearly ready. If there is no sign of Diegis and his chieftains soon then we've done all we can and can turn around. Start asking people whether they've seen him, just so we can say we tried our best. Come on, you can't have been long in the *sacramentum* if you don't know how to slack off.'

'They made me join,' Ivonercus said. 'And I only stayed as long as I did to get a chance to kill him.' He nodded towards the prostrate Ferox.

'Do it, lad, we won't say anything.'

'My orders,' Ivonercus insisted. 'Bring him to Diegis. Maybe once they've beaten some truth out of him, they'll let me have what is left.'

'Why wait? He's here. We'll say he tried to escape and it had to be done.' He grinned. 'Look at the way the bastard's lying still and not moving? That's a bugger trying to escape if ever I saw one.'

Ferox sat up.

'Even worse, he's about to make a break for it. Evil-looking bastard, isn't he.'

Ivonercus stood up and his hand went to the hilt of his spatha. 'You don't mind?' The sword scraped on the bronze top of the scabbard as he pulled it free.

'Why should we? Kill the bastard.'

'That's not what we were told to do,' Vepoc said doubtfully, but he stood and also drew his sword.

'Shall I do it?' the leader asked. 'Be a pleasure.'

'No,' Ivonercus said. 'My oath, my revenge.' He swished the blade through the air, hefting the weapon in his hand. 'I have waited a long time for this.'

'If you are sure, lord?' Vepoc hefted his own sword.

'Lord?' the leader asked. 'Just who are you?'

Lightning sprang down from the clouds and just a few moments later the great booming roar of thunder rolled over them. Big drops of rain pattered on the leaves above their heads.

Ivonercus spun and drove the spatha through the man's beard and into his throat. Vepoc swung down, hacking into the skull of another deserter, who fell forward into the fire. Sparks flew and the other three were shouting and reaching for their weapons. Two died quickly, the Brigantes cutting them down, and the last tried to run past Ferox, who stuck out his legs to send the man sprawling. Vepoc wandered over and thrust down into the deserter's back, twisting the blade until the man stopped moving. His hair was slicked down by the driving rain.

'I don't think anyone has seen us,' he shouted to Ivonercus to make himself heard. Lightning flashed again, and for an instant he saw hundreds, perhaps thousands, of Dacians plodding up the valley.

Ferox managed to get up, hands still tied and the two Brigantes moved to be on either side of him. The thunder boomed out again, a little further away. Ivonercus wiped his spatha on his trousers and sheathed the sword only to draw a knife.

'Do you trust us now, centurion?' he called as he cut the bonds, using the language of the tribes.

'You are Brigantes,' Ferox shouted. 'The Brigantes keep faith. This I have always known. You are held by your oath.'

'We are, but the queen is queen and if I doubted her before I do not now. We are her people and will follow her and obey, wherever it leads us.'

'That is why I have trusted you,' Ferox said. 'And have been pleased to have you by my side.'

Vepoc nodded. All of their eyes were stinging from the rain.

'You have done more than enough if you wish to leave me,' Ferox said. It was two nights since they had left Piroboridava, Ferox creeping ahead of the others to kill two guards. Apart from that, it had been easy getting away, for almost all of the attackers were marching down the valley and the ones left behind were deep in exhausted sleep. Sosius had slipped off almost immediately, and although Ferox did not trust the man, he felt easier in his mind not having him with them. Perhaps the slave was dead or perhaps he would reach the Roman army before them, but none of that was up to him.

It was much harder getting through the Dacian army, and for a long time they had stuck to the woodland on the south slopes of the valley, going slowly and keeping out of sight. In the first day they went barely seven miles, having to hide more than once when bands passed nearby. The second morning their luck had turned when they saw a pack mule, which must have got loose and strayed to the edge of the forest, and soon afterwards two horsemen searching for it. Ferox had suspected that the men were less than enthusiastic about the battle, so taking their time about their errand. The ambush was quick and easy and Ivonercus had suggested that they pose as deserters in the king's service, bringing a prisoner to Diegis, for that would mean that they could ride in the open and go faster. They had talked their way past everyone they encountered, until they had fallen in with the deserters who had clung to them for the rest of the day.

'The queen will count your service more than fulfilled, and see your families restored to lands and honour,' Ferox said.

'We have come this far,' Vepoc called.

'And done it well, but getting to our army will not be easy, and we may well fall at the hands of our own men. If I am killed, they may not believe that you are loyal to Rome and treat you as traitors and deserters.'

'Hold up your arm, prince of the Silures,' Ivonercus said. Both he and Vepoc were rolling up their right sleeve.

'This is an honour,' Ferox told him, and his face was lit up by another flash of lightning. He took the knife and ran it across his skin, making a line of blood that instantly washed away. Vepoc took the knife and did the same, then held up his arm so that Ferox pressed his against it. The knife went to Ivonercus.

'Before I do this, I must ask whether the king died well.'

'He did,' Ferox shouted. 'Aviragus fought like a prince and a man, and it was a fair fight for he had more warriors on his side than we did.'

'So be it.' Ivonercus drew blood and joined it to the centurion's cut. 'The old oath is no more, and a new one binds us to you and you to us. It is done.'

Drenched to the skin, the three men stood, arms pressed together until the two Brigantes, as if on a signal, stepped back.

'Remember this, Roman or Silure or whatever you call yourself. This is a bond of warriors, a pledge always to fight at the other's side whatever the cost.'

'I understand.'

'Then we should go,' Ivonercus said. 'If we run across Dacians I shall talk. If they are Romans, then it is up to you.'

'Fine,' Ferox agreed. 'But one last time I beg you to stay here and wait for me. There is no need for you to take this risk, so I beg you as brothers to wait. If the Romans come this way and you have not heard from me then ride to them and tell your story if you wish, but let me try on my own first.'

Vepoc put his hand on Ferox's shoulder. 'We will come with you, whatever you say.'

'The Brigantes are a stubborn people.'

'And the Silures rarely give their word, but when they do, they keep it, is that not so?' Vepoc said.

It was strange to hear the same proverb twice within a few days.

'Then if we fall, it will not be your fault,' Ivonercus told him. 'Nor will we live and wonder whether we might have saved you had we not stayed behind.'

'We're coming, brother, whether you like it or not,' Vepoc said, and his tone reminded Ferox of Vindex and made him wonder once again whether the scout and all the others were still alive.

'Let's go then,' Ferox said.

The fort at Piroboridava
The next day a little before noon

T**HE STORM** left the air far clearer, and during the morning the clouds fled to leave a sky that was a brilliant deep blue and a sun that blazed down. Brasus sensed that the end was close and felt nothing, neither joy nor fear. Diegis was beaten, the army shattered in spirit and with a quarter of its warriors dead, captured or left on the field wounded and at the enemy's mercy. The commander had ridden hard in flight, reaching the bridge many hours before the other fugitives, accompanied by only a few dozen warriors as escort. His temper was poor, as he roundly blamed everyone but himself for the disaster and bawled at Brasus for not yet having overrun the entire fort as he had been told.

'You had five hundred men and a simple task to complete and you have failed,' Diegis had almost screamed the words at him. Brasus sat cross-legged on the ground while the commander had a stool. He wondered whether the king would chide the defeated commander as bluntly. Diegis had lost battles before, if never one as big and important. Afterwards he also wondered whether he should have argued and whether that might have made a difference. He doubted it. Diegis was lashing out, giving way to rage and bitterness without regard to the truth in a way that was shameful for a man supposed to be one of the pure and honoured as such. Brasus listened in silence, disgusted by the whole display, even when Diegis took this as insolence and threatened to have him flogged.

His warriors began to murmur at this, humming like bees. Sixty or more of them had gathered, sufficient to outnumber the commander's escort.

'Silence!' Diegis' voice had become shrill. 'Silence at once!'

The humming grew louder and men started to stamp their feet in rhythm. More of his men began to gather from their tents.

'You will be quiet!'

The warriors ignored the shouts and the general's escort shifted uncomfortably.

At last Brasus had raised his hand in the air and his warriors had stopped and stood still.

'Take this place!' Diegis had spoken more softly, but the words still dripped with hatred. 'Take this place tomorrow and kill or take prisoner all who are inside. Only then may you leave this place and bring your spoils and captives away.' He had stared defiantly around the gathering of warriors. 'The king chose me to lead and until he revokes that appointment this order is as one from the lips of the king himself. Take that fort!'

Tired though he was, Diegis had climbed back onto his sweat-streaked horse and led his escort away without resting any longer. After him, the ruins of the great army began to come straggling past. Brasus remained where he was, sitting on the grass, his back rigid, and still said nothing.

'We should go, lord.' The old warrior who had been with Brasus from the very start hesitated before touching his shoulder. 'Diegis is no lord, only a vain fool and he is not the king. The king, were he here, would not order such useless folly.'

Brasus had stared into the distance as if he did not hear. Lightning flashed further down the valley and thunder rumbled.

'Lord, he has lost this battle, not us. To kill these last few Romans achieves nothing and has no honour now, for they are brave.'

At last Brasus stood up. 'Tell the men to leave if they wish, but I must stay. Fool or not, his word is the king's and I serve the king, and it is not for me to question what he bids me to do. Go, all of you. I must do what I must do.'

No one had left during the night, and that convinced Brasus that his path was the one for honour. He would sacrifice neither them nor more than he needed of that pitiful band of survivors who had defied them for so long. Two hours after dawn he had all the men go up to the ramparts and wait. 'Show yourselves to the Romans, but do not attack or shoot unless they attack you.'

'Lord?' The old warrior was puzzled, but obeyed.

When the others had gone Brasus prepared for the last fight, cleaning and oiling his armour, sharpening his falx and a smaller dagger he would take in his belt. When the sun was almost at its highest he walked through the main gate of the fort and paced down the road towards the last stronghold. Brasus did not hurry and he had not asked for trumpeters to herald his coming. The Romans would see him and if this Ferox was the man that he thought him to be, he would know what it meant.

There was a murmur from the warriors up on the walls,

and muttering and calls as those who could see him spoke to the ones who could not. Faces peeped over the barricades. The Romans could not have any arrows left by now, but even if they had, he trusted them not to shoot.

Brasus stopped at the junction between the two roads, ahead of him the scarred arch of the principia was filled with a barricade.

'Come forth, Flavius Ferox!' he shouted in Latin. 'Come and fight me. I am Brasus, son of Cotiso, and one of the pure and I swear that if you fight me none of your people will be harmed. Whether you die or I am slain by your hand, you have my word that we will leave you in peace and go on our way. Let us meet as warriors, fight as men, and let the rest go as strangers!'

Brasus turned and shouted the same words back towards the ramparts, this time in the tongue of his own people. The old warrior was up there and raised his hand in acknowledgement. Then Brasus faced the Romans again and spoke to them in Greek.

'Ferox is gone!' a man who sounded like one of the Britons called back to him. 'Will another do?'

Somehow Brasus had not expected Ferox to die, even though so many on both sides had fallen. Doubts filled his mind for this was not as he had felt it should be.

'I will fight your bravest and best in his place,' he shouted.

Brasus waited. There were raised voices from within the Roman compound, angry words and complaints.

'Come, do you accept?' he called.

'We do, but please give us time to choose.'

Brasus rested his oval shield against his leg and put the point of his falx on the ground. His armour gleamed, but rather than a helmet he wore the tall cap of his rank to honour his opponent and because it was easier to see, hear and move fast without the heavy bronze helmet.

At last a couple of the barrels forming the barricade were pulled aside and a chill came upon him as the queen stepped through the gap. She wore a gleaming white tunic with a red border, felt Thracian boots and had her red hair coiled on top of her head. A small round shield was held in her left hand, its field dark blue and the stick figure of a running horse painted over it in white, but she wore neither corselet nor helm. In her right hand was a sica, like the ones used by his own people, but there was a scabbarded gladius on her left hip.

'Don't do this, lady!' a Briton called after her.

The queen ignored the man and came on. 'I am Enica of the Brigantes, called Claudia of the Romans,' she said in fluent Greek, and her voice was softer than seemed right for a woman armed so well for war. 'I am queen of my people and descendant of many women – and men – of honour and power though their names would mean nothing to you.

'I do not wish to kill you, but if that is the only way to save my folk then that is what I will do, Brasus, son of Cotiso.' She gave a pitying smile. 'You should make peace with your gods.'

'Lady, I live to prepare for death and ascent.'

The woman's eyes never left him as she began to walk in a slow circle. Lightly clad and smaller than her opponent, she must have decided that speed was her best chance. Well, let her think that. There was no honour in killing a woman, but this was no mere woman but a queen, and just the way she balanced each step and held blade and shield poised and ready showed a warrior of rare skill. Her magic had held this place against their attacks, so perhaps this was the most fitting way for it to end. Brasus did not relish killing her, but this was his task and once it was done, he could send his men away and then take his own knife, place it against his throat and free his soul. Thus it would be.

Brasus had his shield up, his falx held one-handed like an ordinary sword. That gave the blows less power while retaining its reach. Still they circled, watching. He took two paces forward, falx high, but she gave way the same distance, then followed as he in turn retreated. She was fast.

Enica glanced to one side, and even when he did not take the bait, came on, slashing with her sword. He parried the blow on his shield, swung the flax, but the queen had danced out of the way and her sica moved as fast as the storm's lightning and came under his shield to strike low on his armour. A scale snapped, but the tip of the blade did not go through the padded jerkin onto which it was sewn.

They clashed again, twice, with no more than splinters from shields and light blows that did not break through his armour. When they were close Brasus saw that there was a livid red bruise on the queen's cheek and that one of her eyes was darkened. The sight was oddly unnerving, for such blemishes did not belong to the queen, let alone the demon or the witch she had become in his mind.

Brasus' back was slick with sweat for the day was hot, a day for a man to sit in the shade by a stream and dream of love and long life.

Brasus threw his shield at the queen, forcing her back and making her slash wildly to push it away. He took his falx in both hands and went at her, cutting down and slicing a quarter of her shield from the left side. A great sigh went up from the watching Romans, until she ducked, running towards him, dodging a second strike by the falx and slashing so hard at his side that scales split and he felt the edge bite into his flesh. She was past him and he turned to face her, his thigh wet as the blood flowed down.

The Romans cheered and Brasus roared, falx high, feinted a blow at her shield so that she raised it, then switched to the other side and brought it slamming down. The woman raised her curved sword to protect her head and there was a clang as the blade was snapped by the much heavier falx. Someone screamed from behind the barricade as she only just pulled out of the way. She flung the stump of the blade at his face, but he batted it away with the falx. Many hours of training over many years let him wield the great weapon with the speed of a light stick. He stamped forward, slashing down, and the rest of her shield fell into pieces.

The queen jumped back. Her left arm hung loosely at her side, numbed or even broken, but her right grasped the handle of the gladius and drew it. Brasus' trouser leg was wet with his own blood, but his strength was still there and the pain seemed to have gone. He went forward, cutting down to the left and then to the right, but always she dodged and he turned too fast for her to reach him with her short sword. He was struggling for breath, sweat in his eyes. She was tired too, her tunic clinging to her body.

The queen lunged at him, ducking under the falx, diving to the ground and then pushing up to hurl herself at his legs. He hissed as the wound throbbed, but she was smaller and lighter and the force did not knock him down, although he was forced back, sliding in the dirt. He let go with his left *hand and grabbed hold of her hair to hurl her away. She squealed, an oddly childlike sound, her sword fell and she landed on her back. It was over.*

Brasus raised the falx, gripping again with both hands. The queen stared up at him, still defiant and the fear that anyone must have felt at this time did not show. Again the bruises to her face shocked him, for they made her seem vulnerable – just a very pretty girl rather than some sorceress.

Suddenly she rolled, reaching for her fallen sword, but Brasus was faster and kicked it away. There was silence now all around the fort. The queen was gripping her left arm, which was surely broken. Her green eyes seemed large and images from his dreams flashed through Brasus' mind. He lowered the falx, letting go with his left hand, so that it could grasp his knife.

Shifting her weight the queen tried to get away, the only sign that she was human and fearful that she was showing and Brasus did not think less of her for it. He followed, the falx pointing down, ready to lunge into her chest.

'Death is nothing,' he said to her softly, almost like a lover. 'It is only the beginning of the journey.'

Then Brasus raised the curved dagger to his own throat and sliced hard across it. There was pain, more than he had expected as he started his journey.

XXX

Near Dobreta
The day before the Ides of June

'IT IS A truly extraordinary tale, is it not?' Hadrian said. 'So strange that one would scarcely believe it.'

'Sir.' Ferox's leg was sore, and he wanted to go looking for a poultice to put on it rather than the oily concoction the medicus had lathered all over the wound. He had taken an arrow in the thigh when he and the two Brigantes had come to the Roman outposts. Shouts – and thoroughly Roman curses – had convinced the picket of archers that they were friendly, but he had had to be carried in through the lines. The *sesquiplicarius* in charge of the archers had been upset to learn that one of his men had shot a Roman and a centurion by mistake. He was even more horrified when he saw that the wound was a slight one. 'At that range, sir, it's a disgrace. Should have got the face or chest at least.'

Soon he had been brought before Hadrian, who greeted him with delighted surprise and promised to send cavalry galloping to the fort as soon as the army had rested. True to his word, the legatus with some six hundred cavalry had set off before dawn, but Ferox was forbidden from going with them because of his leg and the Brigantes because 'they deserved a rest'. Late that same day a despatch rider on a foam-covered horse had brought the news that the survivors were safe, with some details. More reports had come on the next day, by which time Ferox was in a bumpy waggon as the main force marched back to the river and fresh supplies. Most of the news was good and arrangements were being made to bring the survivors back as soon as was practical with so many injured.

Ferox ought to have felt happy, but his instincts told him that something was wrong, and since he had hobbled over to answer the legatus' summons, his fears had only grown, and were fuelled when he saw Sosius leaving just as he arrived. Not that Hadrian was anything other than kind, for he had been offered wine and food and told to sit. They were in a large tent of the type senior officers used on campaign, and in spite of the heat of the day a fire burned in a brazier. Hadrian had a table and chair, both designed to fold up for ease of carriage, and several other chairs, to one of which he beckoned Ferox. There were writing tablets on the table, including the ones Ferox had brought out of the fort. Hadrian had several of them open in front of him.

'Extraordinary is the only word I can find for it, although at times reading through we must add heroic, or mulishly stubborn which often amounts to the same thing. The late tribune Piso writes with some style in his account and is most generous towards you among others.' Hadrian pursed his lips. 'Your own narrative is different, with an old-fashioned Roman simplicity about it, reminiscent of Cato, although unlike him you do name others. Indeed, reading it, one would scarcely know that you were present – at least if the reader is not inclined to infer. You have not quite Caesar's knack of a vagueness about some of his own deeds which naturally makes each reader add all the heroic details from his imagination.'

'I am no hero, sir,' Ferox said. 'I did my bit, but so did plenty of others.'

'Perhaps this reticence is more Spartan than Roman – or does the tribe of your ancestors value modesty? No matter. I have not yet polished my report on what happened after you had slipped away into the night, for words sometimes fall short. Your wife is remarkable, if a little terrifying. Do you know that at the last she went forth to fight a duel with the Dacian leader?'

Ferox gripped the arms of his chair. 'They should not have let her.'

'From what I heard, they tried to stop her, but the only men up to the job were limping or otherwise wounded and she does have a forceful personality.'

'She won, I take it.' Ferox had received word that the queen was alive, if no more.

'Not quite, but she survived, although with a broken arm. At least there is not a scratch on her exquisite body.' That was an odd expression to use to a woman's husband, but the legatus showed no awareness of this. After all, Ferox was a mere centurion and his wife only of equestrian rank. A senator could say what he liked about or to such folk. 'All in all, it is worthy of Homer, although I doubt that I shall quote the blind poet in my report as the army and the emperor does not care for such flamboyance. She lives and her opponent is dead by his own hand, so there is no shame only glory.

'And yet,' he paused.

Here it comes, thought Ferox.

'And yet,' Hadrian repeated, 'some of what occurred is unfortunate to say the least, and one would wish that it had not occurred. You have been told that Piso is dead, but none of the details.'

'No, sir.'

'Your wife killed him.' Hadrian stared at Ferox. 'The news does not seem to surprise you?'

'I imagine she had good reason.'

'He tried to rape a freedwoman of yours. She stopped him and he tried to rape her, so she stabbed him to death.'

'The law is on her side, then,' Ferox said, 'and none would call that murder.'

'So the garrison thought – what was left of them at least – for the deed was immediately made public and approved. But do not be obtuse. None of this is heroic.

'The tribune came from a once illustrious family – indeed from several illustrious families for the reluctance of the old aristocracy to procreate with their wives has meant many adoptions to preserve each family's name. His father is a mildly dangerous fool, but the son had never been accused of disloyalty, at least not in public. Ostensibly he was here because the emperor is a kind, forgiving man and wishes old families and senators in general to prosper and win fame under his leadership.

'Piso's role in the shambles at Sarmizegethusa is ambiguous at best, but no one will ever remember that. Only the story of Longinus will survive, because that is the one the emperor will have everyone tell and that is what good Romans will want to believe. An old soldier who was captured, but took his own life rather than be used as a hostage by a hostile king. No matter if the truth is a little different.'

'It wasn't suicide then?'

'Do not ask foolish and inappropriate questions, Flavius Ferox, and take thought instead for those dear to you.

'Piso escaped, and if the manner was questionable, everyone approves success. Even by your account he played a brave role in the later days of the siege. Remember this was a young nobleman who had never before served in the army or fought for his life.'

'He did well, sir. Better than I had expected.'

'So that is a good story, which means that we cannot have the dashing young hero stabbed to death as he tried to ravish a respectable – if admittedly unorthodox – lady of decent enough family. While we may have to play down her amazonian exploits in case they make our good citizens nervous for the natural order, I am sure we can talk a lot about her courage and how she inspired her own tribesmen and the other soldiers. Better leave out the flag with the tits as well.' Hadrian shook his head in mock distaste. 'Yes, I saw it, you Britons are strange folk.

'Now where was I? Ah yes. Privately Piso is better dead, for it will prevent his idiot parent from thinking that he can lead a rebellion and start his own dynasty. And no one really knows whether the son would have been as troublesome as his father or have stayed loyal. It was important that the lad get a chance to serve the res publica, better if he showed bravery and best of all if he did not return from his exploits. A captive in the hands of the Dacians might have been embarrassing in the long run, so it was good that he escaped, a slight pity that he was not killed in the attempt, and acceptable that he came to join you. If he had survived, I had in mind sending him to negotiate with the Roxolani.'

Ferox may have blinked, but did not think so. Hadrian paused and was watching him expectantly. 'The tribune did not strike me as a diplomatic man,' Ferox said after a while. 'Dealing with the clans can be delicate and dangerous.'

'Quite so. I was relying on him to upset them and pay the price. That would have been a brave enough death for him. However, there is no need for such an expedient. He joined you at Piroboridava. To everyone's delight – at least everyone who matters – he fought bravely and did not survive. No need for scandal, no need at all. When the story is written, Piso will not make it back to your "acropolis".' Hadrian shook his head at the word. 'He will die letting others reach shelter – with piles of his foes slain around him, if you like.'

'It did not happen that way.'

'That is neither here nor there. Sulpicia Lepidina is a shrewd enough woman to keep silent, especially if the emperor is willing to foster her husband's career. Ambitious man, that, for himself and his sons.'

As always Ferox feared some undertone suggesting that Hadrian knew the truth about the youngest boy.

'He has three does he not?'

'I believe so, sir.'

'And a daughter too, while his wife is a clarissima femina. Yes, that is a man hoping to rise.'

'He's a fine soldier, sir.'

'Good, because I have asked that he be sent to my legion as narrow stripe tribune and it is tiresome to have to manage a fool in such a post. As I say, the lady will say nothing, while your wife is eager to have her accession as queen made formal. That means that we can count on her discretion. Of the others who were there – well, who would believe any of them or listen to what they say? Which just leaves you.'

'There are the tribune's reports, sir?'

'These?' Hadrian picked up two of the tablets. 'Yes, of course, I was forgetting. All written and dated after he had died so bravely.' He stood up and went over to the brazier, before tossing the tablets in. The coals were hot and in a moment the wooden pages began to burn. 'Ah, there we are, problem solved.' Hadrian rubbed his hands together as if cleaning them. 'And so we return to you.

'Crispinus, among others, told me that you have a mulish obsession with telling the truth. In this case that would be unwise and unhelpful. Surely you do not want scandal surrounding your dear wife? Least of all when her hopes are so close to fulfilment and she may truly become queen and perhaps even bequeath the title to one of your children?'

Ferox said nothing.

Hadrian sighed. 'Then let us consider the problem from another angle, as one of my tutors was fond of saying – ugly old goat that he was.

'Now that the record shows that the tribune fell so bravely, from that moment you were once again senior officer at Piroboridava. Yet you abandoned your post, sneaking away through the enemy lines in company with a known deserter and leaving your command to its fate.'

'I was ordered, sir.'

'By a dead man whose written instructions are turning into ashes as we speak.' The wax on the tablets gave off a strong scent as they burned. 'And let us cast our eyes back on your record.

'On the day you arrived at Piroboridava you slaughtered several of your own officers and let others desert. Then and before the desertion rate among the Brigantes placed under your charge was appallingly high. In the days that followed there were several attempts on your life, which you survived but speak of very poor discipline. And you did not prevent the murder of a centurion – of my legion, blast your eyes – by one of your men. Then when the time came and your fort was under attack, you let the enemy overrun its walls and the remnant you abandoned was only saved by a miracle – and the prompt actions of a worthy legatus.' Hadrian gave a studied cough. 'All in all, it is not a pretty picture, and given your already chequered past, surely demands severe punishment.'

Hadrian came behind Ferox and took him by the shoulders.

'Hercules' balls, man, all we want is for you to hold your tongue about a man who is dead and gone. I really doubt that your wife wants people to whisper about the attack, and wonder just how far things went before she managed to kill him. "Oh poor girl," they will say, "isn't it terrible", while they imagine all sorts of lurid things. Spare her that at least.'

'What do you want from me, sir?'

'That's better. Your part in all this will be allowed to fade away, even more than it does in your own self-effacing version. Piso will gain posthumous glory which will warm the hearts of every senator, especially as they'll never have to meet the little cuss. Let your wife be praised by the emperor and I will help in every way I can to secure her recognition.

'You will be forgotten, apart from a minor reprimand, and we certainly do not want you going back to Britannia, let alone to the north. She may rule, but for the moment she will rule alone. Instead, I will find some uses for you in the years to come. Serve me well – and the army and emperor of course – and one day you may be allowed to go to her. Refuse to do what I ask now, or fail me and the best you can hope for is dishonourable discharge. The worst is exile to an island for adultery, along with the lady.'

Ferox must have flinched and Hadrian felt it.

'So, it is true.' Hadrian could not hide his satisfaction. 'Crispinus thought so, and a glance at the boy made me wonder.' He pulled his hands away and walked around so that he could face Ferox. 'You really have no choice if you want to protect the ones you love. Do you?'

'No, my lord.'

'Good. And if you continue to serve Rome so well then all you do will help her cause and that of your children – quietly at least. Doubt that there will be much recognition for you, not for a long while at least, but I will do my utmost to help Claudia Enica.'

'I should like to see my wife, sir.'

'Not yet. Perhaps one day, when you have shown that I can rely upon you for your service and absolute discretion, then perhaps I shall arrange for you to see her. But today, you must leave this camp, although if you wish to write a letter I shall ensure that it is delivered. Its contents will be the first test of your discretion.'

Ferox stood, his leg throbbing. 'Where am I going?'

'South, at first. Word has arrived that the emperor will get here soon and I do not want you complicating matters.

'Once you are healed I will want you to see whether we can persuade the Roxolani's main clans to abandon Decebalus.'

'In place of Piso, my lord?'

Hadrian grinned with all the warmth of a tiger. 'I believe you do have a gift for diplomacy. And I do not need you to become a dead hero.'

'What about clubbed to death while a fort burned?' Ferox was sure Sosius had attacked Piso all those months before and did not doubt that it was on the legate's orders.

'I cannot imagine what you mean, centurion, to ask such a tactless question.' Hadrian glanced down, then flicked his eyes back to fix on Ferox. 'If you need to disappear, that could already have been arranged. Be assured, I do not want you dead, but I do want you to be useful.'

'To you, my lord?'

'To Rome, Ferox, and to our princeps – to whom you have sworn an oath. I am merely a servant of both, doing my best to ensure their success. In order to do that I must use the best tools I can find and ensure that those tools are wielded as well as possible.'

Ferox could imagine Vindex smirking.

Hadrian glanced at the brazier where the tablets were still burning. 'After you have helped with the Roxolani, who knows?' he went on. 'I – and other sensible men – will make use of you for the good of the res publica.'

'And how will you serve the res publica, my lord?'

'As best I can. You will soon hear, but there is talk of splitting Pannonia into two provinces, which means that the princeps will soon require a legatus to govern the smaller of the two and command its legion.'

'Congratulations, my lord, if it is not out of place to say so.' Ferox could sense Hadrian's delight, and guessed that it was as much at his own cleverness in winning Trajan's favour as joy at the promotion itself. 'You saw what others did not and won your battle.'

'We were both right,' Hadrian replied and almost appeared sincere. 'But save the congratulations until the final decision is made.'

'From all I hear, my lord, our princeps is shrewd enough to appreciate true talent.'

Hadrian chuckled. 'Perhaps it runs in the family. Now, I have more work to do and you need to go.'

'One request, sir. The two Brigantes who came in with me. I'd like to see them before I go.'

'Ah, that was regrettable. I fear their heads are on spearpoints above the camp's gateway.'

'What?' Ferox shouted, hands gripping the arms of the chair.

Hadrian banged his fist onto the table. 'Mind your manners, centurion! A reliable source told me that you were duped by those men, for they had been sent by Decebalus to murder the emperor, getting close by posing as deserters returned to the fold. Another group of deserters has been arrested and executed in the last few days, for it seems that the king sent several, anticipating the emperor's arrival.'

'They were good men, and I do not believe that they were traitors.'

'What you believe is neither here nor there, centurion. The evidence was clear, and I for one will never take an unnecessary risk when there is a threat to the emperor's life.' Hadrian's voice was as level as it was unrelenting.

Still Ferox did not believe a word of it or doubt that Sosius was the source or at least had provided the justification. Presumably unmasking the alleged plot would be another way for Hadrian to show his ability and loyalty. Already flush with the victory over Diegis and the relief of the garrison, uncovering a plot was bound to add to the emperor's favour. No wonder Hadrian was confident that he would receive the post of governor of the new province.

The legate had calmed and was watching him, one hand rubbing his bearded chin. Even if Ferox tried to tell the truth and was believed, Hadrian would be seen as overzealous in his enthusiasm to preserve the emperor's life, even if sadly mistaken. He would still get his province and Trajan's favour and if Ferox spoke up then he hurt Claudia badly, and might ruin the life of Sulpicia Lepidina and his son. Trajan had made a great show of enforcing the adultery laws with severity, especially when anyone of senatorial family was involved. It was imagination, no more, but Ferox felt the cut to his arm throbbing for he knew that he had failed the men who had sworn to him and that there was no chance of vengeance now or perhaps ever.

'May I have their bodies, my lord, to honour after the manner of their tribe?' he asked.

'Sorry, they went in the river.' Hadrian reached for a papyrus and unrolled it on his table. After a moment he glanced up. 'Anything else, centurion?'

'No, sir. Other than to say that you really are a bastard, aren't you?'

Hadrian smiled, for he had won. 'You would have had to ask my parents about that, I suppose. But in the sense that you meant, I would hope so. Rome needs bastards in charge, as long as they are clever. Now close the tent flap as you leave and go and write your letter. I shall read it, of course, before it is delivered, so please bear that in mind. Good luck to you, Flavius Ferox. I should not bother to make you one of my men unless I had the highest opinion of your worth. When they are recovered I will probably send you some of your Brigantes to command. They strike me as handy men. Together you will do great things in the service of Rome and that is a noble end even if the means are sometimes ignoble. Now go!'

Ferox limped out of the tent. The camp was bustling as army camps always were, and the sentries on duty were immaculately turned out. A trumpet sounded for the start of the third watch.

'*Omnes ad stercus*,' he said under his breath, and went to write to his wife.

Historical Note

The Fort is a novel, its plot and the majority of the characters either wholly fictional or greatly embellished from the little known about their real predecessors. However, I have done my best to set the story in as accurate a context as possible, given our limited sources for this era. More details of the sources can be found at my website, adriangoldsworthy. com

Trajan's Dacian Wars were major conflicts, eventually resulting in the acquisition by Rome of the new province of Dacia, its heartland in modern-day Romania. Conquests on this scale were fairly rare after the death of Augustus, Rome's first emperor, in AD 14. Rarely did a Roman emperor want to spend years off on campaign outside the empire, and even more rarely did they trust anyone else to do this for them, lest they become a dangerous rival. Trajan was one of the few exceptions and has gone down in history as a great soldier, who spent almost a third of his reign on campaign. As far as we can tell, his military record before he became emperor was fairly modest and a large part of his quest for military glory came from a desire to justify his rather weak claim to rule. Dacia, a former enemy who had inflicted several humiliating defeats on the Romans in recent memory, offered an ideal opportunity for an aggressive and glorious war.

Trajan's First Dacian War (AD 101–102) brought victories and was widely celebrated, but left Decebalus of Dacia in charge of much of his kingdom. The Second War (AD 105–106) resulted in the abolition of the kingdom, the suicide of Decebalus, and the formal creation of the Roman province (which was subsequently divided into three provinces). Both wars required the commitment of substantial numbers of Roman troops, with perhaps a fifth or even a quarter of the entire army involved and an even higher proportion of legions contributing detachments or vexillations. Warfare on this scale was expensive, but Dacia, rich in mineral resources, especially gold, which appears to have been a royal monopoly, was a great prize.

The loot from Dacia funded the construction of Trajan's Forum in the heart of Rome itself, enough of which is still visible to give an idea of its grand and lavish scale. At its heart was Trajan's Column, 93' high on a 20' pedestal, decorated with carved reliefs telling the stories of the two wars – it was claimed that the height was to show how much earth had been excavated from the hillside to permit the construction of the complex. The sculptures are very detailed, depicting soldiers marching, parading and sacrificing, building roads and forts, and fighting battles and sieges. In most cases weapons were added as bronze miniatures, long since plundered and recycled so that apart from a few carved swords and bows, men wave empty hands at each other. Much is stylised, so that ships and buildings are shown on a smaller scale than the figures. Trajan is prominent, but depicted as only slightly larger than everyone else – this is no great king smiting his feeble foes. Legionaries are marked out as clearly distinct from the regular auxiliaries, let alone the irregulars, and everyone is dressed as an audience in Rome would expect, rather than with strict accuracy, so that the Dacians in the main are generic barbarians, with shaggy hair, beards and baggy tunics and trousers. Debate continues to rage over the accuracy of the scenes.

Trajan wrote an account of his campaigns as *Commentaries*, just like those written by Julius Caesar. However, only a single line from this has survived. Nothing at all has survived directly from the many other accounts celebrating the victories, or from narratives of the earlier campaigns under the Emperor Domitian. All we have are a handful of fragments, and the only remotely complete account is provided by writers of the Byzantine period, who summarised the fuller account written by the senator Cassius Dio in the early third century AD. What we have is brief and at times confused and we have no real idea how much fuller or reliable the original was.

Thus the Dacian Wars, for all their scale and importance, are very poorly known. Archaeology helps to a degree, not least in giving more sense of Dacian society, culture and the sophistication of their architecture, as well as the establishment of Roman forts and subsequently cities. Excavation is rarely suited to helping us to understand the faster moving events of individual campaigns and instead reveals longer term trends. At fort sites, attention naturally focuses on the later, more permanent phases of occupation, usually built in stone, rather than the initial establishment of a base. Trajan's Column clearly tells a detailed story, presenting the official line and quite possibly representing in art many of the incidents Trajan had described in his *Commentaries*. Yet it is rather like trying to understand the Bayeux Tapestry, but without the captions and with very skimpy knowledge of the history of 1066.

This is even more true of the fascinating monuments at Tropaeum Traiani (modern Adamklissi in Romania, not far from the Black Sea). Dedicated to Mars Ultor – Rome's war god Mars in his role as the avenger – these include an altar and a cenotaph, a memorial to the 'bravest of men' who fell, presumably during one of the conflicts with the Dacians and their allies. (Among the units listed is one from Britannia, which might well make this the first extant memorial to British soldiers.) On the great drum-shaped Tropaeum itself, there were sculptures of captives, and a row of scenes or metopes depicting battle scenes, where Roman legionaries and auxiliary infantry and cavalry parade and fight against barbarians until these are killed or captured. There is a story in these images, but we do not know what it is, in part because we do not even know the original sequence of the metopes, let alone the precise date of the incidents depicted.

The cenotaph has the space for some 3,800 names, but is badly eroded so that most of it is illegible. The first man listed was a praefectus or prefect, and while his name is lost, it states that he was born in Pompeii, but now resident in Neapolis (Naples), which means that he died sometime after the eruption of Vesuvius. Some scholars believe that the names are those of men who fell in a great disaster, perhaps one of the two major defeats suffered under Domitian. So many fatalities make it highly unlikely that the monument commemorated a hard-fought victory, but that leaves the possibility that it includes the names of all the men who had died during the course of one or both of the Dacian Wars. As with so much concerning the period, we simply do not know. The sculptures give a better idea of the true appearance of the peoples of the region and also what Roman troops looked like in the field.

The Fort makes use of the little certain information we do possess. Trajan's First Dacian War imposed a treaty on Decebalus, including a ban on hiring Roman deserters and on seeking allies. It also resulted in the establishment of Roman garrisons within his kingdom, mainly in the lowlands and the valleys leading to and from passes in the Carpathians. There was a Roman detachment at Decebalus' capital of Sarmizegethusa Regia and part of its substantial defensive wall has been excavated, although the details of the post are not very well understood.

The peace proved temporary and there is a fair chance that both sides prepared for hostilities long before they resumed. One of the most visible signs of this was the great bridge across the Danube, which was opened by the end of AD 105 and part of a wider programme improving communications in the area. The base of only one pier remains to this day, but confirms the scale of the project, which was described in some detail by Dio and is depicted on Trajan's Column. Trajan left Rome for the Danube on 4 June AD 105, so that much of the campaigning season was already spent before he arrived in the theatre of operations, and it looks as if he was taken by surprise. Trajan's Column also shows a number of Roman forts under Dacian attack before the emperor arrives, while Dio told the story of the capture of Longinus. Rather than be used as a pawn in negotiations, the Roman officer committed suicide, using poison obtained by a freedman. The narrative does not make clear whose freedman this was, but claims that Decebalus demanded his return after the man escaped, offering his remaining Roman hostages as payment. Trajan refused.

The Fort takes these fragments and depicts an uneasy peace with men on both sides anticipating a renewal of war and trying to gain an advantage. Sosius in our story is fictional, for we know nothing about this freedman, nor does the summary of Dio hint at foul play behind the scenes of Longinus' death. As stated at the start of the book, there was a Roman fort at a place called Piroboridava occupied at this time, but it was not located where it is in the story. Our Piroboridava is fictional, loosely based on the remnants of early phases of forts, such as the site at Rācari in Romania. Counter attacks or large scale raids were a feature of Dacian war-making, partly for plunder and prestige, but also to wrong-foot the enemy. The heartland of Decebalus' kingdom lay high in the mountains, which meant that it was virtually impossible to attack it on a large scale during the winter months. Thus delaying any Roman campaign was well worthwhile. When Hadrian became emperor, he had the Danube Bridge decommissioned, removing the road and leaving just the pillars and arches, which still looked impressive four centuries later. The Romans were not usually fond of bridges on their river frontiers, and some, like Hadrian, appear to have seen them as vulnerable spots. Trajan's construction of the bridge was a sign of confidence, even bravado, which his successor did not share. Our story offers a reason for Hadrian's fears and subsequent action.

The Roman army is depicted as accurately as possible in the story, just as in the *Vindolanda* trilogy, but there is much that is guesswork and more detail can be found on my website and in books such as my *The Complete Roman Army*. Epigraphic evidence as well as logic suggest that a legion would have had an unusually high proportion of veterani some twenty years after its initial formation, although it is far less clear what was done with these men for the last period of their military service. In later centuries the *frumentarii* expanded their duties far beyond the organisation of supplies and became a form of secret police, bringing information to the emperor about the activities of his officers in the provinces. Hadrian is credited with starting this process, so there seemed no harm in suggesting that the idea had already occurred to him long before he became emperor.

Ferox is fictional, as is the irregular unit of Brigantes placed under his command. Such tribal units were increasingly common in the early second century AD; Trajan's Column depicts bare-chested barbarians wielding clubs fighting alongside regular auxiliaries as well as legionaries. In later years the vague term of numerus or unit was often associated with these regiments, but at the time of our story they were usually referred to by an ethnic designation and listed as 'under the care of' (*sub cura*) a named commander. Little is known of their internal organisation and equipment, and there is a good chance that such units varied considerably, being composed and organised to meet a local need or simply on the basis of available manpower.

Ferox will be familiar to readers of my *Vindolanda* trilogy, as will Vindex, Enica, Philo and co, and the story of the Brigantian rebellion. Sadly all are fictional, as are the majority of the men at the fort and elsewhere. Sulpicia

Lepidina and her husband Cerialis were real, attested in the Vindolanda writing tablets, although their stories have been considerably fleshed out in my novels. No trace of their lives has survived for the years before they came to Vindolanda and after they left. A Lucius Tettius Crescens is recorded on an inscription from Sardinia, noting that he was merchant in Dacia at the time of the war. A centurion and Roman citizen named Petrullus is recorded a generation later as having come from Britannia, so our Petrullus is meant to be his father whose loyal service gained the family the franchise.

Maximus – fully Tiberius Claudius Maximus – is known from his tombstone, which records his career as a legionary cavalryman, who subsequently rose to become a decurion of auxiliary cavalry, serving as standard-bearer, a member of the acting governor's bodyguard and scout along the way. He led the party that chased down Decebalus at the end of the Second Dacian War, and is depicted on his own monument and on Trajan's Column riding forward just as the king slits his own throat. Highly decorated, Maximus' career appears less distinguished than might be expected, which may suggest that he was one of those soldiers very good at fighting, but perhaps less suited to peacetime routine.

Apollodorus of Damascus was one of the most famous architects of the era, the man in charge of Trajan's Forum complex as well as the Danube Bridge. Hadrian had a deep passion for engineering and architecture, most obviously expressed in the variety and scale of his villa at Tivoli, and in his restoration of the Pantheon in Rome, with its great domed roof. There is a tradition that Apollodorus lacked patience with the amateur's enthusiasm, dismissing his fondness for domes as mere pumpkins. Later Hadrian is supposed to have sent plans of a temple he had designed, which featured giant statues of seated deities. Apollodorus was unimpressed, tartly mentioning that if the god and goddess chose to stand then they would go through the ceiling. One source claims that Hadrian grew so tired of Apollodorus' condescension that he ordered the man's execution.

Hadrian is remembered as one of the better Roman emperors, an essentially good ruler under whom the empire prospered and enjoyed a great measure of peace. His decision to build Hadrian's Wall in Northern Britain, give up some of Trajan's conquests in the east and avoid aggressive wars appear pragmatic compared to Trajan's enthusiasm for expansion. Yet Hadrian was not a popular emperor, most of all with the senatorial class who more than anyone else shaped the memory of each ruler. A little of this came from the shift towards a more cautious, defensive strategy. Rather more was due to the execution of a number of senators, particularly in the early months of his reign. While this was scarcely a widespread reign of terror, good emperors did not kill senators unless they had no other choice. Nerva had exiled Crassus Frugi, the father of the Piso in our story, after a truly inept plot. Trajan recalled the man and then exiled him once again, but Hadrian had him executed. The son appears on an inscription in the family tomb as the last of the line. Nothing more is known about him, and I would hope that he cut a rather better figure than the character in our story.

Hadrian was openly ruthless at times, which meant that he was never loved by the aristocracy. It was said that after his death the Senate hesitated to deify him, the usual routine on the death of an emperor, hence Vespasian's supposed dying words of 'I think I am becoming a god.' Hadrian was tactless, which did not help, for instance in his spectacularly public affair with and then mourning for the youth Antinous. Such things were supposed to be managed discreetly and not paraded. Even in smaller matters, Hadrian appears to have been a clever man who could never resist showing off his cleverness by correcting those around him and always had to be right. He was a competent, perhaps gifted ruler in spite of not being an especially nice person.

Trajan was the cousin of Hadrian's father, although the precise details of the relationship are unclear, and when Hadrian's father died, Trajan became one of his two guardians. This was before Trajan was adopted by the Emperor Nerva. Trajan's widow and other members of court subsequently claimed that, while on his deathbed, Trajan adopted Hadrian. Whether or not this was true, it is highly significant that this did not occur earlier. There were clear traditions about marking a man out as successor and Trajan extended none of these honours to Hadrian – or indeed to anyone else. He never appears to have made a public effort to select a successor, although some anecdotes claim that he hinted about senators good enough to do the job. Hadrian was given the emperor's grand-niece as wife, but his career under Trajan was good without being truly spectacular.

In AD 105 Hadrian was one of the praetors, but did not serve the normal year of office. At some point he was instead appointed as legatus legionis of I Minervia and was decorated for service during the Second Dacian War. Once again he did not remain in this post for very long and sometime in 106 was promoted when Trajan decided to split the province of Pannonia into two, creating an Upper and Lower province. Hadrian was the first legate of Pannonia Inferior and simultaneously commander of the single legion in garrison there, II Adiutrix. In that sense it was a sideways transfer, but the prestige of governing a province was considerable, and the rapid succession of posts in such a short time suggests a display of some trust and favour on Trajan's part and there are hints at this in our sources. Our story offers an explanation as to how this all might have happened.

Dacia and the Dacians are not as well understood as we would wish. As is almost always the case, their side of the story is not preserved and we must guess on the basis of meagre and garbled accounts written by more or less hostile outsiders. Contact between the Dacians and Romans began in the first century BC, and Julius Caesar planned to mount a major expedition against them before marching against Parthia. His assassination prevented both projects, but in the decades that followed the Roman frontier pushed forward and contact became more frequent and periodically hostile. In Caesar's day the Dacians were united under the capable King Burebista. Like Caesar he was murdered by his own followers, and after that the kingdom fragmented into tribal groups. Decebalus managed to restore much of the old unity and power late in the first century AD and as a result was seen as a serious threat by the Romans. No doubt Dacian views of Rome were similar.

The Dacians worshipped Zalmoxis and their faith appears to have inspired great bravery in battle as well as a willingness to commit suicide if things went badly. Little is really known about their beliefs, and I have drawn from passages from Herodotus, who wrote more than five centuries before our story, and Strabo who wrote a mere century or so before our setting. As foreigners describing another race whom they considered to be barbaric, the reliability of their accounts must be doubted, but if we reject them then we have nothing at all. Herodotus tells of the five-yearly sacrifice of a Messenger to the god, of shooting arrows into the sky to calm it and of belief in a blessed afterlife spent in the company of the god.

From quite early on, the Dacians had traded with and learned from the Greek colonies on the Black Sea. Later, Decebalus in particular encouraged Roman deserters to join him and in the treaty with Domitian was given technical and military advisors. Dacian fortifications were formidable, exploiting the rugged terrain to the full and adding well-built walls and towers. Unlike any other tribal army in Europe, they used artillery and other siege equipment. Archers were common and effective, and in addition to composite bows there is a good chance that they made use of 'belly-bows', small handheld catapults a little like a crossbow. Many fought with straight swords, javelins and spears, but most famous were the curved one-handed sica and the larger falx, which could probably be wielded in one or both hands and was capable of penetrating armour and inflicting dreadful wounds. Apart from the Dacians themselves, at various times their armies were joined by allies from the Roxolani, a Sarmatian people, and various Celtic, Getic and Germanic groups, with the Bastarnae notable among the latter. Many of the warriors on the Adamklissi metopes have their hair twisted into a side knot, which was seen as a characteristic of the Germanic peoples, especially the Suebi, and use falxes, and may well be Bastarnae.

Much of this story is invention because we simply do not know how Dacian armies were organised and functioned, and indeed have many gaps in our understanding of Roman practices. The *monâkon* or 'one-armed' is the type of catapult more often known as an onager. Use by the Romans is clearly attested only in Late Antiquity, but the type had been invented in the Hellenistic period, although no one knows how often it was used in practice. I took the opportunity to present a couple of these machines to Ferox as something that would be possible, even if not very likely.

In some ways possible if not necessarily likely sums up the whole story. There is so much about the Roman period that scholars simply do not know. When writing a non-fiction history I feel it is my duty to be honest about this. For a novel I try to make the story as accurate as possible, but filling in the many gaps gives me the chance to explore ideas and at times simply use what makes a good story.

Glossary

ad stercus: literally 'to the shit', the expression was used in military duty rosters for men assigned to clean the latrines.

agmen quadratus: literally a square battle-line, this was a formation shaped like a large box and used by a Roman army threatened by attack from any side. Units were deployed to form a rectangle, sheltering baggage and other vulnerable personnel and equipment inside.

ala: a regiment of auxiliary cavalry, roughly the same size as a cohort of infantry. There were two types: *ala quingenaria* consisting of 512 men divided into 16 *turmae*; and *ala milliaria* consisting of 768 men divided into 24 *turmae*.

auxilia/auxiliaries: over half of the Roman army was recruited from non-citizens from all over (and even outside) the empire. These served as both infantry and cavalry and gained citizenship at the end of their twenty-five years of service.

Bastarnae: a tribal group living to the east of the Danube. Tacitus, writing a few years before our story, believed them to be akin to the German tribes in terms of language and customs. They had a reputation for bravery.

Batavians: an offshoot of the Germanic Chatti, who fled after a period of civil war, the Batavians settled on what the Romans called the Rhine island in modern Holland. Famous as warriors, their only obligation to the empire was to provide soldiers to serve in Batavian units of the *auxilia*. Writing around the time of our story, the historian Tacitus described them as 'like armour and weapons – only used in war'.

belly bow (gastraphetes): an early type of siege engine, rather like a large crossbow and operated by one man. It was loaded resting the specially curved ends of the staff against the stomach, hence the name.

beneficiarii: were experienced soldiers selected for special duties by the provincial governor. Each carried a staff with an ornate spearhead.

Brigantes: a large tribe or group of tribes occupying much of what would become northern England. Several sub-groups are known, including the Textoverdi and Carvetii (whose name may mean 'stag people').

burgus: a small outpost manned by detached troops rather than a formal unit.

caligae: the hobnailed military boots worn by soldiers.

canabae: the civilian settlements which rapidly grew up outside almost every Roman fort. The community had no formal status and was probably under military jurisdiction.

centurion: a grade of officer rather than a specific rank, each legion had some sixty centurions, while each auxiliary cohort had between six and ten. They were highly educated men and were often given posts of great responsibility. While a minority were commissioned after service in the ranks, most were directly commissioned or served only as junior officers before reaching the centurionate.

centurio regionarius: a post attested in the Vindolanda tablets, as well as elsewhere in Britain and other provinces. They appear to have been officers on detached service placed in control of an area. A large body of evidence from Egypt shows them dealing with criminal investigations as well as military and administrative tasks.

clarissima femina: 'most distinguished woman' was a title given to women of a senatorial family.

cohort: the principal tactical unit of the legions. The first cohort consisted of 800 men in five double-strength centuries, while cohorts two to ten were composed of 480 men in six centuries of 80. Auxiliaries were either formed in milliary cohorts of 800 or more often quingeniary cohorts of 480. *Cohortes equitatae* or mixed cohorts added 240 and 120 horsemen respectively. These troopers were paid less and given less expensive mounts than the cavalry of the *alae*.

colonia: a city with the status of colony of Roman citizens, which had a distinct constitution and followed Roman law. Many were initially founded with a population of discharged soldiers.

commilitones: 'comrades' or 'fellow soldiers'.

consilium: the council of officers and other senior advisors routinely employed by a Roman governor or senator to guide him in making decisions.

curator: (i) title given to soldier placed in charge of an outpost such as a *burgus* who may or may not have held formal rank; (ii) the second in command to a decurion in a cavalry *turma*.

Dacia/Dacians: a people occupying lands centred on what is today Romania. The Greeks and Romans believed them to be kin to the Getae. They were perceived by the Romans as a significant threat under King Burebista, a rough contemporary of Julius Caesar. The latter was planning a Dacian campaign at the time of his murder. For several generations Dacia appears to have been weakened by internal divisions, until emerging again as a powerful independent kingdom under Decebalus.

decurion: the cavalry equivalent to a centurion, but considered to be junior to them. He commanded a *turma*.

equestrian: the social class just below the Senate. There were many thousand equestrians (*eques*, pl. *equites*) in the Roman Empire, compared to six hundred senators, and a good proportion of equestrians were descendants of aristocracies within the provinces. Those serving in the army followed a different career path to senators.

*falx***:** a long, curved sword employed by the Dacians and some of their neighbours. They could be wielded with one or both hands, which gave the blow considerable force. The edge was on the inside of the curve and the pointed tip seems to have been designed to punch through helmet or armour.

*frumentarii***:** soldiers detached from their units with responsibility for supervising the purchase and supply of grain and other foodstuffs to the army.

*galearius (pl. galearii)***:** slaves owned by the army, who wore a helmet and basic uniform and performed service functions, such as caring for transport animals and vehicles.

Getae: were a group of people of similar language and customs (at least to outside observers), living in the wider Balkan area.

gladius: Latin word for sword, which by modern convention specifically refers to the short sword used by all legionaries and most auxiliary infantry. By the end of the first century most blades were less than two feet long.

legate/legatus (legionary): the commander of a legion was a *legatus legionis* and was a senator at an earlier stage in his career than the provincial governor. He would usually be in his early thirties.

legate/legatus (provincial): the governor of a military province like Britain was a *legatus Augusti*, the representative of the emperor. He was a distinguished senator and usually at least in his forties.

legion: originally the levy of the entire Roman people summoned to war, legion or *legio* became the name for the most important unit in the army. In the last decades of the first century BC, legions became permanent with their own numbers and usually names and titles. In AD 98 there were 28 legions, but the total was soon raised to 30.

lillia: lilies were circular pits with a sharpened stake in the centre. Often concealed, they were a comman part of the obstacles outside Roman fortifications.

lixae: A generic term for the camp followers of a Roman army.

medicus: an army medical orderly or junior physician.

Monâkon: a single armed catapult described in Hellenistic manuals. The type was widely used in Late Antiquity, when it was often known as the onager, and continued in use throughout the Middle Ages.

omnes ad stercus: a duty roster of the first century AD from a century of a legion stationed in Egypt has some soldiers assigned *ad stercus*, literally to the dung or shit. This probably meant a fatigue party cleaning the latrines – or just possibly mucking out the stables. From this I have invented *omnes ad stercus* as 'everyone to the latrines' or 'we're all in the shit'.

optio: the second in command of a century of eighty men and deputy to a centurion.

pileatus (pl. *pileati*): the 'cap wearers' were the nobles in Dacian society as opposed to the long haired mass of the population.

pilum: the heavy javelin carried by Roman legionaries. It was about six to seven feet long. The shaft was wooden, topped by a slim iron shank ending in a pyramid-shaped point (much like the bodkin arrow used by longbowmen). The shank was not meant to bend. Instead the aim was to concentrate all of the weapon's considerable weight behind the head so that it would punch through armour or shield. If it hit a shield, the head would go through, and the long iron shank gave it the reach to continue and strike the man behind. Its effective range was probably some 15 to 16 yards.

praesidium: the term meant garrison, and could be employed for a small outpost or a full-sized fort.

prefect: the commander of most auxiliary units was called a prefect (although a few unit COs held the title tribune). These were equestrians, who first commanded a cohort of auxiliary infantry, then served as equestrian tribune in a legion, before going on to command a cavalry *ala*.

procurator: an imperial official who oversaw the tax and financial administration of a province. Although junior to a legate, a procurator reported directly to the emperor.

res publica: literally 'public thing' or state/coomonwealth, this was the way the Roman referred to their state and is the origin of our word republic.

Roxolani: or 'red alans' were one group of Sarmatians, but are likely to have consisted of many subsections rather than a coherent and politically united tribe. At times they were allied with Decebalus, at times with the Romans, and often hostile to both.

sacramentum: the military oath sworn to the emperor and the res publica.

salutatio: traditional ceremony where people came to greet a Roman senator – and especially a governor – at the start of a working day.

Sarmatians: another blanket term used by the Romans and similar to the Greek use of Scythians. Reality was no doubt more complicated, but broadly speaking there were nomads originating from the Steppes. They were famed as formidable cavalry, employing bows and lances. Some were heavily armoured.

scorpion (*scorpio*): a light torsion catapult or *ballista* with a superficial resemblance to a large crossbow. They shot a heavy bolt with considerable accuracy and tremendous force to a range beyond bowshot. Julius Caesar describes a bolt from one of these engines going through the leg of an enemy cavalryman and pinning him to the saddle.

seplasiarius (or *seplasiario*): a military pharmascist working in a fort's hospital.

sica: a curved, one-handed sword particularly associated with Thracians and Dacians. The edge was on the inside of the curve, like a sickle and like the larger *falx*.

signifer: a standard-bearer, specifically one carrying a century's standard or *signum* (pl. *signa*).

Silures: a tribe or people occupying what is now South Wales. They fought a long campaign before being overrun by the Romans. Tacitus described them as having curly hair and darker hair or complexions than other Britons, and suggested that they looked more like Spaniards (although since he misunderstood the geography of Britain he also believed that their homeland was closer to Spain than Gaul).

spatha: another Latin term for sword, which it is now conventional to employ for the longer blades used mainly by horsemen in this period.

speculator: a soldier tasked with scouting.

tesserarius: the third in command of a century after the *optio* and *signifer*, the title originally came from their responsibility for overseeing sentries. The watchword for each night was written on a *tessera* or tablet.

thetatus: the Greek letter theta was used in some military documents to mark the name of a man who had died. This developed into army slang as thetatus meaning dead/killed.

tribune: each legion had six tribunes. The most senior was the broad-stripe tribune (*tribunus laticlavius*), who was a young aristocrat at an early stage of a senatorial career. Such men were in the late teens or early twenties. There were also five narrow-stripe tribunes (*tribune angusticlavia*), who were equestrians and had normally already commanded a cohort of auxiliary infantry.

triclinia: the three-sided couches employed at Roman meals.

Turma: a troop of Roman cavalry, usually with a theoretical strength of 30 or 32.

valetudinarium: A military hospital.

vicus: the civilian settlement outside a Roman army base.

vitis: the vine cane carried as a mark of rank by a centurion.

About the Author

ADRIAN GOLDSWORTHY studied
at Oxford, where his doctoral thesis examined
the Roman army. He went on to become
an acclaimed historian of Ancient Rome.
He is the author of numerous works of
non fiction, including *Caesar*, *Pax Romana*,
Hadrian's Wall and *Philip and Alexander*.
He is also the author of the Vindolanda series,
set in Roman Britain, which first introduced
readers to centurion Flavius Ferox.